The Edge of Temptation
Gods of the Undead 2
A Post-Apocalyptic Epic

By Peter Meredith

Fictional works by Peter Meredith:

A Perfect America
The Sacrificial Daughter
The Apocalypse Crusade War of the Undead: Day One
The Apocalypse Crusade War of the Undead: Day Two
The Horror of the Shade: Trilogy of the Void 1
An Illusion of Hell: Trilogy of the Void 2
Hell Blade: Trilogy of the Void 3
The Punished
Sprite
The Blood Lure: The Hidden Land Book 1
The King's Trap: The Hidden Land Novel 2
To Ensnare A Queen: The Hidden Land Novel 3
The Apocalypse: The Undead World Novel 1
The Apocalypse Survivors: The Undead World Novel 2
The Apocalypse Outcasts: The Undead World Novel 3
The Apocalypse Fugitives: The Undead World Novel 4
The Apocalypse Renegades: The Undead World Novel 5
The Apocalypse Exile: The Undead World Novel 6
The Apocalypse War: The Undead World Novel 7
The Edge of Hell: Gods of the Undead 1
The Edge of Temptation: Gods of the Undead 2
Pen(Novella)
A Sliver of Perfection (Novella)
The Haunting At Red Feathers(Short Story)
The Haunting On Colonel's Row(Short Story)
The Drawer(Short Story)
The Eyes in the Storm(Short Story)
The Witch: Jillybean in the Undead World

Prologue
Akron, Ohio

Bob's wife left him, screaming at the top of her lungs, which was a point of pride with him. If he'd had his way, he would have stuffed her mouth with a toilet brush and eaten her alive as she choked on its yellowed bristles.

But he had kept the *urge* in check. The urge was always on him, and yet he went to work every day so that the faceless masses could have their cable television. Bob didn't understand the TV. To him it was simply a box of colored lights. Thousands and thousands of pinpricks of light.

They formed no images in his mind and the words that came from it were bodiless, and worse, soulless. The laugh track that went along with most of the shows made more sense to him. The radio, too was conceptually beyond him. Every channel was static that pulsed. Easy to ignore.

What he liked were people and being around people, and yet there was nothing more than he hated than people. He hated them with the greatest passion and was jealous of them with a passion greater than that. They were diamonds and didn't know it. They were loved and didn't care.

They were gifts that were left half-unwrapped and they were toys that rusted from not being used properly, and the only time that anyone truly cared about them was when one went missing.

Bob had made quite a few disappear...but not his wife. That had been a great win. The ones he had taken and eaten were never as close as his wife. Little Jimmy with the gap in his teeth right in front...little Jimmy from next door who smelled of skid marks and macaroni and who kept coming into Bob's yard to look in his dirty basement windows because he could swear he had heard a child crying; he was also still around. Another win. Another victory over those who hunted him.

4

He could feel the priests when they came sniffing around. He could feel them from blocks away and even though he knew he should run, he never did. Instead, he would freeze. Running was bad. Running meant giving up this sham of a life. He was like a child in a toy box who, when threatened by the coming of other children, tried to cover his toys with his arms splayed and his chest hunched over his prizes.

Bob had many prizes.

He had been collecting them even before his wife had left him. When she was away at work he would dig, and when she slept, he crept away and dug some more. He had gone deep into the dark earth. Surprisingly deep. It was a wonder how deep one could delve when sleep meant nothing and blisters were to be marveled at.

When his shredded hands were remarked on at work, Bob wore gloves everywhere.

"Cold, are you?" was what people asked next. They seemed satisfied when he answered: "Yes," and then smiled. People seemed to like it when he smiled and so he smiled often.

He smiled as he went down into the earth where the hated priests couldn't find him. Every night he dug deeper and deeper. When he was a hundred feet down, and the heat had ticked up noticeably, and his body felt "misty" from lack of oxygen, Bob began forming his cells. He burrowed pits twenty feet deep and ten feet wide.

By the time his screeching wife had left him, he had six built, but only four had been filled. He had room for her, but in a tremendous display of self-control, he had let her scream into his face about how much he had changed and what a jerk he was and other things that were entirely meaningless to a demon.

He had even smiled at her, but this time the smile had not had its previous effect. She left and that night Bob went to find another soul, because he loved people and hated them in equal measure.

That night he found one that screamed and cried and begged. She even tried to joke, and laughed a crazy laugh as tears coursed down her face.

She begged for mercy and he gave it to her.

Her name was Bernice and she had been wasting her life cataloguing insurance forms at a white-bricked hospital. But he had saved her from that hell and now she felt life like she had never before. Life was suddenly more precious to her than she had ever known, and boy he knew that better than any.

Bob didn't have a life and didn't have a soul. He craved both, holding them close, hugging their bloody, screaming bodies to his. He wasn't a sexual creature and yet he never felt more connected than when he was stabbing his piece as deep as he could into them, male or female.

Sometimes they died and that was ok. What was left over was just as precious; not their rotting carcasses, no, these were buried where they died. It was the souls Bob craved. Each of the pits were lined with his symbols, anchoring the souls in place. In death they were pure light both to be hated and loved. He could only stand to be around them for so long and then he would go to the next, hoping to capture it for his own.

Bob's soul was long gone, corrupted into nothing. In life he had denied his soul and in death he had denied the maker and now he was undone and desperate.

Desperate, he went on and on, going through the motions. When next Bob looked at the calendar that sat magnetized to the fridge, he realized it had been three months since his wife had left him and two since he had been to work where he helped the people get their cable.

In his pits he had only one being left. It was a man, scabbed and skinny as a wraith. He had asked for a ride on a rainy night and when Bob had tried to take him, he had fought.

It had been a lovely fight. So much blood and fear. The man had been so strong, but now he was frail and his breath came in a rattle that made it seem as though his lungs were curtained in phlegm. He would be dead soon, which bothered Bob. He loved the souls, but he also liked the screams and the actual bleeding body—in hell, souls were utterly fantastic, but on earth the bodies were good, too.

They were always so warm.

Bob spent the day making the man eat things. A handful of dimes. His own hair. The urine-smelling mud at the bottom of the pit. It should have been the end of him, but the man kept breathing, much to Bob's delight.

And yet, he knew that it wouldn't last. So sad.

And also, not sad.

Finding the next one was always so sweet. It was like falling in love. Hearing the screams and feeling the raking claws. Bob wasn't much to look at anymore. His smile was no longer so sweet. It was now repulsive, and his beard was a wild thicket and his balding head was a patchwork of lesions, and his eyes were so insane that they caused people to blanch and turn away.

He knew something had changed but not what. The mirror was another thing he didn't understand. It took concentration to connect the image in it to his present form; frequently, he assumed it was just a picture.

But he had his sunglasses and his gloves and his turned-up collar and the hat that read: *World's Greatest Husband*. These had always been enough to allow him to blend in with the others, only now he was too hungry to care what he looked like.

He went out that night looking like a nightmare and even if he had known it, it might not have bothered him all that much. He was very hungry for everything…so much of everything, and so far he had been lucky. The priests came and went, always searching in the wrong places.

"They'll never get me," he growled. "Not in a million years."

This wasn't just a cliche to Bob. Time to a demon was a lot like the picture in the mirror, it was flat and wide, and hard to connect with the rising of the sun. He was immortal, just as everyone was, but unlike them he knew it, and wasn't that the problem? It was supply and demand. He had an endless supply of time and that made every second a valueless spec, and of course a minute was only that much worse and an entire year was a torture.

What he needed was something to fill in those seconds, what he needed was to be near someone who really appreciated time. A woman wasting away on a couch watching gameshows could not appreciate time, but a man a second from death loved time and always begged for more with such wonderful urgency.

That thought, as aways, made him grin and he drove, enjoying the feel of the road beneath the tires: so smooth, so accommodating. He drove to where the feast of humanity was the hottest and the smell was greatest. He loved the smell and sights and the little things that no one noticed. He loved the fact that *they* gestured with their fries or smiled with spinach in their teeth or stewed through their bowls with forks looking for that one last piece of meat.

And really, wasn't that exactly what he was doing?

He stewed Akron and found a street where the ladies hung out on the corners and stoops. When he stopped, they would jerk their thumbs up at the brick buildings behind them, inviting him up. He would shake his head in spite of the fact that he was so hungry. It wasn't safe for him to be out in the open. What he needed were the ones who lingered in the alleys where there was nothing but the dark and the drip of rain and the distant glow of the street lamps.

These were the lonely ones who were the most desperate to feel life and he was desperate to help them feel it in all its hideous glory. On that night, most of these little alleyways were frustratingly crowded, and he drove for miles back and forth until he found an alley that held only a girl, so small and slim. He saw that she was denying herself, not eating her fill. She could have been a round-bottomed thing, but she was holding back, not drinking life to its deepest.

Bob would fix that.

Letting the car prowl up, he rolled down the window, hoping that his old smile would do the trick, but ready with his gloved-hand on the door handle just in case she wanted to breathe deep and stretch her muscles one last time in a mad sprint. He loved that. They were always so alive when death was right on their heels—they didn't know how precious those few seconds were to both of them.

He beckoned her to the car. She shook her head and patted the dank, urine-smelling wall she leaned against. Her clothes were black; her hair was blonde and plaited in a tense braid that hugged her skull. She was grinning but it was tight.

And that was so good. She was scared and excited, but as he stepped out of the car, he smelled that she was wasn't nearly as afraid as he had first thought. She would be a tough one and that was even better.

"Hi," Bob said, showing teeth that were rotting out of his head. He knew he should take better care of the body, but he always got so caught up in the minutia and the fun and the simple things of this world that so often went unnoticed.

"Why, you-all don't look so good," the woman said. Her odd accent didn't register, nor did the fact that she kept one hand tucked behind her back. He was too busy breathing her in and enjoying the smell of sweat and anxiety hidden under the chemical mixture of perfume.

"You look good. You look healthy." To Bob that was a compliment.

"Thanks," she said, a little smirk playing on her lips. Louder, she said again: "Why, you-all don't look so good."

Bob showed his teeth wider. "You just said that. Maybe you…" He stopped. There was a sudden tone in the ether around him. It was like a tin bell being rung. Right along with it came the heady smell of blood. Bob was drawn to the smell. Four steps to the right of the woman, there was a man kneeling behind a dumpster; his forearm was slit open and a steady drip, drip, drip of that wonderful, rich blood came from the wound.

Mesmerized, Bob watched. When each drop of blood stuck the filthy alley floor, they didn't splat as they should have, instead each formed a glyph and with each drop the man spoke a single word.

In a flash, Bob knew this was a spell, an anchoring spell to be precise.

"Stop," Bob said. It was a word of command. The man faltered and the next drop splattered instead of forming a glyph, as did the next. Bob and the man stared into each other's eyes as the next three drops were also wasted, useless for any spell and ruined in their purity by landing on the reeking alley floor.

A drop of sweat joined the blood as the man grew grim. He was straining, where Bob was barely using a tenth of his strength—then again, he couldn't use much more, not in this body. To use more would mean burning it out and using it up.

The next drop of blood formed the word: *Hrsta*, and the man spoke it through gritted teeth.

"No!" Bob cried in fury. He redoubled his efforts to break the man, but they both knew it was useless. This was Visha Ra-aye—the Demon Slayer. It could be none other. Only one human breathed the tongue of the *First* in such a way. "I could break you," Bob said. "If I was not in this warm flesh."

The Demon Slayer ignored him and when the next drop struck, he said: "Ast-ri-mhra."

Bob turned from the man, only he couldn't move precisely; his feet were planted in place and his legs were like stone and his hips were locked. He could only torque his shoulders and his neck. He was seconds from being *held*, and he was very close to throwing off all pretense and giving up the body of "Bob."

He had not started off as "Bob." He had begun life eons before and his name was hidden and a secret. He had been spawned in the lower pits where the blood was old and congealed and constantly in need of being stirred. But even from the depths of hell he had heard Old Bob's call and, more importantly, he had smelled the virgin sacrifice that Old Bob was offering. Old Bob had hated his life. Old Bob was a damned fool. Bob hated the woman who loved him. He thought she was a nag when she only wanted the best for him, even if it meant changing him.

Old Bob had seen the news clips and read with greedy eyes all about the ghouls and demons that had turned New York into a ghost town of littered bones and burned-out buildings. He had begun to plan, thinking that he could have a better life when in truth, his life was already wonderful and so full of a thousand possibilities every day.

Old Bob had thrown all that away. He had opened the gate between worlds by drawing glyphs in stolen blood. They had been childish, simple.

And they had worked! A very hungry demon had come through and had taken up residence in Old Bob.

Now, a demon can't simply step into any body it chooses. For the most part it has to be invited, although sometimes a "careening" demon can manage to slip into the weak: the nearly dead, or the child with "eyes" who was in that precious state where control was problematic. But how frequent did that happen? Almost never.

In the worst of circumstances, a demon sprung from hell could climb into a cold body. However, possessing a corpse was terrible. No breath, no heartbeat. It was a tease. It was the ultimate broken promise, and yet no demon would ever pass it up. You were just SO close to being free on earth.

But Old Bob, like a fool, had offered his body freely.

It was such a fantastic prize and was the reason why the demon in him ground his teeth, making a whining noise in his throat as he was trapped. He could have broken out, but that would have meant an end to the body and it was just too precious to give up, even so close to being sent back to hell.

It was a horrible feeling and a delicious one as well to know that he had only a few more seconds of real life. They were precious seconds, seconds that he would never in a million years get to experience in hell.

Visha Ra-aye finished his spell and Bob was good and stuck. He fought back as best as he could, but to no avail; the spell had anchored him in place. Bob couldn't move as long as Visha held his concentration.

The woman walked closer and stared long at Bob, her blue eyes running up and down the ruin of his face. Even held as he was, those seconds were fantastic. From behind her back, she pulled out a radio. "It's him. We got him."

His body might have been frozen in place, but his mind was still sharp. He could feel the priests coming. Their ugly glaring white heat had been on his periphery before he had even seen the woman but, foolishly, he had let his hunger for her scent distract him. They closed quickly from either end of the alley. He was glad that he couldn't turn his head to see their self-righteous faces.

He was almost out of time. He sucked in the aroma of the world that none of these beings had the whit to appreciate to its fullest. That one breath spoke to him. It described *her* hopes and *his* fears. It told him the priests were not paragons. One drank to deal with the stress and the other was a glutton and battled daily with his lusts—and lost daily as well.

No matter. They had their despised God. Their ultimate judge.

A cross was pressed against Bob's forehead and words of Latin were whispered in his face. Whisper or not, the words were a sonic boom that split his ears and his head. He tried to fight it, just as his victims had. He struggled for those last few precious breaths, those last few beats of his heart, those last few moments.

Chapter 1
Akron, Ohio
Jack Dreyden

Jack was bent over on his hands and knees with blood leaking down his arm; in the dark it was black as demon blood. Nearby was the knife which would later be sterilized and re-sharpened; the cut had been too shallow and Cyn had nearly paid for it.

He was shaky and cold, his shirt drenched in sweat. As always after a tough casting, he began to shiver. It didn't matter that it was midsummer, he still trembled. He thought that after a year and a half he'd be used to the feeling of putting his soul on the line, of letting it drain away to practically nothing. But no, he still shook.

It had been eighteen months since he had saved the world, a feat that had been underplayed by everyone. Everyone.

Cyn never brought it up, and when she did, she spoke of her mother, or Pastor John, or poor Detective Richards whose body had been discovered among the ruins of a Princeton hospital. Or she would speak of the heroics of Lieutenant Neilson and his platoon of Seals or the Pope or the soft spoken Father Paul.

Cynthia Childs was his lover, his best friend, and his third cousin, and yet even she never mentioned the fact that he had practically bled to death for her and had saved the world in the process.

She never did, and when he was straight, when his soul was intact that is, he was glad that she never did. Yes, he had saved the world, but he had also twice committed murder, stolen the blood of innocent people, and had made sacrifices to the Mother of Demons, all just to save his worthless skin. He had been a monster, and who wanted to bring that up?

The only people who ever brought up his heroics were the constantly hovering government officials. They were the most backwards thinking people he had ever met. They acted as though *he* owed *them* something! In fact, they acted as though they owned him. For the last year and a half, Jack had lived and worked with an indictment hanging over his head. In a fit of honesty, he had foolishly admitted to two murders as well as culpability in fifteen million others. The government men never let on which they thought was worse.

They dangled a prison sentence over Jack's head and made him go here and there, chasing down stray demons —it was why he was in Akron where the humidity was off the charts and the people bowled for fun—hideous.

Jack didn't trust himself to stand up just yet. His insides were vibrating like a banjo string in a beer keg. He felt empty and shaking. What he had done was what he dubbed: *Free Form Sorcery*, and it wasn't easy.

But there was no other way to hold the demons. They were just too strong, even when they were encased in the *live* ones. "Back off, Father," Jack said, his voice hoarse.

"We…talked…about this…Jack," Father Timmons answered between great gusts of air. By his own admission, the forty-eight year old priest hadn't run more than a mile all told in the last thirty years. It had only been in the last few months that he had given any thought to his conditioning and he wasn't nearly in proper shape for this sort of work. He had sprinted a hundred yards and now he was bent over the demon, trying to spew Latin and breathe at the same time.

"Yes, we did talk about it," Jack answered, half his mind still on the spell he had conjured to *hold* the demon. Any lapse in concentration would free the creature. "And I told you that we need the demon. He might have information."

"He is…a man…we respect that."

The second priest, Father Jordan came up then. He took out a vial of Holy Oil and began dribbling a circle around the demon. His Latin wasn't nearly as good as Father Timmons' and he went slowly, sounding the words out like a first-grader reading aloud for the first time. The moment he was done, Jack sat back and looked up at the night sky. The demon was now pinned in place.

Cyn stepped forward and gazed down on what had once been Bob Chapman. He was rank and hideous. "I think he might be too far gone," she said, wrinkling her nose at the smell of death coming off the man. "You should let us keep him. Really, if this bloke doesn't fit the criteria, then none of them do."

"That's just it," Father Jordan said, "None of them fit *our* criteria. He is human; that's all that matters. He is a possessed person, not a thing, and we will not be a party to torture."

Jack glanced down at his arm, thinking that they didn't seem to mind his suffering. The cut was across his bicep; there were three more below it and five across his forearm, all freshly scarred or scabbed. Along his side were five pink lines and above his belly-button were six in the shape of sergeant's stripes. There were others on his legs.

He was bleeding himself dry capturing demons and always letting them go, figuratively speaking, that is. An unbodied demon was a weak thing, unable to resist the pull of hell for very long. "This isn't working, Captain."

The last person on the squad, Captain Metzger of the US Army, had been across the way, perched on the roof of a back-alley Chinese herb shop. Akron had a hundred and seventy of these types of shops. Since the *Event* in which Jack had accidentally helped to release hell on earth and then nearly died trying to make amends, the herb shops had sprung up like weeds: unregulated and immoral, selling anything from ground tiger penis to crypt dust. Akron had more of these shops than they did McDonalds.

"I agree," was all Metzger said. He was tall and broad, prone to moodiness and rarely spoke, at least to Jack.

"Then do something or piss off," Jack snapped. "My God, Metzger, sometimes you are next to useless. Try growing a spine."

The captain ground his teeth. He was in a tough position; he had zero authority over the priests. Yes, they were American and yes, they worked with the *Rapid Anti-Demon Response Squads*, what everyone called *Raiders*, but they took their orders from Rome and no amount of threats or screamed orders would budge them. If Jack didn't need them so badly, he would have tossed them from his squad long ago. As it was, he did his best to switch out the priests he worked with as quickly as he could, hoping to find one that would listen to reason.

So far none would.

They came in pairs, already prepared to deal with Jack and his "satanic" ways. There were fourteen *Raider squads* fighting and exorcising the many strays, but Jack's *Raider squad* was different. *He* was different. The Event had changed him. He had come out of the ordeal stronger...far stronger.

He was, as far as he knew, the world's only sorcerer.

It was true that he only knew three spells, but that was three more than anyone else knew...except for his cousins: Robert and Cyn. Robert was no sorcerer. He was a necromancer dealing in sacrifices, stolen blood, demons and the dead.

And Cyn...well, Cyn was just a girl. Barely twenty-one and could already boast about having a hand in saving the world. She could boast, though she never did. She was "just" a girl and had no more pretensions than that. The secret that only Jack knew was that she wanted to be shut of the entire fight.

If she had her way, she would find a farm in Wales and raise geese. When they were alone in bed, with Jack trying to ignore the pain of his latest cut and the emptiness in his chest, she would talk about raising geese. The idea fascinated her and yet, when Jack, in true American fashion, asked if there was a market for goose meat, she was utterly perplexed at the question.

She wanted only to raise the geese; she didn't want to sell them and surely didn't want to see them die.

Jack loved that beautiful innocent, naive outlook. It was as precious as it was ridiculous. She would describe Hobbit burrows where the geese would live and local children who would come by in yellow rain slickers and boots, pink boots for the girls and muddy blue ones for the boys—to feed the growing squadrons of mellow-minded birds.

He would laugh at these strange fantasies, but the laughter was usually fake. Yes, Cyn knew spells and she thought she knew what it took to cast them, but she didn't really.

Jack hid that part from her. It was easy. He smiled, enjoying the stretch of skin and the working of the muscles on his face; he touched her arm, relishing the million of cells involved in the simple act; he kissed her hungrily as if he had never tasted lips so wonderful.

And he hadn't…even if he had just kissed her a minute before. The spells drained him. They drained every part of him. They took that part of him that remembered these tactile experiences. They took the love that he and Cyn spun. And that was both good and bad.

It was good because he was constantly falling in love with her. Every day it was a new love. Every day it was exciting…but also everyday he would wake up feeling only a fraction of what he had felt the day before. It frightened him because what would happen if he missed a day with her? Would he forget his love for her entirely? Would he wander? Would he care?

Caring was a real issue with Jack. He looked upon Bob Chapman and wondered why they weren't beating information out of him. It wasn't an evil feeling, not like when he was sacrificing the blood and the souls of others; that had been horrible. This was just a lack of empathy.

Clamping a hand over his latest cut, he struggled to his feet and went to the edge of where the Holy Oil had been poured. The proximity of it made his already squirrelly stomach flutter. For a sorcerer, the concept of God could be just as hard to deal with as that of the Devil—they both took you. They both owned you. They both demanded obedience and sacrifice.

As Jack watched the priests exorcise the demon in Bob, Cyn pulled her medkit out of the backpack she had kept stashed behind the dumpster. She cleaned out Jack's self-inflicted laceration, smeared it with bacitracin and then wrapped it tight; the process took all of a minute—she'd been doing this for over a year now and was quick and thorough.

She then unzipped the light jacket she wore and pulled off the Kevlar vest that had been hidden beneath it. She was red-cheeked and sweating from the heat and with a practiced hand, she spun her thick blond hair into a bun to get it off her neck.

"Who's ready for sushi?" she asked, as if there wasn't a filthy, diseased ravaged man lying on the floor of the alley, screaming his lungs out.

"What I want are new priests," Jack said, jumping back into his argument. He too pulled off his vest and forearm guards. "These two aren't cutting it."

"I can't fire them without cause," Metzger replied. In spite of the humidity and the warm night, he stayed "gear-up," his shotgun at the ready. Akron wasn't the same as it had been. It was dangerous now and the screams of the demon and the prayers of the priest were attracting a crowd.

"Here's a cause: they suck," Jack shot back, uncaring that the two priests were five feet away and well within earshot. "You saw how long it took Timmons to show up and don't get me started on Jordan. Really, Jordan, what the hell was that about?"

"If you can't tell, I'm a little busy here," the younger priest hissed. The two priests were panting and sweating with the spiritual effort of forcibly removing a demon from a living host. The ones that had been invited in were always the hardest to evict. They had their claws dug in deep. They acted as if it was their body and they fought tooth and nail to stay.

"Maybe Jordan is getting shy," Cyn suggested in a low whisper. When the two men looked at her nonplussed, she leaned in closer and said in an even lower tone: "That's English for saying that maybe he's becoming a coward."

The suggestion was certainly not unheard of. Facing even one demon was a difficult thing, but to do it on a weekly or even a daily basis was hard on the psyche.

"All the more reason he should go," Jack said, also keeping his voice pitched low. More than anyone he knew the fear and the stress of fighting the undead and for the first time in a month he felt a tinge of empathy for the priests.

Even this logic didn't stir Metzger. "In case you haven't noticed, there is a worldwide shortage of priests. There are very few who want to be on the front lines fighting a war on demons and even fewer who want to work with you, Jack."

"Me? Why wouldn't they want to work with me? I'm a sorcerer for goodness sakes."

"It's precisely because you are a sorcerer," Metzger answered. "They are Godly men, Jack, and you with your blood and your pagan symbols. It's extremely off-putting. Also, you're a bit of a jerk."

Jack threw his hands in the air. "A jerk? Me? Cyn, can you believe this guy?" She only shrugged, which shocked him. "What? You think I'm a jerk, too?"

Another shrug. "You can be a little tough when we're on the job. I know it's the stress and the spells and the fact that no one has heard from Robert in so long."

After the dust had settled from the Event, meaning after the blame had been well established—Jack and Cyn getting more than their fair share, mainly by being honest about the events that had led up to the destruction of the city—they had been flown to Egypt under escort to search for Robert.

It had been a waste of time and sweat. Despite money being splashed around and the Egyptian government fully on board, no one could remember seeing Robert anywhere near any of the hundreds of historical sites that dotted the country. They had been there for three months poking about. During that time, Jack had worked on his tan, which became a warm brown, and also worked on his spells which drained the tan away.

There was an amazing amount of leeway with the spells...well not his own spell, perhaps. A portal into hell was either there or it wasn't; he could get it to encompass larger or smaller areas, but so far that was it.

Robert's spell to control the demons had implications that Jack had yet to test. He thought it was possible that a few changed words within the spell could allow him to control demons that had already come through the portal. The one problem was that he had yet to find an incentive for a demon to comply. The original spell allowed entry into the world as a reward for doing the bidding of the spell's master, but if a demon was already here what would make it go against its nature and serve Jack? So far that was an unknown.

Although it had seemed to be the weakest of the three spells, Cyn's protective spell was Jack's "go to" spell, especially as he practiced and discovered that his soul was both a source of power and the finest of tools. He had discovered his ability to manipulate his blood by accident.

He had been battling a demon in a Sarasota neighborhood. It had already killed a priest and two soldiers, and things could not have been worse. Jack's sword arm was mangled; there were three deep scores in it that went right to the bone. The demon's poison was in his system working its way to his heart and his blood ran in waves down his arm, but that was nothing compared to the predicament Cyn found herself in seconds later.

She had thrown herself at the beast to protect Jack

With her shotgun empty, she had gone to her sword. She was laughably inept with it and the demon attacked and attacked until she broke and fled. She took off around the house, but the demon easily ran her down.

In a perfect state of terror, Jack hobbled after. "Hey!" he had cried, miserably, trying to get the creature's attention. "Hey! I'm doing a spell. I'm calling a fiend!"

That had earned Cyn one second of grace and she used it to dive into the pool that she had been trapped against. She had planned to simply swim to the other side, but the demon had blown its ice breath over the top of the water, freezing it and trapping her below.

The demon had then turned on Jack, who was light-headed and close to blacking out. He had dropped to one knee with a brush in hand and could do nothing but try to throw up a protective ward around himself to buy time, but unfortunately his left hand was inept at drawing and the pain of the poison was so great that the glyphs dribbled and smeared. Panic nearly seized him, but he forced his mind away from the fear and directed all his energy to the spell, and when the next drop of blood fell from his wound it was almost as if he "caught" it in midair.

The blood slowed and he simply *willed* the next glyph into proper shape.

His mind alone had formed the glyph. The drop had struck in the exact shape he had needed. It had been amazing and had Cyn not been trapped under the ice and likely seconds away from drowning, he would have laughed aloud.

Instead, he forced his mind to do more and it responded with alacrity. The spell was formed exactly as he needed and then he spoke: "*Prt m hrw Hrr vahl Evi ah hurrumm fd. Hrr ah huroon ksa hrer, mkr*,"...My sacrifice *holds* those called to walk in the day and *binds* those unbidden to remain in its place of darkness.

Somehow this worked and the spell froze the demon in place.

To say that the beast fought this imprisonment was an understatement. It went wild and, seeing as only the force of Jack's mind held the spell together, it was a hard battle that was fought between them. They fight was wholly in the mind and in the realm of the will.

It was a strange battle and not one that Jack was used to. On top of that, he was deathly afraid for Cyn, who had been under the ice for close to a minute. Jack began to sweat and to shake and there was what felt like a stab of molten steel in his brain. The demon slowly strained forward until it was almost within reach and in another second it would have killed Jack with a swipe of its bone-claws, but just then there was an explosion from the frozen pool.

Cyn had detonated a grenade in the shallow end. Breaking through the ice, with her ears bleeding, she had lurched out of the water, sword in hand, looking like an avenging angel, hell bent on slaying the demon—and she had.

Unnerved by the sight of the girl, the demon's will had faltered and just like that, Jack had basically nailed its feet in place, allowing Cyn to slash it into pieces.

"I risk my life everyday and I'm the jerk?" Jack asked incredulously, coming back to the matter at hand.

Cyn only shrugged and Metzger sighed, saying: "Maybe I shouldn't have said anything. Come on, let's find out who this is." He headed for Bob's car. Jack didn't follow.

"Isn't that the police's job?" he asked. "They usually get pretty touchy about people messing around at their crime scenes."

Metzger paused in stride and glanced toward where the crowd of youths were edging closer. Many had swords belted on their hips; wearing swords, blessed or not, was a current fad and a dangerous one. "There's not just a deficiency in the number of priests," he said, his voice low. "Akron doesn't have much of a police presence anymore."

"That bad?" Jack asked. He knew that the "Second Depression" they were in was really putting a squeeze on local governments, but it was a shock to suggest there wasn't going to be an investigation of a demon possession. There were always quite a few corpses associated with them and large numbers of worried family members to break the bad news to.

Jack was rarely a part of any of that. He was usually too exhausted and his soul too spent to care about the clean up and aftermath of these battles. Generally, he would go back to whatever hotel they were staying in and sleep an entire day away—but even he thought that *someone* should go check out Bob's house.

"Yeah, it's that bad," Metzger answered. "I was told that if we found our monster, to call it in and that they would get to it, eventually."

A tired sigh escaped Jack as he pulled the heavy vest back on and went to Bob Chapman's car; it stank of death. In the glove compartment, there were three wallets; in the back seat, there were four purses; in the trunk was blood. A lot of blood.

Chapter 2
Akron, Ohio
Cynthia Childs

"You're not a jerk," Cyn assured. A car passed them going in the opposite direction and she tried not to flinch. A year and a half of living in America and she still got wigged out about their driving. It was bad enough they all sped and only used turn signals if the fit caught them just so, but worse was the fact they drove on the bloody wrong side of the road.

"No, I am a jerk," Jack said. He powered the rental forward. It was a brand new Lexus, and still had a new car smell, which he wasn't going to have ruined by allowing Bob Chapman to ride in it. Bob smelled like rot and disease. His teeth were grey and his eyes yellow, and this was without the demon inside of him.

Now that Bob was free of the demon, he and Captain Metzger, as well as the two priests, were driving in Bob's old Chevy Camaro, which had too much incriminating evidence in it to simply be abandoned to the mob. Akron was filled with dismembered cars, resting on their rusting axles, their tires long since stolen. The mob, which had started with a single ruffian, sullen and rude, an unlit cigarette dangling from his lower lip, had gradually grown as a hundred more just like him had sauntered close, drawn by the commotion. They would have pieced-out the car, leaving little more than the frame behind.

"I don't think you're a jerk at all, and you know that," Cyn said. "Would a jerk risk his life every day for strangers? Would a jerk always watch over me?" Whenever she played the part of bait, which was every time they went out, he hovered close, always ready to throw himself at any creature, no matter how terrible, if it meant saving her.

24

It was the only reason she kept going out night after night, putting her life on the line. She was always the one who hung around in the dark alleys or the empty parks or the lonely streets. She was always the one playing the "defenseless" damsel.

The demons never suspected she was nobody's damsel. They didn't see beyond the intentionally streaked mascara to note the silver dagger in her boot or the vial filled with holy water tucked into the back of her skirt, or the triple blessed cross she wore under her shirt. More than any human, the demons saw what they wanted to see.

Still, they were right nasty and entirely dangerous.

But if her weapons didn't work, she always had Jack close by, ready to bleed for her. She'd had men buy her roses and drinks and dinners; she even had one fellow offer her a car once, but she'd never had a man *bleed* for her. And she'd never had a man change on such a fundamental level for her as Jack had.

They never talked about it much, mainly because it was an embarrassment for him, but Jack hadn't started out as a sorcerer. No, he had been a necromancer like their cousin Robert…and like Cyn. She was one as well. She felt the pull. She felt the need to spill blood. She felt the hunger for power that only the *King of Death* could wield. But she hadn't given in and she never would. Jack had taught her that lesson.

He had been addicted to death. The power of necromancy had whisked him up and had taken him whole. It had owned what was left of his black soul, and it seemed that nothing on earth could have stopped him from calling forth an army of demons and usurping their cousin, Robert as *the* necromancer. And yet, Jack had given up a power so great he could have ruled the world. He had given it up for her. He had simply set it aside.

Yes, he could be moody after draining his soul to fight evil, but that didn't make him a jerk. Far from it in her eyes.

"Does Akron even have a sushi place?" she asked, changing the subject. Judging by the dark streets and the many boarded over businesses, she guessed not. "You need sushi, Jack." He needed to eat. His strength always came back faster after he ate. Sleeping was good for him, but food was better. He also liked sushi, something he'd always been too poor to try back when he had been a student.

He ignored the talk of food and brooded, finally saying: "We're getting close."

She could feel it as well. A hint of death hung in the air, setting her nerves on edge. Seconds later, Jack turned onto a side street and another turn later, they parked in front of a house. It was dark as could be and when she stepped out into the humid night, she knew right away that the damp in the air would make everything they found inside that much worse. One sniff confirmed her suspicions. A sick, wet smell of decay struck her.

Jack paused as he stepped out of the car, his hand on his sword. Light splashed over him as Metzger pulled in behind them in the Camaro. When the captain cut the engine, the night was dead silent. Bob's house sat on the edge of the suburbs, surrounded by a whole lot of nothing.

It was too perfect as a murder house, almost as if it could be nothing else. Cyn couldn't picture a family living there, at least not a happy one.

"Can he speak yet?" Jack asked. He meant Bob who stood dully, blinking slowly, a line of drool hanging from his mouth. Sometimes the possessed remained vegetables for life, sometimes they snapped out of it quickly. "Hey, Bob!" Jack snapped his fingers under Bob's nose. "What are we going to find in there?"

The drool swung gently as Bob turned at the sound of Jack's voice. His eyes; however, remained blank orbs. Cyn guessed he would recover in time, but for now he was hollow inside. Hollow and horrid; his mind that of an imbecile's.

"Forget it," Jack said. "Anyone have an extra light?" Everyone including the two priests had their phones out, using the sharp light to illuminate the brown grass at their feet; the yard was unkempt and dying, littered with trash and feces, none of which was canine in origin. Cyn stepped with extreme care.

Captain Metzger handed over a palm-sized flashlight as if he had been expecting Jack's question. Jack hadn't had a cell phone in all the time Cyn had known him—she was his only family and in truth, his only friend. He had no one to call and even if he did, Cyn wondered if he would bother.

Jack didn't thank Captain Metzger for the light—he also tended to forget his manners when his soul was drained. When he was like this, everything, simply was. If he asked for a light, you either had one or not, and he would have made do either way.

"Here, eat these," Cyn said, handing him a box of *Junior Mints*. He liked candy, especially *Reeses Peanut Butter Cups*, but, with all their wrappings, they were not easy to eat, and he would have tossed them away in frustration after the first. He palmed a handful of mints, shoved them into his mouth and started for the house.

"Let the captain go first," Cyn said, holding him back. Metzger moved ahead, shotgun in hand. The door was unlocked and the smell inside, mean.

The priests were still so new to the team that they paled from the stink; Metzger, who had been tempered by six months of battle, only made swallowing noises in the back of his throat. Jack looked as though he were walking through a park. The smell was nothing to him and, sadly, the same was true with Cyn. She was sure the stench was horrible and yet she carried on, shining her light ahead of her, following Jack as he pressed into the house, pushing past Metzger.

He could sense something just as she could. She hadn't been to the edge of hell as he had, but she could still feel things that others couldn't. It was part of her birth right. It was part of being a necromancer.

Jack led them right through the house and down into the basement. In a back corner was a hole that went down into the earth; the smell here was three times as bad as it was in the rest of the house, and it would only get worse.

"There's a person down there," Jack said. "I can feel him. He's willing to deal." A shiver crawled up his back, twisting his shoulders. After a second with her eyes closed and her mind focussed, Cyn understood what he was saying. She could feel *him*. There was a man in the pits beneath the house, though now he was only barely a man.

His pain radiated up to them, but what was worse was his desperation. He was projecting the feeling out into the universe. He was letting everyone and everything know that he was so desperate that he was willing to make deals with his soul as currency.

First, Timmons crossed himself and Jordan followed right behind. They could feel it as well.

Jack opened his mouth and looked as if he were about to make some remark about them crossing themselves— when his soul was drained, he grew petulant and snappish with the priests. Once in a slurred drunken ramble, he admitted to Cyn that he thought their light exposed his darkness, throwing shadow where there shouldn't be shadow.

Cyn handed him more *Junior Mints* and he shoveled them into his mouth.

As he ate, Captain Metzger went down an aluminum ladder that poked up out of the hole; it rattled as he went down. When he reached the bottom, Jack stuffed a double handful of mints into his mouth and followed after, the sword at his hip clanking against the ladder with every step. Father Timmons started to go next, but Cyn pulled him back by his black shirt. It wasn't smart for anyone but her to get too close when Jack was in one of his moods— he could be dangerous.

Drained or not, he had a reserve of power at his fingertips.

She followed him down, her nerves rattling worse than the ladder. They had never been to the home of one of the possessed before; they had always left that particular horror to the police and the local priests. She was just beginning to think that was more of a blessing than she knew—it might have also been a mistake.

Metzger and Jack stood in a cramped little hand-carved tunnel where the dirt trickled off the walls and the dark was absolute. There was no pause in Jack; he was pulled along by a calling he couldn't ignore. He pushed past Metzger, and Cyn nudged past the captain as well and followed along after. She thought she was feeling the same pull as Jack, but she was wrong.

They went down a stunted passage that ended at another hole and another ladder that went down to a third sub-level. There they walked hunched over, dirt cascading off the ceiling until they found yet another hole, going deeper still. At the very bottom was a black tunnel that went in two directions; Jack immediately turned left, while she was drawn to the right.

"Hold on," she hissed at Jack. "There's something this way." Yes, she could sense the poor man in his feces and urine stinking cell. He was a raw line of power. His soul was laid bare, open to the highest bidder, but what lay to the right was far more insidious and subtle...and dangerous.

Ignoring her, he went left, while she, the unblooded necromancer, was drawn to the right. Metzger, wavered, not knowing which to follow. After a few seconds of looking back and forth, he chose to follow after Jack and the priests followed after him. Only Bob considered the right corridor. He stared, his filthy face open in a look of longing, but he was hustled after Jack by Father Timmons, leaving Cyn to face the insidious evil alone.

It was an old evil. It had been the first evil perpetuated in that pit of despair, and it was an ancient evil. The dirt passage opened up into a hollowed square of a room where the ends of worms decorated the dirt walls and the floor was covered in a white sheet pulled as tight as a sail in hard gale.

The decomposed body of a naked child lay in the middle of the sheet; it had been slit open from the throat down through its genitals. What was left of its organs was a black sludge that was rounded and bulged as swamp gasses built up inside. For all her toughness, Cyn was sure she would hurl if the bubble popped when she was in the room.

As it was, the outrageous stench made even her stomach knot and twist.

Around the body of the child were glyphs. For the most part they were ordinary hieroglyphs, though what they spelled out was hardly ordinary: it was a summoning spell. It was a crude spell written in a crude hand, and it shouldn't have worked, but it had and for two reasons.

Bob Chapman had sacrificed a child to bring forth a demon. He had offered the purest of innocent souls to bring forth his demon and it wasn't just any demon that came into this world to possess Bob. The demon had been named Menet-rah.

The glyph that bore his name was unlike the others. It was written in a curious poly-heiroglyphical script. The cuneiform wedges set it apart, making it not only different, it made it unique. It also made it terribly frightening.

There was no way that glyph could have ended up in a crappy little suburb of Akron by accident and it was inconceivable that someone as insignificant as Bob Chapman would have his hands on it. He was a nobody from a nowhere town. He had likely never been to Egypt and if he had, he had gone as a tourist and these sorts of glyphs weren't exactly lying around waiting for people to find them.

"Jack!" she yelled, her voice flat and suppressed as if the tons of earth between her and the night sky was squeezing the air, taking the life out of it. "Jack! You have to see this." There was no answer and a squirm of worry crawled into her belly. She suddenly felt very alone.

With her hand on her sword and the wavering light leading her, she retraced her steps, hurrying down the rough-hewn passage. When she came to the bend, she finally heard something other than her own fearful breathing. It was the sound of a struggle.

She ripped her sword out and raced almost blind in Bob's dungeon of horrors, sprinting past short passages which ended in foul smelling pits that held the moldering bones of his victims. At the fifth of these passages was a sight that stopped her: Jack had Bob by the throat and was lifting him off the ground with just his left hand, while both priests clung to his sword arm trying to hold it from skewering the man. Captain Metzger had Jack from behind, one thick arm around Jack's throat, the muscles bunching with all his strength.

Jack looked as though he was just about to get *really* angry and that would have ended up in three more deaths.

"Stop," Cyn said and this time her voice was alive and it cut through the grunts of the two priests and the swearing of Captain Metzger and the odd garbled gobble that Bob was making as Jack choked the life out of him.

All sound fell away as Jack and Cyn stared at each other. Ten seconds passed and then Jack, still hoisting the man in the air said: "You don't know."

"I know enough," she answered. "He deserves to die, but not yet. He has answers."

"But the demon is gone."

Cyn laughed a harsh, ugly sound that deflated Jack. He dropped Bob as if his arm was suddenly aware that there was no way on earth it could lift two-hundred pounds, and his sword was pulled out of his grip, Timmons grabbing it and backing away with it pointed at Jack.

"One demon is gone, but the original is right there and when we get our answers I will show him the way to hell personally." She held up the sword and it gleamed as if in anticipation.

Chapter 3
Akron, Ohio
Jack Dreyden

Jack blinked at Cyn and even that seemed to take more strength than he had left in him. "There were two demons?" he asked, feeling dull-witted. Even if it were possible, he would have sensed the second demon in Bob and surely the priests would have as well.

"Bob's human, but only barely," Cyn said, advancing on the man. Jack knew her well enough to see that she was close to gutting him; he had been feeling the same thing only seconds before. "What I meant," she said, "is that he's a demon in training. There's something back there that you have to..."

She was cut off by a whimpering sound coming from the pit they had been tussling next to. When she looked in and saw the horror of a person who was down in the hole, her face went white. Jack had seen then skeletal man as well and the sight had sent him nearly mad.

The scant figure was so pale that Jack's first glimpse of him had made him jump. He had thought for a second he was looking at ghost or a wraith. And the man was so thin that when he turned sideways on he almost disappeared and yet that wasn't what had sent Jack to the end of his rope. The man stood on broken ankles; the lower parts of his legs were bent at 90 degree angles and the same was true with his wrists. They were so warped that his fingernails touched his forearms.

It was sick. And still the man tried to scramble up to them, tears in his blind eyes—there were golf tees in both eyes, jabbed just as deep as they could go.

It was seeing that which had sent Jack off the deep end. He didn't know the full extent of his power, nor how to control it, or what it's limitations were, but there were times like this that he didn't need to know, he just needed to unleash it.

"I...I can't understand this," Cyn said, her eyes filling with tears. Upon seeing them, Jack felt the surge of power in him again, but it was weaker and easier to control, and besides, Captain Metzger still had his arm across Jack's throat and it was like a bar of iron.

"Let's deal with what you saw," Jack said, softly, thinking he would steer her away, but she would not be moved. She had compassion enough for both of them—exactly what Jack loved and needed from her.

She disentangled Metzger from around Jack and pointed to the pit. "Get him out of there. All of you. I'll watch Bob. I promise I won't kill him...yet," she added when Father Timmons raised an eyebrow.

Another ladder was found; Jack led the way, followed by Metzger and then the priests. They weren't all needed; certainly Jack wasn't. The man in the pit, naked, stinking, his body running with pus from the half-healed remains of hundreds of cuts, hugged Jack as soon as he stepped into the pit.

It took all of Jack's remaining strength not to thrust the horrible being off of him. He stood perfectly still, his face set in a grimace of disgust. Finally, Father Timmons came down. "There you go my child. You are safe now. Let's bring you up where the light of the stars will fall upon you."

Metzger bent the broken man over his broad shoulder and carried him up the ladder as if there were nothing to him...and really there wasn't much to him. He had almost translucent skin, weak bird-like bones, and hair that consisted of only a few wisps. There wasn't an ounce of fat on him and his muscles were strings, barely able to pull him around.

When they had left, Jack could feel what had drawn Cyn away to the right hand tunnel. "There are more glyphs?"

"Yes," she answered and then led him to where Bob had sacrificed a child to the infernal gods of the undead.

"Give me your light!" he demanded. The one Metzger had given him was gone, lost in the scuffle.

Without question, Cyn handed over her phone and he knelt down next to the remains of the child as if it wasn't even there. He had seen it of course; however, his focus remained on the hieroglyphs; this particular *spell* wasn't new to him. It was an internet spell. It was a downloaded copy of part of a funerary text, making it pure crap. Alone, there was no way the spell could have brought forth a demon, but there was also a dead child, properly sacrificed and one glyph that didn't belong.

"*Menet-rah,*" he whispered, reading the glyph and feeling not just the name but also the memory of the demon. For him, speaking a demon's name elicited more than just the sensation of sound. There was always a strange uptick in the aura around him as if someone or something had pricked an ear. He could feel it even though it wasn't the demon's true name. Menet-rah was more of a nickname.

Next to him, Cyn shivered. The sensation which came with speaking the demon's name was probably worse for her. It was the sort of name and glyph that a necromancer would drool over. It was power and compulsion and an ugly greed. Their strength came from the netherworld. Their strength was in their knowledge of it and their connection to it.

Cyn was a weak necromancer. She cared more for the child than she did for the glyph. "That poor thing," she said, her hand out, almost, but not quite touching the corpse.

At first Jack didn't know what she was talking about, and then he truly *saw* the child for the first time. "Emily," he said. Around the child and the glyphs was an echo of the spell that had been used in her death and a sad memory. "Her name is Emily Druggins." He knew much more but the rest was only pain and tears and a fright that still set his nerves on edge.

"Was," Cyn corrected, though in this she was wrong. Emily was still Emily only now she was owned by the demon.

Jack didn't argue. "There's a lot to be done. First we need pictures." He stood back as Cyn started storing images in her phone. When she finished, Jack unpegged the sheet and rolled up Emily's body in it—the room felt utterly empty when he did.

He then went to the other pits and felt the binding spells in each and the trapped souls and heard their screams in his head. It was strange to shine the phone's light down and not see people staring up at him. He was flicking the light quickly side to side just to see if he could catch the image of one of the ghosts when Cyn asked, "Can we go now?"

She stood white and trembling; again, this was more of a trial for her than it was for him. Souls were the source of power to the necromancer, they were currency. Jack's power went no further than his own soul. He had no desire over any of these.

"You can go, if you wish," he answered, handing her the phone. "I'll be all right." She didn't leave, but only stood at the top of the pit, shining the light on him as he went down to analyze the spells holding the souls in place. They had been carved into the wall with a knife and then dabbed in blood, creating an ethereal connection between the blood used and the souls held. "Interesting," he said in a whisper as he lightly ran a finger over the symbols.

They were very similar to the one he had used earlier to hold Bob in place, only there was a short arc of glyphs curving along the inner ring. These were even more interesting and fantastically more ugly. His hand stung when he touched them.

"Phone, please," he said, snapping his fingers and essentially nullifying the word "please."

Cyn dropped her phone down to him and then she was up there in complete darkness—he could feel her, but not see her. He stared up into the empty darkness, searching for her and it was as though she was just a spirit like the others in the foul dungeon. *That* cut through the emptiness inside of him.

He shot the light in her direction; she was pale almost to the point of being chalk-white and because the darkness behind her was so absolute, she threw no shadow and again the idea that she was only spirit hit him. "Talk to me, will you?" he asked, finally feeling something in his chest beside the dull beat of his heart.

There was a long disquieting silence before she asked, "Talk about what?"

"I don't know, maybe your goose farm?"

It was what made her happy, and she began to prattle on about the geese and what sort of enclosure she would make for them, though she never used the word "enclosure." For her, it was always a "goose house." When she started, her breath came out in shaky sort of manner, but gradually her words firmed up as she described the "house" and its seven bedrooms and twelve baths.

"Geese need plenty of water," she explained. It was all mindless blather in his opinion, and yet the words centered him and held him in place. She was his anchor; she kept him human when he felt altogether alien. And the words made her real and gave her form.

He took pictures, concentrating on the glyphs along the arc. "They are for pain," he whispered. It was a form of torture—a *soul-wrack*. They made him uncomfortable being so close but he had nothing to fear. The glyphs had been personalized; each soul had their own glyph. It was a sign of love—the love of pain. He hurried through the inspection of the pits; there wasn't much else to be discovered unless he wanted a primer in the art of torture, which he did not.

After a long climb to the surface where the air was clean and cool and the stars inviting, he swept past the poor man with the twisted limbs and the eyes that sported golf tees, as if he weren't there. He went right for a garden hose and washed his hands and then his boots with the rust-smelling water.

"You need to eat more," Cyn said, handing him the box of *Junior Mints*. He ate them mindlessly as he watched the priests on their hands and knees, praying over the man they had hauled up from the pits. There was a soft glow around him and in the strange light he looked unconscious, something that was hard to tell what with the golf tees.

The two priests were healing the man. It was skill that not all clergy possessed, but was mandatory in the *Raider Squads*.

"I wouldn't waste all your energy on him," Jack suggested. "We have a lot more work tonight. And you'll need to get someone over here to break the holding spells down in the pits. Those are real nasty."

Father Jordan looked up, sweat coursing off his brow. "Waste our energy? I don't believe you, Jack. This man is suffering and we are going to do everything in our power to ease his pain. That is our calling, just like being a callous ass is yours."

Too tired to care, Jack only shrugged at the rebuke and munched down more *Junior Mints* until he was thirsty and then he glanced down at the hose. "No, drink this," Cyn said as he reached for it. In her hand was a bottle of water; he drank, forgetting to say thank you.

After he chugged the entire thing, he tossed the plastic aside and said to Metzger: "Torture Bob. Cut off his parts or whatever, I don't care; just find out where he got the glyph." A question rose on the captain's face, but Jack waved it away. "Ask Cyn, she'll tell you what glyph I mean. Now, I need some sleep."

He was close to falling unconscious right there on Bob's scrubby lawn. By a force of will, he made it to the back seat of the Lexus, crawled in and was snoring in seconds. When they woke him a little after midnight, he was almost his old self.

"Did we get the info out of Bob?" he asked Cyn the moment his eyes popped open.

"With the help of Father Jordan, we did. That bloke is bloody useful when questioning a suspect. You have to give him that."

Every priest seemed to have the innate ability to tell when a lie was being told in their presence, but Jordan's was a little more advanced than others. He could "glean" things. It took a lot of getting used to, having human lie detectors around all the time; not that Jack was much of a liar. But even white lies caused eyebrows to rise around Jordan.

"The man who Bob got the glyph from is back downtown," she said, going on. "We were only two blocks from his store when we picked up him up and judging by what that jerk said, the man we're after is probably a necromancer."

The idea of facing a necromancer didn't faze Jack just then. He was too hungry to worry about that. "Back downtown? That's good. We passed a Mexican restaurant on the way here. I could use some fajitas. Does that sound good to you?"

She shook her head, giving him a tired chuckle. "It's almost one in the bloody morning. Nothing is going to be open."

A glance at the dashboard clock showed she wasn't lying; his stomach rumbled. "I hope we can find a twenty-four hour Taco Bell. Say, how's...uh, how's that guy, the one from the pit?"

"Better. All of his limbs are straight now and he can almost walk, but they're going to have to bring in someone with a bit more mojo than our two priests to heal his eyes."

This wasn't exactly great news to Jack. He still had to deal with the man who had given Bob the glyph and, necromancer or not, it was almost a guarantee that he would be trouble. Jack would've liked to have gone after him with his team at full strength.

Cyn could practically read his mind. "We could get him in the morning. He might not be going anywhere." Jack couldn't take the chance. If there was one thing that could be counted on with the scum who peddled demon paraphernalia, it was that they had a sixth sense when trouble was coming.

A knock on his window; it was Captain Metzger. He was the only one of the five who looked ready for business. "Are you good to go?"

"Five by five," Jack replied. "Hey, sorry if I was too big of a jerk before."

"Nothing I can't handle," Metzger said. "Are you up for taking out a necromancer?"

"Sure, piece of cake." That was true. Jack could swat necromancers all day—it was the undead and the unkillable things that they brought into the world that were the problem.

After dropping off Bob's victim at the local cathedral and swinging by the nearest Taco Bell, the team, with Bob in tow, hurried to "the shop" as Bob called it. The place was, ironically enough, another of the many Chinese herb shops specializing in items of dubious origin and quality that were "guaranteed" to repel demons.

Captain Metzger pulled up just down the block with Jack and Cyn in the Lexus right behind. Jack sat in the driver's seat for a moment, munching a *gordita* and feeling the aura in the air— it was dead. No spells had been cast recently. Disappointed, he grunted and took another bite.

"Maybe the lack of spells means he doesn't know we're coming," Cyn suggested.

Jack didn't believe it. A necromancer left traces and the only undead presence was the lingering taint around Bob; more than likely their bird had flown the coop. With a nasty Taco Bell burp, he zipped his jacket over his Kevlar armor, grabbed his to-go bag and his sword and strolled toward the darkened store. Cyn, toting a shotgun, joined him on his right while Captain Metzger had his left.

"Chalupa?" Jack asked, offering the bag to the soldier. "I was saving the gordita but you can have the chalupa."

Metzger shook his head, his eyes at squints; he wasn't scared. Jack had never seen him scared. Instead, he got hyped up, his blood running fast, his eyes twitching at any shadow that didn't look entirely kosher.

Cyn was more relaxed. Demons were her big fear and there weren't any around and it wasn't likely that one could be called by the time they kicked in the front door of the shady store.

Both priests were drooping from exhaustion, so Jack counted it a lucky thing that they wouldn't find a demon inside. The only one who looked truly scared was Bob. He was no longer the empty shell that he had been; he had come alive and now his haunted eyes stared into the store.

Jack should have taken that as a cue, that and the fact the place was devoid of graffiti. It was the only establishment on the street that could make that claim, which suggested that the local scum were too afraid to tag the building.

They strode to the door. It was glass and steel…and it was unlocked. It pointed to a quick exit by the owner, but in fact it was an invitation.

Confident that he would find the place empty, Jack walked in and paused, scanning the eclectic and sometimes obscene goods for sale. It was a haphazard and unruly store that was part Chinese herb shop, part voodoo parlor and part tourist trap. From the walls hung antelope horns and silver swords. On the shelves were glazed ocelot eyes, and crosses made from jet and ivory and cedar. In a glass case behind the register was a burnt piece of wood that was supposedly part of the True Cross.

Deeper in the store were darkened alcoves where tarot or palm readings occurred, and in one of them was a figure that sat so unbelievably still that Jack missed him at first.

It was Metzger who nudged Jack and pointed with his shotgun.

"So far you are disappointment, Mister Dreyden," the man said. His voice, made sinister by the dark, was marred by a Chinese accent which was thick, mangling his words.

"Wait until you get to know me," Jack replied. "I'm pretty sure that I'm more of an embarrassment than a disappointment."

"Yes."

Jack glanced at Cyn with a raised eyebrow and said to her: "Yes? That's all he has to say? He's a pretty cool customer seeing as he's outnumbered five to one. What do you think? Is he tougher than he looks?" Cyn only shrugged. He could see the fear building in her eyes and he wanted to reassure her; however the man took that moment to stand.

It was like watching a shadow of a kite unfolding and growing. Only his face was fully visible, looming larger, threatening...and yet, in the last, the person who came to stand across a low, knee-high table from them was a head shorter than Jack and thin as a reed.

The danger that surrounded him was not in proportion to his size, however. It was a magnitude greater. This was no necromancer, this was something more. Jack pushed Cyn behind him. "Wait outside and take the priests with you. I got this."

The man chuckled, low and evil. "Leave them to stay, Mister Dreyden, my glory will only be greater."

At that exact second, Captain Metzger clicked the safety off of his shotgun. The metallic *snick* was a trigger in itself and things took on a slow motion quality. Jack saw blood and more importantly, he felt blood. He knew the blood and what it meant.

The man clenched a fist, the source of the blood and very quickly the source of the spell. Jack had misjudged the man in a huge way. This was no shopkeeper looking to make a buck, and this was no necromancer letting a demon fight his battles for him.

This was a sorcerer.

His hand clenched and drops of blood fell, forming, not a hieroglyph, but a Chinese character. It was tinged silver—the soul of the man; the power of the spell.

The fist with the blood glowed. He raised it and brought it down. Metzger bellowed an order that was ignored. Cyn flinched. There was no other way to put it. She saw the glow in the man's hand and her muscles bunched uselessly in anticipation of what was coming. The priests started to trace the sign of the cross in the air but they were too slow.

Only Jack did anything constructive and his moves were dictated by the erratic nature of fate and his own instinct. There was a low table separating him and his opponent. He leapt over it, just as the man brought his glowing fist down on the floor, yelling: "Shishin Ighn!"

Blinding light flared and there was an explosion of thunder as silvered electricity blasted outward from the man's fist. The bolt separated into six blazing streaks of light, each one crackling across the floor and then up the legs of Jack's team. They convulsed as the power ran up their bodies and then they fell, twitching.

Jack couldn't spare them a glance. He had been in the air as the lightening passed beneath him and he watched it in amazement and fear. The power it took for that spell would have left him useless for a day and yet the man wasn't through.

By some secret means, he opened up another cut on his left wrist; another avenue to his soul. It was access to more power and a second spell. Jack knew he couldn't count on getting lucky again and so he threw himself into the attack, desperate to keep his opponent dodging his sword thrusts instead of casting spells.

And the man could dodge.

When it came to the sword, there were very, very few people on the planet who could best him man to man, sword to sword…and yet this man slipped and ducked and dodged his sword time and again. They danced all around the store, upending bottles of ginger, knocking over warthog teeth and breaking furniture, and yet Jack couldn't touch him.

Jack wanted to think that his inability to skewer the man was because he was using a heavy "zombie" blade, one that was hell against the ghouls and animated corpses because of its heft and the weight of its edge, but the man was a ghost. It was like trying to stab smoke.

He was, in a word, magical. No one could move that fast. Jack would have had more success hacking a fly in two.

And it was just a matter of seconds before the man would slam that glowing fist against the floor and fry Jack in place. In desperation, and realizing there wasn't anything more desperate, Jack abandoned the sword. He basically launched it at the man, knowing that he would dodge it—and he did.

Then Jack launched himself as well. His arms spread, desperate to catch the man, to pin him down, to turn the tables so that he would be on equal footing. Jack was quick; blazing quick. It was the only thing that allowed him to get his strong, fencer's hands on the man.

There then came a desperate struggle in the dark.

No longer was the Asian trying to plant the glowing hand on the ground. Now, he was trying to plant the knuckles square on Jack's chest where the electricity would blacken his heart like an over-done roast.

And yet the advantage passed to Jack. The Chinese man had the bones of a bird and the muscle mass of a fourteen year old boy. Jack lifted him clear off his feet, threw him down on his back, and was delighted to hear the whoosh of air shoot out of him.

The glow died in his hand and the hitching in his throat meant that another spell wasn't going to happen anytime soon, or so Jack thought.

"Where's my cousin?" Jack demanded, staring deep into the man's black eyes; Jack had him straddled, basically sitting on this chest and holding his arms out from his body. "Where the hell is Robert? And don't lie! The glyph that Bob Chapman had in his possession could only have come from Robert Montgomery. It wasn't just an Egyptian hieroglyph, it also had the cuneiform wedges and that meant it was the original script, the original language of man."

The Chinese man grinned, showing oddly small and blackened teeth. "It no script of man. What you say is opposite of truth." His grin became strained and there was sweat in his black hair; it looked like oil. He struggled against Jack's strength. Although he was small and thin, he was also wiry and strong in a slippery sort of way. He twisted and squirmed like a bag of snakes.

"Stop!" Jack hissed. "Or I'll..." The wrist Jack had thought pinned and useless shot to the right and suddenly the man's hand was free. Jack didn't freak or panic. He had everything *but* the wrist under control and he knew that in order to cast a spell, the man would have to cut himself. It was the only way to open a new port to his soul...and somehow he did cut himself.

He jerked his arm and suddenly his wrist was bleeding. Desperately, Jack grabbed the wrist in an iron grip but it was too late. "Shishin Ighn!" his enemy cried as a single drop of blood hit the floor of the shop. It formed one tiny glyph, intricate and beautiful. Up close, Jack saw that the character wasn't Chinese; it was a proto-hieroglyph, only it had been rendered into something that resembled art by the man's skill or power.

The glyph was altogether fascinating to Jack and its lines and swirls etched themselves into his memory, though why, he didn't know. With the Chinese man's fist glowing, and sparks arcing between his knuckle and Jack's chest, he was never going to be able to use it.

All it would take for the man to kill Jack was a single touch.

Chapter 4
Akron, Ohio
Jack Dreyden

The tiny arcs of electricity stung the flesh and dazzled the eyes. They also glinted off metal and Jack saw how the man had cut himself. There was a razor blade woven into the fabric of his pants right at hip level. His clothing was what Jack would have described as "oriental." They were loose, black, and soft. They were more like stylized pajamas than real street clothes.

And they shouldn't have razor blades in them...unless the man had so thoroughly prepared himself for battle that he had considered every possibility, including being straddled by a much larger man. The implications were frightening.

"Who are you?" Jack asked in amazement as well as to buy time. His grip on the man's wrist was becoming slick with sweat and the arcs of electricity were causing his muscles to twitch.

"I am man who send you on and for you it is no peace. Your soul is marked."

There was time to wonder about what that meant. Jack had been concentrating so much on the man's wrist and the flashing power in his fist that he hadn't kept control of himself. He was over balanced. Before he knew it, the smaller man had used Jack's weight against him and he found himself under the Asian who was pressing down with all his strength.

More arcs, more pain, another glint. The man didn't have one razor blade sown into his clothes; he had many and in odd places. And he had one perilously close to the back of Jack's right hand—it wasn't perilous for Jack, however.

Grunting with the effort, Jack forced their locked hands to the side and felt the razor slide across and into his skin. It was a cold feeling, followed by a rush of warmth and the *knowledge* of his soul. It was right there bubbling up from the laceration.

Jack felt it with his mind; he took it and directed it. The blood/soul mixture trickled down his wrist to drop onto the floor where Jack formed it into a curious and beautiful glyph. The Chinese man saw it and his eyes were suddenly big and round. Jack had the advantage now—his hands were clamped on his enemy's wrists. When the lightning came, it would course directly into those wrists and up those arms and even if it didn't kill his enemy, it would likely turn him into a mewling, drooling shell.

"Shishin Ighn!" Jack cried, but just as he did, the man literally flew off of him. It was more magic and though Jack had lost his chance to end the fight, he still marveled at the strength of the man. He had used the lightning spell three times already *and* he had been doing some spell that added to his agility, and yet his hand still glowed and his eyes weren't dim.

The two men faced each other with twelve feet of littered floor between them. Although Jack was tired and almost drained, he felt as though he could win the fight. Cyn was groaning and Captain Metzger was groping for his shotgun. Time was on his side.

Magical power was on his opponent's side. In a blur of speed that only magic could have caused, the man leapt in the air with his glowing fist raised and then brought it down as though he was trying to destroy the building. There was a flash and a crack of thunder—this was followed a fraction of a second later by another flash.

Jack had been expecting the move and even though he was slightly slower, he managed to release the magical energy pent up in his fist almost at the same time. The two bolts raced at each other in a blink and there was a third flash as they collided. The room was saturated in a strobe of light that dazzled the eyes momentarily. Jack turned away, grimacing and thus didn't see that his weaker bolt was overcome and that his enemy's bolt raced the remaining space across the floor and then ran up his legs.

The pain was harsh and bitter, but also relatively weak. Jack's bolt had drained it of some of its force. It traveled up his legs to about mid-thigh and then lost its power. Jack fell forward, with a strangled cry, unable to feel his feet. Everything was numb from his knees down, while north of his knees his legs felt as though they were on fire—but he was alive and what was more, his enemy was spent.

They both were. There was no more magic left in either man. Two steps away was Jack's sword. He crawled to it as his opponent looked around for a weapon of his own. He had not prepared himself for every contingency; he was backed into a corner with a furious but ice cold man in front of him.

At that moment, Jack was, in essence, soulless. He was the demon in the room now. He lurched forward, his feet coming alive with the feeling of a thousand burning needles jabbing him; it didn't help his mood, which was altogether black.

"Where's my cousin. Where's Robert Montgomery? And before you answer, know this: I want you to lie to me. I want you to give me an excuse to slide this blade into you. So go ahead and lie."

From behind him, Cyn said: "Jack, please take a step back. You're not yourself." This caused the Chinese man to give Jack a sly smirk.

"Don't let him hurt me," the man said, his accent suddenly thicker. "I give up."

He lifted his empty hands; they shook as though with fear. Jack knew the man wasn't afraid, though he should have been. "I asked you a question," Jack demanded.

"Please, Jack," Father Jordan said. "Don't do anything stupid."

That was the wrong choice of words. Jack leapt forward, swinging the sword. Without his magic, the man wasn't nearly as quick as he had been and he could only save his face by sacrificing his left arm, which he raised in a defensive move.

Jack's razor sharp blade was three and a half feet of heavy steel; he could have hacked off the man's arm if he wished. Instead he felt that *death by a thousand cuts* was more appropriate. The blade went a half inch deep into the man's ulna just below the elbow.

It had to have hurt like a bitch, but the man only snarled a foreign curse as the arm fell limp to his side, bleeding without any of the telltale silver. Behind Jack, he could hear Cyn's gasp and could feel the priest's outrage. But Jack didn't care and he was just getting started. No gasp was going to tear down the mountainous rage within him.

"One more time, where's my cousin? Only he has access to the glyph that you sold to Bob Chapman."

There was a pause; too long of one for Jack in his state and he again attacked. Just as he did, Cyn cried out again: "Jack, no!"

She was his anchor. She was his soul when he didn't have one. He turned the blade so that it struck with the flat instead of the edge. It wouldn't draw blood but it would leave a healthy mark since he didn't pull the swing this time but brought it down full force on the man's shoulder. There was a hardy *smack*; it was completely unsatisfying. He wanted blood. A second blow was a little better and a third broke all the fingers on the man's right hand as he tried to block the blows raining down on him.

Cyn grabbed Jack's arm and anchor or not, it was a near thing to hold back the fury in him.

"Maybe everyone should leave," Jack said through gritted teeth. "Me and this evil piece of filth need to have a talk...a real talk." As the others glanced around, not knowing what to do, the two sorcerers eyed each other. The man's face bent in disgust, twisted in impotent fury and then sagged as he finally realized that he had been beaten and that there were only a few minutes left to him.

He nodded at Jack and there came an understanding between them. Then he bowed his head and said: "My name is Truong. I sought out you cousin in hope for exchange of ideas or knowledge. I search for wisdom."

Father Timmons surprised Jack by saying: "You mean you were after more power."

Truong gazed at him blandly. "It two sides of same coin. One is equal to other, but, yes, I seek power. You cousin is now strong. His dead sorcery is very strong. His knowledge is very great."

"You found him then," Metzger said. "Where is he?"

"A land of Sudan. There is much death in this land and many bodies for him. No one notices if they go missing. No one talks of this. The people is much very afraid. I do not know what he was doing in this land, but he was north of Khartoum in desert land."

Jack glanced back at Cyn. "The Pyramids of Meroe. It has to be." She nodded, a little crease working in between her eyes. Jack addressed Truong once more. "How did you find him? He's become an expert at covering his tracks, so how did you do it?"

Truong became guarded; Jack saw it in his eyes. "I am from a secret peoples. Only Chinese. Only sorcerer. None can know of them. My tongue would rot out of my mouth before name is spoken. It no can be spoken. They have knowledge of much thing in world, even the whispers of dark things; of secret things. They know your cousin."

"A secret society of sorcerers?" Jack asked, trying to understand what Truong was saying. When the man nodded, Jack followed up, stating as fact: "You will tell me how I can find them."

"I can not. Is no possible."

"He's not lying," Father Jordan said as Jack began to bristle.

"Of course I no lie. Why would I lie?" Truong asked. "My life is no longer mine."

Cyn looked into Jack's face. "What's he mean by that?"

Jack flicked his empty eyes at Truong; they were two soulless creatures, but at least Jack had an excuse. Without a hint of remorse, Jack explained: "He's going to tell us everything and then I'm going to kill him. I'll make it quick, though. That's our deal."

There was a general uproar around the two sorcerers, but neither moved or took their eyes off the other. Jack couldn't take the chance, there was no telling how quickly Truong would recover his strength.

"You can't do this, Jack!" Father Timmons warned. He was angry and thrust himself forward, but he wasn't stupid. Jack's eyes were flat grey and Timmons didn't dare get too close to him. He squeezed to the right of Cyn, partially using her as a shield and added, "We are supposed to be the good guys, here."

Good...Jack couldn't understand the term with his inner core so empty. With a shrug of indifference, he said: "He would kill me."

"We don't stoop to their level," Cyn said. "Remember your trial when dealing with Robert's army. You would've *become* Robert if you had failed. Don't fail now!"

A grunt escaped Jack. These were all fine platitudes and he supposed he didn't want to be a "bad guy," however, that was defined, but he did want to be a "live guy" and that wouldn't happen if he let Truong go.

"How about I put it this way, he will kill me if I don't kill him first. That's just the way of it. Right Truong?" The Asian only shrugged. He couldn't exactly lie with the priest right there; this was the closest he could come. Jack stabbed him with the sword.

Truong tried to dance back, but without his magic, Jack was faster. He lunged forward, unfurling like a whip so that he was in full extension when the tip of the sword slid through the muscles of Truong's chest and ground on the bones of his ribs. The placement of the strike was precise and purposeful.

An epee would have slid through the intercostal muscles and buried itself in lung tissue, possibly causing the lung to collapse—Jack didn't want to kill Truong just then; he wanted to hurt him. They had a deal and that one shrug had been practically an admission that he was backing out of it.

There were cries around him, all of which went ignored. "Tell them," Jack growled. There was no need to say: *Or else*. The *Or else* was obvious in his eyes and in the way he was a coiled spring; he was quite ready peel the flesh from Truong's bones.

"Yes," Truong said, glaring. "He not wrong. It is way of sorcerers. Power is from slay others. Power is from soul. Power is from enemy defeated. I would slay my enemy and take his spell. That is the way."

"It's the way of all things," Jack said. "The cat grows in strength by eating the bird. The wolf eats the rabbit. The man eats the deer. It's natural and it's the only way."

Cyn shook her head, saying: "It's not the only way. The mother *gives* her milk to her child, freely."

Father Timmons also spoke up: "And the Christian gives to the needy from his bounty."

Truong gave Jack a sly smile and a knowing look. "Is way of sorcerer. And necromancer, too, Miss Cyn. Your cousin knows this. Your cousin will kill you. He is strong. He stronger than Truong. He *knows* much and see much. He play game better than you. He is cunning. Ahh, but now is time."

"Yes," Jack answered, slowly, wondering why Truong was asking to be killed. It seemed smarter to draw this out. He could buy time by playing on the sympathies of the weak, or yapping through another long explanation of the nature of sorcerers. That's what Jack would do. He would do anything in the hope of getting lucky, or...

"Hey!" Metzger suddenly cried, interrupting Jack's train of thought. "Bob's gone!" The others spun around; however, Jack kept his eyes dead on Truong. The smile on the man's face was like poison, killing any rationality in Jack.

"He has book of spells, too," Truong said. "So sorry, Mister Dreyden. So, so sorry."

The sword in Jack's hand began to quiver. His immense fury was almost out of his control. Through gritted teeth, he said. "Find him! Break into two teams. Metz, take Cyn in the Lexus. Timmons take Jordan in the Camaro."

"But..." Timmons began.

"No buts!" Jack screamed. "If you want to save a hundred innocent lives, find and kill Bob. If you want to *try* to save one guilty one, then by all means, hang around and yap."

They actually paused to consider the choices and Jack was within an ace of beating them with the flat of his sword. Metzger came to his senses first, grabbing Cyn and Timmons and dragging them out of the store with Jordan following, casting looks over his shoulder.

"They are weak," Truong said, getting to his knees and stretching out his neck to the fullest. "And they make you weak, but I make you strong."

Chapter 5
Akron, Ohio
Cynthia Childs

They drove the streets slowly, Metzger screaming into his phone, demanding police backup, only none would come; he had made the mistake of mentioning that they were part of a *Raider Squad*.

"You're on your own," a lieutenant told them. "Akron is now a *Sanctuary City*. Try not to make too big of a mess."

Metzger looked at the phone as if he had never seen one before. "What in God's name is a Sanctuary City?"

It was basically the city's way of announcing that they had given up. In much the same way some cities had given up on fighting the war on drugs or illegal immigration, Akron went with a: "We can't stop it so why bother trying" mentality and, as any sane person could have guessed, the problem hadn't gone away, it had quickly exploded.

Jack's team was basically on their own.

For two hours, Metzger drove in ever-widening circles, as Cyn reached out with her mind, attempting to feel demonic activity—the city was dark with it. Everywhere they went, the air had a bad feel. It infected their mood and neither of them would have been able to scrape together a smile if their lives depended on it.

After hours of searching, they came away empty handed and frustrated. Finding Jack in the alley behind Truong's shop didn't help their mood. He was passed out behind a dumpster, his bloody sword across his knees, the once forgotten Taco Bell bag, torn open and empty, lying discarded by his elbow. Truong's head sat on the pavement next to the bag and in his mouth was a balled up chalupa wrapper.

In Jack's hand was an empty bottle; he reeked of whiskey and he snored like bear.

"Oh Jack" Cyn said.

His eyes came open; they were bleary and had trouble focusing on her. "Hey, Cyndia. Whatcha doin?"

What am I doing? She didn't know the answer to that question, though she asked it of herself ten times a day. She had been crisscrossing the country and the globe for a year and a half and she didn't know why. It wasn't because she was such a valuable member of the team; any halfway decent looking girl would have sufficed; demons just weren't that picky. All they seemed to care about was that their victims had an aura of desperation around them—and she had it big.

She was desperate for Jack, when he was whole that is, when his soul was a real force and not some tattered remnant as it frequently was. She loved him when he was a full man, the only problem was that he rarely was. His self-appointed task was killing him and he was rarely a happy man. At the best of times, he was a man driven by guilt.

Guilt over his cousin and guilt over the murders that sat heavy on his conscience, and guilt over scenes like this —though this was a first for Jack. He had executed Truong. There really was no other word for what he had done. Jack had likely wrapped up Truong's "trial" in a minute, declared him guilty and now he was like this: bleary and having trouble sitting upright.

She actually liked *Drunk Jack*, she just never liked the reason behind the alcohol. Stepping past the severed head, she took the sword from him and set it against the wall. She then kicked the bottle away; it rolled funny and she saw a strange sediment at the bottom that looked familiar.

"Wait a second. Wasn't there a snake in that bottle? I saw it on the shelf when we first walked in." With a sinking feeling she began looking around the alley floor, hoping to see its remains.

"There was," Jack said with a grin. He tapped his head and said: "Truong say there is strong magic in adder. Potent magic. Make you strong and fast."

Cyn looked him in the face, fully expecting him to hurl up the snake and the alcohol at any moment. "When did he tell you that? Before or after you killed him?"

"After." Again Jack tapped his head. "He said it right here. Like an echo. He also said that you make me weak. That's why he got the ol' chalula wrapper in the mouth routine. He wouldn't shut up. He said that you would kill me. He said I could be more the most powerful sor-sor-er-er. But I said I love Cyn and ya know what he said?"

"What?" Cyn said, breathlessly. She was afraid to find out.

Jack smiled. "He said then we could enjoy ourselves when we were both in hell together for eternity. Wasn't that nice? Eternity sounds nice. Am I being loud? We should try to keep it down, ya know. It's night time an' peoples are sleeping."

"Speaking of which, let's get you to bed," Metzger said, stepping forward, careful not to kick Truong's head. The captain lifted Jack to his feet and was about to drag him back to the Lexus where Jack would likely vomit and then pass out.

Cyn stopped him. She stared into Jack's face, trying to look into the pits of his eyes. "You can hear Truong in your mind?"

"Jus a whisper now, but yeah before he was loud."

"And what did he say about me? Tell me that part again."

Jack looked her up and down, his head making exaggerated moves. "Robert will use you to get to me. Buuuut, I don't really think that'll happen and iffin' it does, he'll rue it. Tha's a funny word: rue. Rhymes with poo and moo and..."

"Don't believe any of this, Cyn," Metzger said. "Jack is drunk and Truong...he was a bad man."

"Yeah, tha's why I killed him," Jack said, again nodding his head way up and way down. "You have to believe me Cyn. He was eeeevil. And we couldn't take him to jail. He knows magic and would just, like break out, no problem. And you know what? He used Bob. Ya know that stupid guy who had the demon in him. He gave Bob the spell, knowing that he would kill all those people. He did it so I would come and then he was gonna kill me. Tha's way more eviler than me, right? Right? I had to kill him, Cyn. You believe me, right?"

He was begging, his eyes teared over. Jack didn't want to be the bad guy. He wanted to be good, straight through from one side of his murky soul to the other, but it never seemed to work out for him and that was why Cyn stayed. Jack deserved something that made him happy and she did her best, even when she was hurting, like right at that moment.

"Yes, he had to die," she said, and it was the truth, the hard to swallow and much harder to live with truth. Cyn loved the idea of a goose farm and little golden chicks running around under foot. Deciding who got to live and who got to die was not a life she wanted to lead, and yet someone had to. Someone had to do what no one else would or could. It was why she was there holding Jack's bloody sword and wondering if she should do something with Truong's head.

With a great deal of disgust and whimpering, she took the surprisingly heavy head by the hair in two pinched fingers and brought it back into the store and set it next to Truong's body. Then, after taking three deep breaths, she searched him until she found a set of keys—one key went to his car, another to the store and a third, likely to his home. She then left, locking the door behind her.

Surprisingly, Jack didn't hurl up his Taco Bell and nor did he pass out. He stared out the window with a vacant expression until they were at the hotel. They made a strange group in their body armor, carrying shotguns and

Jack's bloody sword; the lone front desk clerk stared as they trooped by.

Jack even showered before bed; it was a long, steaming shower and it was five in the morning before the two fell asleep. Jack was out for fourteen hours; Cyn not nearly as long. He spoke in his sleep, something he did on occasion, though this time he spoke in Mandarin, something he had never done.

"I killed Truong," Jack said when he woke.

"I know."

He wouldn't look in her direction. "Did you watch? I can't really remember too much."

She tried to make light of the situation. "Do you remember eating an adder? It was the free prize found at the bottom of every bottle of Chinese whiskey."

"That I do remember. It felt alive going down. Truong said not to chew so...wait...he was dead then." Jack got up and went to the mirror and looked deep into his eyes; they were blue all save for the "whites," these were fantastically red.

"Do you feel different?" Cyn asked.

"You mean now that I've hacked a man's head off with a sword and stole his essence? Yeah, now that you mention it, I do." He laughed high in his throat, looked miserable for a second and then blew out a deep breath; this was all the depression, sadness, anxiety and plain craziness he would allow himself.

"So did anyone get Bob yet?" he asked.

Cyn checked her phone and the answer was: no. Metzger, who had demanded help from his boss, was out looking with two FBI agents tagging along. Fathers Timmons and Jordan, along with a gaggle of local priests and Ignatius Gourman, the Bishop of Cleveland, were in the deep pits beneath Bob's house, trying to break the ring of glyphs and free the trapped souls. It wasn't as easy pouring Holy Water on the glyphs this time; these glyphs hadn't been drawn by the hand of man.

"Maybe you should go take a look at them," Cyn suggested. "You're stronger today, aren't you?"

"Yes, quite a bit. Maybe half-strength; stronger than I should be, but I should save it for Bob. When I catch that guy...well, we'll see what happens. We'll see if he's learned anything from my...I mean from Truong's book of spells. A part of me sort of wishes he has."

Cyn worried about that part of Jack—the part that could absorb the power of a dead sorcerer. She feared what it meant, she feared that it would be as addictive as necromancy was, and necromancy was ten times worse than any drug ever invented. Cyn had never cast a full spell and yet she could feel the urge and the need.

She feared that the ugly desire colored her thinking; was it necromancy that had her suggesting they go to Bob's house? "How about we just go look at the pits?" she said. "Maybe there are some clues as to where Bob might be hiding."

Jack agreed, and after a heavy, hangover reducing dinner, they drove out to Bob's place on the edge of nowhere. They both went prepared for battle; however Bob didn't represent the same sort of threat as Truong. They wore their armor, but their vests were on loose, their helmets left in the car and their weapons holstered or sheathed.

As they entered the house, the stench assaulted them and they both felt the power of the spells in the air, though it was weaker than before.

There were a pair of aged and exhausted priests sitting at Bob's filthy kitchen table, their faces lined and worn. They had their elbows amongst stained and crusted plates and glasses. The wood tabletop was scored and splintered and there was ancient egg yolk petrified in the grooves and black ketchup splattered like blood. The two men ignored the mess—compared to the lower dungeons, the table was practically sterile.

They seemed to know Jack and Cyn by reputation and their eyes narrowed. Jack's narrowed right back. The burger he had eaten hadn't been greasy enough to cancel his hangover out completely and Cyn could see his mood disintegrating.

"Let's leave them on their break," she said and escorted Jack through the house. On Bob's couch was a third priest, sprawled out in what had once been a white robe but was now stained with dirt and feces. He snored like a chainsaw, his mouth hung open showing a white tongue; even his breathing sounded tired.

They made their way down the maze of ladders and deep into the pits where the darkness clung to them and closed in around them. The nearness of the spells was dizzying to Cyn and she was drawn to them, the necromancer in her screaming out to study the spells, to absorb them and then to slice open one of the priests and use his pure blood the way she was meant to.

The temptation was so great that her hands were slippery with sweat on the rungs of the ladders.

"H-How's it going so far, Father?" she asked Father Timmons. The priest was standing facing the dirt wall, leaning his head against his arm. He took up most of the narrow passageway. The only light came from seven candles stabbed into the ground around him and it was as though he stood in a shifting golden puddle. The rest of him was angular shadows and a wheezing breath.

Before he could answer, Jack said: "You know what? There was…there was a spell. Damn! It's on the tip of my tongue. It was in Truong's mind. It was for light, but how did it go? Sha-shi nai something. It was in Mandarin, I think."

As usual, Timmons was uncomfortable being so close to Jack, and he especially didn't like it when Jack spoke about what he called his "pagan practices."

"We're getting more flashlights," he said, "so, you can keep your witchcraft to yourself. We have quite enough of that down here already to last a dozen lifetimes. My goodness, those spells the demon cast are doozeys. It's like trying to pray away an iron wall. Even the bishop is having his troubles and the man is a veritable fountain of power. The Holy Spirit is great within him."

Timmons then paused, looking uncomfortable, and smiled a smile that was the closest thing to a lie that would ever pass his lips. "Speaking of the bishop, uh, he's not a man who puts up with much nonsense. He's very old school."

"Meaning what?" Jack growled.

"Meaning that maybe it's best if you come back another time. Your brand of magic, though it may not stem from a place of evil, surely doesn't stem from God's love and soooo...uh, it's not, a uh..."

"It's not what?" Jack demanded, an unhealthy gleam in his eye.

The priest gave a little shrug and finally admitted: "It's not welcome. I tried to explain the situation to his Excellence, but there is a certain stigma to what you are doing. In his view and in others as well... and mine as you know, it's thought that at best you are mistreating the gift of your soul that the Lord has given you. At worst, you are little more than a witch. Do you understand why I'm telling you this?"

Jack didn't answer; his eyes were narrowed in anger. Father Timmons, a very brave man, put his hand on Jack's shoulder. "I don't mean to anger you. I mean to save your soul. That's why I joined your team. I didn't come here to fight demons, I came here because of you, Jack. Your soul is as valuable as any other, and I think we both know that witchcraft will destroy it."

"I'm not a witch," Jack said, momentarily taken back. He seemed uncertain what to say in the face of Timmons' stark admission. "I-I'm a sorcerer. It's different."

"Fine, you are a sorcerer. From an outside perspective, there isn't that much difference between a sorcerer and a necromancer. It's not the discovery of God's love that moves you. And it isn't the thirst for wholesome knowledge or understanding or wisdom you are after. That's why I wonder if you've changed. I have to wonder what brought you down here. Is it the spells? Are you hoping to add them to your repertoire?"

Jack glared and Cyn started pulling on his arm. "Maybe we should go," she whispered.

He resisted. He had his back up and his chest puffed; he was spoiling for a fight. "You think I need to see those spells? Hardly." A knife, deadly sharp was suddenly in his hand and Cyn was sure he was going to cut himself and do something he would later regret, but instead he dropped down, and in the glow of the candles, drew out both of the spells that were found in the pits.

The necromancer in Cyn flared up and she found herself staring at the spells, the glyphs slowly etching into her memory. Before she could finish memorizing them, Jack had her by the arm and was dragging her back toward the first of the ladders. "Can you believe that? I thought I was here to help," he griped. He gestured for Cyn to go up ahead of him but she hesitated, her eyes slipping back to where Father Timmons stood over the circle of glyphs and the arc within it.

She stared until he kicked dirt over the symbols. She then gave Jack a weak smile that went unseen. They were both shadows and she was glad for that. She hated the thing in her and at times like this she feared that Jack would be able to see the need in her eyes.

"You are helping," she insisted. "Maybe you should poke around the house and look for clues. I'm going to wait outside, if you don't mind." She practically fled into the sweet air of the evening. She didn't want to be anywhere near any spells just then. The temptation on her was very great.

It was full dark out when Jack finally strode out of the house, heading for the Lexus. "Find anything?" Cyn asked.

"Nope," Jack said, climbing into the car. He stared at the clock and admitted: "I can't get that spell out of my head. It's growing on me. And not for the reason Timmons thinks. I don't have to learn it. I'm not obsessed and I'm not destroying my soul…well I am, but it always grows back always stronger than before. The thing is, I feel as though I need the spell. You heard Truong...wait, did you hear him? When he said that Robert had grown strong?"

"Yes, I did and it scared me, deeply."

He nodded, holding the keys an inch from the ignition. "It scared me, too. And everything that we've been through this last year scares me as well. It's all building up and it doesn't seem to be getting any better. That fear is what's pushing me. I know Robert, he isn't sitting on his laurels. It's why he's in the Sudan. He is looking for stronger and stronger spells and the names of greater and greater demons." He paused and chuckled. "And here I am feeling that I have to justify myself trying to master a simple light spell."

"You don't need to justify anything with me," she answered, truthfully. Only the night before she had been staring at him in disbelief with a head sitting next to his knee. When he told her that Truong had needed to be executed, she had agreed. She knew the score; she didn't like it, but she knew that Jack was holding back a dam of evil and if he wasn't around, it would fall to someone else, likely someone less noble.

She caught a glance of herself in the rear view mirror as she buckled her seatbelt. Her blue eyes locked on her reflection. The burden would fall on her. She had helped cause the evil and she had power equal to either of her cousins. It was a power she never wanted to taste, or so she told herself.

His smile was one of relief. "I knew I could trust you," he said. She smiled back, but there was just the smallest edge to it. They were leaving Bob's property behind and she felt her longing for the forbidden spells amp up in a quick flare and then the house was behind them, hidden by a battalion of trees; she breathed a sigh of relief.

The relief was short lived. Night in Akron was dreary. The dark hid things; it hid people that liked the dark, it hid those who worshipped in the dark. Cyn could feel the evil in the air. Bob was out there and if he wasn't captured or killed, he would only add to the misery of the dying city.

Before the "Event" the city had been losing a thousand people a year to sunnier climates; since then, the number was closer to a thousand a month. There were entire neighborhoods that sat empty and brooding, where it seemed every window was broken and every door hung like a crooked picture.

Downtown was still alive enough to justify streetlights, however what they illuminated was the essence of sadness: dealers on the stoops, drunks in the gutters, and hookers on the corners. Anyone with any sense of decency was inside their homes behind locked doors and barred windows.

All save Cyn and Jack that is, and she didn't know if they constituted decent people. She didn't think she did especially as they pulled up to the herb shop and there came over her a sudden lust. It crept into her chest and set up a thrumming. Someone was *summoning* a demon; she knew the flavor of "her" spell. Her birthright had been the protection spell that dictated who or what or how many demons came through the portal from hell.

The spell had either been used recently or was being used even then.

"Do you feel that?" she asked.

"I do. I think it drew me here."

After stepping out into the warm night, Jack took his sword in hand. Cyn had her shotgun and, as much as she wanted to rush forward, she let Jack go first. Yes, he was the stronger, and he was tougher, but what held her back was the fact that she was still strong enough to resist.

She followed just behind him, the gun at the ready. She wasn't afraid. The spell wasn't complete and the caster wasn't strong. It was likely Bob Chapman or another loser just like him. If he was dangerous, it would be because he had a gun, meaning she should take center stage for once.

Jack went to the door, naked steel in hand. It was locked and so Cyn stepped forward with the key.

"Wait," Jack said, his eyes slightly unfocussed. The shop was dark. She could see the body of Truong through the window; the blood around him was blacker than the shadows. "There's someone here," Jack said.

He seemed confused. Of course there was someone there. Spells couldn't be cast from thin air; there had to be blood, there had to be sacrifice, there had to be innocence, not lost—it had to be taken.

For some reason Jack hesitated as if he couldn't sense the clear danger in the air. Her mind felt there was someone in terrible danger. Not a child but also not an adult. It was someone in between. Someone who had been lost and had been found by the wrong person.

Cyn stepped forward into the shop, the shotgun, a veritable cannon in her hands. It would drop any man and make a demon think twice.

"Wait," Jack said, his eyes still unfocussed. He was confused. There was a lot riding in the air, but what she felt were the spells: the spell to open the gate, the protection spell, but where was the control spell? Only a fool would twice bring a demon into the world without one. Bob should have learned his lesson and yet, amazingly he was trying to bring Menet-rah back.

Its vile name was on the air, roiling it, but there was also a confusing aroma of blood. Too late Cyn smelled and felt the blood. There was Truong's blood, old and useless, and there was the sacrifice's blood, young and tasty, but there was also a third blood fountain. A third source.

There shouldn't have been. It meant that another spell had been used.

Too late, Cyn paused to sniff and feel. Someone spoke a single word in an ancient language and then she screamed. The sound ran along the tourist trap buddhas and the incense sticks. It shook the bottles of lizard spleens and the snake whiskey. The scream went on and on. She was becoming unglued. Her very essence was being ripped apart.

Her soul was being stripped from her body. It was peeling off the inside of her self. It hurt. It hurt more than any physical body could tolerate. Her *soul* was being torn apart. No one but the dead knew that feeling.

Chapter 6
Akron, Ohio
Jack Dreyden

Jack was slow to see, and he was slow to feel, which meant he was slow to understand. Too many things were happening at once for him to process. Within the store there were spells and there was hot blood and there were bodies, living and dead. There was also danger; it was all around him, ringing alarm bells in his mind. But there was also such pain in the air! It was pain that few could endure for very long.

He didn't know which way to turn first. With so many feelings and fears assaulting his senses, he had stopped just outside the door of the shop; however Cyn had pushed through and now she was screaming fit to wake the dead.

That was his first thought. Somebody was killing her in order to bring a demon across. Menet-rah. Its name popped into his head and that meant: "Bob!" Jack yelled, striding into the shop, his sword in hand. There were a thousand things to process, but killing Bob took precedence.

The herb shop was *mostly* dark. There were three spluttering candles giving Jack just enough light to see the glyphs painted in blood on the floor, though in truth, he hadn't needed to see them to know what they were.

These were the same glyphs found in the pits beneath Bob's house. Cyn was being held in place by them. She writhed and screamed and wept as her soul was being tortured and there was nothing Jack could do. Although the glyphs hadn't been drawn by a demon, he still needed Holy Water to destroy them and he had always relied on the Priests to carry some.

Cyn's screams cut right through him, igniting his fury and he stepped around the woman he loved, knowing he would have to kill Bob quickly in order to save her. "Bob! Show yourself, you coward!"

There was a harsh laugh and then Bob Chapman showed himself: naked, covered in blood—someone else's blood—holding a shotgun and laughing through a sneer. "You call me a coward and yet you hide behind a girl... and this isn't the first time is it? She's always watching out for you and making excuses for you and fighting your battles for you. I shoulda known this time would be no different."

Bob edged closer, the gun pointed square into Jack's chest. He was so close that Jack could smell the snake whiskey on his breath. If he pulled the trigger, there'd be no dodging the blast; no one was that fast, except for maybe Truong. Jack didn't know Truong's speed spell, meaning he didn't have any way out of this jam, unless Captain Metzger would suddenly appear to save the day.

"And now you're hiding behind a gun," Jack said, glancing back in the vain hope that the rest of his team would suddenly show up and save the day. The street was empty.

"At least I fight my battles. I don't rely on four other people to fight them for me. And what I do isn't for the weak or the cowardly. I put my very soul on the line."

Keep talking, you moron, Jack thought, stealing a look around the shop. There were three bodies sprawled out: Truong, whose head was nowhere in sight, a naked teenaged girl whose throat was cut and whose panties were caught up on one ankle, and, finally what looked like a fourth grader. This last person was still alive and staring at Jack with wide, teary eyes. She was bound, naked from the waist down, tied spread eagle and there was blood coming from her.

Cyn's screaming and the awful sight of the girl and the corpses and Bob's smug look had Jack on the edge of a volcanic reaction, one that was going to get him killed. He almost didn't care, but what pulled him back was the leather-bound book sitting in the dancing light of the candles.

It was Truong's spell book.

The yearning in Jack was immediate, almost overshadowing the screams of Cyn and the desperation in the eyes of the little girl. Bob saw Jack's hunger and his smug-ugly face broke into a grin. He knew what Jack was feeling. He knew the lust for power, and just then, Bob had all the power he needed. Bob had power over everyone in the room. He had the spell book and soon he would be gloating over Jack's corpse.

It was infuriating, and all Jack wanted to do just then was light that spell book on fire and shove it up Bob's ass. He could picture this desire in vivid detail. He had everything he needed: lit candles, snake whiskey to get the flames going, the book and finally Bob.

It clicked suddenly that the fantasy could be at least half-real.

"You think you're tough and brave?" Jack said. "Prove it. I'll toss aside my sword, you drop the gun and we settle this man to man, sorcerer to sorcerer. It's the only way to steal my power the proper way, and isn't that what you want? My power?"

Bob smirked. "Nice try. We both know you'd wipe the floor with me. It would hardly be a fair fight, but you had one part right. Drop the sword."

"Coward!" Jack pretended to seethe, while in truth he was calculating distances. "You battle only defenseless girls." He pointed the sword at the fourth grader. The second Bob's eyes slid off of him, Jack tossed the sword. Not at Bob. There was no way he could hope to spear Bob on the end of it; it simply wasn't weighted properly. And hitting him square in the head with the pommel hard enough to knock him out was a one in a thousand chance.

He tossed the blade side-on so that it struck the whiskey bottle, knocking it over. As he hoped the whiskey poured and the adder slid out as if alive. The blade then spun in a short arc, knocking down two of the candles and then:

"No!" Bob screamed in such a high tone that he seemed almost to be joking. The last candle lit up the whiskey, just as the amber puddle reached the spell book. Bob made a break to save the book just as Jack made a break for him empty handed.

Jack had no choice. He was uncut, which meant he had no portal to his soul. And even if did, there was a waist-high counter between him and Bob, and he didn't think that his electricity spell would go through it. Not only that, Cyn's shotgun was frozen in what Jack feared was a death grip and worse, both she and the gun were still within the circle of glyphs. He couldn't reach across the blood words to get it without suffering the same fate as her.

Jack leapt the counter, took two steps and that was when Bob spun and shot him.

There was no pain. His senses were overwhelmed. The harsh orange and white light blinded, the explosion deafened, and the impact stunned. He was thrown back, his muscles losing their tension so that he became a discarded rag doll hidden in a mist of red.

Even when he landed in a crumpled heap, there wasn't any pain. He was in too much shock for pain. He was stunned and couldn't breathe. His lungs failed him. No matter how hard he tried to suck in the tiniest sip of air, his lungs were closed for business.

His only consolation was that Bob had lost the spell book, or so he thought. Seconds after the blast, his head was yanked up and he found himself staring into Bob's face. Behind him was a glow as the shelves of dried herbs went up in a whoosh of flames.

"Nice try," Bob said. In his hand was the spell book; a single edge of it seared black. He shook it in Jack's red face. "Say, does that hurt? It sure looks like it hurts." Bob smiled as he watched Jack tried to breathe. Jack looked like a landed fish, his jaw opening and closing uselessly. Bob smiled right up until he saw the Kevlar vest. In the dark he had missed it, but now that the fire was licking the ceiling, it was obvious.

The vest was shredded and there was blood seeping from the remains. Bob poked a finger into Jack's chest and held it up so the red glinted. "Still gotta hurt," Bob said, but he looked less certain. He stood and pumped the gun once, kicking out a shell that clinked on the ground. "Maybe I should give you one more to make certain. You see, Jack, you don't bring a godforsaken sword to a gunfight. That's just dumb."

Bob's smile was back in place, wide and insane. The fourth grader was screaming; the fire was eating up one of the shelves next to her bound hands and they were beginning to blister. Cyn had never stopped screaming, her mind tearing itself apart. It should have been tearing Jack apart as well, but he was too filled with hate to find love.

The hate cut through all of the noise and the chaos with one overriding demand: *Kill Bob!*

Had he been able to take even one breath, it would have been easy. He had his blood and his portal to his soul —in fact, he had fourteen portals. The bullet *resistant* vest had done everything its makers had said it would: it had resisted the blast, but it hadn't stopped it. Had Jack been seven feet further back the vest might have held. As it was he was bleeding from fourteen different points, but thankfully none of the individual pellets had actually penetrated beyond the bone and muscle of his chest to hit his vitals.

He couldn't breathe simply because he had the breath mule-kicked out of him and that meant he couldn't do magic.

Spells needed magic words. He could've called lightning just by saying: *shishin Ighn*. Just then, the concept of magic words was ludicrous and foolish. What purpose did they serve?

There wasn't any actual power in them; the power was all in Jack. His soul was what gave the energy to his spells. The only thing he could think of as Bob lowered the barrel down to touch Jack's forehead, was that the words shaped the spells in some fashion, turning soul-energy into electrical energy.

That was likely and yet Jack didn't even know what *shishin Ighn* meant. For all he knew it meant: *Go-go-gadget, electricity!* Or: *Shazam Lightning!*

Logic suggested, and Jack was filled with deadly, cold logic in the face of death, that saying the words had little outcome on the spell if one could visualize the spell and the glyph with complete awareness.

Jack saw the glyph in his mind—no it wasn't a glyph or a rune, it was a character and it said: *shishin Ighn* which meant: lightning. To Jack, it meant lightning, even if it didn't. He concentrated his entire mind on the word and it became lightning and lightning formed in the blood leaking into his hand. It burned and it zapped, and little arcs of blue-white light danced from finger to finger, stinging him, but he didn't care.

Bob cared, however. He cared a great deal when Jack touched Bob's leg and ten-thousand volts passed into his body and sent him flying back with the ugly stink of burnt flesh filling the room.

As if the magic had released more than just ball lightning, Jack suddenly found his breath and as he struggled to his feet, he wheezed and sucked air and smoke into his bruised lungs. He stood and swayed with the fire baking into him fanning the hate that ate him up head to toe.

Jack ignored everything in the room as he stalked over to Bob's body. Bob was dead. He was good and dead. His body was half in the fire and was billowing the foulest, reeking smoke Jack had ever smelled, and that was right and proper, because Bob had been the foulest creature Jack had ever met. And standing above him, his hate only increased as his numbness deserted him and his pain came on in an avalanche.

His chest felt broken. Each breath was accompanied by a dozen lancing pains as though he was filled with shards of glass. It made him meaner. He clutched his chest and did not think of Cyn, instead he wanted to kick Bob's corpse in the face. He was almost drained once again and compassion and caring were far down his list of needs and desires.

What stopped his foot was that he caught sight of the spell book; it sat flapped open, blaring its wonderful secrets to the word for anyone, even those not worthy, to see. Craving struck him. Naked hunger. He just needed to step over a child, a child in misery, to get it.

"Please, help me," the child whimpered.

Jack looked at her as if seeing her for the first time. Her face shown with tears, they were crystals that grabbed the firelight and blazed almost like magic. For a flash, Jack saw her as an enemy, another sorcerer and his blood-covered fist came up, a spell on his lips.

"No," she whimpered, her lower lip shaking and her eyes wide.

She's afraid of me, Jack thought, amazed. That didn't make sense. Wasn't he the good guy? Wasn't he here hunting evil and saving the world? A distant part of him cried out: *Yes! You should start by saving her.* It was a fine idea but what about Cyn? She was bound in place as her soul was being tortured and what about the book? How was he going to save the world without the book?

Suddenly he wanted all three with equal desire and he turned from one to another, wasting seconds he didn't have.

The girl was closest and the easiest to save. Her bindings were hemp and his sword was a step away, its blade resting in the fire glowed orange. The pommel was hot, but not yet blistering. Jack went to snatch it up, forgetting that he was riddled with holes and that his chest was wheezing like a broken accordion.

It hurt to bend over and it hurt to stand and it hurt to breathe even tiny sips of air. Thankfully the edge of his sword was keen and the ropes parted like butter.

After being bound for who knew how long, the girl tried to stand too quickly. Her skinny, bare legs couldn't hold her and she lost her balance, lurching into Jack, who wasn't in any position to support her weight as he could barely hold himself up. They both tottered a few steps and then fell against the low dividing wall.

Beyond the immediate pain, almost all Jack could think was that he was now further from his spell book. Almost the only thing. A part of him screamed: *Cyn is right there!*

She was and the young girl was wobbling around the wall and heading right for her. "Get away," Jack hissed. The girl shied back, again afraid of him. He tried to add what he hoped was a dollop of sweetness to his voice: "It's ok, just go around her and whatever you do, don't touch the glyphs...the writing on the ground. You'll die a very painful death if you do."

The girl edged as far around the circle of glyphs as possible, staring her big brown eyes at Cyn.

Cyn had stopped screaming and that was worse. She was twitching and jerking uncontrollably. Seeing her hellacious pain erased all thought of the spell book. This was the girl he loved. Just then his soul was dingy and worn thin; he knew the love as a fact more than he felt it as warmth.

But there was still a little warmth.

He came to stand just outside the circle, his mind racing, trying to think of some way to change the spells he knew; to rearrange them in some fashion in order to break the ring of glyphs. Unfortunately, he knew only four spells. He could open a portal into hell, he could call forth a demon or one of the lesser imps, he could control it, and lastly, he could summon and direct electricity.

"Maybe I can fry the glyphs," he whispered.

There was only one problem: if the spell failed, he would have almost nothing left in the tank; his soul would be paper thin.

But no other idea came to him and so he felt inside for the power. There were plenty of holes in him and more than enough blood; instead of bellowing the spell, he whispered: "S*hishin Ighn*." The electricity shot from his hand, hit the ring of glyphs and rebounded. His body jerked and his jaw snapped shut with a hard click, locking a scream behind his teeth.

It was over in a flash and all that was left was the echo of pain and the steam coming from his hand. It mixed with the smoke that filled the store; the fire was raging now and there would be no stopping it. Cyn would die here, he realized. She would die and her soul would be trapped in agony forever. The glyphs were magic. They would linger forever. Even when the building was gone and the land reverted to forest, the glyphs would have her.

As far as he knew, the only thing that could break the spell was Holy Water...that or a priest. Jack suddenly remembered Father Timmons had spoken of the power within the Bishop of Cleveland. Yes, a priest could break the spell.

Jack looked back at the door, not eight feet away. It was more of a chimney now than a door. Smoke was pouring out of it in great gouts and for a second, Jack blinked stupidly at it, as it dawned on him that he was going to die here as well.

Unless a priest suddenly showed up, that is.

"Hello!" he yelled in desperation. "Father Timmons! Father Jordan! Anyone?" There was nothing but the roar of the growing fire, while the world outside was so black that the doorway could have been an entry into hell. He was alone.

He turned back to Cyn, his face twisted in sadness and grief. Slowly, he reached out, feeling for the spell—it was there, just inches from his fingertips—it was nasty. He could feel the evil of it, the blood spilled and the life taken. He needed its opposite. He needed a priest. He needed someone or something pure, and he wondered briefly if he

74

could run and grab the girl he had freed and take her essence…not her life or her power, just her innocence.

Jack felt, as weak as he was, that he had the strength to break Bob's spell; he just knew that he lacked the *goodness*. He had tried to be good; it just never seemed to work out. Even when he was murdering people and offering souls to Eveina rha—the Queen of Demons, he had been doing it in an effort to fight evil and save lives.

But he couldn't take the girl's essence, not even for Cyn. That went over the line…besides, she was probably long gone.

Which left Jack the choice between running away and saving his miserable soul or simply throwing his life away in a vain attempt to save hers. There really wasn't much choice in the matter. Without Cyn, there wasn't a reason to live. He knew himself too well. He would gather power for the sake of gathering power and, yes, he would eventually fight his cousin, but it wouldn't be for the right reason. It would because of what Truong had said: *He's grown strong in death magic*.

Jack would want that power and his cousin's spells; he would kill for them. Likely, he would kill for *any* spell. Perhaps not at first. At first he would make feeble attempts at retaining his humanity, but when it came down to it, if he didn't have Cyn anchoring him, he would give in to temptation and people would die.

It was unpleasant to realize that he was indifferent to the idea even then, even kneeling next to the body of his love as her soul was tortured. It meant his soul was now as worthless as the dregs at the bottom of the teacup. It was an unpleasant thought, but also somewhat liberating. His soul was worthless and the idea of giving it up to save Cyn wasn't so bad.

Jack looked up; the ceiling was hidden by a layer of smoke three feet deep. "Please God," he said—it was the closest thing to a prayer he had uttered in a year. He didn't just believe in God; he *knew* God. He knew His power and he knew His goodness, Jack's problem with God was that he didn't feel he deserved *His* love.

Jack was a sinner and an unrepentant one. It was hard to say sorry when he was so full of excuses and rationalizations. He knew that if he ever went to confession every other sentence would be *but it wasn't my fault*. He was also sure that he would end up repeating the same sins over and over again.

But he was down to it just then.

"Please God," he whispered again and then bent his mind on the spell and exerted the last of his strength as he reached out with just his fingers. Immediately, titanic pain shot through his hand and up his arm and into his chest where his pitiful soul resided. The pain was beyond the scope of conscious understanding. It was horrific, searing and yet the pain wasn't the worst aspect of the experience. Cyn's inner screams ran along his nerves. They were loud and desperate and oh, so sad; and they hurt in a place Jack had never felt. The screams were worse than any pain that Bob's spell could ever exert.

Jack screamed as well, or his soul screamed, he didn't know which, but there was definitely a shrill sound blotting out everything including the voice in Jack's head that was demanding…no, begging for him to run away. He could've broken away if he wished. The holding spell that Bob had weaved wasn't strong enough to pin two people in place, it had been written and spoken only for one.

He could run away. He could pull himself out of the well of misery, but he wasn't there to run. He was there to free Cyn or die trying.

With her face in his mind, Jack exerted his power to break the ring of glyphs. He felt himself stretch, thinner and thinner and thinner until his soul wasn't just see through, it could be breathed through. There were pores that quickly became holes and soon, there was more hole than soul and then there were only strands. His soul, which started as something as thin as a sheet, now had the same construction as a wind-riven spider's web.

And yet, Bob's spell hadn't cracked or diminished in any way. Jack suddenly realized he was killing himself for nothing. He couldn't free her, at least not from the outside. And with his last action, Jack threw himself into the circle of glyphs.

Chapter 7
Akron, Ohio
Cynthia Childs

Jack tried to save her, and failed. The pain took him.

No words could describe the pain. It had made Cyn absolutely insane, but now it was suddenly half of what it had been and she did what any drowning person would do, she clawed her way across the floor as if she was clawing her way up the side of a stone cliff.

Shockingly, amazingly, she was free of the pain, but before she could cry with happiness, she found herself in a new hell.

The last thing she remembered before the eternal pain, was rushing forward into the shop, eager to fight Bob—then there was the pain. It was everything. It went on and on. It was unending and unbearable and the world outside of it ceased to exist to her. She knew nothing about Jack's fight, or the fire or the girl.

Now she stared. Her nerves burned and twitched, the pain still an echo that was slow to dissipate. She shook from head to toe as she stared, her mind trying to recover and right itself. What assaulted her eyes didn't help. The herb shop was an inferno; the heat made her cringe; the smoke shriveled her lungs. She saw dead Bob Chapman going up in flames and there was a teenager who had been bled dry.

And when she turned, and there was Jack in a circle of glyphs, his eyes peeled back so that the whites were gigantic. He had his mouth open as though he was screaming, but he made only a keening sound, like the rushing of wind.

"Oh, God," Cyn whispered, remembering suddenly a ghostly image of Jack trying to control his hands long enough to pull her out of there.

He had tried to save her and he had failed. His power…or rather his goodness was too weak. Light drove out darkness and Jack's soul wasn't a good soul. She had known it before on an intellectual level, now she knew it on a deeper one.

She felt sorry for him.

That was her first feeling, when her mind righted itself and she could feel anything at all. She was sad for Jack. She hadn't just seen his soul and its dreadful thinness, she had felt it. He was a desperate man, or he had been a minute before. Now, his desperation was a thousand times worse. She knew the pain he was feeling on an intimate level; that had been her a minute before.

And that would be her once more.

Now it was her turn to save him and she knew she could. The glyphs had been drawn to hold one person, not two. She would grab him and roll out of there. But it would hurt. Oh, God it would hurt. It would be similar to licking an electric socket a second time. It was one thing to wonder how much it would hurt to do it once, it was another to know how horrible, how utterly dreadful the pain was and then lick it again.

The idea of facing such pain made her hesitate. She stood on the edge with her face screwed up and twice she had said: "One, two three!" But hadn't budged. Only the fire coming closer and closer finally drove her into action. With a cringing whimper she stepped into the circle.

Just like that, her world was pain; every single nerve ending cried out. It shocked her, but what almost shocked her more was Jack; she could feel his essence and it wasn't thin or stretched or even gossamer, there was nothing to it but a whisper and a faint one at that. It was scary how far he had pushed himself to save her.

And she would do the same. She had power though she never used it—she used it then in an attempt to hold back the pain. It went fast, eaten up by the evil of the spell. *Grab Jack!* her mind screamed.

The holding spell wasn't meant for two and she wasn't meant to endure that sort of pain. She scrambled and kicked with desperate strength until they were both out of the circle and lying on the floor of the shop with the super heated air and the choking smoke and the blistering temperatures—all of which was a relief.

She wanted to lie there soaking up this new hell, because it was a vacation compared to what she had just gone through, but there was a crash from somewhere near and some part of the building deep in the smoke let out a loud urgent groan. She stood on shaking legs, but Jack would not move. He stared at the ceiling with blank eyes and a mouth hung open. There was so little soul left to him that he didn't have the will to command his own body.

Cyn bent and dragged him across the warping boards. He was dead weight and she was panting by the time she managed to lug him out into the night, where he just laid there unblinking and unmoving. "Jack! Hey! Look at me," she yelled. It was July but compared to the inferno it felt like deepest January and she began to shake and cough.

Jack only stared.

Eventually, a firetruck arrived, its sirens wailing and its lights flicking. Indifferent firemen stepped out to gaze at the fire. The miserable concept of a *Sanctuary City* had infected them as well. Few wanted to put their lives on the line for a city that no one cared about. There were whispered jokes: *Let it burn—It could take out the entire block for all I care—Anyone got any marshmallows?*

They were even blasé about Jack. Perhaps out of curiosity, two of them came by and glance down at him. "He's breathing," one stated and then turned away as if breathing was all that mattered.

"Get back here!" Cyn demanded. "He needs help. He's bleeding and he needs oxygen."

"We aren't paramedics, lady. They'll get here soon enough, so calm down."

Cyn reached down and produced an ankle holstered, snub-nosed .38 and advanced on the firemen, pointing it expertly at the first man's crotch. "You will help him right this second or I will pull the trigger. Now move!"

That got their attention and right quick. In a minute, Jack had an IV running into him and an oxygen mask over his face. His vest was removed and his wounds were being inspected when "her" priests arrived. That's how she thought of whichever priests were assigned to Jack's team at any time. Some lasted a single mission and she forgot their names within days of them leaving.

Until they left or were killed, they were hers.

"Okay, that's enough. Get away," she said to the firemen. When they backed off with their hands in the air, she practically threw herself down in front of Father Timmons and begged: "What can you do for him?"

They were hers but they weren't her servants or her underlings, they were the people she turned to when she couldn't turn to Jack, which was more than he knew. She thought of them as her personal priests and she was constantly going to them for spiritual advice, again, more than Jack knew. She was secretly a devout Catholic.

"He's got almost nothing left," she said in a rush. "I mean, nothing."

Father Timmons knelt down and touched Jack's hand; a shiver ran up him so that his shoulders shook in a spasm. He then bent his ear to Jack's chest, listening for a long time before sitting up. He looked both confused and afraid. "Yes, he's alive…but his soul…I don't feel it."

Jordan was slower to touch Jack and when he did, he left his palm flat on his sternum for so long that Cyn was practically out of her mind. "Please say something!"

"His soul is within him, still," Jordan said, eventually.

"Thank you, God. Thank you, God," Cyn whispered, her head bowed, tears running onto the pavement.

"His soul is there, but barely," Father Jordan said in a warning tone. It suggested that she should not get her hopes up…only sometimes that's all she had, and besides she would never count Jack out. She would hurt and she would cry, but if someone came to him with his body torn in half, she knew that there would be a part of her that firmly believed he would sew himself back together and give her that devil-may-care look of his.

"But is there something you can do?" she asked again. "You know, to help him?"

"I was thinking of asking you the same question," Timmons said. "You know him better than we do."

She liked to think so, but she knew she was only fooling herself. He was a puzzle with a thousand pieces and no picture; he was a broken man; a warped man; he was ice in a fire pit; he was evil and deadly and an uncaring bastard, and he was good through and through and there wasn't anyone she could trust more than him.

"We will pray for him," Timmons said when she only shook her head. "I don't know if we can do anything else. You should hold him and speak to him. He always listens to you, Cyn."

For the next hour, she whispered into his ear: "Hey, Jack? Listen to me. Listen to my voice…" The words ran out of her with all the emptiness of air, but also with all the love of an angel. She spoke until her mouth went dry and, after guzzling a gallon of water, she went on.

The paramedics arrived and she waved them off; really, she hissed them away. What could they do? Her priests could take care of the holes in him better than any doctor. They had progressed from strictly spiritual healing to the physical side of things, though it usually took a lot out of them. Timmons and Jordan were both tired, and yet they drained themselves until they were both staggering with exhaustion. They prayed over him until his eyes closed and his heart ran steady and the blood stopped leaking.

She begged for more, but they had nothing else to give.

Eventually, Captain Metzger arrived with his FBI backup and then another priest arrived. He was old with large, knobby knuckles and blue veins showing through his flesh. He had heard of Jack by reputation and it was clear that it wasn't a good reputation.

He didn't know how much Jack sacrificed. It was the same with most of the priests; they only saw what appeared to be black magic and felt the aftermath when Jack was an ass and dead inside. They had to face the acid of his tongue, not realizing that this was his way of venting his anger. He had never asked for the position he was in, no more than Cyn asked for hers, and in a way her position was less enviable.

She appeared as little more than a strut or a girder, when in fact she was the keystone in the arch holding things together. She suffered in order for Jack to suffer. She felt every pain of his and hers as well. He could afford to be an ass, but she could not. She was the keystone, pressured from every side: the priest's goodness, Jack's mercurial nature, and then there was the government in the form of Metzger.

"We're going to the Sudan just as soon as Jack snaps out of this," he informed Cyn after a glance down at Jack's blood and soot-covered body. Jack was breathing and like the firemen that was all that mattered to the government.

Going to the Sudan meant there would be more death and pain. These weren't things Jack could hear just then and so she spoke of the geese and the soft earth of Wales, where the rain was sometimes as delicate as the sunlight.

The geese, a secret that only Jack knew about, and the ridiculous farm that she envisioned were her only way of venting, and like any normal person, she needed to vent; she needed a release. She wasn't hopeless and doomed and her soul wasn't torn apart upon on a weekly basis as Jack's was, but that didn't mean she had it easy.

She was twenty-three, and an orphan. Her future was demons and swords, guns and fire…and in all likelihood hell was her final destination. She could only put her soul on the line so many times before it was taken in this game of chance.

The geese were her way of dreaming of a real life, a normal human life; they were something that could connect her to the world. For the last year and a half, she had been the dutiful girlfriend, the frantic lover, the maid who cleaned up the blood and vomit, and she had been the bait as the men did the fighting and the killing.

The geese were her way of going to one extreme—the polar opposite of what her life had become. She spoke of them as much for her as for him, and she spoke long into the night after the fire had reduced the herb shop to a smoldering pit.

Eventually, he cracked an eye and whispered, "You can't name a goose: Ducky. That's confusing."

She was too drained for anything but a smile. "I said Donnie. As in Donnie from *New Kids on the Block*."

"That's even worse."

Chapter 8
Khartoum, Sudan
Jack Dreyden

A week passed in slow agony. It wasn't his body that pained Jack. No, the priests had done their job and physically, he was better than ever. And nor was it his soul repairing itself and growing back to fill his empty innards that bothered him; that worked in the same way his fingernails grew, it just happened and he never knew when.

No, what pained him was the waiting.

Jack was eager to get moving. They finally had a destination, they finally had some place to begin looking for Robert. At first Metzger seemed just as eager. He rushed them out of Akron, something they were all grateful for, and back to Washington DC where there was talk of an imminent departure planned for early the next day, but that was put off for a day and then another and another.

It quickly grew annoying, especially for Jack and especially in the first few days when he went about with all the feeling and expression of a dour manikin—except of course, when he was annoyed.

It was up to Cyn to keep Jack from tossing Metzger out their seventh floor hotel window or punching Father Jordan in the throat when he suggested that going to Mass might do Jack some good. At these times, Cyn took Jack to a museum, and there were many, many museums in Washington.

They were all pretty much lost on Jack. He would go about with his robotic expression whether they were at the Holocaust Museum or the National Gallery of Art. The one he seemed most in tuned with was Madame Tussauds Wax Museum. He even had a child poke him to see if he was a display.

On the fourth day he was little improved and so Cyn took him to a pet store and bribed the cashier to let Jack sit in a back room with a dozen puppies. Finally, he smiled. And yet he still chafed at the waiting. They all did. There was a certain amount of finality in the air. If they could swoop in and snatch Robert, their days as demon hunters would be practically over. Sure, there were still strays running about but eventually, they would be hounded down and killed.

When they were finally given the green light, Jack had packed his gear in five minutes.

"Pretty soon you'll have that goose farm of yours," Jack told Cyn as they were sitting in an airport in Addis Ababa. She smiled thinly and covered her nose with her hand. Ethiopia was a land where everything smelled of goats and feet.

Jack was reclining in a plastic chair with his legs pitched up on a piece of luggage that held his body armor. In a shipping tube next to his elbow was his sword. Perhaps the best thing about flying with Captain Metzger was that Jack could carry his weapons if he chose—and he always chose. And he was especially glad he had them at that airport.

Planes were still hijacked in Ethiopia from time to time.

Stifling a yawn, Jack looked around, and for him it was easy to spot at least two of the other teams that had secretly accompanied them. The priests on the teams were all African-American and dressed to blend in with the Ethiopians: loose pants of a variety of colors with a long white shirt over the top. Even undercover the priests looked rigid and nervous as if God was judging them in this minor deception.

They were covert because the government in Khartoum had said no way to the idea of what was basically a paramilitary invasion. This had been the main reason for the delays.

Metzger's bosses had decided that sending in a single team of demon hunters to an area that could be simply crawling with the undead, wasn't a smart plan. Diplomats were brought in to negotiate a proper sized force: the US wanted two-hundred trained soldiers, operatives, priests, as well as sixteen helicopters and five armed drones.

A small detachment considering the mayhem that Robert had caused in the past.

The Sudanese had put their foot down. They had the right and proper fear that Robert would "go big" if confronted with a small army and it would be their country who would be left dealing with the thousands or maybe hundreds of thousands of undead. And they were probably right.

After six days of bickering back and forth, the two sides had agreed on a tiny number: ten. Jack had only shrugged. He was feeling strong and hungry. Timmons and Jordan had said: *This must be God's will.* Metzger complained in a stilted, formal manner which came across as though he was simply *uncomfortable* going in with so few men.

Cyn wouldn't hear of such a small number and had made a fuss which could be heard down every hall of the "Coordinating Building" on L Street where five departments and agencies: Homeland Security, Defense, CIA, FBI and the State Department came together, pooling their assets to form what was supposed to be a temporary task force: *The Panel on Supernatural Displacement.*

As Cyn was integral in controlling Jack, her complaints and their volume carried a lot more weight than anyone else's complaining, and she had been reassured that there would be "others" around to help out, though who and what sort of "others" these would be wasn't answered.

During the long flights and the longer layovers, Jack and Cyn had played "spot the spy."

The priests were harder to spot than the rock-hard soldiers who stood out among the slightly malnourished population. The soldiers hadn't been chosen simply because of the color of their skin; each one was tall and strong. Their confident eyes roved everywhere, assessing every possible risk.

Most of the soldiers were posing as archeologists or students, but Jack had never seen archeologists with biceps the size of his head before. Neither had anyone else and so there were also "helpers" around. People who not only spoke the local language but who also seemed to have endless wads of discreet cash on them to make questions go away.

Their stopover in Ethiopia was a grueling seven hours of heat and stink. Next, they flew in a puddle jumper into Khartoum, and soon they were missing Addis Ababa; it smelled like a rose garden compared to Khartoum. The city was beastly hot and dry and the people weren't inclined towards bathing regularly, so there was an uncomfortable "presence" around the locals.

Cyn was keyed up, her eyes going to every face; there were too many for Jack to peer into, besides, faces could lie. Jack felt with his mind, searching for evil and finding it in plenty of it in the city. From the air, the city had appeared to be a sprawling mess cut up into three sections by the convergence of the White and Blue Niles. Where they got their names, Jack didn't know. The waters of both rivers were silty brown except where oil sheens spoke rainbows on their surface.

It was a crowded city, a busy city. Khartoum was an interesting mixture of new and old, ugly and beautiful. Good and evil—and the evil was ancient. It made Jack shudder.

Still the evil was buried deep and it seemed to slumber. There wasn't that harsh awareness that sometimes struck Jack when he was close to a demon.

"Dis way," a man said the moment they stepped out of the airport. He took Jack's bags, giving him a wink and a gold-toothed smile. He was slim but not skinny and his eyes were wary, not of Jack, but of his surroundings.

Metzger nodded, an abrupt and abbreviated move that Jack read: *It's ok, he's one of us.*

In keeping with their surroundings, Cyn, Jack, and Metzger got into the lead car: an ancient Volvo that had all the style of a shoebox. Still, it ran and the air conditioning worked, pumping out blessedly cold air and that's what counted to Jack, who had feared that he would have to roll down his window and choke on the smell of the city to avoid heatstroke.

They took a number of turns, a dizzying number, so that Metzger constantly had his head cranked around back over his shoulder to make sure that the other cars in the line kept up. Somehow they all did. At one point, the driver unexpectedly pulled over. He parked for all of a minute and then just before he stepped on the gas again, a gentleman in a wilted beige suit got right into the car, nudging Cyn over with his rear.

"Hi, hello there, hi," the man said in a flat American accent. He wasn't a balck man, and he wasn't a white man exactly either, he was pink as a pig. The pink started beneath the wisps of his thin brown hair and went deep beneath his collar and possibly all the way to his toes. "Sorry about the heat. It's like this at least once a year: 110 in the shade and that's if you can find shade, ha-ha."

His laughter was high and oddly stilted. "So, one of you is a necromancer? You can raise the dead and all?" His eyes shifted, flicking quickly as though afraid one of them was going to put a hex on him if he wasn't careful.

"Who are you?" Cyn asked.

"Oh, right. I'm terribly sorry. My name is Milt, and I'm with the embassy. I'm your handler so to speak while you're in country. Sorry about all the cloak and dagger business, but if there's going to be trouble we don't want US interests to suffer from the fallout. With that in mind, we'll want you to steer clear of the embassy and certain industrial areas."

"I can't guarantee that," Jack said. He had a wicked desire to begin mumbling some made-up voodoo, simply to scare Milt. Jack was in a good mood despite the heat and the smell. He felt he was close to ending things with Robert.

Milt burst that bubble. "Oh, well, okay. This might all be for naught one way or the other. There doesn't seem to be any arcane funny business out at Meroe."

"How could you know that?" Jack asked, his words slow with a hint of danger to them. "You didn't send anyone up there, did you, because I was pretty clear on my instructions: no one was supposed to go before we got here. We don't know Robert's resources. We don't know what he knows or how he gets his information."

"You must be Mr. Dreyden. Yes, well, it wasn't any of our men, I assure you. The Sudanese were nervous and so they sent a team up there. The good news is that there wasn't any evidence of what occurred in New York. The pyramids are all still perfectly intact. No mummies running around killing people."

Jack sat back and looked out the window. "And now Robert likely knows we're here. Damn it! If they blew our chance…Cyn, can you feel Hor or Amanra? Or any of the others?" When it came to feeling the undead, she was more in tune than he was.

She closed her eyes, her brow sporting three little lines just north of the bridge of her nose. "I don't feel them, but there are other, uh, things in the city."

"Old things," Jack said, nodding. This happened in some of the older inhabited cities on the planet. Sometimes creatures were summoned or found their way to the human plane and became trapped. Jack hoped that they would remain that way. Some of the beings radiated power that was well beyond his fledging sorcery.

Milt's lips were twisted and drawn back and he edged away from Cyn, though there wasn't much room to. "Should I take that as good news or bad? Aren't we worried about new stuff? You know, fresh corpses walking around?"

"I don't know what's good or bad just yet," Jack said, still with his eyes on the passing city. It was an old city, older than most people realized. Deep below the city streets and the hard baked sand was the remnants of another city, one in which the people had wielded bronze weapons and burned dried dung to cook with, one in which human sacrifice was a daily occurrence in order to appease the walking demons who posed as "Gods." Jack could sense it and it made him shudder.

"That's not for us to worry about," he whispered to the window.

They were quiet for a while until Metzger said: "Then I guess it doesn't matter if we send in the drones." It was his way of asking Jack's permission.

Jack blinked, pulling his face from the window. "Can you wait until evening? I'd rather play this as if the Sudanese hadn't butted in."

"It is their country," Milt said.

"Sure," Jack replied and then ignored the man. "We send the drones in around nine and we go in once we have an idea of what might be there. Make sure that the vehicles are ready and the train conductor has been properly bribed."

Milt frowned. "He is I assure…"

"Hold on," Jack said to him. "Metzger, *you* make sure the pieces are in place. Now, if everyone can clam up, I could use a nap."

The driver snorted a laugh and wound through the city traffic. Jack didn't actually nap. He worried with his eyes closed. What if Robert was already long gone? What if he had already picked up what he needed and zipped? They'd be left chasing ghosts once again…unless Robert left them a surprise, that is. He had done it before. Bodies or partial glyphs, and twice he had left demons behind.

On neither occasion had it been Jack who had discovered those unfortunate traps, and people had been killed. It left him with a paranoia of opening doors and being the first to step into any room. He would do it, but he was always cautious.

Since the embassy wasn't putting them up, they were staying in the finest hotel in Khartoum, registered under an oil conglomerate. It was nicer than Jack expected. The sheets were wonderfully soft and Jack took his nap there after sampling from the minibar. Cyn took a long soak in the tub—a very long soak. She half-floated in warm water for two hours in her own form of meditation.

Then, in a strained silence, they strapped on their armor. Cyn prayed in a corner as Jack sharpened his sword. She would have prayed in the closet to keep out all distractions, but Jack had said once that he thought it was "weird," and that it made him feel alone. She hadn't done it again.

They then laid out their gear, checking each item. Jack had new items. After the fiasco in Truong's shop, they each carried two bottles of Holy Water and two of Holy Oil. He had started filling his belt pouches when Cyn cleared her throat; she held a silver necklace in her hand, dangling from it was a simple cross.

"It can't hurt," she told him after he had looked at it skeptically.

He slid it over his head and immediately cringed. "It burns!" he cried, earning him a punch in the shoulder that made his arm go numb.

Then they were in Metzger's room waiting on the video feed from the drones. There were three of the little birds up: two hummed at about a hundred feet and a third was invisible at a thousand. They ran on state of the art batteries that could keep them on station for two hours at a time; there was a second trio waiting to take over— Metzger didn't want a break in coverage.

So far what they were seeing was a whole lot of nothing. The infrared cameras showed only lonely pyramids and a quickly cooling desert. Nothing whatsoever moved. There wasn't even a real archeology team on site to make things complicated. July was a hard time to spend in the *Barunli Desert* where the last recorded rainfall had been seventeen months before.

How anyone had ever lived there even in ancient times was beyond Jack. "What do you think, Cyn? Everything the same?" She had actually been to the Meroe Pyramids once before on a dig with her mother.

She was squinting mightily at the image. "Can you center on number thirty-six? That one there."

Metzger gave an order over a secured sat-phone and a minute later, the image changed, focusing on one of the odd little pyramids. They were nothing like the Pyramids of Giza, which were not just huge but also amazingly symmetrical. These were sharp angled and much taller than they were wide and some looked strangely positioned as if they were on the verge of tipping over.

"Okay, I guess they're good," she said, leaning back. "I don't see any signs of a new dig."

Jack agreed. It was all disappointingly normal. "Well, we can't blame the Sudanese if Robert has bugged out."

Metzger added: "And nor can we blame Milt."

"Milt," Jack said, rolling his eyes. "Is he really coming along? Is he even trained?"

"Yes. You read his jacket. He's not State, he's CIA. Maybe he's a little on the older side but he still knows what he's doing. Besides, the CIA demanded to have eyes on the ground for this operation."

Cyn stood and stretched, looking relaxed. "Luckily, it doesn't seem as if this is much of an operation. No new digs, no overturned graves, means no big fight."

She was relaxed; Jack was disappointed. "Just in case, we still go in as planned," he ordered. They left the hotel soon after, stepping out into a surprisingly cool night and a second later, climbed into the same Volvo that had dropped them off. The driver was different; he was beefier, and he smelled of gun oil. He came with them as they entered the train station, carrying Jack and Cyn's bags as if he were a porter.

Other teams boarded the over-night train in discreet twos and threes, making sure to spread out so that no two groups shared a car. The train's engine began to grunt and cough and soon there was a lurch. Jack had his eyes closed and his mind open. Next to him Cyn sat rigidly upright.

"Nothing," she whispered.

"Yeah," Jack agreed. The people on the train were people with the usual amount of evil and good radiating from them. None stood out, and most definitely, none were demons. Metzger stood, tucking a newspaper beneath one arm and walked the length of the train: it was the all clear sign.

An hour into the ride, the train slowed. A conductor came through speaking in Arabic. Jack knew he was saying: *Sorry, track repair. It'll be just a few minutes.* It was their cue. The driver who had accompanied them stood, grabbed their bags and left the train. His name was Ringo and no matter how much Jack pressed him, he wouldn't admit to a last name. He was an American of Sudanese heritage and he had a gift for languages; he spoke six as if he was a native and three more, though haltingly.

He had volunteered for the mission and was absolutely infatuated, not with Cyn, though he appreciated her as any hot-blooded man would, but with Jack. There was a disquieting lust for power within him that reminded Jack of his own. The difference being that Ringo was good to the core and Jack could only fake it.

The teams were no longer discreet. There was no point. They hurried to the cars waiting out in the desert. Not even pausing to sort themselves out, they piled in and drove off. Fifteen names were read off by Metzger and the radio crackled repeatedly with "Check, check, check."

It was an hour drive to the Pyramids. At the fifty minute mark, Ringo said: "It's time." He stopped the car in the middle of the road; there was no traffic and likely there wouldn't be any for the next month, save for the stringy goats that passed as livestock in that horrible part of the country.

Luggage was broken into and the men armed and armored themselves. Once they were decked out, Jack went among them, keeping his eyes from their faces. If any of the men died that night, he knew that their faces would invade his dreams, haunting him with guilt.

He kept his eyes down and checked their gear. For the most part, they were fine, except for one man who carried a stupid amount of knives. Jack counted eight. "Why?" he asked and then didn't wait for an answer and moved on, shaking his head. Against demons, one knife was too many; knives were just about useless against the undead.

Then it was time to go.

With tension building, they drove until the pyramids could be seen as sharp shadows jutting up over the dun-colored sand. Then Jack and Cyn exited the vehicles alone. They split up, cutting a "Y" with their prints in the sand for about fifty yards.

Jack knelt, and touched the ground, a grimace on his face. There was nothing here. The ether was as neutral and bland as the sand. They had missed Robert.

Chapter 9
Meroe, Sudan
Cynthia Childs

Jack unbuckled his kevlar vest and tossed it behind him, where it sat ignored and likely forgotten the moment it left his hands. He walked forward to the pyramids, as though pulled by a string. Cyn could see the disappointment in him, but then a strange look overtook him, one that was rare and one that was only a memory for her.

It was the rapture of discovery. He was, at heart, an archeologist and here were the famed Meroe Pyramids. Jack slid and slithered down the shifting sand dunes and bounded along the ancient red stones until he came to the first of the tombs. He touched it cautiously, as though he knew shouldn't but just couldn't help himself.

This was who he was meant to be.

Jack wasn't supposed to be a sorcerer. He was born to be an archeologist, a man dedicated to finding history and uncovering it, exploring it, understanding it.

There were over two-hundred pyramids at the site and yet Jack stayed at the first, going round and round it, exploring every inch, measuring it with his eyes, breathing in the limestone and, unlike any other archeologist on the planet, feeling with that magical part of him for the least echo of soul.

For an hour, he explored this one, not very large pyramid, constantly touching the hand-worked rock with reverence and with love. Finally, Metzger came up and asked: "What sort of clues are you finding?"

"Clues?" Jack asked, confused.

Sitting in a pile of her armor and gear, looking as though she were reclining at a beach, Cyn laughed. "Jack has forgotten all about clues and monsters and all that,

Captain. What you're seeing is a different version of my cousin. This is the Jack Dreyden that was supposed to be."

"Supposed to be?" Metzger looked from Jack to Cyn and then back again, his face growing red. "Jack, we have over two-hundred people taking part in this mission, some of whom have been sitting on pins and needles, thinking that at any moment a demon was going come busting out of that pyramid."

Jack was looking at Metzger as if only just seeing him and was slow to catch up to his words. "Oh, sorry. Have them relax. There are no demons here. Maybe tell them that this is my process, you know, what I need to do to stay sane."

"We've talked about this before, Jack. No one thinks you're sane. The agency even brought in those shrinks, remember?"

The psychiatrists had been a mistake. They had been the government's way of trying to fit something they couldn't understand into a neat little box with a stilted and officious sounding name so that it could be regulated and perhaps taxed.

"I remember the shrinks," Jack said. He was still in his happy place and didn't growl the words out like he normally would have. "Then tell the men that this is my process for staying functional. It's one thing to read about these pyramids and see pictures, but this is so much better. You can breathe in the age! And you can almost taste the sweat and blood of the slaves who died creating these wonders."

"Metaphorically speaking," Cyn added. She was more in tune with death than Jack and she couldn't feel a thing; five-thousand years had swept away all the ghosts. "I think it'll be good to give Jack a few more hours on this. Why don't you have the men split into smaller teams and inspect the other pyramids? Have them look for any signs of digging or excavating that appears fresh. Tell them not to worry, there's no danger here."

It wasn't just busy work. Robert had been there after something, probably something very big, something significant, but that didn't mean Jack was the only one with eyes. The men fanned out and soon there were teams at every tomb. Sixteen of them were discovered to have suspicious marks and what appeared to be fresh digging nearby.

Fifteen of these were false alarms; the scrape of pry bars or the claw marks of hammers were all old, sometimes centuries old. Dutifully, Cyn checked each mark to make sure it matched the records her mother had established during six months of sweat-stained work, three years before.

Only at one of them were the signs fresher. "That's *Beg, North, Number 22*," Cyn said when Metzger pointed. She knew the one. She knew all forty-four tombs in the northern cemetery. *Beg 22* was only interesting because it was set off away from the others.

It was the tomb of Natakamani, a King of the Kush who had ruled right around the birth of Christ. There was little that was known about him, but what was known didn't suggest he had any magical power or really much normal power, either. Historically, he was rather insignificant.

"So why 22?" she asked herself, going around the pyramid, letting her fingers trail on the stone. Like most of the other tombs, it had been "re-sealed." Everything of value had long ago been stolen and to protect what was left, heavy granite stones had been cut and fitted in the doorways. Human hands alone couldn't have moved them.

It didn't stop people from trying. Every few decades, someone would make the attempt...but the marks on the granite of *Beg 22* were new.

And there was blood. "Get Jack," she said over her shoulder to Metzger. The blood was dry, probably a few days old. It was the blood of a virgin. A shiver ran up Cyn's back. She hated that she knew this.

Jack came up while she was still staring at the blood; there wasn't much, only a smear on the inner aspect of the antechamber doorway. These pyramids differed from their Egyptian counterparts in that before their entrances were two rectangular "columns." The blood was found here and only Cyn's ability to sense things of a deathly origin allowed her to notice it at all.

"Virgin?" Jack asked, touching the blood. The interior was darker than the night and he didn't see her nod. It didn't seem he needed to. "And the significance?"

"Who knows? Could be the whole 'pure blood' angle that the ancients were all on about or it could be coincidence."

Taking a flashlight from Metzger, Jack peered in close at the blood and even went so far as to sniff it. He then shrugged. "Maybe it's coincidence, but we should never count on that with Robert. Ok, step back will you?"

Cyn and Metzger edged back into Milt, Ringo and two other soldiers crowding the entrance. In silence, they watched as Jack went around the small antechamber with a growing sternness darkening his features. Lights were pointed where he demanded and every inch of stone was inspected.

"No," he said, his eyes going back and forth from the scrape marks on the granite to the blood. "One of these doesn't fit." He then looked down at the dirt at his feet, before toeing it with the tip of the dusty boots he always wore. "Come here, Cyn. What do you think? Can you feel anything?"

She went to the dirt and touched it with her bare hand. "Yes, there's something down here." More blood, it called to her. They went down on their knees and began scraping back the sand and the loose rocks. When nothing was immediately uncovered, Metzger ordered in two of the soldiers, who produced shovels and began to dig.

"Careful," Jack warned. "Even this dirt has value to an archeologist."

"Are we here to fight demons or to find artifacts?" Milt asked.

Cyn heard the sarcasm in his voice, but Jack took him seriously. "I'd like to think both. Let's hope we get lucky." He was grinning at the idea and seemed confused that he was the only one.

A foot and a half deep, they uncovered the first of the "base" stones that supported the approaches to the pyramids; they were wide and immensely heavy. There was blood on them. Cyn and Jack hurried forward and began blowing away the remaining sand with puffed cheeks.

There was a circle of a dozen glyphs drawn in the blood of a virgin. Jack and Cyn knelt hunched over it, their eyes bright with eagerness. Metzger stood over them with his light blaring and behind him were six other men. "What's it say?" Ringo asked, a tremor in his voice.

Jack looked back with narrowed eyes. "Maybe we should clear the room. Some things are best kept secret."

When Metzger glared the others back out into the night, Cyn asked: "If things are meant to be secret, why did Robert leave this?"

"Possibly because he didn't think the spell worked," Jack answered, after scratching beneath his chin. "It's an opening spell and clearly nothing opened when he thought it should have. The seal on that door is caulked with cement and it's not even cracked. Even the pry bars didn't scratch it."

Cyn stepped closer to the granite slab inspecting it. "There's nothing magical about it. I'm not feeling a thing."

"Yes, there's no magic to the door or to the ring of glyphs," he agreed, suddenly grinning. "You see why, right?"

She had read over the glyph the same as Jack and everything seemed as it should. Slower now, she re-read the poly-hieroscript. "Mother of Demons, accept this sacrifice, open the way and unlock the gates that bar...Oh, wait I see it now. Robert wrote 'lock' instead of 'unlock.'

Wow, what a blunder. I guess it is just a matter of forgetting that one wave under the glyph, but still a costly mistake."

"I wonder if it was. Let me see your mother's notes on *Beg 22*. As far as I remember there wasn't anything here to steal and I'm sure everything has been cataloged and I'm not feeling anything at all behind the slab. There could be a secondary level of rooms below the burial chamber, though I highly doubt it. This tomb has been pawed over a hundred times. Even that damned Italian came through here with his dynamite."

"Maybe...maybe, but there could be more of those odd glyphs that we found at the Waldorf and like Bob had back in Akron. Perhaps in puzzle form to keep the spell secret? Should we look? We have this opening spell. It would be nothing for you."

She was excited and so was he. They were practically giddy with the delight of discovery. "Let's do it," Jack answered. "We should get geared up before we go in, but first things first. We shouldn't ever leave this sort of thing out." From his belt, he pulled out his bottle of Holy Oil. He doused the ring of glyphs and then lit it on fire. It burned blue at first, then sunk to gold and then died away so that only a pleasant smelling smoke lifted into the air. The blood was now charred and unreadable.

He then took her by the hand and led her outside into the cooling desert air where the crowd of soldiers and priests stood waiting on them. For some reason seeing them there cleared her head and doused her initial excitement at opening the pyramid. She found herself looking back at *Beg 22*, feeling odd, as if she was missing something.

Jack was also looking back, his face no longer lit by eagerness. His shoulders suddenly slumped. "You know what? I think it's clear that this is a trap of some sort," he said.

Metzger, who was in front of the rest of the group, took a step back, eyeing the pyramid warily. "But you said it was clear. You said there isn't anything magical about the place."

"Maybe I was wrong. Or perhaps there's a bomb in the tomb, or it could be something else entirely." He squinted at the pyramid for a moment, thinking, and then turned to Cyn and spoke in a confiding whisper: "I thought the glyph was a typo, but now I'm not so sure. The scratch marks on the door make no sense. There were too few to indicate that anyone was really trying to break in, not to mention we are dealing with a necromancer who could call up an army of undead to tear down the walls, so why use pry bars at all? And the blood sitting out where we could see? He had to have felt it and smelled it. Why didn't he hide the evidence of his passing?"

"You're right," Cyn agreed. "Robert's been nothing but a ghost for a year and a half and now he's just leaving clues lying around? No way. And leaving a nearly complete spell sitting just beneath the dirt? I think you're right, Jack, this is a trap, one meant for us. The only question is what do we do about it?"

Despite their whispers, Metzger heard everything. "Perhaps you're being paranoid. How would Robert even know you'd be coming? The only way we know he was here is by a string of circumstances that he couldn't have controlled. To start with, Robert couldn't know what Truong was going to do with the glyph he'd been given. And then…"

Cyn laughed, a sound that was part pain and part mirth. "Are you kidding me? Robert should have killed Truong. Here was a bloke who 'supposedly' tracked him down; that should have been reason enough to kill him, but Robert not only lets him live but also gives him a glyph to bring a demon through the void? No bloody way. Robert would never do that simply out of the goodness of his heart. He's jealous of anyone with power and really, I don't think he has goodness left in his heart. We should've seen it before."

"Exactly," Jack agreed. "Which begs the question: what do we do about it? Whatever is in there can't be simply ignored. We are supposedly the experts."

"But we're not bomb experts," Cyn said.

That wasn't entirely true. All of the men among the *Raider Squads* had been trained in the military and at least a third of them were demolitions experts. Three were chosen among them to inspect the pyramid. They found no trace of a bomb and no evidence that the tomb had been broken into.

With Cyn sitting comfortably in the sand, nearby, Jack went round and round the tomb for an hour until he finally laughed. "What's the first thing we know about Robert? Above all, he's a necromancer. The answer to this riddle lies with the dead."

Chapter 10
Attamhim, Sudan
Jack Dreyden

The town seemed as dead as the pyramids. It was dark, dusty, tired. Nothing moved and no dogs barked. Jack wondered if they even had dogs. He also wondered why anyone would live there in the middle of the desert. Without casinos, he didn't see the reason for anyone to live in a desert.

Attamhim, the nearest village to the pyramids, was ugly squalor and the cemetery, a mile outside of town, was worse. It seemed to double as the town's trash dump.

They followed a rutted dirt road into the boneyard and right away Cyn sucked in a breath. Her hand squeezed Jack's as she asked: "You feel that, right?"

How could he not? A hundred eyes stared up at them as they crossed the boundary dividing the land of the dead from the land of the living. The dead stirred in their graves and the hate was like poison in the air, wafting up out of the ground. "Yeah, I feel it. Ringo, you may want to stop."

They were surrounded, but for some reason the dead weren't digging out of their graves to get them. Taking his sword in hand, Jack slid out of the Volvo. "This is not at all what I expected," he said, "but it may explain some things."

"You mean like what Robert's been doing all this time?" Cyn asked. "He's been building a secret army."

Jack grunted: "Yup. He could have raised thousands of these little cemeteries and we'd never know since we're halfway around the world."

Metzger and Fathers Timmons and Jordan came up behind them, each staring around, unnerved by the proximity of such a large number of undead. "But why this cemetery?" Father Timmons asked. "Is it just because he was in the neighborhood? I would say that doesn't seem likely. This town isn't exactly on the way to anywhere. Not even to the Pyramids. Shendi would have been a better choice; you have to travel right through it."

"Maybe," Jack said, going down to squat over a grave. It was unpleasant to say the least. Evil lay just below the surface...a very odd surface. He pushed away some of the trash and made a noise in his throat. "This grave has been recently dug up. Can I get some light?"

Cyn had her flashlight already out and beamed it down. In the turned up dirt were bone prints. "What in bloody hell? These ghouls have been up and walking around!"

"Maybe Robert needed some work done," Jack suggested. "May I?" he asked, taking her flashlight. He tromped off towards the edge of the cemetery, noting that indeed, every grave had been dug up. Ringing the graveyard was a slat wood fence, three feet tall and badly in need of painting. The east side of it—the side that faced toward the Meroe Pyramids—was torn down.

It didn't take an expert tracker to see that the ghouls had crossed and recrossed here. Jack jogged off down the "path" that had been created by the passage of the ghouls, with his team coming right behind. Timmons, who was the oldest, only lasted a hundred yards before going back for the cars which followed them at a discreet distance.

Meroe sat two miles away over a string of low hills and the path ran straight toward the pyramids, but stopped a hundred yards away; at the west end of the last hill to be precise. There they found odd mounds of dirt and sand; the ghouls had been digging.

They had burrowed straight into the side of the hill; that much was obvious; however the tunnel entrance was covered in rocks. Jack didn't say a word as he started heaving away the stones.

"Slow down, Jack," Metzger said. "I'm calling in the help we were promised. We don't know what's in there."

Jack paused, with a stone hefted near his shoulder. He didn't want to stop and it wasn't the power of spells driving him or some evil force. The simple fact was that he wanted to explore! He wanted to discover. He wanted to creep down the tunnel with a torch in one hand and a treasure map in the other, just like he had always dreamed.

"Let's let them do their jobs," Cyn said, her smirk playing on her lips. She knew his heart...in this case, his childish heart. He tossed away the stone and went to stand with this team as the "others" that had been promised were called in.

In minutes, four black helicopters swooped down out of the dark. They were amazingly quiet and by their odd, angular appearance, Jack guessed that they were stealth helicopters. Thirty men leapt out of them and hurried to the tunnel. They were *Knights,* the military's answer to the demon problem. Their arms and armor were black, all save for their silver crosses and shining swords.

There were four priests with them and they too were armed.

Cyn did a count of the full group. "Fifty men. Let's hope that will be enough." She meant it as a joke, but she was nervous as the rocks were pulled away and a hole ten feet wide and ten feet tall was revealed.

With the guns of fifty men and the one woman trained on the opening, Jack inspected the tunnel. It had literally been "hand-carved." Gouges in the walls and scrapes by the thousands showed where fingers were used instead of shovels. The hole sloped downward, disappearing into the earth.

A squad of *Knights* went first; nine men and a priest. Then Jack's team and then a second team of *Raiders.* They went slow, their flashlights illuminating everything. They checked the ground and the walls, inch by inch, looking for booby traps, trip wires, buried mines. They went slow, and they went without fear.

The priests were working as a team: one setting the power of the Lord against the possibility of fear, another against magical darkness, another against the cold. Timmons and Jordan walked behind Jack, ready with crosses and Holy Oil. Outside the tunnel, the other teams prepared themselves for a fight, with one team set facing the way they had come just in case the creatures from the graveyard should pop up out of the dirt and come after them.

The tunnel ran straight for ninety yards and then began to angle up until it came out in the burial chamber of *Beg 22* and what they found there was something out of *Indiana Jones*. The room, a square maybe twenty-five feet on the side, had a peaked roof, the walls leaning into each other, coming to a point twenty feet above their heads. Directly beneath that peak, sitting on the dusty floor was a golden sarcophagus that was nearly ten feet long.

"No one move," Jack said, as two of the Knights began edging toward it. Jack worked his way slowly around the coffin, his blessed sword at the ready. There was nothing else in the room and when he had made a full circuit, he asked: "Is everyone as confused as I am?"

Heads nodded all around. "I don't have my doctorate," Cyn said, with her smirk playing on her lips, "but I'm pretty sure that isn't Natakamani, the guy who was once buried here. As well, a golden sarcophagus isn't on any cataloged list of items to be found in this tomb or any other in Meroe."

"Sarcophagus?" Metzger asked. "Is that a coffin? Why's it so big? What sort of creature is in there?"

"Just a man," Jack explained. "There will be another sarcophagus inside this one and likely another inside that."

Metzger was relieved. "So what do we do?" he asked. "Do we open it?"

Jack went around it a second time, paying close attention to the floor. There were no scrape marks. It had been carried in and placed perfectly in the center of the room. "I want to say, no. Especially not in this room. There's no telling what sort of cunning plan Robert has for this. Why don't you, uh, step back, I'm going to touch it."

Everyone set themselves for battle as Jack slowly reached out and touched the gold. He half-expected to be shocked and half-expected the lid to blast off exposing some sort of undead creature. His mind hadn't picked up a thing coming from the box and now his hand did not either.

He gave a contemplative: "Hmmm," before running both hands over the lid. He even gave it a rap with his knuckles. It was solid metal, perhaps even solid gold. It was an impressive piece and most certainly didn't belong in that pyramid. "It makes no sense," he said in a whisper that everyone heard. Louder, he added: "I say we move it out to the surface and open it there."

"What? Why open it at all?" Cyn asked. She was nervous about the sarcophagus and it showed in the fact that her sweet smirk was miles away. "Why don't we take it back to the States? We could open it in a controlled environment, like at agency headquarters."

"You want to open it in the middle of DC?" Jack asked. "Let's say it is a trap and there is something bad in there and it gets out. There's close to three million people within ten miles of the capitol. No, it's better out here in the middle of nowhere. Fewer people will get hurt." Jack looked back at the dark tunnel as if measuring it.

"Can't we just take it through the door?" Metzger asked. "It'll be quicker and I don't like the idea of being in a dark tunnel with this thing." Again everyone nodded, and when Jack did as well, charges were brought up by three of the *Knights*, and in no time, the granite slab was exploded into manageable pieces.

Everyone watched from cover, though it wasn't the explosion that Jack kept his eye on; it was the sarcophagus. And when ropes were brought from the helicopters and the coffin was dragged out into the night, again he watched at the ready.

There was nothing to be seen.

And yet he was still wary.

He simply *knew* that there had to be something dangerous about the coffin or maybe something magical about it. Robert had gone to a lot of trouble bringing it to Meroe. It certainly wasn't a Numidian or a Kushite piece.

Cyn saw him puzzling it over. She was snapping pictures of it from every conceivable angle. "I think it might be First Dynasty or even older. Look at the eyes; look how big they are. That sort of strange proportionality was only common in the earliest finds."

"You're right," Jack agreed, somewhat reluctantly. "Which means it's been brought all the way from Egypt and stuck in the ground. Why? I always get back to why?" He brooded over the sarcophagus while the others watched in silence. Finally, he sighed and shrugged. "So, do you want to do the honors with me?"

She stepped back, hurriedly. "Open it? No, I think it should be the soldiers. A bomb is still an option."

It was a far-fetched option in Jack's opinion. Robert had always held finds such as these with more reverence. Poison gas? That was a possibility. The *Knights* had come prepared. Six of them in protective masks came forward, one at each of the corners and one at the head and another at the feet. With everyone ready for the unexpected and set strategically back with their weapons at the ready, Jack said: "Go."

The six men grunted and then lifted the lid up and off the casket. It was heavy, but that wasn't the reason why it came crashing down after they only took two steps. Two of the men at the closer corners could see perfectly what was inside the coffin.

They dropped their side of the lid and started scrambling for their weapons and for the next few seconds everything happened in slow motion—it wasn't as if time *seemed* to be moving slowly, it really was moving in slow motion.

Jack's hands, always so quick, were sluggish and his feet moved as if under water; even his eyes took forever to haul themselves away from the soldiers to focus on what was in the coffin.

Everyone was slowed except the creature that had been inside of it. There shouldn't have been a "creature" in the sarcophagus at all. That wasn't how these things ever worked and yet a tremendous monster leapt out, its evil suddenly sweeping from it in a terrifying wave.

Moving with blinding speed, it rushed full on Jack. It made sense; he was the main threat. He was a power house, even compared to the priests. He had grown strong, but he was nothing compared to the creature. It was huge; physically at least eight feet in height. Its features were human, though exaggerated: eyes four inches wide, a sharp, thin nose, ears, long and pointed, but flat to the skull. It was old and dead with wizened flesh the color of walnut.

Magically, the creature had power that could not be believed.

Like lightning it flashed at Jack, punching with a fist the size of catcher's mitt. He was looking to cave-in Jack's chest and would have if he hadn't been wearing his Kevlar armor. As it was, Jack flew through the air from the force of the blow, his chest on fire, his breath locked in his throat.

He struck the side of the pyramid and began to slide down. As he did, the night started to light up with little blinks. The men were shooting. The guns lit, but as sound traveled far slower than light, they were silent. With time slowed to a crawl, the blasts didn't reach Jack's ears for a few seconds, and in that time the creature killed half the priests and five of the soldiers.

It had learned its lesson concerning Kevlar and now it went for the throat or the eyes.

Nine men dead in what? A half a second of real time? It was impossible to tell, and impossible to fight against. They would have been doomed, but time suddenly snapped back into place. It was jarring to say the least. Priests and soldiers were suddenly flying through the air and gunshots seemed to explode from every direction.

Jack fell in a crumpled heap at the base of the pyramid. The *Knights* and the *Raiders* oriented on the creature that had, a second before been only a blur moving as fast as their bullets. Now it was stationary and they tried to pin it to the earth in a hail of gunfire.

Guns blasted from every direction, but nothing seemed to happen. The air shimmered around the creature as the bullets seemed to snag on nothing and drop, steaming to the cold desert floor. Holy water was thrown by Father Timmons. It struck the same invisible force, this time with a shock of white light.

It thinned the barrier and maybe another bottle or two might have brought it down, only the creature wasn't going to wait around for that to happen. It raised both of its huge hands, giving Jack a perfect view of the right one; on it glowed a glyph etched in blue light. Jack knew the glyph and knew what was going to happen.

Unfortunately, he was still struggling to breathe and could do nothing but try to get to his hands and knees. The creature was too fast for anyone to do anything. It brought its hands together in a great burst of sound and light, like a thunderbolt exploding. Those who were close to the beast were either blinded, stunned or outright killed.

Thirty feet away, Cyn was thrown off her feet and was lying on her back, one hand patting the dirt, her head going this way and that as if she was confused where she was.

Jack began crawling to her. He was finally able to breathe, but standing was out of the question at the moment. He crawled, furious with himself. This was his fault. He had been too eager to see what was in the coffin. He should have left it for someone else to have opened it. But who? And where?

No answer came to him as he watched the creature pause for a moment. Jack saw that it was tiring. He could feel it weaken and it was no wonder. It had warped time, erected a shield to absorb the energy from twenty guns, and expended enough energy in a single blast to stun or kill forty people.

Now would have been the time for Jack to strike back with some energy of his own, but he was still too shaken and he had to wonder what sort of power could stop the creature...wait, not creature...this was some sort of man. Jack saw the terrible humanity in it as it bent and went lip to lip with Father Timmons. The priest flung out his hands as the light in his eyes dimmed to nothing. His soul had been sucked from in seconds.

Now Jack knew what he was facing: this was a necromancer, one that was thousands of years old. It was impossible.

Jack crawled faster to Cyn. The creature dropped Timmons and strode toward her. It saw in her a rival that had to be destroyed before it got too strong. On the way, it stopped to replenish its strength, feeding on those stunned individuals that were still alive between it and her.

Some of the soldiers gathered their wits and fired their guns, while Metzger threw Holy Water, but the spell warding the necromancer was stronger now and the bullets fell harmlessly and the water splashed onto the ground wasted.

And then it was almost on top of Cyn, who was firing her shotgun and slowly backing away. Jack got to her first, knife in hand, blood already dripping from his palm. He cast his *Holding* spell at the necromancer, which made it laugh.

Jack's strength was nothing compared to it. The necromancer shot out white blobs of ball lightning with one hand, blasting the remaining soldiers, some of whom were bravely charging while others were scrambling to get to their feet. At the same time, the creature reached out and began burning through Jack's spell.

It was a battle of magical strength and will, and though Jack was full of fight, his strength ran out of him as though he had sprung a hundred holes. Thirty seconds was all he could give before he was wiped out and his soul bled dry. But then Cyn was there at his side, her own hand bleeding.

Chapter 11
Meroe, Sudan
Jack Dreyden

In case things went to hell, the American helicopters had been parked a half mile away, their rotors whipping the air, ready to go at the first sign of trouble. Trouble came so quickly that they almost missed it. The battle in front of *Beg 22* was short and savage.

Eager to get into the action, the choppers spun up into the air, unmasking their 30mm M230 Chain Guns. The battlefield was lit by blue-white explosions and muzzle blasts going in every direction, but the eight-foot monster smack dab in the middle of the carnage wasn't easy to miss. The first pilot centered his cross hairs on it and caressed the trigger, giving it just a gentle squeeze, sending sixty hand-sized rounds right on target. He was good and did not miss. The rounds could tear an infantry carrier to pieces and yet, after the air blurred and dust rose, the monster was still standing.

The pilot hit it again and there was so much flame and flying lead that he didn't see the beast raise a glowing hand. Just like that, the pilot's field of vision was suddenly warped; it looked as though the ground was rushing up at him. Thousands of stones of every size raced up as if fired from a gun and pelted his bird. Some of the stones could fit in the palm of his hand, others were bigger than his head. The rotors, circling at 800 RPM, were brittle; a sparrow could chip them at that speed.

The rocks turned them to dust and the chopper abruptly turned over in the air and dropped straight into the earth. It exploded in a fireball when it crashed, as did the other three as more rocks flew through the air so fast that they were nothing but a blur.

Jack watched with a cold heart, a dead heart. His chest was empty of feeling. Even Cyn barely gave him a stir. It was the consequence of being soulless. In this situation it had its benefits. He was able to see past the blood and the moans and the soldier wondering aloud what had happened to his eyes.

He was able to see past his friendship with Metzger, who really was a good guy and who always did his best. Jack's eyes weren't dimmed by any of this. He was able to see the truth of their situation.

The necromancer wasn't an all-powerful creature. He wasn't a demon whose energy, whether strong or weak, was a constant thing. The necromancer was alive, likely some form of a human—a strange, magic-warped being, but a human, nonetheless. His strength ebbed and flowed, and just then it was ebbing big time.

Jack and Cyn had weakened it and the helicopter with its 30mm Chain Gun had done a number on it. Now, after hurling half the desert into the air, it was nearly spent.

And yet it could recharge just by lifting out its hand.

Jack couldn't let that happen.

The necromancer reached out to Metzger. The soldier's face twisted and started to pull in on itself. His soul was being ripped from the core of his being, but Jack saved him. Snatching up Cyn's forgotten shotgun, Jack calmly aimed and blasted Captain Metzger in the head, sending brains, red and grey sheeting onto the desert floor.

Cheated of the soul, the necromancer roared and spun to face Jack and so Jack shot him, too. Though the air shimmered and the buckshot fell harmlessly, the balance of power was now in Jack's favor. Modern weapons were far stronger than the necromancer could have ever imagined.

Jack blasted the creature again and again, not giving it a moment's respite. Finally, it threw up a wall of darkness between them. It was a weak spell from a weakened creature and Jack charged right through it, knowing it wasn't likely very deep, just enough to hide the beast.

It would hide and try to feed and that meant it would need warm bodies. "Come on, Cyn!" Jack yelled, orienting on the feel of the beast and the sudden screech of one of

116

the soldiers. Jack found three *Knights* cowering before the necromancer, their great courage finally undone.

With the necromancer draining them, Jack shot them like dogs. It was sad and yet Jack wasn't sad because he didn't care. Not having a soul meant not having to care. It really was as simple as that. But he would care later if he lived. What he was doing would haunt his dreams and keep him far from the confessional even though what he had done was wholly justified.

He committed murder in order to stop the necromancer. Jack killed everyone within reach and when there was no one left for the necromancer to feed off of, Jack grinned. The necromancer was failing. It tried to run, but bullets were faster and it no longer had the power left to stop time. Jack pumped full loads of buckshot into it until the shimmering in the air was thin as a whisper.

Cyn had come to stand next to him by then, a found gun in her hands, its barrel smoking. Her eyes had never been so cold. She was so white, Jack wondered briefly if she would pass out. He really didn't care about that either. She wasn't going to die and that's what mattered, or so he guessed.

As the necromancer faltered, Jack's gun dropped to the sand and his sword rang as he swept it out; the smell of the Holy Oil on it was like perfume. He could have killed the necromancer with the gun, but that would've been wrong. The sword had meaning. He would *grow* using the sword. His power would double at the least.

"On your knees," Jack said, knowing that the necromancer would never agree. There was five thousand years between them, but they were very much alike. They would fight to the death. They would hold onto every second.

The beast charged and raked with its long claws, but Jack was ready for it; he knew its strength, just as he knew that the necromancer was no warrior. As impressive as it was in size and fantastic in its bearing, it was a creature of magic, and without magic it was just another enemy waiting to die.

It tried, however. It loved its life above all else and the closer to death it came the more desperate it became, but against an opponent who was both warrior and sorcerer, it did not stand a chance.

The edge of Jack's sword was far more keen than the necromancer had ever faced; his armor lighter and yet tougher than anything found in antiquity, and Jack trained constantly, daily, sometimes twice if he had the energy. Jack trained because he had known there would be days in which he would be pitted against some five thousand year old monster.

That day had come once again and Jack's blade was swirling madness. He gave the necromancer no let up, hacking limbs uncaring of the sluggish grey blood that dribbled or the outlandish rotting smell that soured the air when he sliced open the belly of the beast.

All he cared about was that final killing stroke. He could have taken it three different times, but Jack was an artist who craved perfection and got it when he sliced the head of the beast right off its neck. It was a perfect stroke.

When the head with its now dull eyes thumped onto the ground, the monster toppled and Jack grinned. The grin lasted for all of ten seconds and then it faded away to nothing, and nothing was all he felt. Even when he looked at Cyn, he was empty.

She had watched the battle with her gun at the ready. Now she shrugged in an odd sort of way and gazed down at the dead necromancer for a few seconds before staring around at the battlefield and the strewn bodies of forty-five trained men. "Timmons was a good guy," she said, absently as though trying to remember what it meant to feel.

"And Metzger," Jack added. They were silent for a few minutes and then Jack said: "Remember Father Paul?"

"A little," she answered.

"They never found his body. He could still be alive."

"Yeah? That's good." Listless, she walked over to where Ringo laid sprawled. His life had been sucked out of him, his face shrunken and pulled tight to his bones. "I don't like this, Jack. I can't feel that I don't like this, but I know I don't. It's weird."

They were silent again.

"We should look for survivors," he said after a time.

"There are none…I would know."

He knew what she meant. She was empty inside and unlike Jack, she could fix that in seconds; she was a necromancer by birth and she could feel the souls. They were hot in a universe of ice. A shiver ran up her. "They're all gone, except those guys who ran away; they're probably embarrassed."

Another moment, long this time, and then Jack took Cyn by the hand until he found her pack, which had been left forgotten, leaning against the side of *Beg 22*. Inside were two boxes of *Junior Mints*. They shared them as they stood over the necromancer; neither really trusted a dead body anymore—sometimes they came back to life.

When it didn't stir, Jack went to Ringo's Volvo. There was a radio inside, crackling and spitting out words of worry. When Jack didn't immediately answer it, Cyn said: "We'll need a cleanup crew here. I don't think we should leave this for the locals to find. Who knows what they'll think. And maybe we should go after the survivors. I think there were three or four of them. It was hard to tell with so much going on. Jack? Are you listening to me?"

He had been staring at the radio. "I'm listening." He hadn't been; his mind was far away trying to piece together the cunning trap that had been set for him. It was so intricate and detailed that it was hard to wrap his mind around it. "Go on," he said to her.

"Go on? What do you mean? I said that we should go after those guys who ran away, though I don't know where they might be heading. Shendi? If they regained their senses they'd go to Shendi. If not, they're somewhere in this bleedin' desert."

"Right, the desert." The radio crackled out more anxious questions. Cyn reached for it, but Jack grabbed it first and tossed it into the sand. "I think we need to disappear. Robert has us dialed in. He knows us and he's playing us. He allowed Truong to find him just so he could set this up, just so he could kill us."

Cyn looked down at the radio with just the slightest hint of worry in her eyes. "And he almost succeeded. But what about those men? Shouldn't we care? They could die out there."

Jack knew that they should care and in a day or two he would, in the meantime he would rationalize: "They're all trained men and really, it's hard to get lost in this part of the Sudan. There's only one road that runs to Khartoum. It's just west of here. And the sun will be up soon. If they can't figure out which way west is by the stars, then the sun will clue them in."

And dry them out and shrivel them up and kill them if they don't get picked up or find shelter. Jack shoved those thoughts away. Finding and killing Robert was bigger than the lives of a few men, no matter who they were.

"They'll be fine," he added, partly to mollify his own conscience; it didn't take much.

"What are we going to do with that?" Cyn asked, pointing at the body of the necromancer.

Jack hated the idea of leaving it for the government to find. Whatever secrets the body held were best lost for all time. And then there was the sarcophagus...it had not just imprisoned the creature, it had hidden it from both Cyn and Jack.

"I think we need to take a closer look at the sarcophagus," Jack said. He took up one of the discarded flashlights and went to the coffin. It was indeed solid gold; easily a thousand pounds. Inside it were glyphs; he wasn't surprised.

"A binding spell," Cyn said, taking pictures with her phone. They both looked back at the necromancer. "A binding spell *inside* a sarcophagus? Maybe it's not as dead as we think. I mean, it won't re-grow its head will it?"

Jack went back to the body. It hadn't budged. He poked it with a finger. "It is truly dead, I believe. I used a Holy Sword. It unbound whatever evil was holding the thing together." He didn't add: *I hope*. "Just in case, we should burn it."

They cast about for a fuel source and saw only rocks and sand. In the end, they gathered Holy Oil from the bodies of the dead. It amounted to only about a quart, and yet the corpse was rendered to ash as if a bonfire had been set.

Next, Jack went to each of the deceased and rifled their pockets for cash; they would need to disappear and that meant they couldn't use credit cards and it also meant bribes at border crossings.

Lastly, he dragged the bodies of his team, Metzger, Timmons and Jordan to one side and prayed over them: "Lord, please bless their souls. They were good men and each deserves Heaven as a final reward for their efforts."

There was silence for a minute and then Cyn, who looked like a blank slate, said: "I wish I could cry for them."

"You will," Jack replied. "It'll come, don't worry." He would cry when no one was around and he would hurt, and he would dream of the men he had killed and he would tell himself that he had saved their souls; and he had. Of course he had also saved his own skin in the process and when he cried he would know the truth: he hadn't killed to save any soul but his own.

"Let's get moving," he said, heading for the Volvo. "We should try to make it to Wadi Halfa by morning."

Chapter 12
Wadi Halfa, Sudan
Jack Dreyden

Jack wanted to disappear without a trace into the Barunli Desert before heading north to Egypt, but his plans changed when they saw one of the *Raiders* who had run away—he was heading back to the pyramids. It took guts not just to face the possibility that the necromancer yet lived, but also the guilt over running in the first place.

"It's dead," Jack assured him right off the bat as he pulled up in the Volvo.

"I ran," the man said in a dusty voice. There were tear stains running through the dirt covering his face.

Cyn leaned over Jack and said through the window: "And you were smart to run. Everyone who stayed died, so don't look like that. Some things are beyond us. You were able to accept that and you made the wise decision."

The soldier eyed her, his lip curled in self-disgust. "You don't get it. I ran! I ran away like a coward. I left my friends back there to die. I disgraced myself."

This elicited a shrug from Jack. "You did," he said, not seeing the point of belaboring the obvious. "When you get back, I need you to do something for me. I need you to make sure the two of us are counted among the dead. Not among the missing, but among the dead. I want two corpses in two body-bags; one with my name on it and one with Cyn's."

"You runnin' away, too?" the soldier asked.

"No. That trap back there was laid out months ago and if my cousin thinks I lived, he'll start preparing his next one. Clearly, he wants me out of the way so that he can get on with whatever he's planning next and I'd rather he spring it while I'm still around to stop him...if I can."

The idea that he could actually stop Robert was now more in doubt that ever. Where had he come across the necromancer? Had Robert locked it in the golden casket? If not, how did he know what was in it and if so, it meant that he had somehow bested a creature that had nearly won a fight against a sorcerer and fifty of the best soldiers in the US military.

A very scary thought.

Whichever it was, it pointed to the fact that Robert was gaining in strength at a much faster rate than Jack. What was worse was that he had access to the power of seven billion souls. Jack only had his own.

These thoughts haunted him as they left the soldier to make it back to the pyramids on his own and drove north along the Nile. The sun glared from his right as the desert began to bake. He was exhausted and his insides were hollow and hungry. Next to him, Cyn slept with her head lolling against the window, and he glared at her.

She was just as empty on the inside as he was, perhaps even more so since this had been her first time she had let her soul be used and abused. She couldn't have stayed awake if she tried, but that didn't matter to Jack. He was hungry and snappish, only there was no one to be snappish at and so he glared at her and at the desert and when they passed a vulture sitting on the gnarled remains of a tree, he glared at it as well.

To make matters worse, the road was crap. For the most part, it was only a rutted dirt path, except when they passed through a couple of dried-out towns and then the road was paved in white stone. The Volvo felt like it was shaking to pieces.

Cyn sat up bleary and disheveled. "What the bleeding hell? Cobblestone? What century is this?"

"Don't they have cobblestone roads in England?" Jack asked.

She glared, as angry a look as he had ever seen on her face. "There it's quaint. Here it's sodding pathetic. Where are we? Is this still Sudan?" She looked around at the dirty little town. It was one of the poorest places Jack had ever seen. Despite the abysmal heat turning the ground into a frying pan, the children went shoeless and many wore little more than rags.

Before answering, he swerved out of the way of a kicked ball and yawned like a bear. "Wadi Halfa and I need to find a hotel, badly. I need food and I need sleep. And I need you to start acting like you usually do."

"You sound like a baby," she snapped. They glared at each other, neither backing down. A second later, Jack nearly hit a chicken that was running loose in the streets and they both stared at it as if blaming it for all their problems. "I'd eat that chicken if I could," Cyn whispered.

"We'll get something. They have to have restaurants in this town."

Cyn laughed and gestured around. It was a very small town; a few hundred one-story buildings made of desert-baked mud bricks. "Where? I was here three years ago on a trek from Nekhen to Meroe and I don't remember seeing any restaurants. We stopped for some petrol and you can guess what their loo was like." A shiver ran up her at the memory.

"We've had our shots," he answered, taking a left off the stone path and down what he thought was another road but which turned out to be an alley. He had seen a splash of color and had hoped that they had chanced on an out of the way hotel.

It was a feed store and there were more stray chickens wandering about, each skinny and gaunt. Jack figured that it would take six of them to make a decent meal.

After twenty minutes of driving they had seen the entire town. There were two "hotels." They by-passed the first because, with its tin and canvas roof and its scrap-wood covered windows, it looked ready to be condemned. Unbelievably, the second hotel was worse. The rats were like livestock or pets that wandered around unnoticed and there was a smell emanating from the building like that of a decomposing body.

They returned to the original and since they were not husband and wife, they were forced into separate rooms. Cyn took the "Top" room as described by a woman who looked to be just shy of a hundred—and she was right. Cyn's sheets were clean and the mattress was newish; early this century new. What made it the "Top" room, however was the metal box duct-taped into the window that hummed and blew out a steady stream of cold air.

Jack's room had a fan that made a steady *tac-tac-tac* sound but hardly moved the torpid air. His bed listed at an angle and there were odd sounds emanating from beneath the dresser.

After hanging their *Do Not Disturb* signs, Jack, feeling like a teenager, snuck into Cyn's room and passed out as soon as his head hit the pillow. The two slept hand-in-hand for the next twenty hours. Jack had one dream that stretched through every one of those hours. In it, he was facing the necromancer, who seemed eighty feet tall. Jack tried to fight the beast but the shimmering glow around him thinned and his strength failed. Then Cyn grabbed his hand.

His dream consisted of her holding his hand and feeding him with her energy. When he woke, stiff and groggy, the cut on his hand was completely healed and he was halfway to feeling like himself...in fact he felt halfway to feeling like something greater than himself.

Cyn eyed her hand; it too was clean and unblemished. "Your power is increasing," she said with equal parts fear and awe. The strength of his soul had been increasing for months, but in the last week it had doubled and now it had doubled again; he was amazed as well.

Jack flexed his hand and then touched his chest where the necromancer had punched him. The bones were completely knit back together as sound as they had been. "It doesn't make sense," he said. Powerful or not, he didn't see how he could heal himself, let alone her. "Maybe it was you," he suggested. "You were always much more in tune with God. Everyone knows that I'm a..."

His words faltered as he suddenly remembered what he had done. He had murdered men in cold blood. The tally of innocent lives he had taken was growing. His soul was a powerful and filthy thing.

"It wasn't me who healed us," Cyn said with another look at her hand. "I don't really have much in the way of power and I don't really want what I do have."

"I guess I'll never understand that. You could be a great sorcerer. You have the ability, you just have to force yourself. It's an odd feeling but not a bad one."

She shrugged and now her newly healed hand touched the cross around her neck. "I won't do it, because I know it's wrong." She hopped up suddenly and went to a window that was so dirty, the street outside seemed like it was from another era. She laughed suddenly and asked: "Why don't we make this our honeymoon retreat?"

Her attempt to change the subject was jarring, which told Jack not to force the conversation back to sorcery. "What? You didn't like Khartoum? Now that place had charm. Metzger said that Khartoum was..." Jack stopped, remembering how he had killed his friend. With perfect twenty-twenty vision, Jack had seen Metzger's eyes right before he had killed him. Those eyes were saying: *Jack's going to save me*, but he hadn't. Jack had saved his own skin instead.

Cyn knew the reason for the hesitancy and quickly filled the void. "Or maybe Paris. We could go today. I bet we could be there by nightfall. I think. I wonder what time it is?"

"Paris? That sounds nice." Jack put on a fake smile; it was all lip going nowhere near his eyes. His depression wasn't going to be so easily cast away. He didn't deserve Paris; he didn't even deserve the "top" room in Wadi Halfa. At best he deserved to sleep among the headstones at Attamhim where the ghouls lay just beneath the first layer of dirt. Or better yet: New York.

The utter destruction of New York could be traced back to his weakness. He had given in to temptation and now the city lay in ruins, with bleached bones lying everywhere. It was a tremendous city of the dead, the ultimate necropolis.

Jack gave a jerk as suddenly something clicked. "Paris sounds great and we should do that but what about Nekhen? There's a necropolis near Nekhen."

"Don't be so down on yourself," Cyn said, turning from the window. "You did what you had to do, not just to save us, but also to save those men's souls."

"That's not what I'm talking about," he answered, leaping up and pacing. He pointed suddenly north. "Nekhen! Do you see? Don't you remember what my father said? He said that his grandfather discovered the tomb of Rath-ara near the city of the dead! Why didn't I think of this earlier? Robert has been there, I'm sure of it."

Cyn held out her hands. "Slow down, okay? You of all people know that there are hundreds of so called necropoli in this part of the world."

"And how many of them are a first dynasty necropolis? You said it yourself, the sarcophagus of the necromancer was first dynasty or earlier. Robert was there...but why move the necromancer all the way to Meroe to set up an ambush?"

Jack paced and Cyn drummed her nails on the bed frame. There were marks on it, suggesting that it had been used as a scratching post by some long dead cat. "Maybe he wanted to make sure that no one focused on Nekhen," she suggested. "Maybe, he wanted to keep it as secret as he could. And that means he was there for more than just digging a necromancer out of the ground." Her smirk was back and Jack matched it.

Within minutes they had showered and were ready to check out. The proprietor of the inn, using gestures, and three words of English: "Eat, eat, eat," insisted that the two of them stay and have breakfast, which consisted of stiff rice, flavored with curry and dates. It wasn't very appealing and yet they were so famished that they scarfed it down and had a second helping. Next they filled the gas tank of the Volvo, bought four extra jerry cans and filled them as well.

They then moved on to the local market, where they were treated like rubes and were forced to buy supplies of water and food at outrageous prices. As they were swindled, old men hovered around the pair, laughing and nudging each other, enjoying the show, while underfoot, shoeless children ran around with bright smiles in their dark faces. They hinted outrageously, pointing at the baskets of candy.

One little girl with a bow of yellow yarn spun up in her black braids was particularly savvy; she curtsied and then did a little dance. "I'm going to regret this," Cyn said and then handed her five pieces of what looked like saltwater taffy. Within seconds, they were surrounded by children, their pale palms held up in the universal sign of begging.

It took ten minutes and twenty dollar's worth of over-priced taffy to extricate themselves.

There were no roads leading from Wadi Halfa into Egypt and that left them with two choices: a three day drive through the desert in the plodding, thirty-year old Volvo, or they could bribe an official to get on the Aswan ferry. The boat would take them three hundred and thirty miles up Lake Nasser to the city of Aswan, Egypt.

Fearing that the car would never hold up, they went with the bribe which ended up costing them half of their money. A very long day later, they discovered that a second bribe was needed to actually land in Egypt. "Don't freak out, Jack," Cyn said, handing over the last of the cash that they had taken from the dead back in Meroe. "I doubt that Robert is so powerful that he can trace a bank transmission from a dry little town in the middle of the Egyptian desert."

Despite this description of Aswan, it was a tremendous step up from Wadi Halfa and they were able to find a bank and a hotel that had every modern necessity. Still only half recovered, the two of them stayed the night, each enjoying an hour long soak in the tub.

The night's stay in Aswan left them clean and refreshed, and they stayed that way for a full thirty minutes the next morning and then they stepped out into the July heat which immediately wilted them. Cyn, her porcelain skin prone to burning, stood in the shade of the hotel until Jack could get the Volvo and its air-conditioning going. The heat gave it a case of the "vapors" and it a dozen tries to get it to start.

The car rattled and shook for the next hundred miles of empty desert road as they drove out to Nekhen, midway between Luxor and Aswan. At one time, many thousands of years before, Nekhen had been the center of Egyptian culture. Now there was nothing to it but ruins: beige stone buildings that were mostly caved in on themselves, a few rock walls, a leaning obelisk, steps that ended suddenly as if there were invisible buildings just beyond them.

As American students and European tourists tended to drop from sunstroke in the July heat, the remains of Nekhen were deserted when they arrived. It was an eerie feeling.

"What do you think?" Jack asked. "Can you sense anything?"

Cyn got out of the car and stood for long minutes with her eyes closed and her skin slowly turning pink from the heat and the burning sun. "I don't feel anything, but then again, I didn't feel anything back at Meroe."

"Let's try the necropolis," Jack said. A few miles beyond Nekhen was the "necropolis"—the city of the dead. It wasn't a city in any sense of the word; it was a vast and ancient graveyard, though it didn't look like much. There were a few odd stone buildings that had been crumbled by time and a rickety perimeter fence that the Egyptian government had put up years before but had never maintained. The real city was hidden beneath the desert and although Nekhen had been deserted, the city of the dead was horribly alive.

The moment Jack stepped out of the Volvo, he felt the eyes on him coming from beneath the sand. Robert's calling card. Just like at Attamhim, he had raised the dead, but this time it didn't seem like they had come out of the ground to do Robert's bidding. The ground was rock-hard and unmarred by the hands of ghouls.

"You were right," Cyn said, clutching her shotgun and staring all around them. "Robert has certainly been here."

"We should spread out and check for signs of a dig," Jack said. "Go to the left, I'll go to the right and we'll meet on the other side. Just like at Meroe, look for tracks."

They looked for new piles of dirt or the scrapings of a thousand skeletons. There was nothing, the dun-colored rock and sand in the cemetery looked exactly like the tired desert on the other side of the fence. They met at the far side, perplexed.

"Maybe a wider search pattern?" Cyn suggested.

After a thirty minute walk in a wider circuit, they again found nothing. At this point, they were both dripping sweat and chugging the nickel tasting water they had picked up in Wadi Halfa. "I think we should go a little further," Jack suggested. This wasted another hour and they were gasping from the heat by the time they circled back to the Volvo.

Jack volunteered to climb a hill that he thought was only a mile away. The desert air made it seem much closer than it was. Three miles later, he stood looking down at a wide flat area of desert; it was a moment before he realized that this was an immense river bed. The Nile, like every other river in the world, had changed course a number times and it had run here thousands of years before.

He squinted into the glare of the afternoon sun, trying to see anything out of place. When that didn't work, he did the smart thing and let his mind feel what couldn't be seen. There was evil near. He reached out and felt it down in the river valley where there weren't any roads.

The land was flat and baked hard by the sun and Jack figured the Volvo wouldn't be too inconvenienced. It was an hour walk back to where Cyn was laying on the ground in the "shade" of the Volvo and panting. "I'm dying," she said. "Let Robert win. He can have this world. It's just too bloody hot."

"I found it," Jack said. The news didn't excite her into action. Grumbling, she climbed into the car as Jack *rowed, rowed, rowed* the engine until it finally caught. He took it off road, avoiding the deeper sands and the sharper hills. It chugged on, growing more and more unhappy, but it made it to the river bed and after a mile they found a lonely hole in the ground, marked only by a pile of rocks and a hunk of flesh.

"What is that?" Cyn asked. "Is that…is that a piece of intestine?" It was three inches of grey yuck that stank. Jack had his sword out by then, but he would sooner lick the hunk of flesh than let it touch the blessed metal. He nudged it with his shoe.

It was intestine and the wet smear beneath it suggested that it had been "left" there recently, maybe even earlier that day.

"I'm pretty sure that this makes absolutely no sense to me," Cyn said, her throat working and her lips so thin and drawn back that they had practically disappeared. "What is this doing here? Did it fall out of someone's picnic basket? Was it caught on someone's shoe? Does this make any sense?"

"No," Jack said, absently, forgetting the piece of intestine already. The hole down into the earth was calling to him in a way that wasn't natural.

Chapter 13
Nekhen, Egypt
Cynthia Childs

To Cyn, the piece of "somebody" so carelessly left behind was worrisome. It meant that there had been someone standing right there at the edge of the hole very recently. So very recently that there was a chance that the person or persons could even then be somewhere close by; perhaps watching them.

The Volvo, out in the open, couldn't possibly be missed, and anyone with a good pair of binoculars would have no problem picking the two of them out. She felt like a mouse on an open plain with hawks circling above.

Any smart mouse would hop down in that hole just as fast as they could, but the smell coming from it was the smell of death. Something rotting and foul, and from her experience, likely very evil was down in that hole.

Next to her, Jack was buckling on his Kevlar armor, sweating and cursing under his breath. It was hot as blazes and only reluctantly she copied him. She then checked the load of her shotgun, made sure that her Holy Water was in place on her hip next to the extra shotgun shells, and then picked up her flashlight.

Jack had his sword, two bottles of Holy Water and his magic…he also had one of the old plastic jugs that they had bought in Wadi Halfa, and was pouring water right down in his throat. With a final splash on his head and a gasp, he gave it to her. "Drink up," he said, and then knelt down at the edge of the hole. He touched a few of the rocks, sniffing one. "This is the spot, Cyn. This is where our great-great grandfather discovered our birthright. Can you feel it?"

She could. The smell in the air was familiar, like a long forgotten memory, but it wasn't a good memory; there was death down in the hole.

After drinking until her belly sloshed; she doused herself and turned on her flashlight.

Jack nodded, flicked his on as well, and took a step down into the darkness, the beam from his light catching little except for the floating particles that hung in the air. It was a tense moment but then, unexpectedly, Jack laughed. Cyn flashed the light in his face. "What is it?" she asked, slightly alarmed at his odd behavior.

"The spell!" he cried. "I remember it. It just came to me. Man, that's been eating at me for days."

"And what spell is that?" she asked, thinking that he meant the healing spell he had been able to manifest in his sleep.

He grinned and then set aside his flashlight. "Truong's spell. Watch." He picked up a pinch of the hot sand. A mumbled word escaped him and then he blew on the sand. It swept out of his hand as if he had not blown sand but a handful of dust. It swirled down into the darkness, each grain suspended in the air, glowing like a firefly, lighting up a finely chiseled set of stairs.

Cyn kept waiting for the sand to fall to the ground, but the grains floated in the air, lighting a good twenty foot stretch of the stairs. "Will it go away?" she asked.

"Oh I guess, eventually," Jack answered, somewhat vaguely. He was already past the spell and now his mind was centered on the stairs. "Look at these. Look at the workmanship. It's exquisite, especially for tomb. I know the ancient Egyptians were all about death worship, but these stairs don't make sense. This is fantastic."

Despite declaring the stairs fantastic, he turned away from them and the hole to squint all around the river valley. For some reason, he seemed dissatisfied by the view as if empty desert wasn't what he had expected or wasn't right in some way.

"How do the stairs not make sense?" Cyn asked. "They're stairs, stairs go up or down; they don't have to make sense."

Jack took a walk around the hole and the rubble outside of it, his boots crunching grit underfoot. "It doesn't make sense because they're the stairs of a palace not a tomb. Look how wide they are. You don't see that even at Giza."

"Styles changed even in the ancient world," Cyn suggested. "Maybe this was how they used to do it until someone decided it was a waste of time to bother with such an elaborate staircase when there were pyramids to build."

"Yeah, you're probably right," he answered, running a sleeve across his face one last time. Stooping, he pocketed a handful of sand and then stepped down into the darkness where it was cold enough to shiver their souls.

The staircase hung in golden light for the first eleven steps and as he progressed, he whispered: "So beautiful." He wasn't wrong. The stairs looked as though a master craftsman had chiseled each one from a separate piece of marble. The walls were white, again marble, and so smooth that it couldn't be believed.

As they descended, Cyn swept her hand along it, feeling for any blemish; there wasn't a single one. "Impossible. This isn't possible. Have you ever read about anything like this…like this level of perfection?"

"Never. It's why I wonder if this is really a tomb." He took the next step down, slow and careful, his hand on the hilt of his sword. She knew what had him concerned: there was evil down there. Eyes in the dark. Spells woven of an unknown nature. Questions beyond answers, and time out of mind. Time of such an age that the years couldn't be counted and the seconds so infinite that they washed over their consciousness like the individual atoms that made up the air in the wind.

They were descending into another era. The beautiful stairs gave way to an equally beautifully tiled floor, again in marble. It was beautiful, but not perfect. Blood marred the tile. Jack bent and let his fingers run over the brown smears. He made a questioning noise in his throat.

"New blood," he said.

Cyn touched it and knew immediately that it had been there almost a hundred years and yet, compared to the age of the tomb, it was as if it had been spilt yesterday. "It corresponds with our great-great grandfather's time frame."

"Yeah," Jack said in a whisper. The evil was closer now. He pointed his sword, at a doorway that was open but not at all inviting. Beyond it was a heavy darkness that ate up the beams of their flashlights, showing them nothing. He stuck the light down into a loop at his hip and then brought out more of the warm sand.

When he blew the grains out into the room, the golden light lit up a simple marble walled room. In the center was a square of black rock seven feet long, five wide and four feet tall. It was a box of sorts; Cyn could see the lip of the lid.

On top of the black stone was a green metal box with the letters CCC stamped on it. Below that, in peeling paint were the words *Continental Can Company*. It was about the size of a bread-box and it was the first thing that showed the least bit of dust.

They ignored the green box for the moment, because to the right of the black stone was a pile of long decomposed bodies. There were eleven in all and it was obvious that their deaths had been brutal.

Cyn guessed that they were locals, judging by remains of their attire and dark complexions. They had been there a long time. Their blood was brown dust and their eyes were long ago decayed into nothing. Their faces were wizened like old apples and their bones were starting to poke through the thin remains of their skin.

"Dr. Loret said that only one of locals lived through the expedition," Jack whispered. "I guess here's proof that he was telling the truth."

"It's always nice when you can trust the undead." Cyn tried to laugh at her joke but the feeling in the air wouldn't let the sound come out, and so she settled on a smile that didn't feel all that jovial. Jack didn't notice one way or the other. He had turned from the bodies and was now eyeing the green box.

He started to reach for it and Cyn grabbed his hand. "Don't touch it. We both know that there's not going to be anything good in it. If I had to guess, there's something disgusting inside. Maybe a last joke from Robert; who knows?"

"Where's your sense of adventure?" Jack asked. "It could be a box of jewels."

"Please! At best it's a box of hundred year old cans of...of...whatever they canned back then," she replied. "It could be turn of the century liverwurst or peaches."

"Also very valuable," he said. When he picked the box up, something shifted inside and the sound it made was that of bare bone on tin. No other sound on earth was quite like it. "There's a head in there."

Cyn rolled her eyes. "Is that right?" she asked sarcastically. "You sure that wasn't the sound of gold doubloons? Or the Hope Diamond? Pop it open and check, Jack, you never know."

He put the box back on the black stone lid. "Ok, so sue me. I'm a kid at heart sometimes. I like adventure and I like discovering the unknown. And we have discovered something. Now we know there's a skull in the box, but did Robert put it in there? That's an entirely different question and I think the answer is no."

Jack didn't elaborate and Cyn knew well enough to know that he wanted her to figure out what he was hinting at. Normally, she would just stare at him until he explained himself like any normal person, but she was also caught up in the excitement of discovery and had it not been for the evil coming from the place, she would've had the same gleam in her eyes that Jack had.

The gold light from the magic motes was not keen enough for what she needed, and so she shone her light on the green box. She read the dull label and noted the dust...and noted that it had been recently disturbed. Someone had handled the box recently, but hadn't lifted the lid.

That suggested that the head had been in the box for a while. Cyn said. "Ok, I agree, the head was left by our great-great grandfather. Why?"

"Because it's part of a ghoul or demon," Jack said. He pointed at the bodies and shone his light at the dull brown smears on their long white shirts and the tears in their flesh. "The expedition was attacked by a ghoul, killing all the locals but one. It must have been overcome by my great-grandfather and the pieces placed in boxes to keep them from reforming."

"Your great-grandfather?" Cyn asked. "Why not Robert Montgomery or Lord Blackburn?"

"Because the three spells are *my* birthright. I am more in tune with all of the spells than either you or Robert. I believe the original Jonathan Dreyden defeated this ghoul and claimed the spells as was his right as victor. He must have then divided the spells, keeping one and giving the other two to his cousins, who later passed them on to you and Robert."

That made sense, but what didn't was why the spells hadn't been destroyed in the first place. It was something that they hadn't been able to puzzle out. "Without further evidence, I think we can assume you're correct," Cyn said. She gave him a wan smile. They had figured out one puzzle, but a much darker one lay in front of them. Across from the black stone was another opening, and the golden light particles showed more old blood.

Jack led the way down a short hall to a second room, which again had white marble walls and floors. Judging by the sprays and pools of blood, the room had been the site of a long ago battle. Other than the dried blood, there was only an elaborate stone sarcophagus in the room.

"The necromancer," Jack said in a whisper. The lid of the sarcophagus had been cast to the side and had broken into a number of large pieces, but the image painted on the front was the same as the one that had been painted on the golden sarcophagus back in Meroe.

The remains of the coffin were empty and yet the fear in the room was palpable. Both Jack and Cyn flashed their lights all over the room. Cyn saw nothing but the blood, the lower, intact section of the coffin and the larger chunks of the upper part.

Jack saw something else. With excitement in his voice, he whispered: "There's a secret door! Look at the chips and crypt dust from the broken lid." He shined his light down at the floor near the far wall. "Look at this straight line!"

The scatter pattern from the broken upper portion was star shaped and properly random—except near one of the walls, where there was a neat line as if the debris had been brushed back. Jack went down in a squat and shone his light at the stone splinters and then at the wall. He then reached out and first felt the air and then the wall.

It didn't budge. Not even when he threw his shoulder into it. He came away from it, rubbing his arm, but he wasn't the least bit upset. "There's either a lock or it's magically held."

"Then why are you smiling?" she asked. "If we can't get in then…wait! The opening spell that Robert used to try to trap us back at the pyramids! But what if it doesn't work? We've never tried it before."

Jack's knife was already in his hand. "There's only one way to find out," he said, unbuckling his left arm guard and rolling up his sleeve. He made a cut just above his elbow and then half-closed his eyes as the blood ran to the point of free fall. The drops changed in midair, going from rounded blobs to fully formed glyphs, each glowing white for a fraction of a second until the next landed right on top of it, erasing it.

In seconds the spell was written and the words spoken. Cyn expected something out of the movies: a white light around the edges of the door which would then swing back to reveal a treasure room piled in gold and jewels. Reality was much more mundane. There was a simple click as part of the wall swung back showing only another dark tunnel and letting in a noxious odor that made Cyn want to gag. Strangely, Jack looked even more ill than she did. Normally, he was tougher in these sorts of situations.

Now, he looked ghostly.

"Was it a difficult spell?" she asked, digging in the tight pack on her back. The town of Aswan had never heard of *Junior Mints*, but they had heard of *M&Ms* which were better in the heat, anyway. She shook out a rainbow of candy into his hands. He swallowed them with a strange look in his eyes.

"No," he said after he had swallowed the candy and washed them down with the brackish water from the old gallon jug. "It's Father Timmons...I think I know how I was able to heal us the other night."

Cyn began shaking her head. "Don't...no...don't tell me, Father Timmons is in you."

"A little I think. Sort of like an echo or a ghost or a taste. It's not as strong as the feeling I have with Truong, but it's there. Timmons was the last soul that the necromancer stole—and then I killed it. Now I have this over the shoulder kinda feel, at least I did just now when I did the spell."

Cyn went to the puddle of Jack's blood and lightly put the tip of her finger in it. "Huh. I can feel it too." What she felt was a touch of disappointment that was strangely bitter-sweet. "Remember when he said he had joined the team to save your soul? I think you might have saved his."

"Great, now I got priest kooties," Jack, joked. His smile faltered quickly. "I wish he was here for real. Him and Jordan, both."

"And Metzger," Cyn added. It might have been the wrong thing to say. Jack's face grew cloudy.

He straightened and reattached his arm guard, keeping his eyes averted and acting as though he hadn't heard her. Once again he had his sword at the ready and the flashlight in his other hand as he faced the darkened opening where the eyes stared up out of the dark.

The smell was worse down there and the fear greater, but that wasn't what stopped Jack. It was the roughhewn nature of the tunnel that led down into the earth that stopped him. It was drastically different from the two rooms they had passed through. He was an archeologist by birth, inclination and training. "I told you this wasn't a tomb."

Chapter 14
Nekhen, Egypt
Cynthia Childs

She took a long look around, not seeing anything that would dispute the idea that this was anything other than a tomb. "I think the sarcophagus gives it away, Jack. This is a tomb and only a tomb. Do you think it could use a headstone?"

Jack had been edging closer to the secret opening. Over his shoulder, he whispered: "Yeah, I do. What's the one thing we know about ancient Egyptians? They love their headstones. What do you think pyramids are? They aren't billboards for flea markets. They are giant tombstones."

"And not every Egyptian had one. Only the very richest and most powerful..." Cyn paused. Wasn't the necromancer the very definition of powerful? Being rich usually followed closely on wielding the kind of near-immortal status he had attained.

Near immortal were the key words. The necromancer had been *bound*, probably when it was at its weakest, and the beheaded ghoul in the front room hadn't been there to protect the remains of the necromancer, but to keep people from trying to set it free.

"Okay, maybe," Cyn said. "You know what's also missing if this was a tomb? There's nothing here to help the dead on to the next life as with most burial chambers."

"Exactly. It also explains why this is lying at the bottom of an old river bed. Whoever buried the necromancer wanted to hide him away forever. It wasn't enough to completely tear down his home or palace that sat above this place, they shifted the course of a river to ever keep him from being found."

She shook her head in awe. "He must have been quite the jerk to rate that sort of treatment."

This made Jack smile. "You met him. He wasn't a pleasant fellow. Now, there's only one question: what did Robert find out down here?"

"Something bad," Cyn said. "There's at least one demon down where ever that passage leads and it's probably pissed off that it's been stuck down there for the last five thousand years."

"I'd say six or seven. The stone work involved in these rooms is so elaborate and so different from anything else found in antiquity that it was likely from one of those cultures that pre-dates our understanding of ancient Egypt. My father mentioned the Witch-kings."

"Then the demon will be just that more cranky," Cyn said. She took a deep breath and added: "Let's get this over with."

Her attitude surprised Jack. "Over with? This is the best part. Adventure, discovery, a hint of danger. Isn't this what every archaeologist craves? And yes, it's just a hint of danger. Robert went down there and didn't seem to have an issue. We should be fine. The demon and the ghouls are all probably *bound*, otherwise they would have escaped ages ago."

This made perfect sense and yet Cyn had butterflies as they descended into the dark. The stairs here were nowhere near as nice as what was found above. Just like Robert's tunnel into *Beg 22* back in Meroe, what was behind the hidden door was "hand" carved out of rock and compressed dirt. It had been made in secret most likely by ghouls under the thrall of the necromancer.

At the bottom of the stairs was a door of heavy timbers that was bound along the edges in flaking iron. The rust didn't make much sense until Cyn heard a slow drip of water, perhaps the one thing she hadn't expected to find beneath such an immense and harsh desert.

The door stood ajar with an opening of about eight inches. Jack lifted his Mag-lite and fed light into the room beyond. It was somewhat of a disappointment, at least to Jack. The room was a rectangle: fifteen feet by ten. Along the walls were shelves of cedar. Age was slowly destroying them; a couple leaned forward looking as though they were just about to topple.

For the most part, the shelves held mundane items: stacks of odd-smelling wood, strange idols carved of ivory or onyx, and linen bags that were on the verge of crumbling into dust. Inside these were spices and herbs.

One shelf held nothing but semi-precious gem stones: agate, jasper, jade, pearl. Another held stacks of tarnished silver coins. Another held coins of gold.

It was a find of amazing wealth and yet Jack's disappointment stemmed from the fact there wasn't another obvious doorway out of the room. His face grew cloudy as he went to the coins and picked up one of the gold ones that still had a dull shine to it. "Take a look," he said holding it out to Cyn.

Her mouth came open at seeing the writing on it. "Those are the same sort of glyphs that we found in Robert's suite back in New York! Do you think he knows this language? Do you think it's the language of the Witch-kings?"

"I think if we can't find the next secret door, we'll never know," he answered. He turned in a circle. "There has to be one."

Cyn had this one covered. She could feel the dead better than Jack and her hearing was also better as it turned out. The dripping water was coming from the north wall where the shelves of herbs seemed to lean forward. In reality, the left side of the wall and the shelves were two inches closer than they should have been—the entire thing was a door. She pulled it back, showing another hand-carved tunnel.

It went straight for a good ten yards and then dipped down—this was where the water was coming from and where the eyes were staring up.

Again, Jack took point. He moved slowly, walking on the balls of his feet, ready to spring in any direction. Cyn had her 12-gauge at the ready, pointed at the wall to her left, her finger just outside the trigger guard.

The next room they found was much larger than the others. It had been a natural cavern with twenty foot ceilings and rounded walls. The wall on the right; however, had been carved into cells. They were tiny: six feet by three and barely enough room for a small man to stand hunched over. The cells were barred with rusting iron...and there were still prisoners "alive" in them.

Nine living skeletons stood at the bars looking out at Jack and Cyn. All nine of them had eyes that glowed red. They were demons of some power.

One demon was a handful, but nine demons? "I don't like this, Jack," Cyn whispered, keeping close.

He seemed unfazed. "They're still in their prison cells. If they could've gotten out, they would've gone after Robert and whoever left that hunk of intestine behind. We should be fine." To show just how safe he thought the situation was, he slid his sword back into its sheath.

Ahead of them was an immense table of wood and iron. It was grey with age except for where the blood had seeped into the wood. The smell emanating from it was horrible. It was the smell of countless deaths, of infinite screams.

Jack made a face at it, but the necromancer in Cyn couldn't help but touch it. She could feel the ugly zing of evil stretch up into her fingertips. "Bloody hell," she whispered, pulling her hand back. A second table matching the first stood five feet further on, and then there was a third. She didn't touch any of these.

"Well, we know how he got so strong," she said. "There's blood from a thousand people on that first table alone. He was storing up the power."

"That's only part of what made him strong," Jack said. He had his light shining beyond the tables where the water was dripping gently.

"Is that?" Cyn asked in a breathless whisper, her eyes locked on the figure, the penned-up demons now far from her mind.

In front of them was a pool of water that took up a third of the cavern. Its waters were black and could've been a hundred feet deep or three inches. Within the water was an island of rock and on the island was a carved statue of a girl who seemed far too young to be pregnant, and yet her breasts were heavy and her belly swollen with child.

She was sitting flanked by the trunks of two stone trees and between her legs was a hole that went down into the earth. It looked as though her child would drop down into hell when it was born.

The entire statue had been carved out of polished obsidian and was highlighted in gold. Her smile, a small thing similar to the Mona Lisa's was gold. Her fingertips, gold. Her eyes, gold. Her nipples and the mound of her pubis, gold. All gleaming. Even after seven thousand years, the entire statue shone like glass and fire.

"That's the Mother of Demons," Jack said.

"Yes," Cyn said, starting forward. Jack reached for her, but she was in the water and crossing over to the island before even she knew it. She was drawn forward. She was a necromancer and this was an altar to her…god?

She had been drawn to the statue, unable to stop herself; however, the thought brought her up short, midway to the island. She stood in thigh deep water, blinking and afraid. This hell-creature wasn't *her* god. She knew her God. Ever since the Event she had been a devout, fully believing Catholic who went to mass three times week, when she could, and was such a regular in the confessional that frequently she would "chat" with the priest on the other side of the screen as she wouldn't have anything to confess.

"You okay?" Jack asked, coming up beside her.

"Of course, yeah. I was just excited. Adventure and exploration, right?" She tried to grin, but it was strained and pleading.

There was worry behind his eyes. "Maybe you should wait here," he suggested.

After a deep breath, Cyn drew herself up to her full height. "No. I got this. It's just a b-bloody statue. There's nothing to it but that." That was true on a conscious level; however on a subconscious one Cyn knew there was some hidden about the statue.

This wasn't the Mother of Demons, but all the same it contained a part of the Mother. Maybe just an eye...one of thousands, or a small part of her spirit; an avatar, perhaps. Cyn didn't know and tried not to think about it. After all, Robert had been here and came away unscathed, which meant that she should be fine.

Jack paused just at the edge of the island, his feet still in the water. At first he used the beam of his mag-light to pick out the individual aspects of the statue, but it was hard to see it all as it was meant to be seen and so he pulled a pinch of sand from his pocket and lit up the island with a thousand glowing particles.

Now they could see the statue in all of its glory—and it was fantastically beautiful, and frightful. Cyn felt a change in the air, one that had her hands shaking around the shotgun. "Sh-she liked that." The statue's smile was no longer small and enigmatic; it was now a full grin.

Jack turned his head back and forth trying to get a better look at the smile. "It can't be. It isn't alive, is it?" He reached out a hand, not to touch anything physical, but to feel the nearness of magic. "There's nothing I can feel. What about you?"

All Cyn felt was awe and desperate fear. They had to get out of there before something bad happened and she was sure that something bad was only seconds from occurring, and yet she yearned to go to the Mother and kneel before her.

"No," she managed to say.

Carefully, Jack stepped forward and touched the island. He looked back with a shrug. "Nothing." Next he took a step onto the island itself, his hand now on the hilt of his sword as if it could do anything to harm the Mother. Holy sword or not, it was a splinter compared to *Her*.

Cyn followed Jack and then stepped past him so that she stood before *Her*. Cyn trembled as her gaze traveled down the face and nubile body. Up close she saw that it was a girl, her body hairless and small. She was too young to be with child and far too young to have been with a man.

The statue was magnificent but what drew Cyn's eyes was the hole that went down into the earth. The hole was a madness of stench and begging eyes. The hole went deep. It went beyond the bounds of the earth. It went directly to hell.

Cyn dug in her pocket for the golden coin that Jack had handed her. Gold or diamonds or the souls of children were the only fitting gifts to give the Mother of Demons. Almost as if it were a Wishing Well, she was going to toss the coin in, but Jack stopped her hand.

"Are you crazy? Don't put anything down that hole." Jack was sweating, no longer so self-assured as he had been. "I don't think we're going to find anything here. Robert has already taken everything of value."

That was insane on the face of it, Cyn thought. The statue was absolutely priceless—it was worth a million souls easily. That was such an ugly thought that she forced her eyes away from the statue and asked: "W-what do you mean?"

"Right there," Jack said pointing at a pedestal that stood just to the side of the statue. She hadn't seen it before. It had been right there and yet it had been so overshadowed by the statue that it might as well as have been invisible. She was only just noticing the piece of paper sitting on it, face down.

There should have been a book on it. A spell book to be precise. How she knew that she didn't know.

The piece of paper certainly didn't belong in its place and nor did it belong anywhere in this cavern. The paper had come from a tree birthed only twenty years before. It was college ruled with three holes running up one side. Robert had undoubtedly pulled it from his notebook and left it for them in place of the spell book he had stolen.

Jack reached out, picked it up and turned it over. In the glow of Jack's particles, they both read the words: *Don't read this.*

"Don't read this?" Cyn asked, feeling slow in the mind. Jack thrust her behind him as she said: "Why wouldn't we read…"

The doors to the cells where the demons were "trapped" were suddenly thrust open with the sound of metal and wood crashing, splintering and breaking in a single great explosion that rang in the cavern.

Jack was already cutting himself, opening a portal to his soul, bleeding in a room that had been built to collect blood and to feed off of it. Cyn turned from the onrushing creatures and saw the leering face of the Mother of Demons. The smile was gone and in its place was a look of want. *She* was hungry!

A sudden urge overcame Cyn just then. She had the need to stab Jack in the back with her knife. She would slide it in him, just above where he kept his Holy Water, right in the kidney. It would incapacitate him. It would leave him gasping. She would be able to bleed him and oh, what a prize he would be. He was strong. His soul was a powerhouse. He was nearly as strong as a demon.

She fought the dreadful desire, but then he reached out a bleeding hand. It was so much of an invitation that she almost put the hand to her lips and drank.

"I'm going to need your help," he said. It took a second before she realized he wanted her to cut herself and join their souls as they had before against the necromancer. It was a crazy suggestion. Did he not realize what he was asking? Cutting herself this close to the Mother of Demons would be too much for her. She wouldn't be able to control herself and she was just as likely to throw herself into the hell-hole as she was to stab Jack.

The demons were rushing across the cavern and, unaware of her internal battle, Jack waved his hand at her. The blood was too enticing. It was almost erotic. She had a knife. It was blessed and when she cut herself she almost screamed in pain and ecstasy—and then Jack slapped his hand on hers.

There was no time for anything as Jack hurled his spell into the water. Lightning strobed the room as the lake was lit by electricity that ran from one end to another. Four of the demons were in the water; they blew into thousands of hunks of decayed flesh and ancient bone that twitched and jigged.

The other five paused for all of a second before one leapt across the expanse of water. Jack hit it in midflight with another bolt of lightning. Water is one of the best conduits of electricity, while air is one of the worst. The bolt sent the demon flying back where it fell with a rattle of bones.

It was up in a second and the others Jack had exploded were beginning to reform as well. "We'll blast our way through," he said, "and then put a binding spell on the door as we leave."

Cyn felt the energy of her soul rush out of her as Jack hurled another lightning bolt. It blasted two of the demons, charring the rags of cloth draped on them and sending them hurtling backwards. The effect was disappointing to Jack. Not only were they still completely intact and ready to go, there were another two that were totally unharmed.

Jack turned to Cyn. "What are you doing? You're holding back."

"It's *Her*," Cyn said, darting a look back over her shoulder at the Demon Mother. "She's angry. These are her children. She doesn't want you to hurt them."

"What? They're going to kill us. Forget the statue and give me your power!" Though he asked he didn't wait for an answer; he *took* her power.

Cyn resisted. The theft...the rape of Cyn's soul was a direct affront to The Mother, as was the hurling of spells about in her presence, as were the blasphemous words that had come from his mouth.

This time the lightning that came from Jack's outstretched hand was a feeble arc and barely cleared the twenty feet of water and did nothing to the demon it hit. Weak as it was, it drained the last of Jack's power. Cyn felt it. There was nothing but the hard kernel of his shrunken soul.

He was weak and it was her fault. She had taken part of his soul.

It had been utterly natural...and utterly evil. Yet she couldn't help it. The Mother of Demons was there in the room. *She* was staring out of the golden eyes on the statue and whispering up from the hell-hole. She spoke directly into Cyn's soul with a slippery tongue. Her power over a necromancer was nearly absolute and Cyn couldn't help herself as she pulled her hand from Jack's grip.

He fell to his hands and knees. His blood mingling with the water. "Fight it!" he gasped. He knew what she was feeling. He knew because he had gone through the same thing the year before.

She dug out the coin once again and now her blood was on the gold. "Fight it?" she asked, incredulously. "Like how you fought it? Remember how you murdered people, Jack? Remember that? And you didn't even have the Mother watching over you. There's no fighting it, Jack. You of all people should know it. There's only submitting to her power and sacrificing for her love."

The words came out of her mouth and she couldn't believe they were hers and when she moved it was as if someone else had control of her body.

Cyn flipped the coin. It twirled, spinning red and then gold in a blur. Her eyes tracked it, but her mind couldn't grasp the circle or the metal or the colors. She only knew that the coin held more than her blood. A part of her soul had been swept into the coin.

And she hadn't even fought it.

She had been right about Jack. He had sold his soul over almost nothing; over the power of a few spells. At the time he had rationalized about the necessity of it. He was saving the world after all, but it had been the beckoning of the spells that had turned his heart greedy and evil. The Mother had woven her power into the spells, but that power had been altogether insignificant compared to being in *Her* presence.

She was ancient beyond imagination. She was one of the first born. She had power over mortals and could kill them with a thought. The statue held a mere spec of her power and yet she had turned Cyn with complete ease.

The coin disappeared down into the hole just as Jack reached out and took her hand and their blood mixed once again. She could suddenly read everything she ever wanted to know about him. He was going to drag her out of there, even if it meant being torn apart by the demons, even if it was against her will—and it was.

The Mother was in her, turning her insides black, corrupting her, making her a pet, a nothing to be used and discarded.

But before Cyn was discarded, the Mother had need of her. Without warning, Jack screamed, his head thrown back and his eyes wide. The connection between him and Cyn was also a connection between him and the Mother of Demons and *She* wasn't happy with him. He had thrown away the gift that she had bestowed on him. She had made him a necromancer and he had thrown that away for love!

Burning pain coursed through Cyn and into Jack. It was a pain that no man should have been able to bear. He had tears in his eyes and his face was a hideous mask and yet he was somehow able to wrench his hand away. He fell to his knees, his hands in the water of the little lake.

"Give it to me, Jonathan," Cyn heard herself saying. She spoke in a voice that boomed and shook the earth; something fell from a shelf in the outer room with a crash and every word caused ripples in the water.

Cyn marveled. The Mother was in her! Using her body. It was the most disgusting thing that she had ever felt and she thought for sure she was going to vomit and faint; yet she was honored. She was being possessed by this tiny sliver of the Mother and it was an honor. *She* wanted that little bit of Jack's soul that he clung to. *She* was never satisfied.

Jack hissed in pain and then turned his warped face up. "Fight her, Cyn!"

"Why?" Cyn asked in her own voice. "Give it to me to sacrifice, Jack. She will look favorably on me if you do. And if you don't give it to me, they will rip it from you." She pointed: nine fully formed demons were in the water, slogging at Jack.

He was utterly trapped.

Chapter 15
Nekhen, Egypt
Jack Dreyden

He actually considered giving in to Cyn...but just for a few seconds. His soul really wasn't worth much at the moment. Just the hard kernel was left. The little nub that always refused to die. Sometimes that nub was a little pit of anger or hate, holding on out of spite. Sometimes there was so little of it left that it was a ghost of thing, filled with a few memories or the last shred of love left in him.

Just then it was a pinpoint of light in an otherwise dark and empty being. It would be easy to give up if he actually thought it would help Cyn in some way.

Yet that wasn't the reason that he clung to it. He wanted vengeance. Once again, he had fallen into a trap laid out by Robert. The man was cunning beyond imagination.

He had moved the body of the Necromancer to kill Jack, but on the off chance that Jack had lived, he had set this up as well. The demons were Robert's thralls instructed not to come out of their cages until Jack had managed to trap himself.

And he was good and trapped.

On his knees and drained of power; Cyn turned against him; nine demons on one side and the Mother of Demons on the other. His sword was gone. When Cyn had drained the last of him, it had flown from his hands to splash somewhere in the dark water.

All he had left to fight with were two vials of Holy Water. It was only enough to perhaps blind one of the demons with a lucky splash. Otherwise all it would do would piss it off. Out of options, he pulled them out.

"Who's first?" he asked in a whisper. He had meant for it to come out as a ringing challenge, but the whisper was all he had the strength for.

One of the old bundles of rags and bones came forward, a leer on its grinning face. It was interesting to note that the demons had not used any of their special powers: their cold breath, their ability to cause localized earthquakes. They hadn't even used darkness or fear.

They were more concerned with offending the "Mother" than they were in dealing with Jack. Not that they would need even a tenth of their power to deal with Jack. Not just then at least.

Jack went with his only weapon and gave the demon a good splashing with the bottle of water. It hissed and threw a bone arm up, but other than the temporary pain, it hadn't really been hurt, at least not in the long run. Holy Water had its uses but it would take a bucket of it to really harm the creatures...and where would Jack get a bucket of Holy Water right then?

Suddenly, he realized that he didn't need a bucket of water; he had an entire underground lake full of water. What he needed was a priest. What he needed was Father Timmons, the man that Jack had tirelessly tried to get fired from his team of *Raiders*. The man who, even in death, still managed to be disappointed in Jack—he could feel it even then, there was a little pinpoint of light within him that smacked of Father Timmons.

He had wanted to save Jack's soul, but now both of theirs were going to perish and that was too bad. If Jack had saved anything of Father Timmons, it wasn't going to be for long and now the question was should he let his soul get taken by the Mother or her minions?

Cyn was fooling herself thinking that she would benefit from helping the Mother. When Jack died, she'd be next. It would be a wake-up call, but one too late to save her. It would be a bit of a splash in...the...face. A sudden idea hit Jack like a ton of bricks and with a quick motion, he popped the top from his second bottle and splashed the Holy Water full in Cyn's face.

His hope that she would suddenly come to "her senses" was dashed when Cyn laughed and licked her lips.

"I'm not possessed. And you just wasted the last of your Holy Water and you lack the strength to make more."

"The strength?" It was an odd choice of words. Since when was his strength the issue when it came to his ability...or rather his inability to make Holy Water? Strength was never the issue. It was always the fact that he wasn't a priest and yet she hadn't mentioned that fact.

Did the Mother of Demons know something that Jack didn't? Was Timmons really inside his soul? If so, could Jack use that tiny essence of the priest to make Holy Water?

Jack cast a glance over his shoulder at the demons; all nine were standing hip deep in the lake waiting to see if Cyn would take his soul. Cyn was also waiting, her face registering a touch of nervousness; she seemed to have forgotten the shotgun in her hand.

"Do you know how to make Holy Water?" Jack asked her. She knew. They both had seen it done a hundred times. She nodded, looking confused now.

"But you have no strength," she said in a whisper. "She took it."

He smiled a sad smile. "What did Father Timmons always say? *I am only the conduit. I have no power of my own. The power I wield comes from God.*"

"Wait," Cyn said, her eyes going back and forth.

"No," Jack said and before any of the demons could move he crossed himself, whispering: "Heavenly Father, please bless this water, and renew the living spring of life within me..." He paused to see the demons looking stricken, their bony jaws hanging open. "Cleanse this water and destroy any impure evil within it and me, and protect me in spirit."

There was a sudden splashing as the demons struggled to turn with the water frothing and bubbling around them. As Jack watched they seemed to be shrinking as the bones of their legs dissolved beneath them. He went on in the way he had heard so many priests speak: "Bless this water and wash away our sins so we may come into your presence free from evil. We ask this through Christ our Lord. Amen."

By the time he was done speaking, the demons were beneath the frothing surface and the air in the cavern smelled of honey. The sparkling motes were bright as stars. He could barely find the strength to smile at them.

If he had been tired before, he was doubly so now. Next to his hand was one of the bottles that had held the Holy Water. He filled it again and then straightened, getting to his feet like an old man slow and creaking. He turned expecting to face the barrel of Cyn's 12 gauge; however the shotgun sat on the ground, useless and cold.

The Mother of Demons was ancient and powerful; she had no understanding of man-made weapons beyond those that cut or bashed or stabbed.

And just then, that made her weak. Cyn was used up and trembling as though she was about to collapse. "She has lost, Cyn. The Mother knows I have no power left in what remains of my soul and without souls, what can she do? She can't do anything to me or to you."

"You're wrong," Cyn whispered as though she were telling a secret. "She hates you, Jack. She is going to kill me to spite you. If you don't cut your throat, she's going to stop my heart. She can do it. She's so strong."

"Okay...tell her to slow down. I'll do it, but does she want me to do it right here? Or should we go to the tables or what?"

Stiff and robotic, Cyn took her eyes from Jack and stared into the water—the Holy Water. "She thinks your attempts at deception are laughable." She turned to the statue and gestured at the hole at the base. It was black around the edges with old blood. "Just lay your head in her lap and cut open your flesh. It'll be quick."

"Sounds easy enough, but what do I do with this?" The bottle that he had filled with Holy Water sat in his palm. Cyn's eyes went wide and she tried to grab it, but was too slow. He tossed it straight into the hole. A half-second later there was a blinding splash of dark light, somewhat like the after effect of a camera flash and then came the sound of cloth being ripped, except it was multiplied a thousand fold. It was a storm of sound that assaulted them.

Both Cyn and Jack grabbed their heads and fell away. When Jack looked back, he saw the hole was belching huge plumes of black smoke which shot up to envelope the ceiling of the cavern.

"Come on!" he yelled, taking Cyn by the hand and pulling her. She resisted but was too weak and when her boots splashed into the cool water she fainted dead away, practically falling face first into the water; he caught her just in time and laid her on her back.

Although he was afraid that the Mother herself would suddenly climb from the hole like a horrid black spider or that the statue would explode like a volcano or the cavern would cave in, Jack paused to wash Cyn completely. Her eyes fluttered open and immediately filled with tears.

He washed those away as well.

"I'm sorry," she begged. She was sorry; however, Jack knew this was just the beginning. Her remorse would only grow until it would threaten to eat her alive.

"It's nothing. Don't worry about it. Can you walk?" He dragged her across to the other side of the lake and now the cavern was half filled with the reeking smoke. She shrugged. Her soul was as drained as his and she had her regret added on top of that; she didn't care what would happen to her. He understood. He had been there.

With a grunt, he lifted her in his arms. Garbed in her armor and soaking wet, she was surprisingly heavy, and he was weak through to his core. Gasping and lurching side to side, he fled from the cavern and fought his way upward until he was out in the blaring light of the desert.

Apathetic to everything, Cyn didn't move a muscle when Jack put her in the blazing hot Volvo. "I'll be right back," he said, and then ran back down into the pit beneath the earth where the air was clouded black and had the stink of death.

The first thing he did was to grab the green box with the skull in it—he couldn't leave that just lying around; there was no telling what would happen if all the pieces of that particular skeleton were laid out—he rushed down the stairs that led to the necromancer's lab and without looking in, he tossed the box inside the room and then shut the first of the secret doors.

Next, because he was in his heart an adventurer and he couldn't help himself, he grabbed a handful of gold coins and another handful of the tarnished silver ones. He then sped back into the second chamber with the broken sarcophagus, again shutting the secret door behind him.

The door was so well constructed that immediately the smoke ceased to billow up. There wasn't even a hint of it creeping around the edges.

Then he pushed outside, blinking at the glare of the sun as it reflected off the sand. The sky above was a perfect cobalt blue. "I think I'm done," Cyn said. She hadn't moved a muscle from where he had left her and laid there staring up at the ceiling of the car. "I think I need to quit this."

"Yeah." What else was there to say? He couldn't find the energy to think and yet he had a big hole in the desert he had to refill.

"I mean, I'm putting my bloody soul on the line and for what?"

Jack went to the pile of debris that was mounded next to the hole. He started chucking rocks down into the slanting pit. "I agree," he said to her.

"I'm going to go to...I don't know, to Bora Bora, maybe. Or the South Pole. Or the straights of Magellan. I'll go where no one can find me." Jack said nothing to this. He knew this sad train of thought—those tracks were well worn in his mind. He just continued to heave rocks, his head swimming from the heat and his exhaustion.

Cyn was quiet for a long time as he worked. When the hole was half filled she suddenly said: "*He'll* find me, won't he?"

She meant their cousin, Robert. "Yeah," Jack answered.

"Or *She* will," Cyn said, her voice quieter than the desert wind. This kept her silent for so long that Jack had the hole mostly filled by the time she added: "I can't run and I can't hide."

"That's why we fight," he said. "We don't have a choice." She began to cry and so he changed the subject: "Tell me about your geese. Will you put little bonnets on them like in the cartoon movies?"

She blubbered and laughed. "Of course. Why have geese if you're not going to dress them properly?" She was quiet again for a time and despite the heat, she hugged herself. "Can I at least go on holiday?"

Jack paused with a rock at his shoulder. "A holiday? What holiday? We just had Independence Day."

She finally sat up and rubbed the tears from her eyes. She looked like she was trying to be her old self. To Jack it looked like she was putting on a mask. "First off, don't say *Independence Day* to a Brit unless you want a poke in the eye. And second, I was referring to a vacation."

"Oh," he answered and then tossed the rock. He bent for another and paused again, staring around. The heat and his exhaustion were becoming a force. "I think this is our vacation." Her face clouded again but after making an angry determined sound, she pushed the smirk he loved where it belonged.

"Oh yeah? And was that night in Wadi Halfa indeed your idea of a honeymoon? Don't answer that! I could tell that you were going to say yes." She struggled to stand and then came over to the pit and looked inside. Without being asked, she bent and started tossing rocks in as well.

They worked in silence until the hole was filled completely and the only sign that anyone had ever been there was the hunk of intestine. Cyn wrinkled her nose at it. "Robert didn't leave that."

"And nor would he leave the crypt wide open like that. It doesn't make sense that any necromancer or sorcerer would. Truong mentioned Chinese sorcerers. They could probably find the crypt of the necromancer, but would they leave it open?"

"They might if Robert's demons had been chasing them," Cyn suggested. "It might also explain the intestine. Maybe they were attacked and only just got away."

Jack unbuckled his armor and then washed himself with a different jug of the water they had picked up in Wadi Halfa; it smelled of old goat milk. He tossed the jug down; it glugged as the water drained out of it. He sniffed his hand as he asked: "And they left just an intestine and no blood? If I had to guess, it's probably another necromancer who had a ghoul with him to do his digging for him."

"Another necromancer? That's just great. That's just what we need." She was close to crying again and he went to her. She hugged him but for only a second before she pushed him away. "What is that smell?" She tried to smile but there was pain behind her eyes. "I'm sorry," she said, again.

He knew she'd say it another ten times that day and probably twenty the next, and that was okay. He had already forgiven her; the apologies were for her, for her soul. She would beat herself up until she realized that there had been nothing she could've done differently.

And then they would never talk about it. When she wasn't looking, Jack rubbed his chest, still feeling the ugly sting of the hooks that had been in his soul as it was being torn from his body.

"It's nothing," he told her.

Chapter 16
Nekhen, Egypt
Jack Dreyden

It was early afternoon by the time they left Nekhen. Jack figured that they would make it to Luxor, a city of some historical note by evening. From there it was only another long day's drive to Cairo.

They were thinking of going to Cairo simply because they were tired of the desert and the scorching sun and the hot as hell water. Of course Cairo had all these things in abundance, but it also had actual five star hotels where all of that could be ignored. Their plan was to lay up in one of these hotels and recuperate.

The death of the Volvo changed things. It blew a rod some ways out of Luxor and so Cyn and Jack found themselves with their tongues wagging from the heat, tramping, first through the desert and then through some no-name town.

They were pretty sure that the town actually had a name; however neither of them knew Arabic and no one in the town knew English or ancient Egyptian. Since Cyn's phone had been ruined by her total immersion, they were somewhat lost. Still, after much pointing and gesturing with the locals they were able to find the town's version of a *Motel 6*, complete with air-conditioning and running water.

Of course, the water smelled of rust and the air conditioning dripped some sort of oily fluid so that the room was half taken up by a puddle when they woke nineteen hours after checking in. They ate and slept again —they didn't hold hands as they had a few days before after the battle with the necromancer. In fact, Cyn kept very much to herself.

"She'll come around," Jack said as he dressed in the same clothes he'd been wearing for days. They were rancid, smelling of curdled goat milk and old sweat.

It was almost evening when Jack left the hotel alone. They were very much in need of supplies since they had lost all of their weapons in the tomb, and had to abandon whatever was left of their food and water with the Volvo. He felt naked without a weapon and so he went in search of one first, finding out pretty quickly that getting hold of a gun was out of the question and a sword was only slightly easier.

It took some bribing and quite a bit more gesturing before he found someone who was willing to sell him a sword. The man, an old toothless chap, wanted five hundred dollars for what was practically a useless piece of steel. It was a heavy, ceremonial scimitar with a dull blade and gold braiding hanging from the pommel.

"Three hundred," Jack insisted. They settled on three-fifty and Jack was then pointed to another gentleman, a plumber by trade, who took the unwieldy weapon in the back of his shop and put an edge on the hefty blade for only ten dollars more.

Jack gave him twenty and asked about where he could find a church. The question was met by an ugly look. The same thing occurred throughout half the town. It was only when he was being fitted for a loose pair of cotton trousers that someone gave him a whispered answer: "Two block is west. No say of me."

The woman who said this had frightened eyes above her veil. Jack assured her that he wouldn't say a thing. He had two sets of clothes made for him and Cyn. He was dressed in baggy linens of tan and white which made him feel like a bedouin. The clothes he picked out for Cyn were local as well: wide, silk pants that tapered at the ankle and a shapeless shirt covered by layers of even more shapeless wrappings.

She wasn't going to be happy.

Now that he was dressed to blend in, he had the rest of the items sent on to the hotel and, after a final purchase of a few feet of black cotton that he wrapped the scimitar in, he set off for the building that the woman had described. It was a sad little structure of stone and wood with shuttered windows in place of glass. There was nothing to indicate that it was a church: no steeple or crosses, just some obvious fire damage on the door and what looked like human excrement against one wall.

The doors were locked and yet there was light inside and voices. Jack knocked lightly until a man came to an upper floor window and stared down. He asked questions in Arabic to which Jack could only shrug and shake his head. Finally, Jack crossed himself and pointed inside.

He was let in by the same man, a priest as it turned out, though he was as unadorned as the building. He looked like all the other locals to Jack: careworn, fearful eyes, cracked fingernails, brown skin prematurely aged by the desert heat. There were seven men in the church all looking at Jack with suspicion and looking at what he carried with even greater suspicion.

"It's just a sword," Jack said, showing the hilt. He presented it to the priest and then crossed himself before pointing at the sword. This had an astounding effect.

The priest's dark eyes went huge; he was afraid at first, but then he smiled suddenly. Jack nodded expressively, like a stage actor. "Yes. I need you to bless this." Again he made the sign of the cross. This set off a burst of excitement from the priest, directed, not at Jack or the sword but at his very small congregation, none of whom shared in his enthusiasm.

Their scowls doubled in intensity, becoming glowers.

In proper Catholic fashion, the priest set them to saying prayers. When they had their faces nose down in red bound books, what Jack took to be bibles, the priest ushered him into a side room that likely acted as a confessional. It was as sad as the rest of the building. The boards of the floor were rough-hewn and the paint on the walls was peeling in long strips.

Jack was sat in a chair that sagged beneath his bottom and then the priest scurried from the room, coming back with a basin of water and a small vial. Jack figured the basin was Holy Water, but if it was, the priest used it in the most unusual fashion—he pulled Jack's boots off his feet and proceeded to wash his feet.

"I'm good, Father. I just bathed a couple of hours ago." It had taken him a good long soak to get the smell of sour goat's milk out of his skin. He held up the sword. "This is what I need blessed, not me." The priest didn't seem to understand or care what Jack was saying and went right on.

After his feet were washed, the priest brought forth the oil. *Finally*, Jack thought, only again the sword was ignored. The priest prayed over Jack and drew a cross on his forehead. The sword was an afterthought; it was finally blessed only after the priest had finished fussing over Jack.

"Thank you," Jack said, holding the sword up, letting the glow from the weak bulb hanging from the ceiling, glint from its edge. It was suddenly light in his hands and he gave it an easy flick.

This encouraged the priest who grinned and nodded—there was something uneasy about the grin that made Jack nervous. "What is it?" he asked. The priest only nodded some more and began pulling Jack along. They headed for the rear of the church. "Where are we going?" Jack asked, wondering what he had gotten in to.

More nervous grins were his only answer. It was full-on dark when they stepped into the alley behind the church. Jack began to protest, but the priest shushed him and pointed. With the dark hiding the finer details of the world, all Jack could make out were the last few buildings of the little town and then what looked like the desert, craggy and open.

What he *felt* was different.

There was a ghoul ahead and what he had thought were rocky crags was actually a graveyard with headstones of various sizes and shapes. The sensation that he was picking up from the ghoul suggested that it was relatively weak, which made Jack nervous. Was this another trap? Or was this simply a stray, and if so from where, and who had conjured it? Jack paused, slinking down, letting his mind and soul explore what his eyes could not see.

As far as he could tell, it was just the ghoul—but it wouldn't be for long, Jack would see to that. With the priest fifty feet back, peeking around a corner in the alley, Jack strode forward. There was no need to be quiet or subtle; the ghoul would attack as soon as it caught wind of him.

"Hey there, ghoul," Jack said, swishing the scimitar back and forth. "Sorry about this but it's time to go back to where you belong."

The ghoul turned slowly, almost tiredly, something Jack had never seen before. "Jonathan Dreyden? What are you doing out here?" it asked, surprising Jack into stopping cold. Not only had it spoken English, it had spoken in a slushy, winded manner that Jack recognized.

"Dr. Loret? Holy cow, is that you?" The ghoul nodded, again slow and unhappily. Jack came closer, less warily, now. Loret was a weakling as far as ghouls went. "I should be asking you the same question, Doctor. What are you doing here?"

Loret shot Jack a look; however with the dark, and the fact that his features were utterly lifeless, the meaning behind the look was lost on Jack. "I'm working on my tan. What do you think I'm doing out in an Egyptian desert?"

"Right, sorry. You're after Robert, of course. Hey, that was who left that hunk of intestine back at the necromancer's grave, wasn't it?"

The ghoul looked down at his stomach which, at the moment, was hidden beneath an old sports coat he had picked up somewhere. "I left what?" He began feeling beneath the coat. "Ah, for crying out loud! You didn't happen to pick it up did you? Tell me you have it there in a baggy or something."

When Jack shook his head, Loret straightened his coat and managed to look huffy even with his split eyeballs and wormy grey lips. "What sort of archeologist leaves valuable artifacts lying on the ground to rot in the sun? For all you knew that could've been from Ahmenhotep! You wouldn't leave Ahmenhotep's intestines just lying around, would you?"

"You're not Ahmenhotep, so it's a moot point. Besides, who are you to lecture me about how to conduct myself at a site? You left that tomb wide open! Anyone could have happened upon it and then what would have happened? I doubt that even you would want the *Mother* loose on this planet."

A cold light suddenly lit in Loret's split eyes. "The *Mother*? Are you talking about...?"

"Yes. There was an effigy to the Mother of Demons and some sort of avatar of hers possessing it. Wait, you didn't get down into the lower dungeons?"

"*No, I didn't get down into the lower dungeons,*" Loret mimicked in a high-pitched falsetto. "How could I? I'm not a sorcerer or a necromancer. I could tell there was a spell nearby but not where. And even if I knew where, how could I get past the door?" His scowl had been heavy on his face, but then it suddenly brightened. "I could dig around it...maybe come up from beneath!"

Now it was Jack's turn to glare. "You'd be wasting your time. Robert took the necromancer's spell book and I cut the link to the Mother, so don't go messing where you shouldn't mess." Jack fingered the edge of the scimitar, menacingly.

"Of course, oh great master. I wouldn't think of disobeying you."

If Loret guessed that the dig "master" would hurt, he was right. Jack had brought Loret's soul out of the abyss in order to get answers from him and now he was essentially immortal in the disgusting form he was in.

"If you're unhappy with your present state, I can send you back," Jack said, lifting the sword. "From what I understand of where you were, you should be thanking me and not making snide comments."

"I'm a ghoul," Loret said. "What sort of comments do you expect me to make?"

Jack didn't bother pointing out that Loret had been an ass when he was alive as well. "How about we dispense with the unpleasantries and you just tell me what you know of Robert's whereabouts."

"Why don't you tell *me* what you know?"

A sigh escaped Jack. He sat himself down on an ancient tombstone and said: "Sure. He's been desperately trying to kill me. Other than that I haven't a clue what he's up to."

"Oh please! You think he cares about you and that Barbie Doll cousin you've been shacking up with? I really doubt it. He's grown strong, Jack. He's beyond you, now. He's filling his soul. He's gaining spells and strength and power. Here's what I think: he trying to become like the old ones, like that necromancer. Oh, he was something. I could feel the residue of his power. It was luscious."

The word "luscious" caused Jack to raise an eyebrow.

"You wouldn't understand," Loret said, seeing the eyebrow. "You don't know what it's like not caring about money or women. It's all about the power on the other side. It's the only thing that matters."

That wasn't true. Jack had raised his father from the dead and there hadn't been an ounce of hunger in him. He had been happy where he had been, content to spend eternity with his wife. He'd been in love in life and he was in love in death. Based on that, Jack didn't like to think what he would be like in death. Somewhat in the same manner as Loret, he craved power, he could feel the demand for it in him.

He liked to think that the craving was all about finding the strength to defeat his cousin, but who knew at this point?

"So Robert's after power?" Jack asked. "That's not exactly news. Where is he trying to find this power?"

"Not in Africa. He's been gone for weeks; at least that's what the scuttlebutt is. Oh yeah, don't look surprised. The undead community is big here, lot of movers and shakers, lots of talk, lots of gossip. You should hear what they say about you…or should I say what they said about you. Everyone thinks you're dead."

"Keep it that way," Jack said with a hint of warning in his voice.

Loret shrugged, uncommitted. "Maybe…tell me how you defeated the necromancer and maybe I'll keep this little meeting to myself."

That was easy. "I didn't defeat him. He tried to go up against forty-two trained soldiers, eight priests, and four military helicopters."

"And one sorcerer," Loret added. "Don't try to fool me, Jack. I can feel your power. You're not the same. You're not as strong as your cousin, but you're not the same. You're a mishmash, that's what I think. The aura coming off of you is like a sail that's been built of quilts and jackets and pieces of yarn."

A shiver went up Jack's back because Loret had read him with far too much accuracy. He was a mishmash. He could feel the tiny light of Father Timmons in him and the cunning of Truong, and the menace of the necromancer and then there were the demons…so many demons—there was even a touch of the Mother of Demons in him.

Each of these people and creatures had added a little to him, growing his power and making his soul feel like it was a junk yard of odds and ends, making it feel as though his soul was no longer even his own.

He stifled the sudden queasy feeling that had bloomed in his gut and said: "Let's just say he was defeated in a joint effort. I just happened to have lived through it. Now, about my cousin. What's his ultimate goal? It can't just be about power. He has to have more of an end motive."

"Some people might think that power is a goal in itself," Loret countered. "Or maybe since Robert is being hunted on four continents, his goal is simply survival?" Loret paused and then suddenly brayed like a donkey, spewing rotting lung on Jack, who only stared in growing impatience. "Sorry, but that's just funny. Okay, I don't know what he's up to…really, it's true. You know that I've dedicated my life…my 'unlife' to finding him and killing him. Why would I lie to you?"

Jack figured that he probably wouldn't and so he shrugged. "So why are you here?"

This seemed to infuriate Loret. "I'm here because I can't just catch a cab or a train. Do you think I can board a plane with this face? But maybe if I had some money…"

"You want money from me?" Jack asked, incredulously.

"I can't exactly get a job, now can I? I don't need much. A few hundred dollars. It's either you give it to me or I kill to get it. Those would be deaths on your head."

This was a new low, Jack thought. He was being blackmailed for money by something that was only a step above a zombie. And yet what could Jack do? He had created Loret and it would've been justice to send him back to hell where he belonged; however Jack couldn't bring himself to do it.

One day Loret would go back to where he belonged and would likely find Jack there waiting for him.

Another sigh, this one a long deserty sigh, escaped Jack as he dug out the money Cyn had wired to the bank in Aswan. Loret's eyes went big but Jack said: "Naw, don't get your hopes up. First off, this isn't my money and second, I owe the priest more than I can possibly give you."

In truth, he didn't owe the priest a penny; however the state of his church could be described as "ramshackle," and that was only if Jack was being generous; he couldn't leave without giving an offering.

Slowly, feeling disgusting, he peeled away four hundred dollars from the roll and gave it to Loret, making him promise "To be good," without defining exactly what that meant. The ghoul nodded without listening as he flicked back the twenties, counting with a line of drool coming from one of his numb lips.

Jack left him and went to the priest and tried to explain the state of things. It was clear that the priest had expected a battle of some sort with Loret and not a lot of talk, and he especially didn't think that it was right for Jack to have given the ghoul any money.

He was slightly mollified when Loret disappeared into the night and it also helped that Jack gave him five hundred dollars and all the coins he had taken from the necromancer's vault, to go towards fixing the church.

Wrapping the sword once again, Jack made his way back to the hotel. He was sure that Cyn would still be sleeping and he wondered what she would say in the morning when she found out that he had given away the majority of her money. What they had left was barely enough to get to Cairo on the dilapidated and listing bus that came through the little nothing of a town every two days.

These thoughts were on his mind as he entered the hotel lobby and he was slow to catch on that the Egyptian standing at the counter was bigger than the others in town and that there was a gun at his side beneath the long flowing shirt that he wore. Was it the police? The Muslim Brotherhood? Or was it the Egyptian version of the CIA or the KGB? Had they heard that a foreigner was in town trying to buy weapons?

His purpose was unknown and yet the danger around him was heavy in the air. The man turned and his eyes widened as he recognized Jack; he went for his gun and he wasn't slow. Perhaps he went for it just as a precaution, or perhaps he was there with murder on his mind. Jack couldn't take the chance to find out which.

Jack's breath came out hot and strangely full and in a literal blink of the eye, the heavy, near useless scimitar was in his hands and the blade was suddenly a millimeter from the man's neck.

Something had happened. Something fantastic and scary. He had slowed time just as Truong had and just as the necromancer had. Time had snagged on nothing, slowing for everyone but him.

Then it blinked back to normal.

"Don't…please," the Egyptian said with his mouth hanging open and his brown eyes popped wide.

Jack hadn't been fully charged to begin with and slowing time had drained him again, but not as badly as he had expected. Still, he was relatively apathetic towards the Egyptian. Just then he could have sheared his head off or bought him a cup of coffee and he didn't know which the man deserved.

He was mulling the two choices over when something hard nudged into the side of his head. It was the barrel of a gun. Jack could smell the residue; it had been fired recently.

"Drop the sword, Mr. Dreyden."

Chapter 17
Nekhen, Egypt
Jack Dreyden

Slowly, Jack turned. The gun pressed against his face didn't bother him so much; his mind was barely aware of it. He was still dwelling on the fact that he had just slowed time to a crawl. How had he done it and who's whispered breath had come from his mouth? Had it been Truong's, the necromancer's, or had it come from the Mother of Demons herself?

All three had the power and knew the spell, but the breathy nature of it was from the necromancer, he decided. The moment the golden lid of the necromancer's sarcophagus had been lifted off, the creature had shot straight away at Jack and there had been an echo in his mind or in his ears right before the necromancer had tried to bury its fist in Jack's chest. It had been a whisper and it only registered on his subconscious…and clearly his soul as well.

Necromancer or no necromancer, how had Jack done it? He had almost stopped time without even being aware and, more importantly, without having cut himself. How could he do magic without a portal to his soul? Was there a gate to his inner being in his lungs? Or had it simply been in his breath?

"Put the sword down, Jack," the man with the gun ordered. He was one of the *Raiders*. Jack could smell the Holy Oil, and feel the blessed blade that he carried. He was like all of them: tall and strong, short bristly hair, hard eyes.

At that moment, Jack didn't know if he was really in the mood to move the sword off the Egyptian's bare neck —after doing magic, he didn't like being told what to do. His sorcery made him feel special; it made him feel greater than even this captain of men, who was all muscle and grit.

It had Jack wanting to make those he deemed lesser than himself cower in abject fear…

But then he took another breath and he was himself again, the haughtiness gone.

He lifted the sword. "Sure. Sorry about that. I think I was just a bit jumpy after everything that's been going on. You…you're Captain Vance, right?" He had met him twice, both times introduced by Captain Metzger. They'd been friends. Jack's eyes slid away.

"Yes, I am," Vance answered, his voice like ice.

"You heard about Meroe I take it?"

"I heard enough," Vance said. "I heard that fifty men died and yet you walked away unscathed, once again. And I heard that some of the men had been shot to death; murdered in all likelihood. I heard a lot of people are looking into it."

A familiar angry feeling began to come over Jack and now the scimitar no longer felt so unwieldy or heavy. "Then you heard wrong." The sword came up, the tip glinting with the oil. Even with his gun, Vance had to know that he was no match for Jack, and yet he didn't back down. The two faced each other as the desk clerk and the tall Egyptian backed away.

"Okay, forget what I heard. What about what I saw?" Vance asked. "I saw the corpses in bodybags stacked like bales of hay and inside were friends of mine."

Jack glared, feeling the power grow within him. Vance had his finger in the trigger guard; he was too well trained for that to be chalked up to emotion. He was a moment from firing his weapon.

"Stop!" a high voice demanded, breaking the moment and shifting their focus. Cyn was standing on the stairs that led from the upper floors. She was dressed in the clothes that Jack had bought for her. Somehow she made the loose fitting 'shrouds' appear sexy as if they hinted of the fine woman beneath instead of concealing her.

"The truth is the truth, Jack," she said. "Don't pretend it doesn't exist."

Vance lowered his weapon and asked: "What is the truth? What happened to Metzger and the others? They were shot. No one needed to see the autopsy report to know that."

Cyn took a moment to answer. "The truth is that brave men died doing their duty. The truth was that they were facing an ancient necromancer...one of the *Nephilim*, one of the race that ruled the world and enslaved man back even before the Egyptians or the Uruks. They were mentioned a couple of times in the Bible. They were giants, but I didn't know they were magical in any way."

"He was one of the last of his kind," Jack said, speaking words that were mostly just an echo in his head. Some part of the necromancer was buried deep inside of him, but was still alive and would remain alive until Jack breathed his last. "But how do *you* know?" he asked Cyn. She had not slain the necromancer and she hadn't been connected to it as Jack had been.

Now it was her turn to avert her eyes and Jack understood. She had her own connections—*The Mother of Demons; The Queen of Souls*.

"I guess it doesn't matter," Jack said, making light of something with far reaching implications. Whatever those implications were, they didn't bear on that moment. He turned to Vance and handed over his sword. "I liked Metzger, he was a good man and that's why I killed him. I killed him to save his soul and to defeat the necromancer. Cyn will tell you. I need something to eat."

Any sorcery made him hungry, but just then he wanted to get away from Vance and his Egyptian friend as fast as possible. The story of how he had killed Metzger and the others was an open wound that didn't need salt poured on it. Weaponless, he went back out into the town, looking for a bar to start drinking in; however, this was a Muslim country and since the Event, muslims had drawn in and had become even more fundamentalist.

With the ban on alcohol being stringently enforced, Jack settled on a place that specialized in strong tea, strange meats, dates and sticky rice.

He was digging into a plate of what seemed like a combination of all four when Cyn found him. "They're not too happy with my explanation," she announced as she sat down.

"Good for them," he answered and then scooped in another mouthful of food. It didn't taste good, but it was filling and he felt empty, not just spiritually but also physically; his insides were a cavern, echoey and cold.

"It's not good. There's been another 'incident' as they call it." Jack looked up from his food quickly and Cyn shook her head. "No, not another necromancer. It wasn't even a fiend. Just a big bunch of ghouls and a few demons. Vance said: 'two-hundred little and twelve big,' but I knew what he meant."

Two-hundred ghouls and twelve demons—it was too much for all the *Raiders* combined. "How many good guys were on the ground?"

"A few hundred plus helicopters, but they were late to the party. It was a blood bath among the civilians. By the time the *Raiders* got there, basically everyone was killed. An entire town of thirteen thousand, all dead."

Jack stared at his plate, feeling guilt over the fact that he had chosen to hide from his cousin for the last week. "Where did all this happen?" he asked, wondering if he could have done anything to stop it.

"That's the strange thing, it happened in this town in Lebanon that I never heard of, Chaqra or something like that. Anyway, Robert stirred up a graveyard so that he could get what he wanted without being noticed."

"And what did he want?" he asked. She had begun eyeing Jack's plate and she didn't look up as she shrugged. Jack stirred his tea absently and said: "Chaqra. What the hell was in Chaqra?"

She shrugged a second time and then poked around in Jack's plate for a piece of meat. "Well, that's chewy," she said after popping something grey into her mouth. She chewed for a long time and then eventually spat out the hunk into a napkin. "Never heard of it and neither has anyone else. Not even Google…well I guess it has listings like anywhere else but there's nothing there of a historical note."

After gnawing for a time on what Jack was beginning to think was the foot of a goat, he said: "Perhaps nothing that is in most text books, but Robert was there for a reason. Something pointed him to that village…or to that area in general. Lebanon has been well travelled and populated since man started plodding out of Africa. The Sumerians, the Babylonians, the Uruks, all traveled in that area, but where are the ties to ancient Egypt?"

"That's the mystery that the government wants us to solve."

"Just like that? Did Vance even say please?"

This time Cyn tried her luck with the date-rice combo. It was chewy as well but at last she swallowed. "No, but the orders didn't come from him and he wasn't exactly happy about it either. He doesn't trust you."

"And you? Do you trust me?" He meant the fact that she hadn't touched him at all in the last day and a half.

She didn't hesitate. "Yes I do. I'm just in a weird spot and thinking some bad thoughts. And really it wasn't you who I didn't trust."

"You don't trust yourself. I get it, Cyn. I've been there. In fact, I've been there frequently. I second guess myself all the time, but I've never second guessed you. You're my anchor. Here, let's get something out of the way right now." He glanced around at the seedy little coffee house, taking in the patrons, fifteen men, ranging from a table of geezers with wrinkles as deep as river canyons to a few teenagers trying to look tough despite their baby faces.

The men spoke in low voices and looked their way every few minutes, though it was mostly toward Cyn that they directed their eyes. Custom dictated that women didn't belong and yet she was clearly a foreigner and since they needed the tourist dollars desperately they only ground their teeth and made comments they were sure couldn't be understood. They weren't subtle.

Jack waited until no one was watching and then brought out his knife. With a practiced, move he cut the heel of his left hand and then held the knife and his hand out to her.

Cyn began to bite her lip. "Jack, I don't know about this. What if *She* is still in me somewhere? It won't be safe for you."

"It'll be safer if we find out right now instead of in the middle of a fight. And if she's in there, maybe we can evict her or perhaps make her less than she was. Remember, Cyn, this is your body. No one runs it except you. Remember when we were in the necromancer's dungeon? I tried to take the power of your soul and you stopped me cold."

"And I wished I hadn't."

Jack waved away a fly, dripping blood in the process. "That's not the point. You could have stopped her, and you did. Right at the end. Now, cut yourself before I scare the locals more than I am. It's probably gotten around that I bought a sword and then there was Dr. Loret…" Her eyes went big and she started to stutter out a question, but he waved that away as well. "I'll tell you as soon as you cut yourself. Come on, Cyn. We've never been stronger than when we're in things together."

"That's just it, I don't want to be strong. I want to be me, just a girl in love with a boy. I don't want to be Mr. and Mrs. Rulers of the Universe. I have my shotgun…Or I had it. That's all I need to take on Robert."

"Maybe, but I really doubt it."

She pulled not only her hand back, but also her entire body. Without looking up she whispered: "*She* went too deep and now it's all there wide open. I don't think you know what I'm trying to say. I've felt you when you were at your weakest and yet you were still you. Deep, deep down, you were still you, but I…I feel like I've been pierced."

"Yeah," Jack said. "I think I understand." And he did. When he was whole and safe, he knew that his soul really wasn't murky or muddled. It was more of a medley or a stew of different ingredients that only added to the flavor, but no matter what, Jack had always kept that kernel of himself deep, deep down.

He guessed that it was true for everyone and yet few people had ever had their soul tested in battle. Cyn had been tested, only her first test had been against the Mother of Demons—one of the Gods of the Undead. It would be a wonder if her soul hadn't been pierced right through, kernel or no kernel.

"So Chaqra?" he asked, giving her a smile and then wrapping his hand in a napkin.

She was glad for the change of subject. "Yes. They want us to fly out as soon as they can get a proper plane into Luxor. They've had people searching for us all over the desert. When they found the Volvo they knew we were close."

Jack shoved his plate away. "Well there goes any shot we had at sneaking up on Robert. Chances are he knows exactly where we are now."

Cyn didn't agree. "I doubt it. He has every major intelligence agency on the planet looking for him. He is probably so engrossed in hiding that he's forgotten us. And if not, then he's got his own plans he has to worry about." She went for his fork and started to dig around at the odds and ends until her eyes went big. "There's a hair. Oh, that's so gross. Come on, let's get out of here. I just hope the food is better in Lebanon."

Chapter 18
Nekhen, Egypt
Cynthia Childs

They did get to eat, eventually, though they didn't eat at all in Lebanon. From Luxor, Egypt, they flew to Tel Aviv, Israel where they ate until they were round in the belly and sleepy. Then came a three hour drive, which they both slept through, that ended at Chaqra where their appetites disappeared altogether. The destruction and the stench of the corpses that had been left to rot in the sun had Captain Vance and his four man team of *Raiders* gagging.

Cyn and Jack, though no longer hungry, went among the dead unfazed at least when it came to their stomachs. Their emotional state was a different story. Seeing the ordinary people torn apart like they had been had Jack blinking back tears every few seconds.

"It's not our fault, Jack," Cyn whispered, taking his hand. "We wouldn't have gotten in here in time even if we had been with the other *Raiders*."

"Oh yeah? Then why does everyone always keep looking at us as if we were somehow to blame for all of this? Maybe I should get teeshirts made that say: *Not my Fault!* Or maybe one that says: *Am I My Cousin's Keeper?* Do you think they would get it then?"

Cyn gave him a tired smile and said nothing. Besides the *Raiders* and the three tired companies of *Knights* that stood dejectedly around the battleground, there were a few hundred Lebanese soldiers, a cadre of government types and a handful of imams, all of whom were red-eyed and furious; they frequently cast dark glances at Jack and Cyn.

She pulled him away from the dead and he went with her, eagerly. They both knew that there was nothing in the pools of blood and the cast away limbs and the flayed skin hanging like morbid banners that would lead them to

Robert. To get to the bottom of this, they would have to go deeper than this top layer of blood.

After a short conversation that consisted of a lot of gesturing, a Lebanese officer pointed them south and sent a soldier with them to unearth what Robert was really after.

The soldier, skinny and nervous, walked with his head bent back toward Jack and Cyn so much that he tripped on any little thing. Finally, Jack strode past him. "This way?" Jack asked. The soldier nodded to where a drainage ditch cut a third of the town away from the rest. It was an open, slow moving sewer that stank as badly as the city of corpses. Again, Jack and Cyn walked unaffected until they came to a veritable bog of refuse that overflowed its banks.

"What the hell?" Jack whispered under his breath. The drainage ditch had been dammed and now was backing into the town. The soldier pointed around to the left and they followed, carefully until they emerged on the other side of a makeshift wall of rock and dirt that had been erected by hand—by undead hands.

Robert had used a portion of his undead army to throw up the dam. His thralls had then begun an excavation beneath the sewer ditch. There was a tremendous hole, thirty feet across that went straight down into the earth. There were Lebanese soldiers here as well, but they kept well back and had their weapons pointed at the hole as if expecting it to suddenly explode with ghouls.

"Has anyone been down there yet?" Cyn asked.

Captain Vance shook his head. "I asked the same thing but not even the *Knights* wanted to chance it. They say they have no idea how deep it goes."

Jack and Cyn went to the edge of the hole and looked in. The bottom couldn't be seen and the smell coming out of it was that of condensed evil. The hole was perfectly circular and along the side was a carven ledge that spiraled down. "There's nothing here," he said to Vance. "No monsters, I mean. They're long gone. What you smell is the residue of the creatures that had dug the hole. There had to be a hundred ghouls down in there."

"Yeah," Cyn agreed. "Watch." She picked up a stone and flung it into the pit. It fell a long time before there was a muffled thud. Vance waited for a few seconds, with his head cocked, listening. "See?" she said. "There's nothing down there that'll hurt you."

The spiraling footpath seemed safe enough. It was five feet wide and the slope was gentle as it wound down into the earth. Jack and Cyn led the way with Vance and the nervous soldier following. Cyn was once again decked out in her Kevlar armor and there was a new shotgun pitched up on her shoulder. Jack's sword was also new. With great forethought, the quartermaster of the *Raider Squads* kept extra swords and kevlar armor for both him and Cyn on hand.

Jack demanded a precise length and balance to his swords. He knew that these sorts of demands were frowned upon and that they made him look a bit like a prima donna, but he didn't care. The scimitar had been an ugly, hacking weapon and had been tossed away and promptly forgotten at the sight of "his" sword. The scimitar just wasn't a weapon for a fencer.

Though he carried the sword, he left it sheathed. There was nothing to fear in the hole. Yes, it was very deep, well over sixty feet deep, and the darkness multiplied with every step down, but he wasn't afraid in the least. Robert was long gone.

Vance had a flashlight joined beneath his tactical shotgun. It wasn't very practical as a light source. Both Jack and Cyn wanted to study the walls for clues as they descended but Vance was adamant about keeping the gun pointed the way they were going; he didn't trust Jack's assurance that the hole was empty.

As their feet disappeared into the murky dark, Jack fingered a pinch of sand in his pocket and showed it to Cyn. She shook her head at him, knowing that a show of sorcery would only upset the Lebanese soldier, who appeared on the verge of bolting.

"We need the light to figure out what Robert had been after," he whispered. She could tell that all the nasty looks he'd been getting had put him in a mood, one that even she couldn't affect, at least not down in a hole where the smell of blood wafted up.

When they reached the bottom of the hole and the sky was only a dim disk high above, Jack blew on the sand in his palm and immediately the little group was inundated with golden specs that hung in the air. Even though she knew it would cause trouble, Cyn couldn't help smile. It felt to her as if there were a thousand fairies floating above her. The light warmed her soul, but she was in the minority.

With a cry, the Lebanese soldier backed away, his hand feeling the walls as he fled, never taking his eyes off of Jack.

"Impressive," Vance growled. "But then so are these inventions called flashlights. There was no need to make a scene. The Lebanese are half out of their minds already."

"I asked for light on more than one occasion," Jack said. "Next time, give it to me."

Vance gave Cyn a look that she read as: *Control him!* She pretended not to see it. Jack wasn't a dog whose leash she could yank and who she could order to heel.

She walked away to inspect the bottom of the hole. Unfortunately, it didn't appear as though it was going to tell them much. Yes, there was a circle of obscured glyphs and there was a hollowed-out gravesite complete with the *impression* of a skeleton and a few crumbled pieces of bone, all of which amounted to little more than debris and bone dust.

To learn anything, someone would have to take samples to a lab. With a sigh, she looked up at the sides of the hole.

Next to her, Vance tried to wave away the particles floating near his face, which only caused them to spin about him in a dizzying fashion. He had to duck low to get away from them. "Listen, Jack," he said. "There's not going to be a next time. Not with me and not with anyone else. In case you were wondering, your reason for murdering Metzger and the others is complete and total crap. That's pretty much what everyone is saying. There's not a *Raider* team who's willing to work with you now."

Jack didn't look all that upset at this. In fact, it looked as though he hadn't heard; he too was busy studying the walls. "Too bad for them," he said to Vance, absently. Vance's eyes went wide and his knuckles turned white on his gun.

Cyn quickly put herself between them and pointed up at the wall of the hole. "This find is deep, wouldn't you say so Jack? Though it may not be that surprising since a lot could have happened in the last six or seven thousand years to bury it."

"I don't think we're looking at that sort of timeline," Jack replied. "Look at the strata. See how thick it is? That's clue number one. That suggests…"

Vance interrupted, grabbing Jack and spinning him around. "Too bad for them? Really? Did you really just say that? Because I think it's too bad for you. You're hanging by a thread with the Justice Department. Everyone knows that."

This earned Vance a shrug. In Jack's world, there were many things worse than jail. "I only meant that it is too bad more people will die because of that attitude. Now, if you don't mind, there is more to my job than just shooting a gun and complaining about things I don't understand."

Vance started to puff up in anger and Cyn quickly grabbed Jack with one hand and gestured at the walls with the other as if she were a game-show model. "Are you saying this is strata from a river bed? Or a flood plain?"

He eyed Vance for a moment before answering: "I can't tell yet, but the layers are thick enough to suggest a major flood event every forty years or so. You don't get that anywhere else but a flood plain or river bed. Vance, shine your light higher up the wall...please." He had forgotten his manners until Cyn elbowed him.

The light, higher than the glow of Jack's suspended particles, showed more of these deposits of silt stacked one atop another. "I would say flood plain," Cyn said.

"But this is an exceptionally dry land," Jack countered. "I say river bed. We'll get some samples taken and..."

Vance dropped the light, suddenly. "Aren't you going to find out who was buried here? Isn't that more important than whether this was a river or some plain?"

"We're getting there all in good time," Jack said. "But you can go look if you want. If you see a tombstone that says: *Joe Blow*, let me know, but if there's only a few shreds of this or that and the dust of bones, then keep quiet, will you? The first thing we should do is establish a time line."

Still glaring, the soldier stalked away and shone his light down at what was left of the skeleton. Dropping into a squat, he poked a piece of thigh bone with the end of his gun. "Why did the ghoul leave behind these pieces? You know, when it was animated or possessed or whatever you call it."

Jack rolled his eyes at the interruption and let out an aggravated breath. "Because it wasn't animated. There just wasn't enough of it left to allow a demon or ghoul in."

Cyn decided to humor Vance and knelt down next to him. She touched the blood glyphs, feeling the evil in the dried blood. They had been kicked away and were impossible to read.

Next she inspected what was left of the bones and the ground under them. "He was tall," she said. "Close to six foot. And you were right, this isn't six-thousand years old." She held up a crumble of what looked like rust; Jack grunted at it.

"What?" Vance asked, shining his light at her hand. "That looks like rust."

"Exactly," she said. "Which puts this find in the iron age. In the mideast that means that what we're looking at is 3,300 years old at the most. Though I would say that it was closer to 2,000 years old."

Jack finally came to kneel next to the others. In his hand was one of the glowing grains of sand. He set it to hovering over the remains. "I agree. Likely a Roman and at his height, a centurion."

"And you know he was a centurion, how?" Vance asked.

Jack, who had his nose down inches from the bones, said, "First, the age of the find: iron age. The length of the line of rust, just a hair over two-feet, suggests that what had been here was a gladius: the Roman short sword. And see this, what looks like ancient red mulch? It was likely from a scarlet cloak, again common among Roman soldiers. Now the fact that he was buried alone and not in either a mass grave or a mausoleum puts his rank somewhere between common legionnaire and a *Primus Pilus*. Any one of higher rank than Pilus would have been buried with honors, even on a battlefield."

Cyn gave a shrug. "Sound logic, but who was he? Robert went to a lot of trouble in digging this guy up."

"We'll never know," Jack said. "Robert did all of this and killed all those people for nothing. This guy's bones are too far gone to resurrect. I don't even know why he tried."

"Ha!" Cyn cried, jumping to stand tall over Jack and Vance. "Oh, what a rookie mistake. It's elementary my dear, Jack. Robert does indeed know who this was."

Even though she was clearly making fun of him, Jack grinned up at her, sitting back next to the remains of some long dead centurion as if he was in a school library ready to have story time. "Tell us, Cyn, how does Robert know?"

She began pacing back and forth, holding a single finger aloft, feeling like herself for the first time since her ordeal with the Mother. "First, the glyphs. Yes, you can't read them, but, you can tell there's only a single ring. To raise the dead three spells and two rings are needed."

Jack's face lost its pleasant grin. His blue eyes narrowed as he stared at the smeared glyphs. "One ring of twenty-two symbols. That doesn't match any of the spells I know, either."

"Exactly," Cyn said, beaming at her star pupil. "Robert wasn't trying to raise the dead. If I had to guess, he was just trying to talk to the dead, which would suggest he knows who this was. There is no way he would just start talking to random skeletons sixty feet beneath the earth."

They all stared down at the remains until Vance asked: "So who is that? He's got to be someone important."

"He's probably a mistake," Jack said, though for once, he didn't sound so sure of himself. "He must be. There is no connection between a first or second century Roman soldier and the necromancers who reigned four-thousand years before Rome existed. And Rome wasn't known for its sorcery. Babylon and Ur, yes, but not Rome. If I had to guess, Robert didn't know what he was getting and yet… and yet, he came right here. Someone or something directed him."

Cyn reached out to touch the last shard of skull. "So he was important. But how so?"

Jack put his hands out and hovered them over the smeared glyphs and then the flakes of bones and the crackles of rust. He sighed and there was a touch of anger to it. "I'm getting nothing. There was some spell work done but I don't know what was used."

He knelt over the glyphs for a good hour and during that time, Vance stood to the side, looking bored and Cyn collected various samples from the gravesite and a few spots along the walls that she found interesting.

Eventually, when they didn't suddenly divine Robert's current location and plans from some rust and a bit of blood, the Lebanese moved them along to bring in their own "experts," imams of proven valor.

These, it turned out, were few and far between. It came as a shock to the religious world that those spiritual leaders who taught intolerance, and preached death to gays and the murder of "infidels," and who treated women not even as second class citizens but as chattel, were not actually holy at all and had no power over the undead.

Jack's earlier spell work had caused a ruckus among the locals, who wanted to put a torch to anyone who had even a whiff of magic about them. Before a riot broke out, he and Cyn were bustled out of the hole and into a sand-brown truck that rattled so much they were sure that it was losing pieces by the mile. They sped out of the destroyed town kicking up great flocks of fat birds; these had feathers of black and beaks that dripped red.

Cyn couldn't stand the sight of so much death and kept her chin tucked down; however, Jack stared out. His anger at the wonton death was like heat rippling off of him.

When the town was well behind, they leaned into each other and fell asleep, listening to the truck disintegrate beneath them. An hour out of Tel Aviv, they pulled over and they could hear Vance talking excitedly. "I can get there in forty minutes," they heard the soldier say, his words quiet, grim, tired.

"He's done it again," Jack said to Cyn in a whisper, his lips so close to her ear that it tickled. That he meant Robert had opened another gate into hell was a given.

Cyn closed her eyes and tried to sense the spell her cousin had used; she came up blank. "Can you feel it?"

"No, it's too far away. I can usually feel it when he does the spells if it's within about a hundred miles, but he's far out of range. He could be anywhere really, though I would bet he's back in Egypt. Egypt or China. If he knew about those eastern sorcerers, he'd be there in a heartbeat."

It turned out that he was wrong on both counts. "We're going to France," Captain Vance said a minute later.

Chapter 19
Tours, France
Jack Dreyden

"I know where we're going but not why. What's in Tours?" Captain Vance asked as they boarded a fat-bodied military transport, the same plane they had flown in on. The three of them went to the front and found a spot of privacy behind a pallet of supplies. Jack dropped into some webbing which made a hammock of sorts and then shrugged at the question.

Vance grew livid and poked him in the chest. "You're the expert here. What's your cousin after? Is there a museum there? Or a privately owned collection of ancient Egyptian crap?"

Jack could only shrug a second time and Cyn added: "We have no idea what he could possibly want in that little town and neither does Google." Along with her new shotgun, Cyn had received a new cell phone. She had diligently researched Tours but hadn't come up with anything about the town that connected it with Egypt or Lebanon. It made no sense for Robert to unleash a horde of undead on the people there.

"Really, I'm not holding back. If I knew I'd tell you," Jack said. "How long till we get there? I need sleep. I need to be as fresh as possible."

Vance glanced down at a scrap of paper in his hand. "Three hours to the airport and then a chopper ride of about twenty min…"

"Three hours!" Cyn cried. "Robert will be long gone by then." She began pacing, chewing her lower lip.

"It is what it is," Vance snapped. "We can't get there any faster, so we deal with it."

Cyn looked ready to draw blood. Her eyes were lit with a fire that went deep, but then it seemed as though the fire was suddenly quenched. She fell into the webbing next to Jack and asked: "Tell me, are we just chasing ghosts? This'll be the third time in a week that we are hot on nothing but a shadow. How does he just pop up here and there without anyone knowing?"

The army captain gave her an exaggerated shrug. "That's not our job to deal with. Our only job is to fight these monsters and yes, I wish it could be perfect, but it's not. When we finally catch up to Robert, he'll meet extremely swift justice, I promise you that. We have shoot on sight orders. Now, as I was saying, from the airport it'll be twenty minutes by chopper to the town. We'll have three companies of US Army *Knights*, some French special forces—don't ask me how good they are, because I don't rightly know. And lastly, we have what's left of the *Raider Squads*."

"We?" Jack asked, lifting an eyebrow. "I thought that nobody wanted to work with me anymore."

"Shut up and listen. The latest arial recon puts the numbers of undead at about twenty-thousand." Vance didn't seem like the type of man who ever showed his fear, but Jack saw it was there at the edges. "We need all hands. No, don't say anything. We both know that you'll come and do what you have to. And you know that we'll put up with you. Like I said to Cyn: it is what it is and we deal with it."

He was right, but that didn't mean Jack would roll over and agree to everything. "I will go, but you need to know who's in charge: I am, so now it's your turn to listen up. You are going to let me sleep until we land. Don't wake me for anything unless it's to tell me that Robert is dead. And you are going to make sure that whoever you put on my squad knows the risks and accepts that what I say goes. And that includes the priests."

"How am I going to do that?" Vance asked.

"Figure it out," was all Jack said. Vance started to leave, but Jack stopped him. "And when we land, I'm going to want some crepes. Something sweet and I'd like some French bread. And Cyn's going to want some eggs. Make sure they're fresh. We need to be at full strength."

Vance looked as though he was going to tear Jack's head off. He rubbed his temples with both hands as he reluctantly nodded. He left as quickly as he could before Jack could make any more strange demands.

A minute later, as the C17's engines began to rev up, Jack turned to Cyn and said: "Twenty-thousand. It's not going to be easy. Can you look up whatever graveyards are near Tours? I'm going to have to bring at least twenty-five thousand of my own ghouls and maybe more to be on the safe side."

She spent a few minutes researching and then she handed Jack a list. "You got millions of corpses to use if you want them. There seems to be cemeteries on every corner in that part of France. This one here, Saint… whatever that says, is the closest and a good place to start."

"There's never a good place to start," Jack said. He was dreading the idea of creating another zombie army, even a relatively small one of twenty-five thousand. So much could go wrong. The worst of which would be if Jack were killed. Then the number of their enemies would suddenly double. Worse than that; however, was the fact that Cyn would be the only one left who could stop Robert.

Jack hated the thought of that. She had never tried sorcery and the triple-spell to open the portal and control the demons that came out of it would likely kill her.

"I can't worry about that just yet," he whispered under the drone of the engines. He had to sleep; he had to be a hundred percent, on the off-chance that Robert was still somewhere in the town when they finally got there.

Falling asleep for Jack took little effort. He simply closed his eyes and let the engines lull him out. It felt like no time before Cyn was shaking him awake. She said: "We're here," but she needn't have. Even though the creatures were still fifty miles away, he could feel them as an ugly cloud away to the east.

190

As he was still groggy from his nap and had a stain of drool on one shoulder, she helped him up. "Put your arm out. There you go." Cyn dressed him, as though he were a toddler—an armored toddler.

As she was belting his scabbard across his hips, Vance came up fisting a number of brown bags. "I got breakfast," he said, although the sun was just setting. What he was carrying was definitely not crepes and baguettes. The brown bags were from McDonalds.

Jack took one and glanced in. "Yummy. McDonalds, just like mom used to make."

Cyn tried to give him a smile, but it was all teeth and no eyes. She hadn't looked in her bag. "It's the worst we've experienced since New York," she said, waving a hand at the air in the plane as if she could feel the evil with her fingertips. "I really don't like it. There's no reason for Robert to have come here, you know? Do you think this might be another trap? There are so many cemeteries around that town. He could spring something on us as soon as we set down."

Vance had one of his big paws wrapped around a double quarter pounder. He took a bite and said: "Don't worry. We'll have helicopters waiting to evac us in case something bad goes down. We should be…"

"Do you remember what happened in New York?" Cyn demanded, interrupting the captain. "Robert's demons filled that town with so much darkness you couldn't land a helicopter anywhere. He could do the same thing here, trapping us. He could destroy all the *Knights* and all the *Raiders*, as well as Jack and me, in one move."

Captain Vance took another large mouthful. "It's possible," he said as he craned a handful of fries out of the bag and loaded them into his jaw. "Come on, eat up. You got three minutes before the choppers land."

"It's possible," Jack said. "But would Robert really go to that much trouble?" He had suddenly lost his appetite, and yet, he too tucked into his food. He ate standing in the dark cargo hold of the plane. Vance looked as though he was going to reply, but then just shrugged and took another bite. Cyn held her bag and looked miserable.

"Can you pull up a map," Jack asked her. "I want to see what we're dealing with here."

Her fingers flashed over the screen of the phone and in a second she showed him the town. "Here, here, and here are cemeteries," she said, pointing. "I mean they're all over this country. We could use the corpses ourselves to pre-empt Robert, but that feels wrong."

"That's because it is wrong," Vance said. "Though in this case, I don't think we have a choice. The official French position is that it will be considered criminal if you raise the dead. That being said, they're also saying do whatever it takes. They've had at least ten-thousand people killed in the last few hours, but they have managed to hold a line around the town. It's taking everything they have but it's…"

He stopped as the heavy thump of helicopter blades filled the air. He pointed to the map. "We'll head to this cemetery first. Supposedly there's like fifty-thousand corpses interred there. Now, let's move." Hamburger in one hand and a shotgun in the other, Vance left the plane.

Jack and Cyn followed. This was Jack's first time in France and it wasn't pretty. To the east was the constant rumble of artillery, while jets and helicopters zipped back and forth overhead. The air was thick with the stench of jet fuel and the dead—even from miles away, he could smell the bodies.

Thirty or so helicopters settled onto the airstrip not far away and a torrent of grim-faced and sweating *Knights* and *Raiders* bustled towards them. It was an odd sight. They were in their combat gear and ready for battle and yet each man was munching down on McDonald's hamburgers or trying to dip fries in ketchup as they boarded.

When Jack climbed into the lead copter, he yelled over the din to Cyn: "Eat your food. You're going to need your strength. If I get killed…" Just like the others he was eating as he spoke. It was comfort food and just then, on verge of battle, the McDonalds burger tasted far better than he ever remembered—except for that bite. It seemed to get stuck going down.

When he could clear his throat, he said: "If I get killed, you need to take over. You're the only one who knows the spells. You're the only one who can counter Robert."

She had been nibbling on the edge of a burger. Now she looked suddenly green. "I can, but I don't want to. I can teach someone else the words and the glyphs. It's not that hard, anyone can learn."

The chopper suddenly lifted off and Jack almost lost his very recently downed hamburger. He almost lost it a second time a minute later when the copter was rocked by a low-flying plane. Cyn pushed her dinner away. Jack pushed it back. "Eat, please," he insisted. "Yes, anyone can learn the language. That's not the point. If I die, the spells have to go to someone who won't abuse the power. You know how close I was to losing it and going off the deep end."

"And you know that the *Mother of Demons* had me like that." She snapped her fingers.

"Maybe because you haven't strengthened that part of you that has the ability to resist. Now eat." In answer, she threw her bag of food over the side of the copter. She glared at him, but he only smiled and said: "That's precisely why you would be perfect."

Miserably, she nodded.

"I would have eaten that," Vance said, crossly. "They say that you should never go into battle with food in your stomach, but I say hell to that. Get what little happiness you can before you go to your death."

Jack scowled him into silence.

No one spoke much after that. The fires of battle were raging and could be seen blurring the horizon and it seemed as if in no time they were right over them. From the air, the world was black and white. Wonderful and foul.

The countryside was beautiful and softly green, the homes were idyllic cottages, the sky a gentle, cloudless blue—and right in the middle of it there was a line of fire and smoke, and explosions and screams. Old corpses walked in the day and drew blood and feasted. New corpses were strewn everywhere like so much trash.

They had a sad, but perfect view of the battlefield. It was a roiling black cancer, irregular in shape, about four miles at its widest. The perimeter was a good fourteen miles in length, and the French fought stubbornly for every inch.

Closer up, things were far worse. Men fled from the scene, their eyes insane, their minds cracked open. If they were exceptionally tough, they fought and died in place; however, the average man would fire only a few shots and then break and run.

But this was not all bad. The French had learned lessons from what had happened in New York. They held their priests back, keeping them safe where they could bless the men and restore their strength. They also had roving bands of soldiers, designed to scoop up the thousands of deserters, not as punishment, but in order to return them to duty in an honorable way. They were also issued appropriate weapons: shotguns and swords and grenades.

Unfortunately, they lacked in three areas: realistic training, combat experience, and a concept of the amount of ammo that could be expanded in battle. On average it took ten shotgun shells to bring down one of the creatures and as they would only reform thirty seconds later, the French were draining their resources by the minute. Men were going into battle now with eight loads of shells.

It was never enough and the loss of life was staggering.

Jack directed that only his chopper set down where the fight was raging the hottest. "Wait here," he ordered Cyn as they landed fifty yards from the battle. "I'm just checking things out."

She glared but remained in the chopper. The rest of the soldiers and priests ducked out of the helicopter and fanned out around Jack, who pushed through dozens of men, some fleeing, some standing, trying to get their nerve up in spite of the shrill, cried coming from the demon created darkness.

Even with the Holy Oil still wet on their foreheads, the French soldiers were tense and nervous. They gripped their weapons as if they were life preservers and they were about to be tossed off a ship.

"It'll be okay," Jack assured as he whipped out his sword. In weight and length, it was a cross between the supple quickness of a rapier, and a heavier, bone-hacking saber. It blazed like the sun and sang like a song of silver as he held it up.

The men around him cheered and not just because of the sword. The squad of *Raiders* around him were grim-faced and utterly fearless, cut from the same cloth as the fallen Captain Metzger: tall and thickly muscled, with arms like iron. They were clear-eyed and brave.

They followed Jack into battle without flinching.

And what a battle it was. New York had been an endless flowing massacre, but this was a knock-down drag out fight, with neither side giving an inch. It was fought in near complete darkness with only hand flares giving them any visibility. The flares created little spheres of red light that distorted everything, making the smallest walking corpse into a fearsome beast.

The bone-creatures came on and on relentlessly, using everything at their disposal: they spun darkness, and unearthly cold. They exuded a stench that was not only revolting, it was sometimes poisonous. Still, the French soldiers fought until they were torn apart, or cast in ice by some demon, or driven to madness by the fear that radiated out of the darkness.

Only then did they break and run, pelting out of the black clouds. When that happened, and it did every few seconds, more men were sent in. The new soldiers would advance, stiff and robotic, fighting their growing terror as they entered the cloud.

As Jack and his motley team of nine men strode up to the cloud, a man suddenly sprinted from the darkness, nearly colliding with Captain Vance. The captain caught the man who flailed and kicked in spastic fear. Vance didn't berate him or try to smack some sense into him, he only righted him, set him on his feet and let him go. They had all seen it before and knew there was no use trying to talk any sense into the man.

"I'm just taking a look at what we got here," Jack yelled over the din of explosions and screams. "Stay with me, watch my back and don't get entangled in the fight."

The men were well trained and there were only nods, except one man, who said: "Yes, Skipper," which Jack found amusing. He left them and their stern looks and waded into battle with a small smile on his lips. He smiled because he knew this was where he belonged. No one looked down on him here, or made snide comments.

This was his purpose. This was why he twisted and tore his soul. If anything, this was why he was special.

Before them were mounds of bodies and flares burning red and spitting a grey smoke that made the fight not just dark but also hazy. Everything ten steps away was dim, except when there was an explosion or a blast from a shotgun. Then the hell around them was lit for that brief second showing him the horror that Robert had unleashed.

In between the flashes, he could hear just fine. The men fighting yelled and screamed, but since the language of these screams was so pretty to an American ear, it lacked the edge of desperation that Jack was used to. French or not, the fight was fierce.

He wanted to join in, but that was not why he was there. Closing out the sound of the battle, he willed himself to relax and then willed his mind open so that he could feel exactly what he was facing.

The demons stood out in the darkness. They were holes in his mind that burned like acid. He forced himself to count all seventy-six of the beasts.

"Not bad," he said, and began to blink, once again focusing on the battle.

Captain Vance spun him around. "How can you say that?" Jack only looked at him with a puzzled expression, which angered the hot-headed captain even more. "Three men have died while we've been standing here doing nothing!"

Jack turned his gaze to the string of flares. The defensive line was coming apart, eroded by death and desertion. Replacements were slow to come forward and when they did, they came hesitantly.

"Why didn't you say something?" Jack asked. "Wait here." He left Vance snarling like a dog—but like an obedient one. He stayed put as Jack went forward, unafraid despite the terror on the air.

Jack felt strong and light and moved like a shadow, swift and silent. He had given up the desert clothes he had picked up in Wadi Halfa and was now decked out in black with his tactical armor over that. The armor had been made to his specifications; he didn't need it to stop bullets, only claws, and he could move with surprising agility.

He leapt into the fight, not realizing that his smile was still on his lips and it remained there as he struck like a hurricane of steel, sending hands and heads and the ugly remains of flesh flying; soon he was surrounded by piles of twitching bones.

"Your swords!" Jack cried to the French, waving his blade. They each carried a sword that had been blessed, but not one of them had pulled it, preferring to attack from a distance with their shotguns. It was understandable, wanting to keep such deadly opponents as far away as possible, and yet the guns were not as effective as the swords.

The holy nature of the swords caused the darkness in the undead creatures to come unwound, rendering them temporarily "unbodied." The bones would eventually reform, but it would take time. Still they could be killed, or rather, there was a way to send their warped souls back to hell, though it was dangerous and difficult. It was simply a matter of piercing their souls with the blessed swords.

Although it sounded easy, in reality, it was far from it since demon souls were rarely more than little black knots, the size and shape of a raisin, which they kept hidden. The bones had to be searched for these nasty tumors and there was rarely time to do so in the midst of a battle, and just then, the French weren't so much concerned with killing the creatures as they were with simply surviving and holding them back.

Jack was able to rally four of the men who made a spirited attack which kept the line from caving in at this point. They grinned and sent up a lusty cheer. "Keep using the swords," Jack said and then started tromping back to where he had left Captain Vance and his squad. He only made it a few feet before there was a new cry.

A demon had come.

"Damn," Jack whispered. So far, he hadn't used an ounce of magical strength and he wanted to keep it that way. He had to be strong since there was no telling if Robert was just a few miles away in the center of the black cloud. And yet, he couldn't leave this demon unfought.

It was a strange one and that was saying something when demons were involved. For some odd reason, it had stitched two corpses together, linking them at the hip with a length of wormy gut. It was weird and Jack expected it to be an awkward fight. It turned out to be terrifying.

The demon spun as it rushed forward, sometimes using arms like legs and legs like arms. It resembled some sort of pale, two-headed human-spider crossbreed, moving much faster than seemed possible. In a second, it was on Jack, four eyes, gleaming red, four clawed hands swinging; four bony feet lashing out with kicks.

"Damn!" he said again, though this time it was more of a cry of shock. He was fast and slick, but he had never come across something that could attack from every possible angle: left, right, up and down. It was all he could do to whip his blade back and forth in a blur as he gave up ground at an alarming rate.

The French soldiers were running and even the *Raiders* were moving back and Jack didn't blame them. The demon was not only awkward to fight, it was craftier than most. It feinted time again so that half the time Jack's blade whistled harmlessly by the creature, and yet it was Jack who drew "first blood." Having timed the swirling attack, he managed to whack off a hand off at the wrist. He received a kick in the chest for his efforts that would have broken his sternum if it wasn't for his Kevlar.

As it was, he found himself gasping.

The creature didn't wait for him to recover and was on him like lightning, attacking without let up in a confusing melee that left Jack gasping *and* cringing. The claws cut him again and again, sending their poison into him, weakening him and making him stumble until at last his feet were kicked out from beneath him and he fell.

Chapter 20
Tours, France
Jack Dreyden

"Damn," Jack said for the third time, this time it was only a gasp. Taking a deeper breath, he yelled: "Stop!" It was a word of command with a great deal of power behind it and such was the strength of his soul that the demon froze above him. It was "standing" supported by one arm and one leg so that it was sideways, its bodies horizontal to the earth, looking now more like a centipede than a spider.

It stopped for all of two seconds, but that was enough time for Jack to take a proper breath, and roll backwards in a crouch. The next words out of his mouth were ancient: "*Phra-isth rath em.*"

In that tiny span, the demon was above him again, blows coming from both right and left as well as from directly above, but in a blink, the demon seemed to suddenly stop, poised to strike. And it wasn't just the demon, the entire world went from a movie to a picture. Bullets hung in the air, screams stretched out, and the dying were stayed, momentarily from their fate.

Jack had almost stopped time. It was progressing about fifteen times slower than it normally would have for everyone except him. He could move freely in that blink of an eye and yet he couldn't maintain it for long. Stopping time wasn't that taxing, it was maintaining it that drained him, and so he dashed forward and hacked downward with his sword just as he let the spell go.

The edge of the blade sliced right through the run of gut, splitting the demon in two parts. He fully expected one of its bodies to simply collapse and when that didn't happen, he figured that each would be half as strong as they had been as a whole, but he was disappointed here as well.

Both bodies were now independent from the other and were just as strong and quick as they had been, and where before it was an awkward fight because of the crazy angles, now it was a desperate one. The demons—and now Jack understood that there were two separate entities that he was dealing with—were pulling out all the stops.

One would breath ice as the other blasted poison fog. One would come flying in from the side with claws extended while the other shook the earth with a stomp of its foot. Again and again, Jack was forced to use magic.

To conserve his strength he used it in bursts as the eastern sorcerer Truong had.

A dodge here, a riposte there, a dive roll, a flash of his sword. He had no time to show off his form or to display his full power. He had to get the fight over as quickly as possible before one of those claws took out an eye. A poisonous scratch was one thing. They hurt like nobody's business, but there was no recovering an eye in the middle of battle.

As fast and wild as the two demons were, Jack was faster, especially when he controlled time.

One of the demons crouched just to his side, swinging a hand to tear off his face, while the other was eight feet ahead. Jack ducked the clawed hand that hung, outstretched by time, then threw himself forward on his knees so that he slid across the iced over ground and hacked with two hands at the midsection of the further demon, aiming for the spinal column connecting its upper body from the lower.

The force of the blow was a shock that went right up his arms and then he was sliding past the beast. It had been shorn in two and toppled over with a clatter of bones. In spite of that, both parts continued to flail at him and the head tried to spin around on its neck to blast him with more ice.

Jack's slide carried him beyond the beast and, as his feet hit firm, hard dirt, he dove to the side so that the blast passed "somewhat" harmlessly by. His back and left side blistered and stung from the cold. He tried ducking under a poison cloud breathed out by the second demon, but he stumbled and caught some of the green gas in the face.

Hacking and coughing, he rolled like a log out of the cloud, heedless of the sticks jabbing him and the rocks cutting him. When he stopped and could squint through his tearing eyes, he saw one of the demons bearing down on him, looking to finish him off.

At Jack's command, time slowed again.

It was just a blink, a tiny fraction of a second that allowed Jack to leap up and dart forward to get *within* the swing of one of those deadly claws. The demon had not expected for him to suddenly appear so close and certainly didn't expect to feel the shearing blade grating across the vertebrae in his neck where its head joined the rest of its body.

The demon's head fell and cracked wide open; the interior of its skull was alive with black beetles burrowing into a moldy mess. The bugs scattered in fear but no one saw. Like a lumberjack, Jack swung his sword in a downward arc, hacking at the demon's left arm, while it raked at Jack's chest with its right.

Claws dug quarter inch deep furrows into Jack's Kevlar, while his sword took off the arm. Headless, and with only a single arm remaining, any other demon would have been hacked into pieces in seconds, but this demon was used to using its feet as weapons.

It got one good kick in, sending Jack stumbling back over the frozen corpse of some soft-cheeked French soldier, whose face was forever molded in mid-scream. The dead boy—he was no man and couldn't have been much past his eighteenth birthday—reminded Jack of how much he hated this whole affair. Sometimes in the midst of fighting for his life and saving the world, he lost sight of the smaller details.

These were the bodies of real people lying scattered all over the battlefield. They had moms and dads who loved them. They had girlfriends and went to parties and read books and probably had wonderful futures that had been stolen from them by these monsters.

Seeing the boy brought this back. Jack was suddenly furious. Before he was workmanlike, doing his duty, killing because it had to be done, because no one else could. Now he was in a fury.

He picked up the dead soldier's shotgun and pumped round after round into the remains of the two demons, blasting them until no two bones touched another. At last he tossed aside the smoking gun, spat on the quivering bones and then made his way to where Captain Vance and the squad of *Raiders* had been standing watching the fight.

"I want those two demons sent back to hell right this minute!" Jack ordered. The men glanced at each other, a little surprised. During the middle of a battle, and yes, the battle was still raging all around them, it wasn't a normal request to perform an exorcism. Vance barked them into movement and at his command, the *Raiders* didn't hesitate to carry out the orders. Seven soldiers went forward to form a thin line as the two priests began their prayers.

"That was something," Captain Vance said, glancing at Jack out of the corner of his eye. He was no longer the swaggering soldier; he seemed somewhat spooked by Jack. "You, uh, moved so fast. How…how did you do that?"

"Magic," Jack grunted. He turned from the soldier and looked around at the battlefield. The French were only just now sending soldiers forward to shore up the hole that the conjoined demons had caused. "Tell them that they need to use their swords more."

Vance nodded, looking eager to get away from Jack, but Jack grabbed him. "And tell them they need better communications. No radios, of course, but maybe try using old landlines or field telephones. They have to be able to move men up quicker than they have been."

"Field telephones? I doubt they have them. No one has used those in decades, but maybe someone can rig up something. I'll find out." After another sideways look at Jack, Vance left.

Jack stood near the priests, watching as the bones of the demons began to smoke and screams of rage echoed across the battlefield. Although it was so cold that their breath puffed out of them, the priests were sweating with the strain of the exorcism. It was a contest of will: one side desperate to hold onto this earth with everything they had and the other channeling the power of God through their veins.

Although it was not always the case, time and circumstance were on the priests' side and in a few minutes the bones lay in heaps, unmoving and utterly dead. Jack spat on them a second time and said to one of the priests: "Let's get going. This isn't our fight."

He had come into the darkness only to see what they were up against and it wasn't good. He would definitely need to call up his own undead army, something that always sickened him on a level beyond the physical. The dead were meant to rest in peace.

With this breach shored up, Jack pulled the squad out of the darkness and into the light of day, where every one of them, Jack included, stopped to stare up at the sky and breathe in the warm air in great gulps. A few of them shook with the dregs of adrenaline coursing through them and a couple reached down to touch the soft earth.

More screams and explosions turned their focus back to the matter at hand. Jack found Vance. "I need one of the copters to zip me over to this cemetery: Cimetiere de Montmar. Keep the men ready to go. Once I wake the undead and get them moving, we're going to where all this started. Oh, and find out where that is if you can."

Vance gave him a curt nod and then Jack was jogging off to the helicopter where Cyn waited. "Was it a bad one?" she asked. "I could feel something in there, but not what."

"Yeah, it was bad. Sort of like Siamese twin demons; two for the price of one, but Truong's spell made things easier."

"The time thing? Messing with time seems bloody scary to me."

Jack shrugged. "Getting my guts pulled out is worse, trust me. Even with me using my spells, look at what one of those things did to my armor." He pointed to the grooves.

"Oh, you poor thing. Did baby get his Kevlar all scratched up?" She grinned at him; however he could see the worry behind the watery smile. Whether she was worried about him or about the immediate future, he couldn't tell.

"It wasn't really that bad, I guess," he said trying to smooth over her fears.

She replied by kicking him in the shin where he wasn't armored. As he cursed and hopped around, she hissed: "Don't be a git, of course it was bad. And next time you'll take me with you, because I have to tell you, Jack, that if you think I'm going to act as baggage for you to cart around unopened and unused, you're wrong. I'd just as soon go home if you're not going to use me."

Suggesting that she would "go home" was somewhat of an empty threat. She had no real home to go to and certainly no family either. "Fine, but you have to be all in. I might need your, you know, your soul," he said.

"And I might give it to you," she shot right back. "I never said I wouldn't, but I'm not going to have you kicking around in my soul for fun. That's where I draw the line."

"It wasn't for fun," he said, rubbing his leg. "I wanted to see the extent of what we have together. I don't want to be up against something big and not know how much power I can draw from you. What if I accidentally drain you completely? In the middle of battle is the wrong time to figure these things out."

A look of pain swept her face just before she turned to gesture at the helicopter. "Well, we can't do it now. They are waiting and people are dying." She climbed up into the copter and made a great show of checking her shotgun, unloading and reloading the shells. Next, she drew her rapier, a weapon that she only rarely used or practiced with.

Jack didn't force the issue. He sat down on a folding bench next to her and, as the engine began to rev, he closed his eyes. It seemed like a second later that Cyn was shaking him awake once again. "It's time," she said. "Can you do this without my help? Are you strong enough?"

He was tired and the fight with the twin demons had taken a lot out of him, but he felt he had the spiritual strength to cast the three spells. The only question was if he had the mental strength to do it. Allowing demons and ghouls to come into the world, even for the purpose of saving lives was not pleasant.

No one, living or dead wants their body abused by these evil things and it made Jack sick to his stomach even thinking about it.

"Yeah, I can do it," he told her. "But can you do me a favor first? Can you see if anyone had any Pepto?" He didn't want to ralph all over his glyphs.

Chapter 21
Tours, France
Cynthia Childs

They touched down right smack in the middle of the cemetery, the helicopter settling in among the graves softly, almost daintily. The pilot handled his huge craft as though he was afraid that by landing too roughly he would wake the dead, while his four-person crew stared over the edge of the chopper like little kids looking over the side of the bed after a bad dream.

"Thanks for the ride," Cyn said to the crew member with the largest and most flamboyant insignia on his uniform, whom she assumed was in charge. Cyn could barely keep British ranks straight. The young Frenchmen could have been the Grand Poobah of the French air force for all she knew—though she really doubted it.

He was close to panicking. The crew hadn't been blessed and so they were relying on their own personal courage, which had been sapped after their earlier landing within a hundred yards of the undead horde. Though Cyn was, for the most part, immune to the fear generated by the creatures, she knew that it was still strong enough to shake the bravest person if it was their first encounter with its mind-numbing effects.

"You'll come back for us?" she asked, speaking slowly. She was just fluent enough in French to allow her to ask where the water closet was and how to get to the Eiffel Tower. She had no idea how to tell them that they were about to raise a second army of ghouls but that they would be "good" ghouls. "Do any of you speak English."

When they shook their heads, a groggy Jack Dreyden said: "They're going to be in for a hell of a surprise if they hang around. Let me go talk to the pilot."

He was gone for what felt like a long minute as the crew stared at Cyn as if she was a witch who was considering turning them all into toads. Jack had come out of the magical darkness, stinking of evil. His sword was blackened as if from a fire, his armor was scraped up in a number of places with what looked like claw marks from some alien being, and he had that look in his eyes he got after spell casting.

It was a look that made people turn quickly away.

Cyn was being treated as guilty by association. Thankfully, the engines began to work themselves up to full power and Jack came back, pointing for them to get off the chopper. They both stepped out and hurried over the buried bodies of what was soon to be Jack's army, while behind them the pilot didn't waste a second and heaved the helicopter out of there, nearly clipping a cherry tree in his haste.

And then the world was suddenly and eerily quiet. Far off they could hear the explosions and gunfire and even further away was the confused noise of traffic as a million people fled this part of France, but up close there was an air of unpleasant expectation around them.

The feeling had them looking around; Jack with a hand on the hilt of his sword, Cyn with a little quiver as goosebumps flared across her skin under her armor. "Is it me or are we being watched?" Jack asked out of the corner of his mouth.

"I think it's both of us," Cyn replied. They spun in a slow circle, staring out, hoping to see who or what was *spying* on them. Spying was very much the operative word. It felt as though someone was peeking out from behind a curtain at them. "At least it's not the dead."

The eyes that were on them were not coming from below, which was something of a relief. Jack pointed at an elaborate crypt that was just about thirty yards away. It had been fashioned from the whitest marble and, with the carved figure of an angel that seemed to stand guard over it, it stood almost eight feet in height.

"He's over there," he said, his sword coming all the way out. "I can feel him…yes, it's a male."

Cyn had her gun up and she stood on tip-toes, craning her neck. "Is it Dr. Loret?"

Jack, who was far more in tune with magic, shook his head. "No, it's something else. Come on." He jogged toward the crypt, but by the time they got there the feeling of being watched had vanished. They went round and round the crypt a few times, but there was nothing and no sign that anything or anyone had been there.

"What the hell?" Jack asked in a whisper. "Was there an invisible person here? Is that what that was?"

"I don't know. I kind of doubt it. There was a 'seeing' vibe that didn't feel simply like an invisible person. It was more like an invisible spotlight, you know what I mean."

Jack grunted out a "Yeah," and then sheathed his sword. He went around the crypt one last time. "Whatever it was, it's gone now and we're wasting time. Those French guys can't hold out forever."

There was a sidewalk nearby; it was properly smooth and wide enough for Jack to work with, and as he got down on his knees and swept away some dirt and sand with his bare hands, Cyn unzipped a pouch on her belt.

Inside of it were three razor sharp jack-knives and ten short-handled paintbrushes bundled together with a rubber-band. She grabbed one of each and held them out to Jack, her hand shaking slightly. The blood-magic always got her excited in an ugly way and it was an effort every single time to ignore the feeling.

Jack took the blade and cut himself on the left forearm —one quick slash and the red just poured out of him. Cyn turned to look at the serene and quite beautiful graveyard. It was one of the prettier ones that she had been to. The flowers by the tombstones were fresh, the trees hung delicate shade over everything and the grass was a soft green.

She concentrated on that instead of Jack and the mumbled words: "Hrr vahl Evi ah hurrumm fd. Hrr ah huroon ksa hrer, mkr, hrr fd fdhra." He started with what she had always considered to be "her" spell. He then went quickly to the spell that opened the portal into the Duat—the underworld. "*Hrr vahl Evi ah hurrumm fd. Kul hrr hrer hrrfhk. Ahk kul, ahk fd, ahk thul ah fherd.*"

The casting took only minutes and then an ugly metallic tone erupted in their minds and their stomachs went sour with disgust—the first of the four sets of spells was complete. Jack took a swig of the pepto as they hurried away, heading to the easternmost edge of the cemetery. Once there, Jack cut himself a second time and began painting blood.

He was normally stoic; however his face was now twisted. She knew that the spells not only hurt terribly to paint, they were also draining…and yet this time he seemed almost haggard by the time he was done.

"It's different for some reason," he said from his knees. "It's harder than it's ever been before. Like there's something trying to stop me."

Cyn had felt something strange about the casting as well, except with her the hunger was greater and the angry edge that came with it was sharper. "I'm sure it's nothing," she said, wanting to get the spells over with and at the same time she wanted to experience the next spell so bad that she helped him to his feet and practically dragged him two miles south to the third point of the compass.

"Two down and two to go," she told him as she lowered him down to his knees and thrust the knife in his hands. "It'll be okay."

The third cut went off without a hitch; he bled like a stuck pig, but the spell was a trial. He was oddly pale and he began to shake and the further he went around the circle of glyphs the more out of it he seemed, almost as though he were sleep walking through the spell.

"Come on, Jack. The lower part of that glyph is supposed to be a triangle. Focus or you'll force me to do it for you."

"No way. You can't," he said, his words slurring like a drunk's. "Where would you get the blood? If you take mine…"

He had been pulling away from her and so she grabbed him. "I'm not going to *take* anything. I'll guide your hand is all. Here, I'll wrap my hand around yours; it'll be easy." And it was easy, too easy. It was almost as if she were doing the spells. She drew out the symbols, whispering each word as she finished it. As she went around the twin circles, she could feel the power of them building.

When it was done and the third tone rang, he could only stand with her help and it took them twenty minutes to cross to the westernmost part of the cemetery. She wanted to help with this one, too, but Jack rallied his strength. "I'll do this one on my own. Turn away."

"Turn away? Why?"

"Your face," he said, pointing. "It's not the same." She touched her cheeks, wondering what he was talking about, and only then felt the lines and the tightness; she was grinning like a maniac. It was how Jack looked when he had been working his necromancy in New York—when he was murdering people.

Even with the realization that something was wrong with her, it took an effort of will to turn away. She had always been drawn to the spells; they were her birthright as much as they had been Jack's; however, now the pull was stronger than ever. It wasn't even a demand within her to finish the spells, it felt like a *command*.

"It's her," Jack said. "She wants you to kill me." There was no need to elaborate beyond the pronouns of her and she. They both could sense that the Mother of Demons was exerting her will.

"Yes," Cyn agreed. "I'll go. I'll wait over there." Saying it and doing it were two different things. She placed her hands on the sidewalk to push herself up, but suddenly her palms felt glued to the cement. "I'm stuck. Jack! I'm stuck! I can't move my hands. *She* won't let me."

Cyn was suddenly beyond scared; she was close to panicking. She was close to ripping her hands off the cement even if it meant leaving behind the flesh of her palms.

Jack must have heard the fear in her voice. "It'll be alright. I get the feeling that the *Mother* won't hurt you. She wants your soul. She wants you to commit your soul to her by using these spells."

"I won't do it," she told Jack in a whisper.

He was ghost white and when he nodded, it was a bare motion, an inch up and an inch down. "Then close your eyes and don't watch."

Like a child who was afraid of a scary movie, Cyn scrunched her lids down as hard as she could as Jack drew the last set of symbols. What should have taken a minute took nearly ten and during those minutes, he grunted and groaned and made swallowing noises as if he was dry swallowing the skin of a pineapple.

He seemed to be in agony, and things only got worse when the blood-glyphs were drawn and drying on the sidewalk. He had to force the spell from his mouth one word at a time and then there came the tin ringing, in their heads and Jack slumped over. Cyn's hands were suddenly free and she went to him.

Jack made no attempt to get to his feet. He just lay there, looking up at the blue sky. "She wants to drain me to nothing so that you'll be forced to finish the spell," he told her.

"I already said I won't do it." She felt that it was such an easy thing to say, but was it the truth? The temptation had never been greater.

Again he read her. "I've been right where you are, feeling the need. It'll take you over. It'll change you."

"I said I wouldn't do…"

He stopped her with a wave of his hand. "Don't tell me. Tell her."

Cyn smirked, knowing what he was looking for. "I won't do it!" she screamed at the top of her lungs. It was a strange feeling screaming into what seemed like a dead world. Her and Jack were the only humans within miles and yet there were houses just over the fence, and there were cars in the streets and tricycles sitting in yards.

The two of them were in a city, except there were just no people…unless she counted the ones in the dirt. Despite the fact that they were soulless and unanimated, the dead seemed to be looking up at her. There were empty eyes on her, watching and waiting with eager expectations. But she wasn't going to give it to them. "You hear me you bitch? I'm not going to give any of myself to you."

"Now walk away," Jack said. "I'll be fine. But you need to walk away while you still can."

She didn't leave him. She knelt back down next to him and kissed his lips; they were cool and stiff. He was in pain; she could feel it coming off of him in waves; it was strangely, horribly alluring.

He must have felt it as well. "Don't give in, Cyn. Remember this isn't you. The Mother is trying to use you. Get going and don't look back."

A hundred excuses to stay sprang to mind and she opened her mouth to recite them, but Jack shook his head and pointed. He was right. These were foreign feelings and alien urges; she knew it and yet it took all of her will just to take one step back.

The moment she did, she felt ten times better. The step represented a victory. It meant her soul was still her own. *I am still me*, she thought to herself and to prove it she forced the smirk back where it belonged and asked Jack: "Can I at least whistle while I walk?" Not only did she whistle, she gave an extra sway to her hips as she left. In her tactical armor she was sure she looked ridiculous, and when Jack's chuckle carried through the still air to her, she was sure of it.

Each step away was easier than the last and smirk became genuine as she made it to the fence. She followed it around the perimeter and not once did she look back to where she had left the man she loved. It was one of the most difficult things she had ever done. Not only was the hunger for the spell heavy on her, so was her fear for Jack.

The Mother wasn't just weakening him, she was punishing him and Cyn honestly didn't think he'd have the strength to finish the spells; however, he proved stronger than she could have guessed.

She could sense in some deep crevice of her soul that new blood was in the air and that the final spell was being drawn. The air in the cemetery became suddenly sharp and putrid; the smell made her stop and clutch her stomach. "Okay. I'm not going to vomit. I'm not going to bloody vomit. I just have to keep walking." Fifteen steps further on her strength left her and she knew that she had lost the fight against the growing nausea churning in her guts.

Still, she was a lady. She hurried through a gate and went to the nearest car and, as if she were admiring it, she put her hand lightly on the fender, bent over as though inspecting the tires and heaved out a gout of stomach acid. It burned her throat coming up and the stench had her heaving even more.

She tried to fight it; however Jack was getting closer and closer to finishing the spell and the need in her was terrible. There were two choices open to her: run back to him slit his throat and finish the spell as it was meant to be done, or puke up her stomach and cry.

Her hands became claws that scritched over the surface of the car. To be so close to the blood magic was a trial. It ached her soul like a rotten tooth. Time dragged out and the pull became so unbearable that she found herself clinging to the car as if it were an anchor.

"Come on, Jack. Finish it, please!" She had no idea what sort of ordeal he was going through and frankly couldn't have cared less at that point. She was being tested, with her soul on the line. To give in meant becoming a necromancer; a true necromancer like her cousin, Robert. It meant the craving for blood would never leave her and yet it also meant power and strength.

How Jack had managed to hold on in New York, she didn't know. When he had been put to the test, he'd had every reason to give in, and he'd had every temptation right in front of him. She had told him to fight it, but now she knew how silly she had sounded. There was no fighting this. There was only blood and the ruin of souls and the destruction of all creation. There was only one God and she was the Mother of…

The tin sound filled the air, stopping all thought, save one: *Jack has opened the gate to hell!*

"Thank God," she whispered, the need now suddenly and wonderfully gone. Cynthia Childs had passed her test. She cried as she knelt on her hands and knees next to the car. It was a warm day and sweat mixed with the tears that ran along the curves of her face and dripped from her nose to land in the splatter of vomit.

It was a pretty day and all she could see was the mess she had made.

Blearily, she looked around as if expecting the world to be filled with corpses, but the nearby cemetery was still serene, at least for the moment. She knew that soon the souls would come piling up out of the gate and then Jack would send them on to fight Robert's army and France would be saved, and if they were very lucky, they would find Robert in all this mess, and they'd be able to kill him and be done with the entire sordid affair.

In her heart she knew that wasn't going to happen. In fact, it wasn't her heart telling her this. Some other part of her, what felt like that same part of her soul which could sense when the spells were being used, was ringing a shrill tone of danger within her.

It felt as though something was wrong with the spell… or there was something wrong with the gate or there was… "There's something wrong with Jack!" She scrambled for the shotgun she had mindlessly let fall earlier and then ran for the cemetery gate in a full out sprint.

If Jack was dead or dying then no one would be in control of the gate…no person at least. It would be open to the dead to come and go as they pleased and in no time the world would become just another aspect of hell. She ran, thinking that she would have to shut the gate or die trying, but after a mile, when her heart was hammering in her chest and her breath was like fire, she saw Jack far off.

With the distance, he appeared no larger than a toy soldier and yet she could see him climbing to his feet. In front of him lay the gate and from it souls poured out in a pale, glowing fountain. They were gauzy wisps of nothing that soared in every direction; most slipped beneath the earth to find bodies to claim; however a good number, a thousand or so, raced right at Cyn!

Given any chance, they would take her body and soul. One thing that worked against them was a blessed cross. She had one, of course, but she also had a problem with it. It was strung on a heavy silver necklace and sat nestled very comfortably between her breasts—under both her shirt and her armor.

"Oh, hot damn!" she hissed, digging at the front of her vest. She saw very clearly that she wasn't going to get it out in time. In desperation, she flung herself back with a cry as the air warped and shimmered in front of her face as the souls massed there. Perhaps in vain, she held her breath and squeezed her eyes shut.

The souls were nothing like she expected. They appeared as soft as morning mist and yet they felt like nettles, cutting and pinching her, getting at every inch of her exposed flesh. They hurt, especially around her ears as they dug deeper and deeper until she couldn't stand it any more.

"Bugger off!" she screamed, spastically thrashing around with one hand while still digging with the other for her cross. Finally, her finger hooked the chain and out it came. Just like that, the damned souls sped away, leaving her sprawled on the ground.

Her relief was short lived; beneath her the ground began to twitch and shimmy—the dead were digging their way to the surface. She didn't want to be above them when they did. Again she plucked her shotgun from the ground, and sped off toward Jack, who must have heard her cursing and was stumbling in her direction. That felt

216

wrong to her. He needed to be at the gate. The warning feeling was still within her and now that she saw he was alright she knew that there was something wrong with the gate itself.

"The gate!" she cried. Her voice was so weak and her breath so ragged from the sprint that there was no way he could have heard. She began pointing until he finally turned to look back the way he had come; by then it was obvious what was happening.

When they had first touched down in the helicopter, the cemetery had the same gentle appearance as the rest of France: the land was beautiful with gentle swells and easy valleys that looked softly green. Now the cemetery was rising up in a great mound with the gate as its peak.

Something huge and dreadful was coming. It was ancient beyond Cyn's ability to comprehend and it was evil beyond her ability to withstand.

Chapter 22
Tours, France
Cynthia Childs

The mound grew to be a mountain. The earth shook and rumbled as it rose higher and higher. Birds shot into the sky with frantic cries as mausoleums of granite and marble shattered like egg shells, tombstones fell like dominos and coffins erupted out of the earth. In complete disbelief, Cyn glanced back the way she had come and saw that she was staring *down* at France!

She had to be five hundred feet up and getting higher with each passing second. Beneath her feet, fissures opened on the side of the slope. Some were mere cracks in the ground while others looked as though they could swallow her whole. She ran from these, zig-zagging right and left to avoid them.

At first, the mound was similar to a huge pustule growing larger and larger, but then suddenly the ground dipped and undulated like a wave. Cyn found herself running on nothing but air and then she was falling along with the land and she was sure she was going to break every bone in her body when she landed; however, seconds later, the earth felt as though it had reached up and caught her on a gentle slope of grass. She tumbled like a child rolling down a hill until she came right to the edge of a new chasm that was hundreds of feet deep.

"Holy Christ!" she hissed, clawing and kicking herself back from the edge. Somehow she was able to get to her feet and stumble away from the drop off, going from gravestone to weather-faded gravestone as she climbed.

The stone markers sat at cock-eyed angles like the bad teeth of a giant and rarely were they embedded in the dirt as deep as she could have hoped. Frequently, as she pulled herself higher and higher they toppled over, landing with a thud that was lost in the sound of the earth heaving and the shrill scream coming from the gate.

When the screaming had begun she didn't know. At first Cyn had thought that she was making the hellacious noise because she had been screaming in abject fear as she had fallen, but the moment she had been able to catch her breath, she realized that the sound was external and coming from the top of the hill.

It was the sound of ultimate pain and was unlike anything she had ever heard in her life. She wanted to run from it as fast as she could, only she knew she couldn't.

The screams were coming from the gate and were a horrible reminder of the evil that lurked deep beyond it. The gate had to be closed and she was the only one who could do it.

Jack was in no shape to do it. She could see his grey and exhausted face from sixty yards away. He was on an edge of the newly formed hill where the land was particularly sharp and dangerous. Every few seconds, great wedges of earth many feet across and weighing tons would shear away, dropping hundreds of feet. As she watched, a great chunk of the hill came apart beneath him and he fell only to be caught in the branches from a flowering tree that was bent far over. It was practically upside down and had half its roots exposed to the air.

Laboriously, almost in slow motion as if he had a great weight on his shoulders, he climbed limbs and then roots like a ladder. "Get to the gate!" he cried, waving her on.

That was easier said than done. The gate was now high above her at the top of a steep and treacherous slope. A sudden slip or a new tremor in the earth would more than likely see her tumbling down at breakneck speeds. As scary as the slope was, what was perhaps worse was that the earth was beginning to give up its dead.

Bony hands, leering skulls and decayed and foul creatures were everywhere around her, burrowing up into the light of day and, as always, the undead were repulsive, both physically and spiritually. Cyn felt them drawn to her living warmth. She could sense their hunger and hatred and their perverse desire to seize her soul. It made her feel naked and afraid. Foolishly, she looked around for her shotgun in the hope that in all the turmoil the gun would be on the ground somewhere near at hand.

It was nowhere in sight, and so she faced the growing horde clawing out of the tortured earth with just her bare hands balled into weak little fists.

"Keep going! They won't hurt you," Jack called from his perch in the sideways tree. He was no longer climbing; after casting so many spells, he had reached the limit of his endurance and could only lie on the trunk, barely able to keep his eyes open, likely close to the point of passing into a coma.

Cyn put on a good show of bravery, waving to him while straining to keep the grimace from her face. Her guts were going squirrelly with fear as she climbed the slope, weaving in and out of the corpses. They did nothing to stop her; they simply stared with their dead eyes and watched her as she climbed to the top.

The view from the peak had to have been fantastic. She was close to a thousand feet up a new mountain in the middle of the French countryside, but there was only one view for her: the bloody glyphs, the gate, and the monster within it.

Something green and black and huge and horrible was forcing itself through a hole little bigger than a manhole cover. She couldn't tell what the thing was. It might have been a thousand-foot tall toad for all she could tell from the slime covered and oddly bumpy flesh that was jutting up and spilling from the edges of the gate.

Whatever it was coming into the world was beyond her mind to comprehend. It was stunning to her senses. The shriek coming from it became a numb tone; the foul flesh of its body left her eyes blurred and unfocused; the atrocious smell contracted her stomach and cramped her intestines. The sight of the thing even sent her muscles into spasms.

In its presence, she was no longer human. If she had feet, she didn't know. A mirror would have only confused her. Just then Cyn couldn't remember her name or her mother's face. Her mind could only focus on two things: the hell-creature and the overwhelming need to close the gate before it could get out and destroy the world. With stiff, fumbling fingers, she batted like a fearful savage at her belt where she kept four cylinders of silver.

Two of them held Holy Water and two were of Holy Oil. One of the four made it into her hand, where it burned her fingers as if it had been just pulled from a forge.

She heard a new scream, this time coming from her own lips, as she threw the burning vial. Her aim was perfect. There was cry from the creature, a sound like a million crows being crushed under foot; there was a splash of darkness that covered the earth in one tremendous blink…and then there was nothing—total nothing.

Nothing except the sound of Cyn screaming…and then an odd thud that had her looking around in confusion as her mind adjusted to the concept of reality once more. France was suddenly back to the way it had been—or mostly back the way it had been. The mountain was gone and the cemetery was once again composed of the same rolling hills and yet, it was no longer green or beautiful. The earth looked to have been pushed inside-out; there were mounds of dirt everywhere and coffins jutted up in uneven rows like the crops one would only find across the River Styx.

There wasn't a single tombstone still standing and the mausoleums were now ruins. Everything that had been alive in the cemetery was now dead and everything dead was now alive. This included the trees, which had all been uprooted and it was from one of them that she had heard the thud. Jack was lying on the ground next to one of them, making a low groaning noise.

Truly, the cemetery looked like a battlefield except instead of dead bodies lying around everywhere, the bodies were standing. Tens of thousands of ghouls stood staring, not at Jack, who had brought them into the world but at Cyn, or so she first thought. It wasn't until she took a step toward Jack and she heard something behind her that she realized that they weren't looking at her at all.

The gate hadn't been closed. It's bloody glyphs were still shining wet and perfectly drawn and the way into hell was still completely intact. All she had done with the vial she had thrown was drive the awful creature back down into it.

But there was something in its place. A woman stood directly in the center of the gate, her feet suspended on the oily black surface. Cyn gasped at the sight of her and for the second time in a minute, she found her mind becoming unglued from reality as she stared. The woman was utterly naked, utterly flawless, and utterly beautiful. She had hair of spun gold and the shimmering eyes of pearl. Her breasts were full and engorged, her hips flaring provocatively, her skin was the color of cream and her smile, perfectly red lips over the whitest teeth, was simply bewildering.

This was the *Mother of Demons* in the flesh. Cyn knew her in an instant and not just because of the woman's resemblance to the statue in the necromancer's dungeon, there was a deeper personal connection, one that might have begun eons before.

"Don't go to him," the Mother said. "Stay here with me."

Cyn's knees buckled and she fell to the earth. The Mother's voice had not been loud; it had been soft and sweet and wonderfully musical—and it had been powerful. The words coming from those ruby lips had sent a vibration through Cyn that had unwound her muscles, dropping her in place. Even if she had been able to stand or run, the words *compelled* her to stay.

She couldn't leave if she wanted to. Her feet were like the roots of a tree and her legs stiff as trunks. Even her hips were like clay.

"You do not need the man," the Mother went on. "You are powerful. You are a daughter of the Mother. You can give life and you can take it as well. Is that not full of wonder? Is that not greatest of all? Stay here with me. Bring me out. Say the words to bring me out and you will know the power."

Suddenly, Cyn was craving this unknown power. "What words?" she asked. Her own voice in her ears was so soft and weak that she didn't think it could be heard; however the woman heard and answered.

"Beg the Mother of Demons to come into this world. Give her all that you are and she will come to you and you will share in her power. Is that not the greatest of all?"

The way the Mother spoke was so beguiling and full of charm that Cyn found herself nodding even through her confusion. "Yes, that is the greatest…only what was that middle part?" Cyn was sure that whatever the woman had said really was the greatest…except the part about giving all that she was. That little sentence got hung up in her awe-addled mind. It jarred her and awakened the rebellious streak within her which just happened to be both deep and wide. That part of her put on the brakes to the conversation right quick and it demanded to know what was meant by giving "all that she was."

"It means your essence," the woman answered the question that Cyn was sure hadn't been spoken aloud. "We will join essence. We will become one once again and it will be the greatest."

"Once again? When were we ever one? I'm pretty sure I would have remembered that."

It was a simple question and yet the answer spanned universes. The woman attempted to show Cyn the truth of her words by sending pictures directly into her mind. It was too much information for her to comprehend in so little time. Ten million years' worth of pictures were shot into her mind and instead of filling her with understanding, it short circuited her brain and Cyn fell once more to the earth. How long she laid in a groggy semi-state of consciousness she couldn't fathom.

If asked, she would have been sure that a thousand summers had passed before she could move again and she knew that she must have aged into an old crone, but when she put her hand to her face, she was surprised that it wasn't grey and wrinkled. It was as soft and white as it ever was.

"Do you see that we are the greatest?" the woman asked in her musical voice. "Do you see that we are one?"

Again, Cyn found herself nodding and as before it was simply because she was compelled to by the Mother—if she wanted you to agree, you would agree even if you didn't know what you were agreeing to. Cyn had not understood a billionth of what had been forced into her mind, but she knew one thing: the Mother of Demons was in fact a woman. A human woman, or she had been at one time.

"Who are you?" Cyn asked.

"I am the greatest. I am the woman. You are my daughter. Come and free me and you will have my power. Do you want to know my power?"

Before she could collect her wits, Cyn found herself nodding again. She tried to catch herself: "No actually, I don't…"

Too late, the Mother of Demons sent more images into Cyn's head, and with them came a surge of something wonderful and terrible. Again, the sensation was overwhelming, dropping her to the earth. Time went in and out. The sun spun on its golden wheel and the grass grew. Eventually, Cyn was able to blink once more and her mind slowly grasped the world around her as it reformed itself into her perception of reality. "Please, don't do that anymore. It's too much."

"You did not like the power?"

Cyn had to think about that. Saying no would have been a lie. There was a curious and enticing thrum of what felt like electricity coursing through her. It made her feel huge inside as if her soul was supercharged and could burst out of her in a great ball of fire. *It's magic power*, she thought to herself. It was what Jack had to feel when he was casting his spells.

The sensation was amazing and at the same time there was a tinny, gritty undertone to it, the cause of which she couldn't put her finger on except to say that the power was also ugly. "No, I like it. But…but it also feels wrong somehow."

"There is no wrong," the woman said, anger showing in the smallest of frowns. The frown affected not just her face but the entire world. In seconds, the pretty blue of the sky grew dark with clouds as if it was only the Mother's smile that kept the sun lit. "I do not do wrong. I do what is right and what is needed. So shall you, Cynthia Childs. Free me. Give me essence and speak words of power and you will be one with me. You will be one with the Mother of Demons, the Mother of All."

Suddenly, Cyn found herself being dragged forward, pulled to the edge of the gate into hell, her boots leaving twin lines in the upturned dirt. She tried to fight the pull. She grabbed rocks and hunks of half-rotted coffin wood. She was still kicking when she had a sudden insight: The Mother was too big, too great to be brought through a gate that was so small, so rudimentary. Her power and her immense essence would destroy the gate if she tried to force her way through—and the Mother didn't want to destroy it. The gate was the only way for her to see into this world with any clarity. It was the only way for her to impose her will on the earth.

For the Mother to come through, a new gate would have to be constructed, and it would take a soul to build it.

Cyn was pulled right to the edge of the blood glyphs and then lifted to her feet. *Say the words!* the Mother said, speaking directly into Cyn's mind, again, nearly blowing the fuses there and making her thoughts muddy and slow as if they were coming to her via a telegraph.

The Mother wanted Cyn to say *yes* and so she would say *yes* and she would give her essence to build the gate and she would then die or cease being as if she had never existed. Cynthia Childs would be utterly destroyed. She would be deconstructed and the original spark of her soul would be taken and reabsorbed.

And such was the compulsion and power of the Mother that Cyn felt she would be just fine with that. It would be both good and right. Cyn wanted to please the Mother. She wanted to do her duty. She wanted to agree to everything.

Chapter 23
Tours, France
Cynthia Childs

Giving everything wasn't just right and good, it was the greatest of all. Cyn found herself nodding again, her chin going up and down and her mouth open and slack. She felt like a complete fool or like a child who was barely able to feed herself and was being offered an ice cream sundae.

"Yes, please, Mother. Take it all. Take all…"

A shadow passing between her and the ultimate glory that was the Mother caused her to jump.

Jack was suddenly next to her. His body trembled so that grave dirt dropped from his shoulders and sweat dripped from the strong line of his jaw. He looked filthy and disgusting. Compared to the Mother, he was little more than a hairless ape.

He placed one of his grubby hands on Cyn's shoulder, and said: "Don't do it. If there's one thing we can't do it's bring her into this world. You know, deep down that would be wrong." His words were not musical. They were harsh and cringe-worthy. They were nails on a chalkboard.

And yet they held truth.

Of course Cyn knew it was wrong to give herself over to the Mother. It was *her* soul on the line after all. It was her soul and yet it was such a little thing, just a tiny gift. And it wouldn't be wasted. It would be a gift to the Mother and wouldn't that be the greatest? Cyn nodded in answer, wondering if she had heard the question or was imagining it or if she was just going crazy.

"Please, Cyn," Jack said, fighting to stay on his feet. Being so close to the Mother was making him wilt and gasp. He had only the breath for whispering: "It's wrong."

At his words, the woman frowned a second time and the clouds grew even darker and began to thrash above them. "I can not do wrong," the Mother said and now her musical voice was hitting harsh, strident chords that made Cyn cringe and Jack blanch. "A god can not do wrong," the Mother said, going on. "Gods describe right and punish wrong."

Jack had his hackles up and, after swallowing loudly and taking a breath that sounded like it came from a broken horse, said: "Now, that's the thing, isn't it? You are no god. You are nothing. You are…" He had been glaring at the Mother, but now his face contorted and his fingers bent into claws and his Adam's apple went up and down convulsively while his legs crimped down. It looked as though he was being turned into an old man right before her eyes.

"No," Cyn whispered, dropping down next to Jack and touching him lightly, as if afraid that whatever was happening to him would run up into her fingers and strike her as well. He was rough and gritty; he smelled unpleasantly of man-sweat, while the Mother was of tulips and cloves.

"Stop it, please," Cyn begged. "He didn't mean it. You're not wrong, Mother. Of course you're not. You could never be wrong. H-he is the one that is wrong, just stop that, please."

Set me free once more, or he will die and I will take his essence, the Mother said, her lips not moving. *Say the words. Give yourself to me.*

"Don't do it," Jack hissed, forcing himself to his feet in spite of the pain that carved his face in anguish. "She can hurt me, but she can't kill me; not when I'm like this. She's like the necromancer. It's all about the souls with her. Don't make her stronger by giving her yours."

"The son is wrong," the mother said and this time she directed her frown at Jack. He cried out suddenly and went to the ground on his knees. "The mother kills whom she wishes to. She gives life and she takes life. At this moment I do not wish to take life. The Mother teaches only. I teach respect. I teach understanding. I teach you where you belong, Cynthia Childs and what your role is. I show that your power is so much greater than his. Your power is pure."

Another scream split the air and then Jack was on his side curled into the fetal position save for one arm that stuck out. It hung, looking oddly long as if it was being stretched by some unseen force. His hand shook and his fingers fought to remain closed but in vain.

In seconds, his hand came open and a silver vial fell, its precious water dribbling uselessly into the dirt. Only then did the Mother snap her fingers, releasing Jack. He immediately went limp, his eyes rolling back in his head.

The entire short episode was confusing to Cyn, whose mind had felt riddled with holes to begin with. That was Holy Water Jack had been carrying. Why hadn't he used it to close the gate? Why had he held onto it?

"Because man is always wrong whether he knows it or not," the Mother said after "hearing" Cyn's unspoken questions. "Man is arrogant and condescending. He thinks he knows everything there is to know. And this one," she gestured with a curled lip at Jack, "thinks that you will chose him over a god. He thinks you will close the gate and shut away your mother forever, simply because he has abused your feelings and has taken advantage of your loving nature. But you know better, to close the gate would be wrong."

At the word "wrong" a harsh wind struck Cyn causing her to put a hand in front of her face. Through her fingers she could see the Mother though not as a whole. Cyn could see parts of her: the top of her arm, a hip bone, the right knee. Each aspect of the Mother was both perfect and imperfect. Each part was flawless and flawed. Each showed that there was much more to the Mother than Cyn knew. The mother was of fantastic size and was only giving Cyn a glimpse.

"Of course there is more to the Mother because I am *She*. I am the eldest of all. I will be the living god if you free me. Come and say the words. Give your essence, freely."

Sudden understanding cut at least partially through the fog of puzzlement that Cyn had been drifting in since first seeing the Mother. "I have to die for you to come through and…and I have to die willingly. You can't force me. Okay, now I get it." Once again she was confronted with the fact that the gift of the soul was the strongest power behind any magic—even at a "godly" level. "I get it, at least I get what you want from me. Though I'm not exactly sure what you are offering in exchange. If I'm dead, if you take all of me, what do I get out of it?"

The Mother gave Cyn her grandest smile yet—and it was enough of an answer. The smile was a reward people would kill for. Cyn wore a goofy grin and her knees were jelly, but some part of her still held onto her love for Jack. "What about him? Why…why did he want me to stop you?"

"He wanted you to choose him over your mother."

Cyn glanced down at her lover, her one actual friend, and the only person she would call family. After everything they had been through together, she knew him on a level that was beyond intimate. She had, on more than one occasion, given him her soul.

"And what has he given you in return?" the Mother asked. The question was so out of the blue that Cyn was tongue-tied, causing the Mother to laugh with the sound of crystal wind chimes. "Has he not given you only trouble? Sadness? Anguish? Pain? Where has the joy been in your joining? There has been precious little. He is a man and thus he is like the rest and has brought you only hardship."

The truth in that statement was evident by the fact that Cyn's eyes slid from Jack to rest on the upturned dirt just next to him. Her mind flashed with images: him stabbing her with a knife, him threatening to kill her with a sword, him stealing her blood and taking her soul. "But…but that was a gift. At least it was supposed to be. I don't think you get it, ours is a different sort of relationship," she said.

"We have a duty and an obligation and a destiny. We support each other in our fight."

With a cluck of her tongue and a shake of her head, the Mother said: "*He* has saved the world. *He* is the sorcerer. *He* is the one who fights and claims the glory. You are there only to clean up his vomit and keep him from getting in trouble. As so many, you do not see. Your heart is too great. You are blind to the fact that he is not the only one with a destiny. You have one as well. You can become one with a living god."

There was that word again. Whenever the Mother of Demons had called herself a god it had made Cyn wince. Everything she had experienced in the last year had pointed to the fact that there was only one source of ultimate goodness, while there seemed to be an endless number of tributaries leading to the foul bog that was evil.

The Mother of Demons was just a very large tributary.

"Good and evil are subjective," the Mother said, her frown coming back, churning the skies, causing thunder to ripple above. "What a god does is by definition, good. Do you understand? Evil and good are subjective. What is good for one may be evil for another. That is simple. That is elemental. You would do well to learn the differences between…"

Her words faltered and Cyn was abruptly jarred from the trance she always found herself in when the Mother spoke. They were being watched. Cyn turned and saw a faint shimmer in the air and felt that strange sensation of being under an invisible spotlight that she and Jack had experienced earlier.

Of course the Mother could sense it with ease. Her frown turned into a glare as she suddenly spun to stare up into the darkening sky. Then with a growl, she snapped her fingers and a bolt of some sort of energy that was a cross between lightning and fire, flashed through the air, passing so close to Cyn that the little blonde hairs on her arms stood straight up.

The bolt scorched the sky, sending up a trail of smoke and for just a brief second, Cyn caught sight of something that was nearly beyond description. Suspended ten feet off the ground was what looked like a pale white worm, a foot in diameter, with strange blood-red "hairs" sprouting all along its curving, squiggly, undulating length.

It stretched away off into the distance.

The worm was "lit" by the Mother's magic. There was a flash of light and a scream and the weird feeling of being watched was gone. The entire episode couldn't have lasted more than three seconds and yet in that short time Cyn found that she was suddenly and completely in control of herself. She saw with perfect clarity the Mother for the demon she was and she saw Jack as he was in reality: just an average man thrust into the unwanted position of being a hero.

And she saw herself: a pawn to the Mother and a lifeline to Jack. She was his anchor. She was what kept him sane. But what was she beyond that?

"I'm just a girl," she said and as always that lie was good enough for her. Frantically, she dug for one of her remaining vials of Holy Water and once again, the silver vial burned her hand as she held it.

"Stop," the Mother said, this time in a gentle voice, one that was so full of charm that Cyn's hand stopped poised above her head. "Consider what you are doing. Consider the power you are giving up. Consider that you are angering your god."

There was that word again: god. "You keep using that word," Cyn said, matter of factly. "I don't think it means what you think it means." At this, the Mother's pearl eyes flashed to black while at the same time, the silver vial burned hotter than ever. Cyn had to throw the vial or drop it. Holding it was no longer an option.

She chose to throw it and it left her hand, tumbling end over end.

Too late she remembered that she hadn't unstoppered it! It flew at the circle of glyphs and she thought that it would either bounce away or be swallowed up by the gate; however, it hit what appeared to be a wall of air, broke open and sprayed what looked like diamonds, each glittering and sharp and each exploding a millisecond later.

There was a white light as pure as the glitter from the stars and then both the Mother and the gate vanished. Cyn took one unsteady step and then fell over, the sky of France spinning high above her. All she saw was blue sky and gentle puffy clouds. Everything was suddenly diffuse and soft, everything except the feel of Jack's hand which found hers.

The hand was warm and strong and fit hers perfectly.

Chapter 24
Tours, France
Jack Dreyden

With a groan and a little cough that had just enough strength to expel the stale air from his lungs, Jack clawed at the dirt, fighting simply to roll over. It was another labor to sit up. Once again, he was drained as deeply as he had ever been drained. The Mother had fought him tooth and nail in order to open a gate into hell…or so it had seemed at first. When he started the spell, he foolishly thought that he was in a battle with the Mother of Demons herself and like a fool, he thought he was winning.

In reality, he hadn't been in a battle at all and if he had been, he wouldn't have had a chance at winning. Jack had been a hero only in his own mind, and once the fourth set of spells had been completed and he had been rendered impotent with all the strength of a mewling kitten, he had been shown the truth: the Mother of Demons had allowed him to "win."

Only in retrospect was he able to see that she had been toying with him and had allowed him to complete the spells only because she had wanted him to. One of the key components to opening a gate into hell was the literal begging for the Mother's assistance and it was up to her to allow the gate to be opened or not. Why she had let him complete the spells, he didn't know, but he didn't think she would ever let him use the spells again.

She was an angry and jealous bitch of a demigod and couldn't stand being told "no." The least bit of resistance was blasphemous to her, especially if it came from a man. It was an affront to her and Jack figured that she was busy planning some sort of terrible revenge and just at that moment, he couldn't have cared less.

The very fact that the Mother would deny him access to the gate into hell was so fantastic that he secretly cried in happiness.

Finally, he was done with this.

There was nothing so horrible as bringing unwanted souls back from the netherworld. Even the dreadful pain that the Mother had thrust upon Jack earlier, what felt like he was being force fed tumors, was nothing compared to the horror of opening a gate into hell. But the tumors were a close second. What she had done to him was beyond description and he could still feel the pain in his innards radiate out as he took little sips of air. It hurt to breathe and it hurt not to. His nerve endings were on fire and he felt bruised on the inside.

But the pain wasn't the reason why silent tears slid down his cheek to drop onto the floor of the graveyard. The pain would fade and in fact it was already fading. He cried in pure happiness. If he never painted those bloody glyphs again, he would die a happy man.

Next to him, Cyn was stretched out in the turned up dirt with her arms flung above her head. Her face glowed white and stood out in stark contrast to the dark earth. Although she was very much alive, she looked as pale as death, and her beautiful blue eyes stared out of her skull seeing nothing, not the beauty of France and not the horrors he had brought into the world: all around them were tens of thousands of foul half-beings. They were creatures that stank of decay and fetid grave dirt and they were shuffling through the graveyard, coming right at the two of them.

She didn't seem to care. "Are you okay?" she asked, finally turning to look at him, her eyes half-lidded.

"Yeah, sure," he said as he passed a hand across his face, swiping at the tears quickly so that she wouldn't see them. He also tried on a smile but could only force the corners of his mouth up by a few millimeters. "Just a little tired is all. Can you give me a minute?"

She nodded and, thankfully, closed her eyes, seeming to drop into sleep. That was a blessing; he didn't want her to see this part of his life. "One last time," he whispered as he slowly groaned his way to his feet.

The power he had over the ghouls and the demons made him different. It made him ugly. It took something evil inside of him to control the evil without and it was an utterly disgusting feeling to command the dead, to rule them as king. It made him feel as though he was a demon himself.

He struggled to take a deep breath and then when he was calm, he sent his will out among the multitude of undead, feeling their warped souls, feeling their evil, taking a part of each of them inside of him. And there were so many of them. He knew their exact number: 42,869 ghouls and 141 demons. He could feel their minds and their temper and, as always, there was some resistance to overcome. Sometimes it was just a little, while at other times the creatures were as unruly as a class of children with a substitute teacher.

It was from the demons that he always had the most trouble.

On a psychic level, one that was unknown and unknowable to science, he battled the greatest demon he had called forth. That was the way these things went about a third of the time. In their world, the demons were petty and petulant princes and few creatures ever had the temerity to make any demands on them and so when Jack began issuing orders, the strongest of them pushed through the crowd to challenge him.

The creature had chosen what was probably the finest corpse in the cemetery to wear: a woman who looked as though she hadn't been in the ground for more than a day. The dead body was tall and slender. Its skin was pale but unmarred, so that the cause of its death couldn't be ascertained. It was covered in a light pink dress that looked splendid, in spite of the fact that it was stained with dirt. The body had gobs of brown hair that had been meticulously styled for what had been thought was a final internment.

The body really was one of the better ones Jack had ever seen and he had seen far too many to ever count. Yes, the body was great, all except the eyes. It did not have eyes. The lids had been glued shut to simulate sleep, but the demon had popped open the holes in the woman's skull and Jack could peer in at the complete emptiness of the corpse.

"You have your orders," Jack said, trying to avoid looking the demon in its borrowed face. Locking "eyes" and staring into those empty pits was disturbing. The demon came right up to Jack, who was suddenly very aware that he had lost his blessed sword somewhere in the cemetery and that he was too drained even to perform the simplest bit of magic. Right then he couldn't have pulled a rabbit out a hat.

"Go!" he snapped, pointing past the demon in the direction of Robert's army. The demon shook its head and smiled with oddly red lips. The corpse's makeup was also disturbing. Whoever had made the woman up in preparation for her funeral had tried too hard to simulate life, and the effect made Jack feel queasy.

The demon could sense the effect its body had on Jack and pressed its advantage, getting close so that Jack was also assaulted by the perfume that had been liberally applied before she went into the ground. Beneath the sachet was the sickly-sweet aroma of decaying meat.

"You are weak," the demon said, speaking in a terrible growl that was again made more horrible by the fact that it spoke with the high voice of the woman. "You cannot command Ghulat. Ghulat was strong when the world was young. Ghulat made kings and feasted on queens. Ghulat…"

"Ghulat needs to shut his trap and get moving," Jack barked. He had heard all sorts of demon bragging in his time and it was wearing. "Find the greatest of Robert's demons and drag it to hell. That's the only thing you need to be concentrating on right now. You came through the gate. You accepted the contract now fulfill it."

The demon Ghulat snapped the woman's teeth closed hard enough to break the front ones off, so that when it smiled, all Jack could see were jagged points. The demon then went through a ritualistic display of fury by tearing open the woman's face and chewing off her overly-red lips.

This actually helped Jack, who found it easier to deal with the demon now that it looked much more like one.

Now came the actual battle. From an outside point of view, it was extremely underwhelming. The two fought with their minds. The demon was ancient and had battled wills for thousands of years. His mind was a tough knot, an old root that would never wither, while Jack was young, barely tested, and exhausted.

Still Jack was a sorcerer, which helped and yet he did not win the battle simply because of that. He won mainly because of the contract that had yet to be fulfilled. The demon wanted to break it and the only way he could was to first break Jack's mind. The attack came quickly and it came without mercy. It felt like Jack's brain was being compressed, crushed inwards by a vice.

He started to sweat, and his head began to pound, but he stuck to his guns. "Go Ghulat. Do as you're told." Ghulat redoubled its efforts and there was what felt like a spike of iron in Jack's mind, but it didn't last as Jack laughed in the face of it. "You are a joke, Ghulat. Go and be a joke somewhere else." It had been a forced laugh and yet it had its desired effect. Ghulat threw another tantrum as it realized it had no choice but to obey. Once it did, the others followed suit and left to hunt down Robert's army.

Then Cyn and Jack were alone in the cemetery and the silence was unnerving.

The two went to the tree Jack had fallen out of and sat on its trunk, not speaking to each other; not seeing much beyond the tips of their boots. Jack was thinking about the land. What had once been beautiful as well as hallowed had been abused and likely would never be built on again. It would gain an evil reputation and would be called haunted.

The land was ruined, which was becoming something of a hallmark of his. He left destruction in his wake. "In Robert's wake," he uttered. When Cyn cast a look at him, he tried on a grin. "So that was the Mother of Demons in real life. Pretty scary."

Cyn's eyes darted away. "That was part of her. She's bigger than that, probably bigger than we can imagine."

"You want to tell me about her?" Jack asked. "You guys were talking for some time."

"Not yet," she answered. "It was a lot to take in… more than I could handle. Well, almost more than I could handle, and that reminds me. I know you trust me to fight my own fights, but next time, if you have the chance to shut the gate then bloody well shut it. The Mother almost had me."

Jack patted her armored leg. "But she didn't. What doesn't kill you makes you stronger, right? You faced the Mother of Demons one on one and came out alive and unscathed."

She shook her head. "Not completely unscathed. She showed me many things and she fed her power into me. It wasn't right and it's making me sick. I can feel it churning my insides, making them dark. I have to get it out of me but I don't know how."

"You can try magic. We both know you have the ability. I can teach you the lightning spell easily enough and there are plenty of targets around here." He waved an arm at the trashed-out cemetery.

"No, I don't think so. Magic is not for me. I won't do that to my soul. I won't destroy it for target practice or for fun."

He brought out a knife and said: "Then there really isn't any other option. I'm drained and I need a boost just in case we find Robert at the center of this mess…

speaking of which, how do we get the helicopters back? The pilot really wasn't any help."

Cyn dug in a pocket and held up a cell phone. "This little gadget is called a phone. It's right handy and allows you to communicate with people far, far away. You should get one." She was smirking as she said this, but then her eyes caught sight of the knife and the smirk became a tense grin and she clasped the phone in both hands. "I don't know if I should give you this power. It's not wholesome. It's hard to explain, but it won't feel like I would be giving you a gift this time. It'll feel like I'd be giving you a disease."

He made a face. "A magical venereal disease? Sounds gross." Her smirk came back and as it always did, it made him love her even more. "Seriously, if there is an issue with this power that the Mother gave you, it would be better if you transferred it to me. I can either dump it with a little target practice, or use it against whatever we find at the center of all of this."

Reluctantly, she agreed and so he cut the inside of their wrists with the knife and then they joined their souls touching new blood to new blood. It was a connection unlike the others they had experienced together—it stung like nettles under his skin. And worse, it made him feel as though he was going to puke all over her. There was indeed something horrible in what the Mother had given her and Jack knew immediately what it was.

It was power, a fantastic amount of power that fully revived him…but it was stolen power. Cyn had been given what Jack, at one time in his life had craved: souls. Inside of her were the shredded remains of dozens of souls. It was horrible feeling them squirm inside of him and worse, he could feel the necromancer in him spring back into life, becoming greedy for more. That part of him did not care about right or wrong, it only cared about its all-consuming hunger.

Jack tried to keep a neutral look on his face; however, Cyn was connected deeper than the surface and knew what he was feeling. She tried to pull away.

"No," he insisted, holding her flesh bound to his through an act of the mind and not of the body. "You can't have this evil in you. It'll ruin you. That's why she gave it to you. She wanted to tempt you with its power. She wanted to warp your soul."

"What about your soul? You may not care about it, but I do."

Again she tried to pull back, using more of her own strength, which Jack found surprisingly powerful. Nonetheless, he was stronger than her and he was stronger than that evil part of himself that he had thought had been killed for good. "My soul has already been dirtied by this sort of thing and a little more won't hurt." That was a small lie that they both pretended was the truth. He took the power of the Mother from her and when he had siphoned it all off, he made to pull away, but, out of the blue, she let a little of herself into him as well.

It was a golden feeling compared to the horror of the souls and it soothed his mind and calmed his conscience. It also kept him from puking, something he had been sure he would do.

But it also fed into the demand for more and he had to get away from her before he gave in to the temptation to *take* all of her. He broke the connection between them and immediately walked away, saying over his shoulder: "Call the choppers…please. I need some time and some air."

What he needed was space. Her soul was pure and sweet and wonderful, while the others inside of him were horrors that screamed in desperate pain, filling his ears with their cries. They weren't full souls. They were the shredded remains; strangely shaped bits of beings that spun and twisted, trying to entwine with the little kernel of what was left of his own soul.

They were searching for something, their other parts, likely. Jack had the distinct impression that they were trying to complete themselves. It was an unpleasant feeling, full of great sadness and horror and, if there wasn't the possibility of facing Robert, he would've set them free. Though in truth, they would never be free. The Mother owned the rest of their souls and thus they were bound to her. Freeing them simply meant freeing himself of them.

"It'll be okay," he whispered to himself. "I just have to give them some time to settle a bit." Keeping his head down, he walked the length of the cemetery, and while he walked he breathed deep and steadily, doing his best to calm the souls. They responded best when they were able to enmesh themselves in the tiny bit of Cyn's soul. They still cried out and thrashed about but it was easier for Jack to take.

When he reached the far end of the cemetery, he didn't hesitate. He climbed right up the chest-high wall and leapt down into the real world where the air was clean and the sanity close to normal. Close, but not quite.

The town was empty, having been abandoned hours before. It was eerily silent and completely still. Nothing moved. It had not been just the humans who had fled this part of France, even the birds and cats and the mice had run off.

"Hello?" he called out, only to hear his own voice bounce back at himself. "Wait…what's French for hello? Uh, bonjour?" His words rang on empty streets. The moment was surreal and became more so when he walked to the nearest corner cafe and, after stealing a croissant and Coke, sat down at a table facing the street. His first impression was that he had been stranded between ticks of a watch; however, a second, much worse thought came to him: What if the rapture had occurred and everyone but him had been lifted up to heaven?

Even though he knew the truth, it was such a depressing thought that he tried not to think about it and forced himself to nibble on his croissant and sip at his Coke, but they only made his stomach roll over and, with a grimace, he was forced to push them away. The bits of souls were not settling down as much as he had hoped, in fact they weren't settling down at all.

"I'm going to puke, aren't I?" He could feel the Coke brewing like a storm in his guts and before he knew it he vomited right across the table. He hurled again and again as though he was trying to puke up the souls and splatter them on the street.

"Stop it!" he shouted and thumped his own heaving chest. "Just settle down in there!"

The shouting didn't work. It only made the souls angrier and Jack groaned, holding his belly. As he did, the *whup-whup-whup* of helicopters came to him. Captain Vance and the rest of the Americans were on their way.

"No," Jack whispered. "They're too early." His army of demons and ghouls had barely begun their fight. He could sense both groups squaring off...and he could feel some of Robert's beasts scattering to the winds. To hunt them down took a level of concentration that he wasn't up to with his mind pulled in so many directions.

"First things first," he said, before forcing everything going on around him out of his mind and concentrating only on the souls. At first, he tried to separate them, each into an individual little penned up section of his mind,, but then he found two of the souls that were perfectly joined together.

They were nearly opposites in shape and texture, but there was a seam on each that matched up with the other; yin and yang. They had been warped through some unthinkable power of the Mother's to fit together like some bizarre jigsaw puzzle.

And if two fit, it figured that the rest would.

Not wanting to be seen huddled over a pool of vomit, he staggered away from the mess he had made and went to a little park where the swings creaked under a light breeze. This little sound in the deathly quiet world was a strange blessing and, with it as background music, Jack worked the puzzle of the souls, going through each and categorizing them: squiggly, straight, firm, soft, hard.

He was still sitting on one of the swings when Captain Vance and Cyn found him. "Having a little play time with your inner child?" Vance asked.

Jack held up a hand. He had just made a discovery about the puzzle: the squiggles of souls were turning into shapes that he knew all too well. The Mother of Demons had not just given Cyn power, she had also given her a very well-designed trap. The souls fit together to spell out the three verses that opened the gate to hell.

"Son of a bitch," he hissed. The spells were more than half drawn in his mind and now the remaining souls were going crazy, desperate to find their counterparts. He wanted to stop; not just because his mind was starting to feel as though it was being torn apart by the violence of the remaining souls, he was also honestly afraid of what would happen when he finished it. Would the gate open inside of him and would he be obliterated by the eruption of souls from hell? Would his own soul be burned out opening it? Would the Mother herself come and possess him?

These were terrible questions with equally terrible answers, but he had no choice but to finish creating the spell in his mind; it was either that or be driven insane by the rampaging souls.

"You ok, Jack?" Cyn asked him and he was dimly aware of her soft hand on his arm. She spoke more than these words, but he couldn't hear, and she touched him on the face, pushing the hair from his forehead and looking into his eyes, but he didn't feel any of that. All he cared about was pinning down those souls and finishing.

"We'll get a priest," Vance said and then began shouting orders into his radio. A moment later, he suggested: "Let's lay him down." Jack was suddenly nose to the sky and saw neither the sun nor felt its warmth. The spell was so close to being done and his head was pounding and the souls were screaming and someone was yelling Latin in one ear and someone else was whispering "I love you," in the other.

Then, just like that, the spell was whole in his mind and the souls quieted and the world was peaceful and calm and everything was silence and serenity except, of course, for the spell and the ugly demand that he use it. It banged inside his head, a steady drum and the demand was so powerful that he almost opened the gate to hell right there in the park, not caring what would come out.

Chapter 25
Tours, France
Jack Dreyden

"I'm ok," Jack said, trying to get to his feet. "I don't need an exorcism. I'm good. I just had a bout of something." For some reason he couldn't point to, he was hugely embarrassed about the spells inside his head.

Cyn came right up to his face and peered into his eyes. "Are you sure? You don't look so great. It was that power I gave you, wasn't it? It was bad. I knew it."

Captain Vance agreed with Cyn's assessment. "She's right, you look like a crap sandwich."

"Thanks for the concern, but I'm fine. Now, can you back off for a moment? I need to check on the progress of my undead army." Although that sounded pretentious to his own ear, it seemed official enough to Vance for him to step away and plausible enough for Cyn to give him some breathing room. The last thing he needed was for her to pester him with a thousand questions concerning the Mother or the exact nature of the power she had put in Cyn.

The spell was there inside of him and wasn't going anywhere, and as long as he kept focused and busy, he probably wouldn't think about the gnawing hunger to use it. And he really did have to check on his army. Demons and ghouls were notoriously slow when there wasn't a firm hand on the tiller. If Jack let his attention stray for too long, the creatures would fulfill their contract, but at their speed, not his, and they would prefer to take centuries instead of hours.

With far more effort than it had ever taken him before, Jack centered his thinking so that he could feel the various creatures. His ability to sense their evil presence had a range of about twenty miles and both his demons and Robert's stood out like black spots in the world—some being darker than others, depending on the strength of their evil.

With only a thought, he could direct his minions here and there, just as Robert surely could, assuming he was somewhere in the vicinity, which Jack doubted. If Robert was still in Tours, then it was likely that his army would be surrounding him, protecting him while he finished digging up whatever he was after.

However, Robert's creatures weren't holed up in a defensive position. They were intent on escaping, trying their best to get away before Jack was able to corral them all. But it was too late for them, they were being bottled up nicely.

It took some time, but once he made sure the situation was well in hand, he opened his eyes and glanced around at the living. Cyn, looking fresh-faced and beautifully young once more, sat on the hood of a little box of a car, checking the bore of a new shotgun; Captain Vance, grim and bristled, sweating under his combat load, leaned against a wall of weathered bricks talking into a cell phone; a priest from one of the *Raider Squads* sat in a reclining chair that he had pulled from somewhere. He was a small trim man with a cross laying across his chest armor; he drank coffee from a tea cup.

"Care for some?" the priest asked, holding his up; strangely, at least for an American, he held a pinky jutting out from the cup's handle. "There are also cold-cuts if you wish." He pointed across the street at another cafe. "I found a full lunch set out, ready to be eaten. It's so strange. And on the next street over are three bikes right in a row sitting perfectly upright on their kick-stands. It was as if their owners had calmly parked them only to *run* away. Does that make sense? This whole town is like something out of the *Twilight Zone*. I know you might be used to this sort of thing, but I can only call it eerie."

Although it wasn't quite true, Jack remarked: "To me, it's just another Monday."

The priest blinked at this and replied: "You know, I think today is Thursday."

"That's even better," Jack said and then turned to Captain Vance. "I think I have the situation under control. The French can stand down and we should be able to move to the 'site.' You have figured out where the epicenter is, right?"

"Sorry, but that's a negative. We know the location of the cemetery that Robert used to raise his undead army. It's south of the Loire but north of the smaller river; I think it's pronounced Levee Du Cher or something like that. Either way the two rivers form a rectangle of about six square miles and it's likely that whatever he wanted was in that area, but so far we haven't been able to pinpoint the exact location. The French have been kind enough to send out two different recon flights, but as of yet we have nothing."

"Then we'll use the helicopters," Cyn said, sliding down off the boxy little Euro-car. "And we must hurry if we're going to have any chance at catching Robert."

She seemed completely over her run-in with the Mother, while Jack was still shaken inside and out and unable to think too much beyond the spells inside of him.

They headed back to the cemetery where the choppers had settled in among the wreckage of coffins and the ramble of broken headstones. At Vance's orders, they began spooling up their engines, and as the rotors turned, they kicked up an odd storm of white silk; what had once lined so many of the destroyed coffins.

Around the thrumming birds the *Raiders* and *Knights* checked their gear in preparation for a fight and the priests went among them, blessing the men. Jack was handed a new sword and had his Holy Water replenished. He paused before getting on the helicopter to check the blade of the sword, and when he turned around he was face to face with the priest who had been sipping coffee with his pinky extended.

"May the Lord cast his blessing on you," he said and anointed Jack's forehead with Holy oil.

Jack couldn't help himself and cringed, expecting to feel the fire of the Lord burning out the evil that the Mother of Demons had placed in him, but he felt nothing more than the slide of the man's finger and a gentle warmth spread through his bones.

He was so relieved that all he could say was: "Okay, good. Thanks."

Next to him, Cyn was pulling her hair back in a ponytail. "Okay, good? You sounded a touch nervous. Do you have everything under control?"

This made him laugh and the laughter combined with the oil and the blessing pushed the thought of the spell deep in the corner of his mind—and that had the effect of making him laugh harder. "I haven't had *anything* under control since the first day I met you."

She gave an odd look at his laugh, but then smirked, saying: "Don't try to pin that on me. You came to me with your crazy story, not the other way around. I was simply an innocent bystander."

"Well, it wasn't my fau…"

Captain Vance interrupted them, yelling over the sound of the turbines. "What the hell? You two got thirty choppers waiting on you. Rap up your flirtations and get on board the damned bird!"

"Bloody touchy," Cyn said, speaking right into Jack's ear. "Makes me miss Captain Metzger even more."

Bringing up the murdered Captain killed Jack's laughter. He missed the man as well, just as he missed Father Timmons and Father Jordan. Though Jack had griped constantly, they had been good teammates, certainly better to Jack than he had been to them—a new regret on his part to add to the thousand he had in the cold storage of his soul.

The pair, the last two to board the choppers, climbed in and held on. Within seconds, the French birds were in the air, leaving the abandoned town behind and flowing over the hills, which all seemed to be covered in grapevines or trees of a thousand different hues of green.

In a double "V" formation, they sped straight west over the blue ribbon of the Loire River to Tours, where the world was thankfully no longer a black storm of horror. Robert's demons were too busy fighting to stay earthbound to bother with the unnatural darkness or the cold or the stench, none of which would bother the undead soldiers of Jack's forces.

Not that the Tours was in any way as beautiful as it once had been. Thousands of buildings smoldered and sent up plumes of smoke, while the streets were strewn with corpses, some looking horribly sad, splayed out and unmoving in disjointed positions, and others fighting tooth and nail with other corpses, tearing and rending each other to pieces. There was a great deal of blood in the streets; from the air, the streets glistened a copper-brown.

Once they crossed the river, orders were relayed to the choppers, so that the formation seemed to dissolve in midair, the birds spreading out to form a long line that slowly swept along and from each, men stared downwards looking for any sign of Robert or what he might have been after.

Jack stared along with the rest of them until there was cry from one of the *Raiders* riding in the same copter. Jack couldn't see what was being pointed at but he saw Cyn shake her head and he knew that it was a false alarm. For the next few minutes, Jack watched her instead of the ground. She was so much more interesting.

Cyn squinted down, her face full of concentration, tiny lines creasing her forehead, her lips, normally full, were now drawn in. In that brief moment, he saw the future Cynthia Childs. He saw clearly what she would look like forty years from then and he liked what he saw. There would be grey in her hair and those tiny lines would be deeper, but she would still be beautiful and she would still have that impertinent smirk.

A harsh thought killed the moment: *She'll still have that smirk in forty years, IF she lives that long.*

"She'll live that long," he muttered, pulling his eyes off of Cyn and concentrating on the ground, or at least he tried to concentrate. He tried to focus on the streets and the buildings, but soon his mind wandered and his vision blurred as the city became a kaleidoscope of ugliness. Within the horror there was a darker horror, the remnants of necromancy, the stench of blood-work. He had felt it as they passed over the cemetery Robert had used to create his army; now, he felt it again.

Cyn could sense the necromancy better than he could and beat him to the punch. "There," she said, pointing down at a complex of white-topped buildings, at least one of which was a church of some sort. "Set us down. I can feel…something. The spells to open the gate, I think, but since there are no cemeteries around, Robert wasn't trying to raise a second army."

This suggested that Robert was after only a single person; the last piece to the puzzle? Jack certainly hoped so, no matter what the danger was. He felt stretched and worn from the long chase and was eager for it to be over with. "Have the pilot land as close as possible. In fact, get all the choppers on the ground. I want to blanket the area. Place teams at every street corner within five blocks and have them detain anyone that isn't already dead."

The orders were carried out quickly, although they weren't carried out with what anyone would call military precision. The orders were too vague and the area too large and sprawling. Pilots chose their own destinations to land generally with the safety of their aircraft in mind rather than simply dropping down among the telephone wires, the street lights and the looming buildings.

The lead helicopter took a calculated risk to land in a church parking lot where there were light poles and sculpted shrubs and a few of the funny little cars that so many of the French drove. There was precious little room to spare for the rotors, perhaps only a few feet on either side, and Jack could see the sweat coursing from beneath the pilot's helmet as he brought them down with a light thump.

"Go! Go!" bawled Captain Vance. The ten *Raiders*, composed of two priests, six warriors, plus Cyn and Jack, jumped out of the chopper and crouched with their weapons drawn and ready, awaiting an onslaught that didn't occur. No horde of undead broke over them. No ice-breathing demons attacked.

After a few seconds, Captain Vance pointed at the sky and the copter lifted off. When it was gone, a deathly silence filled the church grounds. Only their breathing could be heard until Cyn said: "I don't feel any of *them* nearby. I feel the remnants of a spell. It's in there." She pointed at one of the smaller buildings.

Judging by the size and shape of the building, it could only be a crypt, and a crypt of someone of historical note. The entrance was dominated by Doric columns, twice the height of Captain Vance, while the rest of the structure was cast entirely in marble tile. The lettering carved into the stone above the entrance was faded with age, but still legible.

"Can anyone read French," Vance asked.

"That's not French," Jack remarked. "That's Latin."

The neat little priest who had earlier been drinking coffee out of a teacup said: "Yes, it is indeed. It says that this is the final resting place of Gregory of Tours. Very interesting, I'd say."

"Interesting in what way?" Vance asked. "What's he got to do with the Roman guy or that thing back in the Sudan?"

"And what's he got to do with Egypt?" Jack asked. The clues were so oddly distinct and so separated by time and distance that he couldn't make heads or tails out of it. "What's Google say about this guy?"

Vance raised an eyebrow at this. "Google? I thought you were an archeologist. What sort of archeologist uses Google?"

"The kind that knows history is too vast to know everything there is about everyone," Jack shot back. "As well as the kind that needs answers right now. We need to know what we might be facing in there."

"Possibly nothing," Cyn said, her cell phone glowing bright in front of her face. "I was way ahead of you with the internet search, but as far as I can tell there isn't a connection between Saint Gregory and Egypt, or one between him and the Mother or between him and Rome for that matter. He was the Bishop of Tours until he died in 594 AD. Before that he was a hagiographer, which is basically a biographer but one who focused on saints and he was famous in his time for his writings, most notably for a set of books on Saint Martin, also of Tours."

She paused for a time, her eyes scanning the pages. When she was done, she made a face of disgust. "That's about it. The only thing that's of note in my opinion is that he was related to thirteen of the previous Bishops of Tours. They sort of had a monopoly in that field."

"That could easily be chalked up to nepotism run amok," Jack said, coming to stand hovering over her shoulder, squinting down at the screen. The article on Gregory was just as she had said, and none of it looked helpful. When he finished reading it from top to bottom, he scowled first at the phone and then in at the crypt, which was shrouded in shadow. He wasn't afraid of what lay beyond the broken doors. He knew there was no ghoul version of St. Gregory within it. All he could sense was the residue of the spell, reminding him of what he carried around in his head.

"Let's go inside and check it out," Jack said, unable to come up with a better idea. "Maybe we'll find more clues."

The soldiers went first, crouched behind their tactical shotguns. Jack and Cyn strolled in after Vance had declared the room to be: "Clear." It was, sadly, not clear. On the floor in the middle of the room was a fresh corpse, a child with a face forever warped by pain. Around the child were the blotted remains of the twin circles.

Just beyond that was the tomb of St. Gregory; it had been torn open by something strong enough to break a five-inch slab of granite into chunks. Vance moved up to the edge of the tomb and glanced in with a quick peek. "He ain't here, not even scraps."

Jack came up next and glanced in. "Can you point your flashlight inside the tomb?" he asked Vance. "Yes, right there. You can see the faint outline of where a body used to be and that odd substance that looks like mold isn't mold, it's hair. Gregory was definitely here until very recently."

"And now Robert has him," Cyn said. "Ol' Greg must know something, but what?"

"Perhaps he knows something about someone else," suggested the slim priest. "He was a hagiographer. Maybe he knew something about one of the saints. I say we check out Saint Martin since his tomb is the closest."

Everyone agreed and, after another Google check showed that St. Martin's tomb was two miles to the west, they called down their hovering chopper, which came to land once more in the parking lot. Quickly they were buzzing above the pretty trees and the strewn corpses and pools of blood.

They were there in just over a minute. As the pilot gazed down and saw that there was nowhere to land within the vicinity and everyone else was checking out the destruction of St. Martin's tomb, Jack was peering between moments in time.

Their sudden appearance had surprised a sorcerer. It was a man dressed in velvety clothes of black. They swam around him, making Jack think he was wearing a long, flowing a cloak. He ran up out of a huge hole that had been dug under the north end of St. Martin's mausoleum. Only Jack saw him and he did for just a blink; the sorcerer was there for a second and then in the next second, time changed.

The sorcerer slowed time to a crawl so that he seemed to blaze away in an impossible blur. "Son of a bitch!" Jack seethed, knowing that if he waited for the chopper to nose about for a place to land, the sorcerer would be long gone, and he couldn't take that chance. He had to catch the man and find out why he was at the tomb and what he knew about St. Martin and if he was working for Robert in some capacity.

It would mean a fight, but only if Jack could catch him first, and there was only one way to do that: he leapt from the helicopter…from a hundred feet up.

Chapter 26
Tours, France
Jack Dreyden

Scientifically, Jack knew that the velocity of a free-falling object was not static. A falling object accelerated at thirty-two feet per second, and then doubled that speed *every* second. Meaning that in the first second an object fell, it would travel thirty-two feet and during the next second, it would fall an additional sixty-four feet and in the third second it would travel a hundred and twenty-eight feet.

There would be no third second for Jack. He would be just a smidge into that third second before he struck with a sickening thud on the street below, becoming just another corpse in a city full of them.

However, Jack possessed both magic and the knowledge that the speed at which he fell was dependent on time, something he could control. "*Phra-isth rath em,*" he said as he dropped, slowing time to a tenth of normal speed. It was a strange sensation, dropping away from the side of the helicopter and seeing the blades spinning above him, moving in long sweeps like a clock with four "second" hands. The noise of their passage was distorted in his ears, sounding like a long low rumble among a background of distortion.

The edges of the world and everything in it blurred; everything except Jack's sword, which he whipped out of its sheath the moment he landed at a tenth the speed he normally would have.

Thirty feet away, the sorcerer, another Chinese sorcerer, spun about just as time snapped back. The man stood only as tall as Jack's chin and seemed wiry within his billowing cloak. He was somewhat ageless; his tan skin smooth and his hair black as jet, and yet there were wrinkles at the corner of one of his eyes.

The other eye was simply gone and in its place was a charred black crater from which an oily pus dripped. It looked as though someone had recently used his face to put out a torch.

"Go your way, Visha Ra-aye and I will go mine," he said, his hands disappearing within his cloak.

"I just need to know what you were doing in that tomb?" Jack demanded, moving to his right, the sorcerer's blind side. He would strive to attack from that angle if he could.

"I said: go your way, Visha Ra-aye and I will go mine. Do not question me and I will not question you."

Any other day he might have gone his own way, he might have been able to put aside the hyper-aggression that seemed to come over him in the presence of another sorcerer. He might have ignored the *need* to do battle, but just then he had a stronger need.

"You will tell me and then I will decide if I let you go or not."

Anger flared in the one eye left to the sorcerer. "You are a fool. You do not understand the gift I give. I am counted among the waters. I am the Master of the Eastern Rivers."

Clearly Jack was supposed to be impressed by this, but wasn't. "Maybe I am a fool since I really don't care what you're the master of."

"You should care, Visha Ra-aye, because I am allowing you to live. My power is far greater; my magics far more subtle, my knowledge vast compared to yours."

"Your magics are subtle?" Jack asked. "That hole in your head doesn't look all that subtle." The sorcerer glared and ground his teeth, inadvertently showing Jack his "hole card" so to speak. "I see now. You're not 'letting' me live. The truth is you're hoping I don't kill you. You tangled with something too big to tangle with and now you're weak, so weak that some nothing like myself might just wipe the floor with you."

The sorcerer didn't reply to this, perhaps because he knew that Jack would see through his lie. "That's what I thought," Jack said. "Now, since I don't give a rat's ass about what river you're the master of, you're going to tell me what I want to know right now or you're going to tell me once I have my sword run up through your guts."

"No," the sorcerer answered, and then in a blur, he cut himself, spraying blood and hissing: "Kru vah ah-tan!" The droplets of blood falling from the cut on his wrist suddenly changed from red to black, and from rounded drops to sharp angles. Before they struck the street, they changed course and darted at Jack so fast that he only had time to thrown himself to the side. He was too slow and a dozen of the black darts struck him. Eight of them hit his armor with the sound of bacon sizzling and leaving holes in the Kevlar.

One hit the inside of his right elbow; there was a sharp pain and then complete numbness that spread to his bicep. Another hit his wrist paralyzing everything from the spot down to his fingertips, causing the blessed sword to drop with a clang onto the street.

The third and fourth of the little darts struck him on the neck and on the face, making his head cant over and his mouth droop as though he'd just had a stroke. Now, even if he knew some sort of counter spell, he wouldn't have been able to use it.

Unable to wield either his spells or his sword, Jack was out of the fight practically before it started, and yet the sorcerer didn't stop. He cut himself again and another dozen black blood-darts shot at Jack, who could only throw his left arm over his face and try to turn away. The arm went dead as did his left leg.

He fell to the ground and tried to crawl away, looking over his shoulder as the sneering Master of the Eastern River came on, his face screwed up with evil delight. He had won and now he wanted to punish Jack for his insolence; he wanted to hurt him. Before he could; however, a rattle of machine gun fire erupted.

The French helicopter carrying Cyn and Captain Vance had dropped down so that it was forty feet above the street and now the door gunner fired at the sorcerer, but with seemingly no effect. The air shimmered around the man in a glowing bubble that sparked gold every time a bullet struck it and there was enough strikes to cast shadows and make Jack squint against the glare.

With a growled spell, the sorcerer shot a bolt of lightning up through the bubble at the chopper, hitting it in the tail rotor and causing it to begin spinning out of control. Two seconds later, the helicopter dropped out of sight and crashed with a great deal of breaking glass and shrieking of metal. Jack's heart was in his throat as he waited for what he thought would be the inevitable explosion signaling the death of the woman he loved, but thankfully none came.

Jack sagged, both in relief and defeat, and tried to say *Stop, please*; however what came out of his paralyzed face was: "Shnap fees."

This only made the sorcerer sneer all that much harder. "I am Master of the Eastern Rivers. You will now learn what that means and where you rank." More black darts shot out from his bleeding fist and Jack could do nothing but try in vain to roll away. He was too slow and all he did was expose more of himself to the strange numbing venomous darts.

They stung down his back, across his left kidney and his hip. Most struck his armor but enough hit him to leave him nothing but a rag doll, and yet that did not stop the sorcerer. He hit Jack once more with the paralyzing spell —but it was one too many. One of the sharp projectiles hit neither his flesh nor his armor. It hit one of the vials of Holy Water he wore at his side. There was a crack, a flash of silver light and then the air was suddenly filled with a fine mist that rained down in gentle curtains.

Wherever the mist fell, it neutralized the venom and washed away the black holes in Jack's skin leaving him completely unmarred and able to feel every inch of his body once again.

He found it glorious, while on the other hand the mist perplexed the sorcerer, who backed away from the droplets as if afraid to get any on him. This allowed Jack enough time to roll over and snatch up his sword. He attacked without hesitation and without warning. The black darts and the lightning bolt had been proof that he had seriously underestimated the sorcerer's reserve of strength and his magical ability.

The sword cut a silver arc as Jack went on the offensive. The sorcerer countered by slowing time by half and dodging the thrust by the barest of margins. Jack swept his sword in a shining deadly arc once again, saving his magical energy and using his skill and speed advantage in an attempt to wear down the sorcerer; however his opponent unexpectedly pulled a sword of his own out from within the folds of his billowing robe.

It was a slim katana and one that was a bit shorter than most. He raised it assuming a fighting stance; however instead of attacking, he hissed: "Kru vah ah-tan-rahe."

This sounded so much like the last spell that Jack darted in, lunging at the sorcerer before more of those strange blood darts flew at him. The spell wasn't the same. Instead of turning his blood into poisoned darts, it darkened his blade, black as coal.

At the sight of it, Jack hesitated, appraising the new magic and not quite understanding it. "Seems like a bit of a waste of energy if you ask me," Jack remarked, turning his head side to side, trying to see the blade fully. "I mean, if you can run me through, don't you think the poison is a bit of an overkill?"

Jack was fishing for information before he committed to another attack, only the sorcerer was too cagey and remained silent. Strangely, he also stayed on the defensive; a mistake, or so Jack thought. Before his enemy could come up with another, perhaps more effective spell, Jack darted in, looking to stab over his opponent's blade, which was held invitingly low.

Showing some skill, the sorcerer blocked the attack, but for some reason he didn't follow up with a riposte which was normal in fighting sword to sword. Frequently, a blow was only landed after a few passes as each fighter looked to gain an advantage in position.

The sorcerer was content to block and leap back. Again this seemed foolish as Jack was obviously the quicker of the two. It was clear that eventually one of his attacks would get through the defense. Surely, the sorcerer had to see that; instead he was watching Jack with glee in his eyes.

Jack was suddenly very nervous. The sorcerer was fully expecting something bad to happen, but what? He hoped that he could kill his enemy before whatever was going to happen, happened; however as Jack brought his sword up, he saw that the shining metal was no longer shining. It was turning black from the tip on down to the handle.

"What the hell?" Jack cried, struck by indecision. He saw what was going to happen: the sorcerer's paralytic spell would travel right down the blade and into his skin. The only question was: would it only affect his hand or would it completely numb him head to toe?

He couldn't take the chance to find out and so he dropped the sword with a yelp. This had the sorcerer laughing which, for Jack was at least better than being attacked. It gave him precious seconds to dig out another vial, this one was of Holy Oil.

As quick as he could, he poured it on the blade and was happy to see the poison dry up and once again the sword shone like silver. The sorcerer calmly pointed out: "You have one left, only. You will lose." Then he repeated his spell, feeding more poison into his blade. He beckoned Jack to come at him, but Jack declined with a shake of his head.

How could he attack? He would be paralyzed within a second of their swords touching, something that couldn't be avoided. What he needed was some way to drain the sword of its magic, or neutralize it in some way. The idea of throwing his last vial of Holy Water at the sword crossed his mind; however, he knew that would be a very chancy throw of a small amount of precious fluid.

"What if I burned it out?" he wondered, as a plan began to brew. As the sorcerer started advancing with the tip of his blackened sword held far out in front of him, Jack didn't have time to consider the repercussions. After learning from Truong, Jack had embedded razors in his armor at strategic points and he used one to cut his arm, hissing: "Shishin Ighn," and then adding "Rahe," as the sorcerer had with his spell.

Lightening suddenly lit up his blade with a crackling white light. Like the sorcerer, Jack held his blade out ahead of him, although for him it was because he was afraid of getting a little of his own medicine in the form of mild electrocution.

The sight of the glowing sword caused the sorcerer to hesitate, but only for a second, and then with a cry, he sprang forward. Their swords met and the magical energy flashed, alternating dark and light as each tried to gain the upper hand.

Jack was amazed to find that they were very nearly evenly matched, at least at the moment. The Master of the Eastern Rivers had a far deeper capacity of energy; however, judging by his cratered face, he had already gone through some sort of trial that day and was weak.

Three times they crossed swords, the light and dark battling as ferociously as the metal that rang out. On the fourth pass, Jack's lunge was the quicker and his blade sank deep into the left shoulder of his opponent. The cut was deep and yet it was the lightning exploding into the sorcerer that did the most damage. The man was lifted off his feet and blown back to land within the doorway of St. Martin's temple.

"Give up," Jack urged, striding forward.

"No," the sorcerer growled, climbing to his feet. "You fight the Mother. You pit yourself against the Queen of Souls and you will lose and you will suffer, and so will everyone who helps you. I will not help you. I will defeat you and gain everlasting glory. Kru vah ah-tan-rahe!" His blade went black again.

In answer, Jack said: "Shishin Ighn-rahe," although he said it with some reluctance. He knew that he was not only quicker than his opponent, he was a far superior swordsman. The sorcerer was a magician first and foremost and a swordsman a distant second. He was sloppy in his defense and slow in riposting. He had obviously relied in the past on slowing time to gain a speed advantage over his opponents, and yet Jack could equal him there.

It was only a matter of a few more passes and the man would be hit again and probably wouldn't be able to recover, and that meant Jack had a tough choice: should he kill the man or let him go free?

He was bogged down in the dilemma and didn't see the cold calculations behind the sorcerer's remaining eye —he wasn't about to go down so easily. Their swords rang out with a fury as they clashed and then for a moment they were pressed almost chest to chest, and here again was another reason Jack thought he would win: he was also bigger and stronger than the smaller Asian.

In his mind's eye, he saw how the fight would end: with a grunt, he would throw the man back and before he could recover his proper footing, Jack would beat down his Katana and slash him across the throat.

Reality wasn't quite so simple. Unexpectedly, the sorcerer bit down on his tongue and with a bloody mouth breathed: "Kru vah ah-tan." The words came out in a black cloud of paralyzing poison going directly into Jack's face which froze in a corrupted mask of fear.

Jack could see, but only through his squinted lids, and he couldn't move his eyeballs side to side, so he was forced to torque his shoulders back and forth to catch a glimpse of anything on his periphery. His ears felt as though they were stuffed with cotton and his mouth seemed welded shut. He had managed to hold his breath before the cloud struck, but now the poison was crawling up his nostrils and into his sinuses and down the back of his throat. If he dared to take a breath he knew that he would suck the residue of the poison into his lungs and then it would be lights out for Jack.

Frantic, he thrust out with all of his strength, sending the sorcerer reeling backwards. With his sword arm swinging back in forth in a pathetic attempt to keep his enemy at bay, Jack dug for the last vial of Holy Oil. Just as he popped the top off, he saw the dark form of the sorcerer coming at him, his blade held aloft like a black hammer.

Desperately, Jack flung his sword up, taking the blow on the flat of the blade with a flash bright enough to blind them both as he put all of his magical strength into the lightning dancing on the steel. The power shooting from the edge of the sword caused the sorcerer to step back for a moment, giving Jack enough time to splash himself in the face with the oil.

The effect was less than miraculous.

He could see once again; however, everything was a blur of oil and tears within a background of utter darkness. The sorcerer was only a shifting black shadow with a terrible black sword that came down again and again, smashing without any art or skill. He hammered relentlessly straight onto Jack's blade, so that with every blow the black sword came closer and closer to Jack's flesh.

In desperation, Jack flailed with his left hand and caught hold of the sorcerer's robe and pulled him in close. They were too close for sword work and everything was still too blurry for him to see. The sorcerer's fist seemed to come out of nowhere to crack him beneath the jaw, knocking him to the ground and sending his sword clattering away, it's magical lightning draining uselessly into the ground.

At first all he saw were stars and all he tasted was copper blood, but then the sorcerer's face swam into view. "Will you beg for your life like a coward?" he asked, leering again now that he had won. "Or will you beg to die like a man?" In answer, Jack spat into the sorcerer's face, speckling him with black and red. It wasn't just out of anger that he spat, the taste of the old poison in his mouth was foul.

"I won't be begging for anything," he answered in a bit of a slur. His tongue was swelling where he had bitten it.

"For that, I'll make sure you beg, but not for your life, but for the life of the woman. If you kiss my feet and lick my shoes, I might keep her alive. You two have been useful in stirring things up and keeping prying eyes from me. So beg me and I might keep her alive for a while longer."

Jack took stock of his situation. He was flat on his back with his arms straddled and his sword too far away to be of any use. The fact that he couldn't move meant cutting himself was no longer an option and so effective magic was out of the question. He had no choice but to beg for Cyn's life—except he couldn't bring himself to do it.

He loved her and feared that even now she was trapped in the wreckage of the downed helicopter, and would be easy picking for the sorcerer and yet, every time he opened his mouth to beg, his swollen tongue would freeze as if it was still paralyzed.

This odd feeling gave him an idea that was nearly driven out of his head when the sorcerer produced a knife so quickly that it was almost like magic itself. He held the point over his palm, delicately touching the scarred flesh there. "I know magics that will turn you grey with fear. I know magics that will have you tearing out your own bones." He moved the dagger away from his own skin and brought it closer to Jack's face, hovering it just above his right eye.

"You want me to beg?" Jack asked, trying to see beyond the knife. "You want me to beg like a dog?"

The sorcerer nodded and there was a strange light in his eyes. It made Jack think that there was more to this concept of begging than he knew. Was there power in it? Was this how a stronger sorcerer gained power by defeating a weaker one? By stealing his dignity and debasing himself? Jack hoped he would never find out.

"Fine, I'll beg," Jack growled and then clamped down on his aching tongue until his eyes watered and he felt his blood flowing warm and salty. He smiled, showing bloody teeth before he said: "Kru vah ah-tan," the breath from his lungs erupting in an acid fog that burned as it came out.

Too late the sorcerer saw that Jack had turned the tables on him, spewing his own paralyzing spell back into his face. Spastically, he threw himself off of Jack and tried to cover his face with his hands. He partially succeeded, so that he was blind in his remaining eye and the left side of his mouth ran downward in a slant as if his lips were melting; the partial success came at the cost of paralyzing both of his hands.

The knife dropped from the sorcerer's wooden fingers, landing next to Jack's cheek, who ignored it as he stood and went for his sword. It felt good in his hand. It felt natural and he knew that what he had to do with it was just as natural. The sorcerer would have to die. He was evil. He was a danger, not just to Jack and not just to the girl he loved, but he was also a danger to the entire world.

Jack turned back to the sorcerer and saw him huddled over his own sword and already there was blood in his palm. He was trying to work another spell—yes, he was dangerous and yes, he would have to be put down. That's how Jack had to think of it. He was a rabid dog and had to be put down.

And as a reward he would gain from the man's death. What didn't kill him only made him stronger, and he had to get stronger. Robert was gaining strength every day and Jack had to keep up.

These were the excuses he made as he advanced on the sorcerer, coming up from behind, his sword raised. The blade was no longer blessed; now it was the tool of an executioner.

The sorcerer, even inches from his death, was a dangerous thing. Blood dripped from his slack hand as he spoke magic: "Kru vah…"

He wasn't quick enough and Jack took his head from his shoulder, with the spell half spoken. Sadly, it felt good to Jack. The swing had been one of those perfect swings that ballplayers talked about. The blade had hit that beautiful "sweet spot" and the sorcerer's head flew.

Chapter 27
Tours, France
Cynthia Childs

The last clear thing Cyn remembered before the crash was seeing Jack jump out of the helicopter. The sight stopped her heart dead in her chest, while her skin flared with a thousand electric pin-pricks—she had just watched her love throw himself to his death.

Her mind couldn't understand what her eyes had shown it and was still trying to make some sense of what had just happened when her body reacted on its own. Without concern for the danger, she threw herself to the edge of the copter and for a moment had to search for Jack, sure that he'd still be falling, and sure that she had been only quick enough to see him splat on the ground.

Except he wasn't falling or splatting, or dying. He was far below her already standing with sword in hand. It was as if he hadn't been sitting in the helicopter the moment before. She remembered saying: "What the hell?" And she remembered blinking in confusion as she tried to make sense of what was happening, and she remembered Jack fighting against someone who was full of shadows.

And the next thing she knew, the little priest who had been on the copter with them was smiling into her eyes. He seemed to float above Cyn.

"Are you okay?" he asked, his voice hazy and yet able to cut through the sound of alarms blaring from all around them. There was something wrong with the helicopter, but she couldn't see what. Her view of her surroundings was strange and dark as if she had been put in a box.

"Cynthia, are you okay?" Gomez asked, again, louder, now. She should have been asking him that question. The priest…Father Gomez was bleeding from a gash in his scalp. Blood had drenched the side of his head, and his face, in contrast seemed very pale.

Cyn thought that she was fine, only the second she tried to shift from what was beginning to feel like a very awkward position, a bolt of electric agony went up her spine. The pain was so unexpected that it made her cry out and she really looked around for the first time, well she looked as much as she was able to.

The copter had corkscrewed into the ground and was now laid over, not just on its side, but also with its nose pointing downward. Cyn found herself in the cockpit, stuffed in the footwell of the copilot's seat. Where he was, she didn't know. The pilot was next to her, still in his chair, his head caved in on one side. One of his eyes dangled from its socket by a ribbon of something red and gory. It stared at her.

"My back," she gasped. The pain had her eyes watering, but in spite of the agony, all she could think about was Jack…and the co-pilot; where were they? And what was the red mess all over the control panel. And where was everyone else? She tried to pull herself up, but then she saw that her right wrist was cocked at an ugly angle; she stared at the fracture as if seeing someone else's hand.

Father Gomez touched her wrist, lightly. "You are injured and in need of the Lord's blessing." He closed his eyes and his touch became warm and soothing, taking away the pain that was grinding along her nerves. His lips moved in prayer, and it was a moment before she realized that he trying to heal her.

That wasn't something she could allow. Jack was out there, possibly fighting for his life, possibly injured… possibly dead. She couldn't let the priest use up his strength on her, not until she knew what was happening with Jack. "Stop! Don't. Just give me a hand out of here, okay?" When he hesitated, she growled: "That's an order!"

Since she never knew exactly where she stood in the ranking of things, she had never tried to "order" anyone about before, and so she was pleasantly surprised when the priest reluctantly agreed. "Try to slide me out of here," she asked.

Her position in the footwell could only be described as "knotted." She had arms and legs going this way and that, while her body was bent and contorted and in hellacious pain. And it was with a mental strength she wasn't normally known for that she came out of the crushed-in spot without screaming. The pain was immense, but she knew that one peep out of her and the priest would heal her, wasting his precious power on her instead of saving it for Jack or any of the others.

As far as she was concerned, she should be the last person healed. Everyone else had important jobs within the squads, while officially all she ever did was act as bait for demons, which was something a chimp could be trained to do. Yes, it was true that she was also the only person who could keep Jack safe from himself, and it was also true that she was the only person who could keep the world safe from Jack. And yet that could be done with a stiff back. When she tried to stand, she realized that her condition was beyond simply being stiff.

Fainting from pain was a key indicator that intervention was needed.

She woke a minute later with Father Gomez kneeling over her, a warm, white light spreading from his hands. "…and through his blessings, the Lord heals all wounds. Stand, Cynthia Childs and know that you are healed and whole through your faith in God."

Instead of saying thank you, she asked: "What about Jack?" The priest shrugged and Cyn leapt to her feet and swayed for just a second. Her back and wrist were completely healed but her head swam from everything that had happened in so short a time.

"Where is Ja…" She stopped as she saw the destruction around her for the first time. The helicopter had spun into the ground out of control only two minutes before and there were chunks of flaming metal and debris everywhere. And there were bodies.

machine. Some went over the side nervously making Cyn think that they were priests, unused to the more adventurous side of God's calling.

The copter disappeared from view as the pair went around the side of the basilica to where mounds of dirt two-stories high marked the entrance to a demon-made tunnel. It was tall and wide enough for them to walk side by side without stooping. It was also dark and damp and the prints in the earth were mostly odd bone-prints.

Seeing them gave Cyn the shivers that spread throughout her body. They went up her back and across her shoulders. They were in her belly, making her queasy, and her chest and suddenly it was hard to breathe, and then the shivers were in her hands and it felt as though they were no longer hers to control.

"You okay?" Jack asked, stepping near and looking at her closely. She felt as though she was about to shake to pieces, but he seemed perfectly fine.

She tried to shrug but with her body rattling away, it wasn't obvious. "I guess I never get used to some parts of this life. Headless bodies and bone prints, those weren't in the job description."

"And neither were helicopter crashes," he said, putting an arm around her shoulders. It wasn't the most comforting thing. They were now armor to armor and for the first time she noticed that his had dozens of little holes in it, each large enough for her to fit the tip of her pinky in. She wanted to ask about them and at the same time she didn't want to know. She didn't want to know what had driven him to decapitate a defenseless man. What would happen if she didn't find his reasons compelling enough? Would he forever be a murderer in her eyes?

It was best not to know. "I think I just need some light," she said, digging for her phone…her *new* phone… the one that one of Captain Vance's men had handed over without question. It was smashed beyond repair. She had survived the helicopter crash, but for some reason it hadn't. And neither had the man who had given her the phone. He had been one of the ugly piles of jutting bone and torn flesh that lay crumpled in a pool of red.

Seeing the phone triggered her shakes to go into overdrive and she was forced to sit as her muscles turned to jelly.

Jack squatted down next to her and brushed a strand of blonde hair from her face. "It's just a phone, darling. And if you want light, I can help." From his pocket he brought out a pinch of dust and gently blew on it. The grains leapt from his hand as glowing embers of gold. Soon the entire tunnel was bright enough to read by. "You see? No problem."

But there was a problem. The now dead phone that belonged to the now dead soldier had a picture of a pretty woman, holding a pretty baby, as its screen background. Now there were a thousand cracks running through their faces. Seeing them caused Cyn to break down in tears and she wasn't exactly sure why. She didn't know the soldier beyond the fact that he was one of Vance's *Raiders*. And there had been many pretty women killed in the last year and a half and she was sure that many had pretty babies.

So why was this one special? Why was this woman and her baby making her cry?

"It's the adrenaline from the crash running through you," Jack said. "It can mess with your emotions."

"Or it's all of it," she replied. "I think it may be time for me to…"

A voice from up the tunnel cut in on her. It was Captain Vance and he was still limping; a bad sign. "Please tell me that guy without the head is your cousin." Jack shook her head, making Vance sigh. "At least tell me he was a bad guy, then."

"Bad enough," was all Jack replied. "What kind of casualties are we looking at up there?"

"Four dead and four in critical condition. The rest of us are a little nicked-up, but we'll survive."

Jack grunted, a sound, Cyn knew, that meant he had already put the dead and wounded behind him. As always, he was focused only on Cyn. He truly cared only about her. The world could burn and as long as she was alright, he would be fine. It wasn't healthy and yet he could still function in an environment of constant danger which would destroy a lesser man.

"What were you saying?" he asked her. "It's time for what?"

She wanted to tell him that it was time to quit, to run away, only she couldn't. Her simple job of being there for Jack was vital. If she left so would he, and no one else could do what he could.

"It's time for a vacation," she answered. "Once this is done, we are going somewhere blue and tropical and far away."

He grinned. "Sounds good, but in the mean time we have to figure out why Robert was interested in St. Martin." The three went down the tunnel, which ended at a large pit the size of a backyard swimming pool. Jack went down into it and studied the dirt walls and floor.

"What do you make of this?" he asked Cyn and tossed up a bit of what looked like rock to her.

She ran her hands over it only to feel bits break off. "Wood, probably from a coffin. This must be the site of St. Martin's original tomb, but since there isn't another sacrificed body, it's safe to say that they didn't find any more bones. If that was indeed what they were looking for."

Jack poked around a bit more, sending his particles of light here and there to illuminate one part of the pit or another. Eventually, he came out, looking thoughtful. "What do a Roman centurion, St. Gregory, St. Martin and ancient Egyptian funerary texts have in common?"

The easy answer and likely the true answer was: "Nothing," Cyn replied. "As far as we know, neither saint ever went to Egypt. I don't think St. Gregory ever left Europe. The Romans were everywhere. The connection is likely there…except that particular Roman lived right around the time of Christ, while St. Martin lived three-hundred years later and Gregory was a hundred and sixty years after that."

"What I want to know," Captain Vance said, "is what do Chinese sorcerers have to do with any of this?"

"Nothing," Jack told him. "And it's not the right question. It's only adding an unnecessary variable."

Feeling drained, Cyn sat down on the lip of the pit and let her feet dangle. Vance and Jack joined her, one on either side and they each took turns reading from Vance's cell phone. He had looked up both saints to see if there was a connection. Gregory was a biographer, turned bishop of Tours who was "canonized," or sainted, after his death. Martin began life as a Roman soldier who later became a pacifist. He eventually became Bishop of Tours and was also canonized after his death. But what they had to do with a long dead Roman soldier and funerary texts was impossible to discover with what they knew.

"Maybe we are adding our own unnecessary variable," she said. "Maybe Egypt has nothing to do with this. If you take that out, we have a link between the three: St. Martin connects the soldier to Gregory. Maybe the connection has to do with Rome."

Jack thought this over for a time. "It's possible. Gregory never went to Rome and the soldier likely never made it to France."

"So St. Martin is the key to their connection, like Cyn said," Vance stated.

"Except St. Martin was most famous for his sudden turn against war," Cyn noted. "Why would Robert care about that?"

The idea made Jack snort. "He wouldn't. He would only care about what caused him to turn from war. There is a more obvious connection joining the three: Jesus Christ. Robert could be *very* interested in something from that era."

"The Holy Grail!" Vance cried, suddenly. "He has to be after it. Doesn't it give you immortality?"

278

"I doubt it," Cyn said. "The cup of Christ was a metaphor for the belief in everlasting life after death. Besides, how would a soldier end up with it? And if it did make a person immortal, how did he die?"

Jack laughed. "I admit I was thinking about the Grail as well. What about the *True Cross*? The cross Christ was hung up on was drenched in his actual blood and, mythologically speaking, there are many tales concerning its power."

The three were silent for a time, the men thinking and Cyn pouring over the phone. She tried redefining her search adding the term "Holy Grail" along with the names of the two saints and when that didn't bring up anything, she tried the same thing with the words "True Cross."

"Damn it. I'm not getting anything out of Google," she complained.

"It's a computer so garbage in equals garbage out," Jack said, gazing into the pit. "We need something deeper. What we are looking for is a secret so deadly that St. Martin took to it to his grave, perhaps literally." He pointed around them at the pit.

What Jack said struck a chord in Cyn, but not about Martin. There was something about St. Gregory, some little tidbit that stuck in her mind and was gnawing at her. "There may be a different connection between Gregory and the other two and maybe even the funerary texts," she said speaking as fast as the words popped into her head. "According to several sources, Gregory would actually write himself into the biographies of long dead saints, acting as if he had been there and seeing things first hand."

Jack caught on. "Gregory was a sorcerer!"

"Or just a clairvoyant," Cyn said. "And maybe he saw something." She typed on the phone's miniature keyboard, entering: *St. Gregory holy relic*. "Whoa, I got something and it's something Robert would definitely be interested in: the Lance of Longinus."

"The what?" Vance demanded, trying to turn his head at a screwed up angle to see the phone's display.

Cyn pointed the phone at him, but Jack answered before he could begin reading: "It's the Spear of Destiny! The Holy Lance. When Christ was on the cross, possibly right at the moment of his death, one of the Roman centurions pierced his side with a spear and out flowed blood and water, but it wasn't water that came out. It was part of Christ's soul."

"You don't know that," Cyn said, fearing that what was being said was bordering on blasphemy.

"You're right, I don't know; however by the way Robert is going after this thing, I think he believes it. This leaves us with two questions: what kind of power does the spear have? And what's he going to do with it when he gets it?"

Chapter 28
Tours, France
Jack Dreyden

Cyn's smirk was nowhere in sight; her lips were a thin line on her face, which usually meant that she was angry about something. "What?" Jack asked, taking an innocent tone.

"Your assumption about Christ's soul, that's what. The Gospel of John clearly states *blood and water* came from the wound, and you know that."

"Yes, I know what it says, but perhaps John didn't know what he was seeing," Jack answered. "I'm sure it wasn't blood and water. Think about what happens when you mix blood and water. When you have more water than blood, you get bloody water and when you have more blood, you get watery blood."

She looked unconvinced, strangely so. He went on, arguing what he felt was a worthless point: "Maybe it was the power of Jesus then. He had not been conquered or overcome in a fight so he probably died with much of his power still inside of him and it had to be released somehow. That's what makes sense to me. If everything that was written about him was true then he could have hopped off that cross and wiped the floor with the entire Roman army."

"But he wasn't like that," Cyn said, her odd anger calming. "He was a pacifist."

"Just like St. Martin," Jack replied, trying to get the conversation back where it had begun. "Martin started life as a Roman soldier, he then becomes a Christian and then, years later, he suddenly turns pacifist in a time when there just weren't any pacifists. Why? Vance, what would you do if you suddenly came across a powerful weapon, one that was a serious game changer, one that could make you Emperor of Rome."

The soldier shrugged. "Easy, I'd use it. Wait, are you thinking Martin finds this lance, what could be the ultimate weapon and then just says: no thanks?"

"He was tempted," Cyn said in a quiet voice. "He was tempted and didn't give in. Then maybe he kept hold of the lance so that no one else could use it for evil purposes."

Captain Vance wore a look of disgust, as if the idea was repellent. "What about the Roman soldier, the one back in Lebanon? He wouldn't have done that. Anyone who is callous enough to stab a man hanging from a cross is the sort of man who would definitely use the spear for his own gain."

"Not if he had a conversion," Cyn replied, "Which is exactly what happened to the centurion, Longinus, at least according to historical documents."

Jack hopped up from the edge of the pit and stood with his toes hanging off the side. "It's a good hypothesis, Cyn but we could be wrong. Let's just look at the facts as we know them: we know that Robert left Egypt and went to dig up a Roman soldier, but came away with nothing. Next, he comes to Tours and raises St. Gregory, and then takes a pitstop to come here to see St. Martin. He checks his tomb and then digs a big pit, once again after someone or something."

"I say this argues in favor of the lance being Robert's goal," Cyn said. "If we subtract the lance from the equation then nothing makes sense. All the connections fall apart. Without the lance in the picture, there is nothing about St. Gregory's history that would stir Robert to this sort of action."

After a brief hesitation, Jack said: "With everything I know about Robert, I agree. And if we accept that he raised Gregory for information about the Lance of Longinus as true then it follows that he would head straight for the lance. I guess that's here."

Jack expected this to be the end of the conversation; however, Cyn's face clouded. "There is a hole in the theory. Although he had never been there, St. Gregory wrote that he had seen the Holy Lance in Jerusalem. If St. Martin had it in Tours a hundred and fifty years before Gregor was born, why does he mention Jerusalem?"

"To throw people off the scent of the true lance," Vance suggested. "If the lance is as powerful as you two say then it's great only if your side has it and is willing to use it. If not then you live in constant fear that someone will find it or steal it."

Jack nodded in agreement. "That or St. Gregory did indeed have a vision of it in Jerusalem, perhaps at a much earlier time, since it seemed he was able to see into the past. One thing makes sense: something that Gregory told Robert led him here. I have to say that the lance or some other artifact being here in Tours is the only thing that makes sense. Robert wouldn't spare a second on a saint unless there was something in it for him."

"I agree," Cyn said. "Robert is after power. The one question is: did he get it? Did St. Martin have the lance buried here? Can you tell, Jack?"

"No, I'm having a little trouble," Jack answered, touching his chest where the Mother's poison spell sat. "My insides are sort of mixed up with what the Mother put in you…"

Before he could finish his sentence, Cyn rounded on him, her eyes searching his face. "What? What did she do?"

It was too late to try to come up with some sort of lie and so Jack told the truth. "She put the three spells to open the gate into you, Cyn. It was a puzzle. She made it a puzzle that had to be solved and now it's in me." It was in him, demanding to be used…that part he kept to himself.

"That bloody bitch," Cyn snapped, storming off to walk up the tunnel, stopping as the tunnel began to rise. "She couldn't beat me and so she does this?" Her voice came back as a dull echo.

Jack wanted to tell her that "everything would be okay," but he knew better. The Mother was crafty and even locked in hell she was certainly aware of everything going on, and it was certain that her meddling would continue.

"Think of it this way, Cyn: the Mother did me a favor. I can open the gate now without draining my power. It might come as a rude shock to Robert. Either way, for good or evil it's done and I think it's best to put it out of our heads and concentrate on this. For now, I think we need to move forward with the idea that Robert is after the Spear of Destiny or another artifact of similar power. If he has it already, we're screwed, if not, if it wasn't here, then we need to find it before he does. Any ideas?"

Cyn came back down the tunnel, her head down, her blonde hair spilling over the phone in her hand as she did some more research on the fly. "The lance was lost to history for hundreds of years, but a number of 'true lances' were discovered. No one has been able to confirm which, if any, is the actual Lance of Longinus. We'll have to look at each. One is in Rome, another in Vienna, and the last is in a little town in Armenia."

"Then we'll alert each as to the possibility that Robert is coming for them," Jack said. He turned to Vance. "I'm going to need to know where the lances are in each city. I'm going to want a plane ready to go at a moment's notice, and I'm going to need permission to visit each. And I need the security around them increased by a factor of at least ten. And I'm going to need to know where the closest cemeteries of any size are in proximity to them just in case Robert beats us to them. And I want land cleared at each cemetery; north, south, east, and west, for helicopter landing points. Any questions?"

Vance shook his head. "None. Except, well what if he's not after the lance at all or what if he's already found it?"

Cyn answered: "If he's found it, he'll use it and we'll know soon enough. If he hasn't, then we can't sit around waiting for Robert to act."

"Yeah, I hate waiting," Vance said. He was about to leave when Jack stopped him.

"And I'm also going to need new weapons and armor. And I'll need some more Holy Water and Oil. Make it three vials of each this time. Got it?"

"Yes, weapons, armor, oil, LZs, security, and permission. Anything else, your highness?"

"Yeah, don't be a jerk," Jack said, but then grunted as Cyn elbowed him in the side. He quickly amended his request to: "Don't be a jerk, *please*. And see if you can scare up some French food…please. I puked up that burger ages ago and I'm famished. Oh, and Cyn needs a new phone."

She was quick to add: "Please."

Vance waited a few seconds longer to see if Jack was going add any more requests and then, without asking, he snatched his cell phone from Cyn's hand, punched a button, and began barking orders into it as he headed back up the tunnel.

Cyn watched him go, studiously keeping her eyes from Jack. "That spell in you is necromancy, isn't it?" Jack didn't answer which was answer enough for Cyn. "When were you going to tell me about it?"

"Never if I could've helped it."

"Is the need bad?"

She had no idea how bad. Necromancy was so easy compared to sorcery. The power was right there, almost free for the taking, if one had no problem with murder, that is. And it was endless power; just take it and use it. There was no need to recuperate, there was no need for Jack to drag himself around as a fraction of a person for days on end.

Saying anything but yes to Cyn would have been a blatant lie. He tried to appear blasé. "The need is there, a little. It'll probably get worse when I use the spell. Until then, I'm not worried." That was true enough to pass. He had too many other things to worry about.

They left the pit and found themselves in a dark city. The sun had finally set on what had felt like a very long day and yet he didn't have time to decompress. He had an army of undead to command.

As Captain Vance made arrangements to fly them to inspect the three possible Holy Spears, Jack jumped on board a helicopter and ordered it into the thick of the fighting between his ghouls and Robert's. Although he was worn from his fight with the sorcerer, he needed to take control of his army which was just starting to unravel as a fighting host.

Thankfully, it didn't take long to get the situation back under control. In the scheme of things, this had been only a diversion, a means to keep Jack occupied. Robert had used just the right amount of strength to get what he needed.

"I'm tempted to tell you to leave them for now," Cyn said. "Getting the spear has to be our top priority."

"And leave thousands of demons to slip away in the dark?" Jack couldn't have that on his conscience. "The spear should be fine for now. It's not like Robert can take a commercial flight to Rome or Vienna. He's going to have to drive which means we have time."

By midnight, the battle was over. A few demons had escaped, but the great majority were in hell where they belonged. Jack ordered his army to return the bodies they had taken back to their graves and from there he commanded them to return to hell as well.

Then it was just him and Cyn, sitting on the stone wall of the cemetery, kicking their heels and holding hands like teenagers. They had just fallen asleep, leaning on each other when a military helicopter dropped down out of the sky. Captain Vance stood in the doorway taking huge bites out of the side of a baguette, the length of his arm.

When they climbed up into the helicopter, he tore off a chunk of baguette for each of them. "Dinner. Sorry, but I forgot the butter. We're short on time. For some reason, the Vatican is being a pain about letting us see their spear. They want us to rule out the other two before we inspect their's. So we're going to Vienna first. We have a private jet waiting for us. I've never been on a private jet."

"Neither have I," Jack said, glancing in at a duffle bag crammed with new clothes for him, armor and a sword.

"Oh, you'll love it," Cyn told him, but in this she was wrong. The plane was a thirty seater and was nice enough; however once Jack had changed into his new clothes and buckled on his armor and had a sip of white wine offered by a pretty stewardess, he fell straight to sleep and had to be shaken awake two hours later.

Next to him, Cyn was equally bleary-eyed. "Are we here all ready?" she asked. "What about dinner?"

"You missed it," Vance told them. When Jack stood and reached for his sword, the captain stopped him. "They want us to leave our weapons on the plane. I told the ambassador I'd talk to you about it, but that I wouldn't make any guarantees."

Jack buckled the sword in place. "And now you have fulfilled your promise. We're bringing the weapons and when I say we, I mean you as well Vance. No one working with me can go about unarmed, it's too dangerous."

"That's what I hoped you'd say," Vance answered, slinging a shotgun over a shoulder. "I always thought that you were a prima donna, which you are, of course, but at least it's working in our favor this time."

Strangely, they weren't greeted by military men in military vehicles. It was a limousine, long and white, which picked them up. The driver looked at the weapons and the armor with wide eyes, while the American ambassador, an ex-politician with a heavy, braut-fed gut and a double chin, fretted and gave assurances of their safety, and tried to explain the need to cooperate.

In answer, Jack crawled into the limo and put his feet up. "Tell them their choices are I come with my sword or Robert comes with an army of the dead." Unexpectedly, the ambassador repeated Jack's statement word for word into a phone. The stark choice settled the matter in their favor and soon they were being whisked through the dark streets of Vienna to the Hofburg Palace, home of the Imperial Treasury.

Jack had never seen such magnificence. The palace was huge, the size of a city block and was truly awe inspiring. It was a tourist's dream. His head spun as the four of them, Jack, Cyn, Captain Vance and the American ambassador were whisked right past security and into a world that was difficult for him to comprehend. There wasn't a blank wall or a straight line in the place. There wasn't a moment for him to catch his breath. Everything was swirled and adorned and gilt and beveled and beautiful and, in truth, garishly over the top to the American's sense.

As expected they were ushered to a wing of the palace that resembled a small museum. Here the security had been heightened. There were two soldiers at every door, each stern-faced and strong. A woman took to leading them through the museum. She was tall and leggy and strode with purpose as though she was in a hurry, and Cyn had to skip every few steps to keep up.

As they went deeper into the museum, past shining suits of armor and beautiful paintings and stone sculptures, the woman spoke over her shoulder: "Touch nuzsink." Her accent made Jack feel as though he was in a spy movie and when they met the president of Austria, a man with such a Nazi-like aura, he couldn't help grin in spite of the somber moment.

The Austrian president, who made a portion of the palace his home, displayed such a stern, blue-eyed, authoritarian manner that Jack feared their trip had been a waste of time and that there would be demands and negotiations concerning their inspection of the spear. However, the man was more than agreeable. In fact, when it was explained fully what was going on, he took Jack by the hand, a grip he didn't relinquish, and escorted him right to the lance.

Compared to the build up and the palace and the crown jewels that surrounded it, the lance was underwhelming. First, it wasn't a full spear, it was only the head. Black metal, a little over a foot long, three inches wide and tapering to a dull point. Around its middle was an odd sheath of gold; the spearhead had been broken at some point and the gold held it together.

The very idea that the lance could be broken colored Jack's thinking—this couldn't be the real deal. "May I hold it?" he asked just in case he was wrong. This was translated and agreed to. A key to the glass case was produced, and when the lid was pulled back Jack felt a thrill of nervousness go through him in spite of his doubts. If the spear was the real deal and held a portion of Christ's power, what would happen to him when he touched it? Would it burn the evil out of him and maybe turn him to ash along with it?

"One way to find out," he whispered as the long-legged woman stepped aside, giving Jack access to the weapon. It was cool to the touch and sat in his hands like any lump of metal would.

"Zat," the woman said, pointing at what looked like a small arrow embedded within the point of the lance. "Ees a nail, vit vich Jesus vas placed on zee cross."

"One of the Holy Nails; impressive," Jack said, making sure to keep his eyes from rolling. The nail was very small, too small to be a nail used in a crucifixion, at least according to the computer models. As well, the nail was altogether straight. A real nail hammered into a beam of wood and then pried out again would have been bent in some fashion, especially one forged two-thousand years ago when metalworking wasn't very exact.

Next to him, Cyn took a deep breath and then reached out a shaking hand to touch the spear. She caught his eye and there was a look of disappointment in it.

"Ees it rheal?" the President of Austria asked.

A year before…before Jack knew that magic was real, he would have answered: *unlikely* and would have based this on logic, research and the law of probabilities. Now, he simply said: "No, it's not." It is true that the spear that pierced Jesus may not have retained any power whatsoever, or if it had, the power might have faded away to nothing after so much time. It might look and feel exactly like this, only Jack didn't think so.

Neither did Cyn. "There is no energy to this spear, no power. The same is true for the nail."

Jack expected arguing and denial from the Austrians, instead they looked relieved and, strangely enough, an offer was made for Jack to take the spear with him when he left. After what had happened in Tours and Syria, the Austrian president wanted no part of the spear, real or not.

It was even gift wrapped in a pretty box, though hurriedly so and, with the same indecent haste, the four Americans were shown the door.

"I guess this answers the question: what do you give a man who has everything?" Cyn chuckled, looking in the box on the drive back to the jet. Jack laughed, though he was the only one who did. Cyn's joke had been exceedingly English. The fake Lance of Longinus constituted Jack's sole property. He didn't have a home or a TV or a mantle to put the spear on. He technically didn't even own the clothes on his back. The government provided his clothes and his sword and his armor.

He owned nothing…nothing except an old spear and a nail, and for some reason this struck him as hilarious.

Chapter 29
Rome, Italy
Cynthia Childs

Armenia came and went in a blur. The jet sped them southeast and once again Jack slept through the niceties of private jet travel. He unstrapped his sword, placed the fancy box holding his thousand-year old fake Lance of Longinus between his feet, tilted his chair back and slept through both takeoff and landing and everything in between.

Cyn stayed awake long enough to ask for a blanket for both her and Jack and then she too was gone. The last thing she remembered was Captain Vance once again swearing into his phone.

Then they were landing and being shaken awake with the historic city of Vagharshapat outside the little porthole of a window next to her seat. The sun had been up for an hour and the new morning didn't do much to bring any charm to the Armenian city. Aside from a number of beautiful churches, the city possessed little charm. It had been redesigned and rebuilt fifty years earlier by the Soviets with the concept of utility being of greater importance than aesthetics. It consisted mostly of block after block of dreary, two story rectangles.

"How do you like our fair city?" asked the interpreter for the Mayor. Both men were so alike they could be brothers. They were both fiftyish with deep, coarse black hair that was beginning to grey at the temples, and both had webs of wrinkles at the corner of their eyes.

"It's great," Jack lied through his teeth, saving Cyn from having to. They were traveling in the back of a Soviet-era army truck, the only vehicle large enough to fit them all. To their entourage was added a deputy US ambassador, who was clearly afraid of Jack and did everything possible to keep from touching him, a local holy man, whose religion was never established, and a number of armed guards all of whom looked as though they felt that the threat lay inside the truck rather than outside of it.

It made for an uncomfortable ride. Thankfully, it was a short ride to the Manoogian Museum where their version of the lance had been housed for the last three-hundred and fifty years. Jack took one look at the spear head and his jaw grew tight and his smile fixed in place. Cyn understood. This wasn't the spear that had pierced Christ's side, either.

To start with, it wasn't even a real spear, not a military one, at least. The head of it was wide and flat, not sharp in the least and shaped like a diamond from a deck of cards. No soldier would carry such a thing, except, maybe in a ceremonial situation. To make matters worse, there were four holes in the flat head that had been purposefully placed so as to simulate a cross which was most certainly not a Roman symbol used in the first century when Jesus had lived.

"Hmmm, okay…yes," Jack said, acting as though he was considering the thing's potential. Without asking, he touched the metal. The mayor and the guards and the museum's bespectacled curator all watched with anticipation stamped on their faces. Jack screwed up his eyes and gritted his teeth and then sighed, looking sad.

"I am sorry to have to tell you this, but this isn't the real Lance of Longinus." At this proclamation, the holy man grew angry and the mayor showed disappointment and the curator turned snooty. The guards at least relaxed.

There was quite of bit of talk flying around the room, all in Armenian, and during the spittle-inducing arguments, Cyn secretly touched the metal and found that Jack was right, there was nothing to the thing.

"They say you are wrong," the interpreter said. "They say that this has been a relic of the Armenian people for the last two-thousand years, ever since Thaddeus, the apostle of Christ brought it to us. There is no doubt that this is the singular spear."

Jack shrugged and said: "If it is then double…no triple the guard on it. Or send it into hiding with only one man keeping the secret of where it's hidden, and then pray that my cousin doesn't find that one man. I wish I could advise you further, but we have to be going. We'll see ourselves out."

Total time in the presence of the fake spear: two minutes. They left the curator and the holy man deep in another argument, boarded the truck and were soon back at the jet where they found that the engines had never ceased. They were wheels up four minutes after that.

Except for affording them a night's sleep, the trip had been a waste of time. Jack cranked at everyone, until Cyn begged the stewardess for any sort of breakfast. When it came, he ate ravenously, scarfing down two plates of eggs and sausage. From then on, he was as chipper as he could be.

Cyn ate like a mouse. She was nervous about going to Rome. Although she went to mass every Sunday and tried her level best not to sin, she was still in fact a necromancer, and that meant she was inherently evil. What would the Pope see when he looked in her eyes? A shudder ran across her shoulders.

No one saw. Jack's chipper mood had given way to a food coma and he was snoring next to her, while Captain Vance was again on the phone: this time updating his superiors on the useless trip to Armenia.

And it wasn't just the idea of meeting the Pope that had her afraid. If there was a real Lance of Longinus and Robert didn't have it already, they all figured it had to be in Rome and that meant a showdown with Robert. It meant that the end of their long running battle could be only hours away.

And she didn't think she was prepared. She had her shotgun and her imp-like smirk and an evil power that she refused to use. When she added those three things up it didn't amount to much. *What about your soul?* a voice in her mind asked. *What about giving your soul to Jack? He might need it.*

Yes, that should have been part of the equation, except for one thing: the spell that Jack was carrying around inside of him had been meant for her. The Mother of Demons had made it for Cyn and it called to her wordlessly. A connection with Jack's soul now could be catastrophic for both of them. She could picture the spell igniting spontaneously the moment their souls joined and she could picture herself willing the Mother of Demons through the gate.

No, they couldn't join souls. In fact, what made the most sense was for Cyn not to even be in the fight or anywhere near it. She knew that Jack would spend far too much of his energy trying to keep her safe. She knew it and she was sure Robert knew it as well. He would target her with every demon and spell he possessed.

All the more reason to bow out of this one, the voice in her mind said in what sounded like a perfectly reasonable manner, one that was certainly far too rational and logical to argue with, except…except she knew she couldn't leave Jack alone to face whatever nightmare Robert was cooking up.

And she was sure he was cooking up something.

She stood and went forward to where Vance was hissing into the phone about the absolute necessity of clearing landing zones at the cemeteries in the greater Rome area. "Yes, I understand that some of these cemeteries interred bodies that are thousands of years old; however, I'm more concerned with the fact that there are three Children's hospitals in Rome and that there are a thousand schools and five-hundred thousand children who attend those schools. You saw the footage from Tours."

He covered the phone and looked up at her. "I'll be just a minute. These cemetery guys aren't listening to the ambassador or her staff. I keep telling them that if there's an incident, we're going to raise the bodies one way or another. And if they…Yes, I'm still here. No, I don't speak Italian. Yes, I can understand you. Okay, now that's settled, I want you to pay attention to me. In thirty minutes there will be a squad of soldiers at your gates. If you don't let them in they're going to blow up…you know, explode? Yes. They will explode those gates. So I suggest you do what they say. Ciao."

He punched the button and then stared out the window of the jet for a few seconds before turning back to Cyn. "What can I do for you?"

"I think I need a better weapon. The shotgun is pretty good, but…but I worry that it won't be good enough. Do you know what I mean?"

He laughed, but not cruelly. "I know exactly what you mean. Against the ghouls the shotgun is great, and a single demon isn't that much harder to put down, but against the heavy weights, it's just a toy. Trust me, all the *Raiders* feel the same way. The trouble is it's all we have. Sure we can get a missile launcher, but they're too bulky and slow to fire."

"What about grenades? Do you have any of them?"

"Sure. I might even be able to scare up a grenade launcher. You've just got to be mighty careful what you're shooting at, especially what is down range of your target. If you miss you could hit a school bus and you wouldn't want that."

It was his third mention of schools in a minute. "Do you have children?" she asked.

"Three girls all back home," he said and then looked out the window, sighing. "Well, what passes for home these days. We had a house in eastern Pennsylvania, but it was too close to the action. The dead got to within twenty-two miles before they turned back."

Cyn felt her stomach cinch with guilt. "Oh, that was close."

"Ever since then jobs have been drying up and property values crashed. We had to abandon the house six months ago. That really sucked. The bank foreclosed on a house that no one would ever want and we had to file bankruptcy. It's the reason I joined the *Raiders*. Better pay. I had to try and get my family in the red again."

"But you could die," Cyn said, aghast.

He shrugged. "That's what life insurance is for. I'm worth more dead than alive. Hey, why don't you go rest and I'll see about the launcher."

She had been effectively dismissed though she didn't mind. Vance's face had taken on a melancholy cast and she feared saying anything more concerning his family. Melancholy wasn't the best frame of mind to be in right before what could be their biggest fight yet.

"Unless we're just wasting our time," she mused, sitting back down next to Jack. "If the spear in Rome turns out to be fake, what does that mean? And what should we do?"

No clear answer came to her, although she mused on the subject all through the flight. They landed at noon and stepped out onto the airstrip into a sweltering Italian day. The sun blazed down and the sky around it had the appearance of steel. They barely had time to sweat before three black limousines pulled up, each bearing a small flag: yellow and white with what looked like crossed keys on the white half—it was the flag of Vatican City, the smallest country in the world.

The entire city sat on only one-hundred and nine acres and had an official population of eight hundred and fifty-one people.

From the limousines came a dozen Swiss guards, who frisked them and relieved them of their weapons. They were tall and stern and utterly uncompromising, not that anyone, including Jack, raised a fuss. Strangely, Jack seemed completely at his ease among the guards and when he climbed into the back of the middle limo, he immediately started poking about, opening the tiny drawers that were embedded in the wall of the vehicle and sniffing at the various decanters.

"I think this is either cognac or brandy. Is there even a difference?" he asked Vance, who only scowled at him while the two Swiss guards who sat in the back with them didn't bat an eye or make any noise at all.

"There's a difference," Cyn answered. "But I don't care for either. Do they have any vodka and maybe some pineapple juice?" She felt like she needed a drink and wondered why she hadn't taken advantage of the alcohol on the jet when she had the chance.

Jack checked in what was a very mini minibar. "Everything's in Italian. Ah! This is probably vodka and this carton has a picture of an orange. Will a screw-driver do?" When she eagerly agreed, he eyed her. "Are you nervous about meeting the Pope?"

A half-shrug accompanied her answer: "Yes, I suppose. We did help kill the old Pope."

"We did no such thing," Jack snapped. His scowl equaled Captain Vance's as he threw ice, orange juice and vodka in a glass. "Here, drink this. It might straighten your thinking out. We were innocent pawns and we did try to stop him."

He made a drink of his own and Cyn saw that the proportion of vodka to orange juice was two to one. She asked: "What about you? Are you nervous?"

"Now's not a good time to lie, so I'll go with a non-answer," he said with a grin and then took a swig of his drink and looked out the window. "My, Rome sure is pretty, but who knew it would be this hot?"

"Everyone," Cyn replied and then took her own drink —and then made a face. "That's not vodka. Ugh!"

Jack laughed and then took another drink. "I think it's some sort of Italian tequila, but we're beggars and so we can't be choosers."

When Jack finished off his drink and also made a face, Captain Vance remarked: "You look more like thieves. No one said you could drink any of that."

This struck Jack as funny. "Lighten up! This is a limo. You are supposed to be able to relax in a limo. If they didn't want us to have a drink they would have sent a bus or a truck. You really should have a drink and lighten up."

"I'll lighten up when we get Robert," Vance said. "Until then I want you on your best behavior, Jack. We need the Church's cooperation."

"The way I see it, they need me much more than I need them. If Robert summons a million ghoul army, there aren't enough priests in the world to deal with it and who are they going to call? Me. And who is going to have to put his life on the line? Me."

Vance waited until Jack's diatribe was over before he asked: "And what will happen if you start acting like a prima donna and offend the Pope? Robert will take advantage of our division and kill untold thousands. So to keep that from happening, you are going to be on your best behavior. You will call any cardinal you meet *your eminence*, bishops will be *your excellency* and if we do meet the Pope you will kneel and you will kiss his ring if he offers it, and you will refer to him as *your holiness*. Got it?"

"I've got it," Jack said, as he made himself another drink and then polished it off in a single long pull.

By the time they drove up to the gates of Vatican City, Cyn was ready for a second drink as well, only there wasn't time. The roads had been cleared for them and they whooshed along, crossing a bridge, heading for St. Peter's Basilica, its great dome easily visible, dominating the skyline.

Although it was still early afternoon and thus prime time for tourists and the faithful who make pilgrimages from all over the world, St. Peter's Square, the tremendous open area just before the basilica, was completely empty save for a few clergymen going quickly about their business. As they entered the square, the lead and trail limos peeled away leaving their limo alone as they pulled right up to the front steps where a cadre of men, sweating in their heavy garb, greeted them.

"Ciao!" a man in a red cassock said. Though he spoke the word with enthusiasm, his eyes were sharp on Jack's face and he seemed as edgy as a cat. "My name es Tarisio Onisto, Cardinal-priest of Santi Simone." He paused, giving them a chance to bow at the waist, which they did, though somewhat stiffly. He then added: "I am Secretary of the State of The Vatican. I give you welcome. Let me introduce his Eminence, Cardinal…"

He went on to name the other seven men in the delegation, all of whom possessed long Italian names and even longer titles. Cyn was quite lost after the second name and by the time the last man was introduced, she had already forgotten the Secretary of State's name and was glad she could get away with just calling him *your eminence*.

They bowed to each man as they were introduced, but no hands were shaken and no rings kissed. The situation felt awkward and forced and it didn't help that after being introduced, each of the dignitaries would smile perfunctorily and then take their turn giving Jack a closer look, usually through half-lidded and suspicious eyes.

Jack did not bear the scrutiny well. His bows grew briefer with each person introduced, so that the last man: Pietro Cesarini, the arch-priest of the basilica received only a nod, a slight dipping of his head.

"This way," Cardinal Onisto said, holding a hand out, suggesting that Cyn and Jack walk beside him up the stairs. "His Holiness, Pope Romanus the Second, is waiting inside. He understands that time may be an issue and so he has gone for the spear, personally. You should be honored at his attention."

Captain Vance was quick to agree that they were. Cyn nodded along; however, her mind was mostly taken up by the basilica. She was in awe and gaped like a tourist, her eyes darting everywhere. The building was massive, over two football fields in length, supported by tremendous columns that stretched up to the ceiling, which was hundreds of feet over their heads. Cyn felt altogether tiny, as if she was nothing more than an ant.

Jack let out a low whistle of appreciation as he spun around in a slow circle, not once but three times. There was so much to see that it would take a person years to take in every wonderful detail.

"This is some cathedral," he said. "It makes St Patrick's Cathedral back in New York look like a shack."

"And yet, this is not a cathedral," Cardinal Onisto explained. "It is but a church. It is not the seat of the Diocese of Rome, that distinction goes to the Arch-basilica of St John Lateran. But yes, this is very nice as well, grazie."

They walked through the empty building, the ceiling and walls too far away for their steps to echo back to them. It wasn't until they entered a staircase going down that the concept of proportion came back into being, and yet the stairs were as grand as everything else. Rails of finely worked brass, marble steps, pictures and paintings and carved reliefs everywhere.

They went down two levels where the ceilings were actually a bit lower than expected, just a few inches over Jack's head. Here they found more of the Swiss guards standing with their machine guns at the ready. They were guarding a room of red. Everything was red, from the carpet to the plush velvet curtains hanging on every wall.

His Holiness, Pope Romanus, dressed as usual in sharp white, stood out, strangely, almost as if there was a glow about him and Cyn couldn't be sure that there wasn't one. He was young for a Pope, not quite sixty, and was hardy and virile. He was tall and thick through the shoulders. They called him the "Fighting Pope" however he seemed extremely gentle to Cyn.

She was still staring when Captain Vance went to one knee. Quickly, she followed his lead, while Jack was very slow to assume the subservient position.

"Can you please leave us, Tarisio?" the Pope asked, his English enhanced by a light Italian accent. The cardinal bowed and shut the door, leaving the four of them alone.

The Pope went first to Vance and put out his hand. The captain wasted no time and kissed the ring, crushing it to his lips. The Pope then touched his head and said: "You are a good man. Fear not for the future because the Lord sees your works and is pleased."

"Th-thank you," Vance stuttered.

Next the Pope came to Cyn and stood over her in silence for some time, so long that she grew afraid and couldn't lift her eyes from the floor. "I would like to hear your confession," he finally said.

"Now?" Cyn asked. She was quite suddenly terrified, fearing that she was being put to some kind of test and was failing before she had been given a chance.

"Yes, now. When was your last confession?"

Cyn honestly couldn't remember, but that was mostly because she was having trouble figuring out what day it was. Ever since Akron, her life had been a hectic swirl of battle, exhaustion, and plane rides to distant countries. "A week, I think."

Next to her, Jack gave her a look of frank surprise. "I used to have Father Timmons as my confessor," she explained feeling strangely guilty as if confession was a sin itself.

"Ahh, Father Timmons, the martyr," the Pope said. "He guided you well, Cynthia. Now, for this brief time, it will be my turn. Begin your confession, if you can."

If you can? That sounded like a challenge and one that the Pope didn't think she would be able to accomplish. From his kneeling position, Jack put a hand on the floor—he was about to stand and when he did, Cyn knew things would get ugly.

Quickly she began, starting by crossing herself. "Bless me Father for I have sinned. It has been, uh, about a week since my last confession. And I…I…" She suddenly drew a blank. What were her sins? For some reason she was drawing a blank. Embarrassed and horrified she started to stutter: "I…I…I…"

Nothing would come. She put the Ten Commandments in the forefront of her mind as a guide and went down the list—and still couldn't think of anything she had done in the last week that constituted a sin. The closest she had come was when she had *nearly* given in to the Mother's temptations. But in the end she hadn't. That wasn't really a sin as far as she knew.

The Pope waited, expectantly and she blurted out: "I'm sorry, but I don't remember my sins just now but whatever I did, I am sorry."

"Do not be sorry for acts uncommitted," Romanus chastised gently. "Perhaps you could tell me what you confessed to Father Timmons?" Her mouth came open and hung there as she remembered that she hadn't been able to come up with a sin then either. Her look made the Pope smile as he explained: "This is why *She* wants you so very badly. *She* knows your innocence and your goodness and *She* is very jealous."

Cyn knew immediately that he was referring to the Mother of Demons. "Who is she? She was human once, right?"

"Oh, yes," the Pope said, suddenly sounding old. "She was human once with all the failings of our race. *She* was tempted and, unlike you, Cynthia, she gave in to her hunger for power and unearned knowledge. And it destroyed her."

Jack had been on one knee with an arm across it, looking as though he was about to be knighted, but now he leaned back with a look of astonishment on his face. "You…you're not saying that the Mother of Demons is Eve. *The* Eve, from the Bible?"

"That is exactly what I'm saying," Romanus answered. "She was the original temptress, the original sinner, the original liar and the original thief. She stole from the Tree of Knowledge and, seeing as she is immortal, we can assume the Tree of Life as well."

"Tree of what?" Jack asked. "Wasn't there just the one tree in the Garden?"

Romanus gazed sternly down at Jack. "And you call yourself a scientist? You are full of doubt, Jack Dreyden and yet you do so little research. There are two forbidden trees in the Garden and she stole from both. Adam's death is recorded, as is Cain's and Abel's and Noah and everyone, except Eve. She never died."

Cyn caught something in the way he had said *original sinner*. "If the Mother of Demons is the actual Eve, does that mean humans are demons?"

He didn't hesitate or sugarcoat his words: "Yes. The Lord our Father created Adam in his likeness and created Eve from Adam. After that it was Eve who took to creating. Adam called her the Mother of the Living and the Lord never created another thing until he came to Mary in the form of an angel. Our original sin has nothing to do with the apple and the tree. It's simply the sin of being born. It's the sin of being created without the hand of God involved."

"But that's not fair," Cyn said.

"Fortunately for us, ours is a loving God and a forgiving one. His goodness is beyond question. Now, time feels to be spinning quick. I am anxious in my heart and fear we will all be tested soon in ways where right and wrong will be turned on their heads. For now, you are blameless, Cynthia Childs, I pray that you remain so." He held his right hand out to her and she kissed the famous *Ring of the Fisherman*.

Romanus then came to stand before Jack. He did not offer his ring to be kissed and nor did he touch Jack, he only sighed in sadness. "You carry the mark of the Mother in your soul."

"I do," Jack answered, simply.

"Do you understand that the mark was always meant for you? The Mother is a sly deceiver. You have been tempted by her in the past whether you knew it or not, and you were victorious. She then tempted Cynthia and when that did not work either, she forced the mark on her, knowing that you would take it to keep your love pure. *She is hungry for your soul, Jack Dreyden. You are important to her. Do not give in. Remember: For what is a man profited if he shall gain the whole world and lose his own soul?"*

"Well, that's the problem, isn't it?" Jack asked. "It's my soul that's going to be the death of me." He meant it as a joke, but no one laughed, and his own smile was short lived. After a moment, he jutted his chin at the open glass case just behind the Pope. "Is that the spear?" Romanus nodded solemnly. Just looking at it, Jack knew. "It's a fake, isn't it?"

Romanus nodded again. "I am tempted to put it up for sale on Ebay or sell it at the next Vatican garage sale," he said with a little grin.

"But you want to use it as bait, don't you?" Jack asked, grinning right back. When the Pope nodded a third time, Jack said: "I was hoping you were going to say that."

Chapter 30
Rome, Italy
Jack Dreyden

The meeting with the Pope went well right up to that point. After that the two began to butt heads over everything. For starters, Romanus absolutely refused to allow Jack access to the city's cemeteries and catacombs. They went back and forth, each growing hot under the collar.

Cyn had to pull Jack away at one point. "You do realize that's his Holiness the Pope! You don't poke the Pope in the chest. It's just not done."

"You do when he's not listening to reason. Did you hear him?"

She shrugged. "Yes, I did hear him. If you ask me, his plan is sensible and has a good chance of working."

The Pope's plan was to fortify each of the fourteen moderate to large cemeteries that were within a thirty mile radius of the Vatican, stationing two companies of Italian infantry and a score of priests at each. In addition to these forces, CaptainVance had offered the tattered remnants of the *Raider* squads and the Army *Knights*.

With the idea of luring Robert into a trap, Romanus was also secretly gathering as many priests, bishops and cardinals as he could and hiding them within the cavernous halls of the basilica. By sunset, he expected to have at least five hundred clergymen. In addition, he was bussing in another five hundred Swiss guards who were coming in dressed as tourists.

"Tell me how denying Robert access to the cemeteries is a bad thing," Cyn asked. "It will surely mute whatever attack he's planning."

"Yes, he's on the right track. I just think it makes sense to prepare helicopter landing sites at each just in case I need to raise my own army in a hurry. What's wrong with that?"

She rolled her eyes. "To start with, it's against his religion and my religion too, mind you, to desecrate the dead in such a way. I understand the necessity, but he doesn't see any difference between what you do and witchcraft which is expressly forbidden in the Bible. And so your other idea of secretly stockpiling bodies here in the basilica is doubly wrong in his eyes."

"Vance," Jack said, dragging the captain into the argument. "Can you please tell the Pope what a contingency plan is."

"No," was all he said and then went back to coordinating where the supplementary American forces would be placed.

Cyn laughed at the soldier's quick response. The laugh was genuine and full. She wasn't laughing to hurt Jack, she seemed strangely giddy. "Come on, Jack, don't be stubborn. It's a good plan. So good that maybe you won't be needed, which I think is wonderful. I never thought it was possible, but can you imagine, finally sitting out a battle?"

Frankly, he couldn't. It might have been ego, but Jack was sure they were going to need him before all was said and done. Robert was just too slick to be caught in a trap and if he was caught, Jack feared that he was too powerful to be held for long.

At Cyn's urging, he did his best to keep out of the way of the preparations for the battle and he steered clear of the Pope, who seemed to be everywhere, overseeing every detail of his meticulous plan.

Jack tried to nap and he tried to relish the first rate food that was served to him by a friendly priest, who kept saying: "Es good, ay?" And he tried to tell himself that the Pope was a singularly capable man, but at the same time he could feel the coming storm just as the Pope could. Strangely, it built up but didn't explode. At about five that afternoon, the urgency plateaued, neither increasing or decreasing. It was odd which only added to his nervousness. He was on pins and needled and took to pacing in the low-ceilinged room that held the fake Lance of Longinus, striding back and forth in front of it.

After an hour of the pacing, Cyn fell asleep against the wall. With her belly full of carbonara and her cares lightened for the first time in a year, she was able to close her eyes and was soon breathing steadily. Jack watched her as she slept. He ignored the shotgun at her side and the black armor and simply concentrated on her face. Without the worry weighing her down, she appeared younger than when he had first met her.

She was so captivatingly beautiful that for a time he could ignore the oppressive sensation of doom hanging in the air. He wanted to kiss her and tuck her in and be a real boyfriend and live a normal life with her. He daydreamed about it for an hour and then the sun went down and the heavy feeling on his heart grew.

He got up to pace again and was in mid-pivot when the Pope entered the room, causing him to freeze. The older man carried a sheathed sword in one hand. They gazed at each other for a few moments and then Jack began pacing again.

"I feel the same way," Romanus said in his light accent. "The waiting is always the worst part."

It's not the hot blood covering you from head to toe, going tacky, making your shirt stick to your skin? Jack wanted to ask. *It's not the hacked up bodies and the smell of decomp?* "There are worse things."

"And you have seen them, no doubt," Romanus stated, not mentioning the fact that Jack had not knelt or used any of the customary honorifics in his presence. Fighting Pope or not, Romanus had yet to be tested in a true knockdown drag-out fight. He had a mass of power; it radiated off him in waves, and yet, until he was tested, Jack would view him as an equal, and that was for his own good.

When someone amassed so much power that people were afraid to contradict him or point out his flaws, it invariably led to trouble.

"I've seen too much," Jack allowed and began pacing once more. "So, have you come for some pointers on how to fight the beasts?" he asked gesturing to the sword.

Romanus found this amusing and smiled easily. "I do not need a lesson in demons, thank you. I have been studying them and you for the last year and a half." Once more Jack was brought up short, making the Pope's smile that much wider. "That surprises you I see. It might surprise you even more that I received daily communiques from every priest who has ever worked with you. Father Timmons thought highly of you. He found you to be a wonderful human being."

Jack had trouble believing that about Timmons, especially after all the scorn and abuse Jack had heaped upon him. "He must have been more forgiving than I gave him credit for."

"He was," the Pope agreed, a shadow of sadness passing across his face. He opened his mouth to say more, but just then Captain Vance, armed for battle came into the room. He stopped at the sight of the Pope and immediately dropped to one knee.

"Stand good Captain," Romanus said. "And let the soldiers know that until the battle is won, no one will genuflect in my presence. Fighting men fight best on their feet. Would you agree, Captain?"

"Yes, I would, your Holiness." He stood and then gave a half bow to the Pope. After a few seconds of silence, Vance turned to Jack and said: "I'm, uh leaving. I'm heading up a new squad of *Raiders*. We're going to be stationed over at a place called the Catacombs of Domitilla. I can't say I'm all that excited about a subterranean assignment. That place is creepy beyond anywhere I've ever been."

"Do not be afraid," Romanus told him. "You go with the Lord's blessing." The Pope had a silver flask tied on a white cord about his middle; he unstoppered it, filling the room with a sweet scent of flowers. First dabbing his fingers to the top of the flask, he drew a cross across Vance's forehead. He then went to where Cyn was sleeping and, with one finger drew the cross on her head as well.

Cyn blinked up at him and then smiled. "Thank you," she said.

"You are more than welcome, child of God." He then turned to Jack, but as he did, he put the stopper back in the flask and hid it back beneath his cassock. "I rather fear that with the evil you carry about inside of you, a blessing might very well become a curse, tainting both of us. And yet I could not let you go into battle without a gift from the Lord's servant."

He held out the sheathed sword. Jack took it with some reverence. It was old, very old; it's age seemed to radiate up from the hilt and into his palm. It was old, and yet the workmanship had never been bettered. Jack withdrew the blade part way and was shocked at how brilliant the metal was; it shone beyond what was physically possible. "What sword is this?"

Romanus reached out and touched the blade before saying: "The Vatican is filled with an amazing number of treasures and relics, and not all of them are strictly ordinary like the spearhead. This sword is called Almacia and at one time belonged to Tilipinus, the Bishop of Reims. It's the brother of the sword Durendal, the sword of the paladin, Roland."

"Roland? From the Song of Roland? That Roland?" Jack asked, pulling the sword completely out of its sheath. It was marvelously light and supple, and its balance was unlike anything he had ever held.

"Yes," Romanus answered. "It's said that this blade is unbreakable and that its edge will never blunt. I don't know if any of that is actually true, but I do know there is something, I don't know if it's correct for a Pope to say this, but there's something *magical* about the blade. I give it to you, Jack because I want you to use it. Put aside your sorcery. Father Timmons once wrote that you are a marvelous swordsman. For the sake of your soul, use the talents God has given you and trust in Him that they will be enough."

He left them and, for a while, the three stood staring at the sword, until Vance asked: "So where's your battle station?"

"Whereever the fighting is thickest, I guess," Jack said, sheathing the sword.

"And what about raising an undead army?" Vance asked. "As much as I like a Pope in armor, it may still be necessary."

The sword in his hand felt like it was almost begging to be used in battle. "I will do what is needed," Jack answered. "But first, I will give his Holiness every opportunity to win the battle his way."

"Seems fair." Captain Vance nodded and then looked around awkwardly for a moment. "I have to get going. Take care of yourself, Prima donna and take care of Cyn, too." He put out a hand, which Jack shook. Cyn hugged him and then punched him in the chest, her fist *thokking* off his armor.

"I can take care of myself, thank you," she declared wearing her impish smile. He agreed that she could and then with a last sad nod, left them.

The waiting had been bad before; now, it was a trial. The certainty of battle built up in the air and soon Cyn became antsy because she was weaponless. They went in search of the Pope; however, he was in a meeting of cardinals and so they asked the highest ranking Swiss Guard if they could find her a shotgun. He didn't blink an eye that such a small woman could handle such a monster of a gun and in minutes one was fetched.

Then came more waiting. Jack and Cyn hovered close to the communications room, listening to the reports come in. There were three-thousand infantry men and hundreds of priests in place, ready to spring into action at the first sign that Robert was about to open a gate into hell. Twice there were false alarms and Jack was not reassured listening to the near panic in the voices coming over the radio as army units and untested priests rushed to the different scenes.

It was fitting that the first real sign that Robert was finally making his move came exactly at the stroke of midnight.

Jack was lounging on a five-hundred year old baroque couch, with Cyn cuddled to his chest when he *felt* the first word of the spell. They both sat up and stared at each other, their breath held, pent up in their chests, all their senses at full alert as if it were possible to hear Robert's actual words.

But there was no way that was possible, not at that distance. When Robert spoke the second word of the spell, Jack leapt up and ran, sprinting through the cavernous great hall of the basilica. He ran out into the dark and stood panting on the steps. Now, he shut down his physical senses. His eyes and ears were useless. Robert was far, far away, just at the very edge of his ability to sense the necromancy in action.

Next to him, Cyn was on one knee, her eyes at slits as she too, tried to pinpoint the direction and the range. They were like statues.

"What is it?" a bishop asked, breathlessly. He had followed them out of the building at a run and was holding his chest with one hand as he gasped for air. "Can you sense your cousin? Where is he? Is he in Rome?"

"No," Jack answered, his voice only a ghost of a whisper. "He's south, far to the south and he's waking the dead."

Chapter 31
Naples, Italy
Jack Dreyden

"I need a helicopter!" Jack practically yelled, grabbing the bishop's cassock in both hands. When the old man started to sputter something in a mix of Italian and English, Jack let him go and sprinted back inside the basilica, running into the Pope and his entourage almost directly beneath the great domed ceiling four hundred feet above their heads.

Jack stopped, bowed quickly and then blurted: "It's Robert! He's opening the gate right now. I need a helicopter right this second!"

"Yes," Romanus agreed, nodding gently. "I can feel him to the south, but how far?"

"I'm not sure," Jack answered and then turned to Cyn who had followed him back inside. "What do you think? Forty miles?"

She shrugged a single shoulder and said: "I can give direction, but not an exact distance, but if I had to guess, it is closer to fifty. The signal is very faint."

"That's why I need a helicopter," Jack said to the Pope. "I'll be able to home in on Robert's location very quickly. You have to trust me on this, it'll be the fastest way to figure out where he is." *And*, Jack didn't add, *it will be the fastest way for me to raise my own counter-army and stop Robert in his tracks*. If Jack were lucky, there was a good chance that he would be able to trap his cousin at the scene of his latest crime.

Romanus seemed to guess Jack's mind; he turned to one of the younger priests. "Get a helicopter here as fast as you can and prepare Father Bradley's team."

The priest stepped aside and began speaking Italian into a cell phone, the words rapid-firing from his mouth, running together so that it was hard to tell if there were individual sentences in what he was saying or just one long one.

"Who's Father Bradley?" Jack asked. "Is he with one of the *Raiders*?"

The Pope held up a finger and then turned to another of his assistants and spoke in Italian, gesturing excitedly as he did. When he was done, he explained: "Father Bradley is not part of one your teams. He is extremely sensitive to the nature of Robert's type of spell work. You might say that he has a nose for necromancy."

"That's good, but I would prefer a priest with some fighting experience to come with me."

"You will not be going with the first helicopter," Romanus said. "Bradley's team will scout out where Robert is and report back. You will take a later flight. Before you argue, we have twenty-six helicopters fully fueled and ready to go, as well as numerous transport trucks. Depending on where this is occurring, we can have our entire force moved in four hours."

"And I can have this fight wrapped up in one," Jack shot back, his voice growing loud enough to set off a stir of echoes floating above their heads. Cyn gave him a sharp elbow and he quickly added: "Your Holiness."

In answer, Romanus murmured something in Italian and before Jack knew it, two of the Swiss Guards that had been hovering nearby were gently pushing him and Cyn away. "You will wait over here for the Holy Father," one of the guards said. His voice was soft and the push with his free hand gentle, but his eyes were wary and hard, and his finger steady on the trigger of his Steyr TMP machine pistol; which was the Austrian equivalent of an Uzi.

"Fine," Jack hissed. "Just watch it with that gun. You don't want to aim it anywhere near me if you know what's good for you." It was all bluff. Yes, he was a powerful sorcerer, however, bullets could still kill him quite easily.

"It'll work out," Cyn said as they were escorted out into St. Peter's Square. "You'll see. His Holiness knows what's at stake here and he's very decisive and…"

"And he's keeping his best chance to nip this in the bud sitting on the bench," Jack said, interrupting. "We have a real shot at ending this, Cyn! It'll take time for Robert to dig up whatever he's after. I could be there in thirty minutes and have an army ready to go twenty minutes after that. Think about it."

"Think about what? You said you were going to give him a chance." That was true, but now that the final battle was in motion, he was regretting saying such a thing. There was too much on the line. Cyn gave him a hard look and asked: "What are you thinking about doing?"

He hunched in closer to her. "The Pope's trap has have failed and now I need to get on that helicopter." He pointed up at a dark, thrumming shadow that was coming down out of the night. It was going to land sixty yards away in the middle of St. Peter's Square. Nearby were eight men; four of the Swiss Guards and four clergymen, waiting on the descending chopper.

"No," Cyn said. "It's out of the question. They'll put up a fight and they're fanatical, Jack, and that means you'll end up killing innocent people. You could start a war with the Pope and that's not a war you can win."

A part of him wanted to put that theory to the test. Could he win in a battle with the Pope? It was the sorcerer in him. He could feel that part flare up bold and confident…and stupid. There were also two bishops standing above him on the steps, lingering when they should have been off preparing for the coming battle. And there were a dozen Swiss Guards around the square, watching, their hands stiff on their weapons. Jack could take them, he was sure. What he didn't know was if he could take them and still have the power to face his cousin.

"People are going to die because of this delay," Jack said, quietly, his anger dissipating, replaced with the sad reality. "And when he won't let me have access to the cemeteries, even more will die."

"Maybe." She wouldn't look at him. Her eyes were on the chopper as it landed heavily, bouncing on its wheels.

The eight-person team raced forward, bent at the hip. They climbed in and a second later the chopper lifted straight up and then was gone, thumping into the night. "There is every possibility that his Holiness will change his mind when confronted with reality. If not...then we will do what we have to, as always."

"As always," he agreed.

They waited on the steps, feeling the spell of Robert's take shape. Quickly, they were able to confirm that Robert wasn't raising a single being; he was going to raise another army. Cyn guessed that he was in Naples and was researching everything she could about the city, when more helicopters began to land in the square. They would come in threes, pick up thirty or so priests, bishops and cardinals and then lift off again within a minute.

The pope and his closest advisors took the first set. Jack and Cyn were not part of that group. Nor were they part of the next or the next after that. Jack was just about to become irate when he was ushered forward for the fourth set. "Where's Robert?" he asked the Swiss Guard, leading them. "Where are we putting down?"

"Naples!" the guard yelled over the sound of the blades whipping overhead. They were crammed into the helicopter with twelve others, an equal mixture of Swiss soldiers and priests. The latter were praying, their lips moving, their words drowned out by the engines.

"Find me the nearest ceme..." Jack began, speaking directly into Cyn's ear. She pointed to her phone; she had already pulled up the listings for sixteen cemeteries.

"Way ahead of you," she said with a blink of a grin. It was there and gone in the same second and her eyes were wet and quicker than normal to skitter away from his face. A part of him wanted to say comforting things and soothe her; however that would mean screaming over the engine noise. He was sure that his words would lose their impact somewhat.

Instead, he crushed her to him in an embrace that could be felt, armor or no armor. They held each other as they drew steadily south and, as they did, the wicked spell of Robert's took shape and became palpable and caused their fear to ramp up. The flight took twenty-eight minutes all told; at the sixteen minute mark, the spell was complete.

The tinny ring couldn't be heard, yet it was felt like an ugly ache deep in the bones. Around them, the priests ceased their praying and grew troubled. Cyn began wiping her hands on her pants.

Jack wasn't afraid in the least. The hilt of the sword Almacia felt alive and eager. It grew warm in his grip and when he pulled it slightly from its sheath, a bright light had him blinking. Everyone stared, their fears suddenly forgotten.

The next few minutes flew by. They could feel the evil that Robert had brought forth coming closer and closer, and then they were swooping low over a cemetery, the wheels of the chopper skimming the tops of trees. Below them, the ground was shifting and moving, seeming to undulate as the grass erupted with bony claws.

When they began to slow and they were still over the cemetery, Jack grew confused. "Where the hell are we headed?" he yelled to the closest crew member.

In answer, the man pointed straight down. Jack looked over the side of the chopper and saw a hundred thousand strong army of undead swarming from all directions. About two-hundred yards ahead, three helicopters were just taking off from a landing zone that was completely surrounded. In the center, easily visible, like a beacon, or a lighthouse on a dark night, was the Pope, standing with his left hand around a ten foot tall wooden shaft which was topped with a glowing crucifix.

Jack couldn't understand why the Pope was just standing there. Where was Robert? Why weren't they battling it out? Had Robert escaped, and if so, why were they preparing to land in the middle of a storm of undead?

There was no time for answers. In seconds, the helicopter whomped down with a jarring force. "Stay close!" Jack thundered to Cyn and then leapt out, the sword, Almacia in his hand, blazing a blue-white with the intensity of an arc-welder's torch.

The Pope had chosen a small hill on which to make his stand. Around him were the first nine helicopter loads of clergymen and Swiss soldiers, fighting sword and shield against tooth and nail, fire and ice, shadow and fear. They were desperately battling to hold the perimeter open so that more and more helicopters could land.

It was not a perfect circle they fought in, by any means. In five places it was being stove in, if not outright breached. Jack ran to one of the gaps in the line where the growing darkness was deepest.

As expected, a demon of great strength was contending with a bishop. The battle between the creature of shadow and bone and the man of flesh and light was even, at least spiritually. Physically, the near indestructible demon held a significant advantage over the old man who was being forced backwards, step by step. The demon raked with his claws as ghouls bit at the bishop's ankles.

Jack sped right for the demon and the light of his coming caused the ghouls to flee and the demon to hesitate, his red eyes fixated on the sword. Jack did not strike the beast down; he did not have to. The bishop took full advantage of his opponent's inattention and drove his sword into the thing's chest. There was a blast of light and it came apart, like a house of cards. Loose, wet flesh shed like moldy autumn leaves and its bones crumbled in on each other to form a pile of sickening refuse.

Wisely, the bishop dropped to one knee, pulled out a flask of Holy Water from beneath his robes and splashed the bones, which had begun to quiver, almost at once. He knew that they would soon slide back in toward each other and the demon would be whole once more in a matter of minutes.

The bishop couldn't allow it. He crossed himself and declared in a loud voice: "Exorcizo te, omnis spiritus immunde, in nomine Dei Patris omnipotentis, et in noimine Jesu Christi Filii ejus, Domini et Judicis nostri…"

A long wretched scream erupted from the bones as the demon was slowly driven out of the corpse. There were more screams just like it, happening here and there around the perimeter; however, there were other screams as well; human screams. For every ten of the rotting bodies that were brought down, a soldier or a priest was killed.

It was a ratio that couldn't be maintained.

There were just too many ghouls and too many demons crawling over each other in endless waves and even with the helicopters coming one after another, it was only a matter of time before they were overrun.

By himself, Jack bought them precious minutes. He threw himself into the heart of the horde, whirling his magic blade like a scythe, cutting down creatures as if he were the reaper of demon souls. It was a world of darkness and ice and fear. The dead were everywhere, deep ranks of them.

He drove through them, their magical fear washing off of him, their darkness no match for the shining blade, their icy breath, easily dodged by slowing time. He dodged and danced and slew, and all the time he kept his head up, searching for his cousin. Like a whirlwind of terror, he fought, but he could not fight the entire horde. He couldn't fight even a fraction of it and he couldn't go too deep into its terrible mass.

Behind him, shotgun blasts let him know that Cyn was guarding his back. He had fought knowing she would be there. What he hadn't expected was the thirty or so others who had charged into the darkness after him. They hadn't been able to keep up and now they were trapped; a knot of clergymen and soldiers, brave but foolish.

Jack stopped in his tracks, while next to him Cyn hucked air in and out as she reloaded her shotgun. "What are they doing here?" she asked.

"The better question is: what are we all doing here?" Jack wondered. "We couldn't have picked a worse spot to land in."

Cyn didn't have an answer. She topped off her load, nodded to Jack and said: "I'm good."

He led them through the horde back the way they came until they joined the lone group fighting for their lives. It was a desperate and futile battle. Many, if not all of them, were bound to die as a result of their impetuous charge. They were too far from their lines and facing a thousand-to-one odds. It was a mad fight, one that they were quickly losing.

Jack did what he could, but he had to conserve his strength; and he couldn't risk sacrificing his life or Cyn's for a doomed cause. He fought his way back into the middle of the knot, where he found a man he recognized: Tarisio Onisto, Cardinal-priest of Santi Simone. His olive-skinned face was haggard and pale; his blessed sword was covered in black ichor and notched up and down its length.

"I fear that I have failed his holiness," the cardinal said, grabbing Jack's hand and pulling him close. "It seems that I will be a shepherd no more. Guide them back. Keep them safe."

"What do you mean?"

The cardinal only smiled and then raised a hand to the heavens saying: "I am the Lord's wrath. I am the Lord's holy wrath. I am the Lord's life-giving light." His smile began to falter and his jaw twitched. "I would turn away, Mister Jack and do not look."

That was an impossible request. The cardinal's eyes were glowing as if there were a spotlight burning in his head, and there was a glow coming from his mouth that was white and hot and blinding.

Jack was still staring when, out of the blue, Cyn tackled him, knocking him to the ground and covering his face with her body. Even with her on him, he could feel the light of the Lord burn as it blasted out of the cardinal.

The dead withered in a vast circle. A thousand of them turned to ash—and so did Cardinal Onisto. His skin became a fine, white powder that blew away to the south and then his bones went next, just so much dust. In seconds, his vestments crumpled to the ground, empty.

Cyn crawled off of Jack as soon as the cardinal was no more. He had blasted the dead in a great circle and those not destroyed were cowering with their hands across their faces. The soldiers and clergymen wept, some going to their knees and crossing themselves.

Some glanced at Jack; when the cardinal's light was burning the night, only he had screamed in pain and only he had clawed at his armor as if it had been on fire. The moment Cyn stood, Jack scrambled to his feet and looked back at where he had been sprawled on the ground, fully expecting to see scorch marks and he did.

There was a circle of black burned into the ground, a circle of glyphs. For a happy moment he thought that the Mother's evil gift had been burned out of him, but it was a short-lived moment. The spell was still there as evil as always. The scorch marks were only God's reminder that he was carrying the blackest sin around in him.

As if I need the reminder, he thought, unhappily and then yelled: "Back to the lines! Form a square. Fighters on the outside, clergy on the inside. We fight as a team and we will live as a team."

It was Cyn who actually led them back to the lines. She was safer in front. The greatest danger came from behind as the living corpses came on, snapping at their heels. They learned to fear not just the Holy sword but also Jack's avenging fury. The cardinal's death weighed heavily on his conscience. It had only been a minute earlier that Jack had been unable to sacrifice himself because he was "too important."

Now, he felt as though he was just another sword. He had been humbled by the cardinal's ultimate sacrifice.

They made it back to the lines, which had swollen to three hundred men—three hundred dead men in Jack's eyes. They were all very powerful in their own right and yet the way of evil was too easy. Robert took his power at the edge of a knife, and it came as easily as drawing that red line in the flesh. These men had to fight and bleed and cry, and sometimes they had to give their very souls just keep back the evil for a brief time.

There were helicopters overhead and there were dead men among the living, sprawled in poses of greatest anguish. The venture was futile. The Pope had made a tremendous mistake coming here and in Jack's opinion, the only thing left to do was to retreat. They had to stop bringing in more men and start getting those that were here out. It would mean men left behind. It would mean a last few sacrificing themselves for the rest.

The Pope didn't see it that way. His Holiness came rushing up as soon as they reentered the lines. "Did you see Robert out there? He was right there when we landed." He pointed to a lone body that was so much different than the others. This one had been opened up with a delicate and horrible touch. There were two circles of glyphs painted next to it.

Jack stared, forgetting himself. "No. He was here? Which way did he go when you showed up?"

Romanus pointed nearly do west. For a moment, Jack wanted to head in that direction and leave the horde in the hands of the Pope and his small force, but then he remembered the sacrifice of Cardinal Onisto.

"We need to evacuate these men," he said. "You need to stop landing men and begin saving the ones you have."

"At what cost?" Romanus asked.

Jack thought he understood the question. "At the cost of a few who will hold the LZ open for the rest to escape."

"You are short sighted in this. The cost is greater than a few men left to die. What of the thousands or millions that the demon horde will devour when we flee? Or do you still plan on raising more evil to combat the evil in front of us. Evil begets evil, Jack."

"Or I'm fighting fire with fire," Jack countered.

Romanus smiled, showing old world teeth, dark and crooked, but friendly. "I value your soul above all others, Jack Dreyden. A thousand men could die here today, but if I lose one soul then I have failed. Do you understand? Cardinal Onisto only died, nothing more. We will stick to the plan and bring in more men. We will dig in and allow our enemies to wreck themselves against the wall we create."

"And if we all die?" Jack asked.

"Then we all die," the Pope answered simply.

Too simply for Jack's tastes. While they fought and died, Robert would get away and then who would be left to fight his next horde? A few ragged survivors? This was the flower of the priesthood that was being sacrificed on the altar of good intentions.

Jack couldn't allow that to happen. "I'm not going to stay and watch the slaughter. My fight is with Robert. Your fight is with common sense."

"I'm sorry you feel this way," Romanus said. "You are free to come and go as you please, but you should know that if you leave it will lower moral. We need you, Jack."

"And I need to fight a fight I can win."

Chapter 32
Naples, Italy
Jack Dreyden

"Find me the closest cemetery to this one," Jack whispered to Cyn as he strode away from the Pope. "I'm going to save him even if he doesn't want to be saved."

The perimeter had shrunk so much that only one chopper could land at a time and it was so small that there was no way the pair could get on a helicopter as it was about to leave and not be noticed.

Men stared; they began to whisper and point. They were calling him a coward, Jack was sure and, just like the Pope, they wouldn't be happy in the manner in which he was going to save them. That was too bad.

Cyn and Jack jumped on board the first helicopter to land. Cyn went to the cockpit and yelled: "Fontanelli cemetery. We have to go here." She pointed at her phone's screen.

The pilot shook his head. "No. To Vatican. We pick up…uh, a soldiers. And a papas."

"No priests," Jack said. "Fontanelli, first. Do understand? Drop us off and then you can go to the Vatican. Capiche?"

After a moment, as the pilot assessed Jack and his gleaming sword, he answered with a single word: "Capisco." He then pointed for Jack and Cyn to go back to the cargo area. When they were seated, the helicopter jerked upwards at a slant, nearly spilling Cyn off the side.

Jack caught her and held her tight as they flew over the battlefield. It was frightful sight seeing the hundreds of thousands of dead swarming toward the little hill. In the distance were a scattering of blinking lights; helicopters heading in. They were so few in number that he found it sad.

"How can Romanus think he can win this?" Jack murmured. "Maybe he could if he had all four thousand of his men right here, right now. Even then the casualties would be outrageous."

"He has faith," Cyn answered. She had her legs dangling two hundred feet above the army of undead. She leaned back into Jack, showing that she had faith in him to keep her safe. So far he had kept her safe and yet, he was the first to admit that so far he had been lucky.

The chopper cleared the boundary of the cemetery and for some reason did not go higher. It remained at two-hundred feet for a few minutes heading northwest over the city of Naples, and then it started circling slowly, a searchlight beaming down on a church perched on the side of a steep hill. There wasn't a cemetery in sight.

"What's he doing?" Jack yelled to one of the crew members. "We need to go to Fontanelli!"

"Si, Fontanelli," the man yelled back, pointing down at the church. "Fontanelli." There was no room to land and so the pilot swept the chopper east two blocks and set down on a soccer field.

At first Jack refused to leave the chopper. Why strand himself in the middle of Naples when he needed to get to a cemetery? Then Cyn said: "It's underground. Like the catacombs, ok?"

Jack felt he was a relatively brave man and yet the idea of going down into the earth to raise the dead gave him a case of the willies. Of course that wasn't something he could let show, especially since Cyn appeared altogether confident.

"Well, that's different," he said, stepping down onto the deep, green grass. With a wave to the pilot, they hurried out from beneath the spinning blades and toward the hill dominating this part of the city. It was struck in gloom and altogether quiet, which was very much in contrast to the rest of the city.

It was one in the morning and yet the city was alive, not with gunshots or screams, but with car horns and the slap of running feet. The city was being evacuated. Every street was filled with people and cars, every street except the one heading to Fontanelli. People moved away from it, casting nervous glances up at the hill; many of them crossed themselves and a few spat on the ground in its direction.

"That's not so comforting," Jack said with a little laugh.

"Just superstitious people," Cyn replied. "Lucky for us, if there were demons in there, we'd know." Jack laughed again, this time at himself. Cyn didn't seem to notice. She was staring down at her phone as she walked. "Wow. There may be four million corpses in there. The cholera epidemic and the plague are said to have filled the caves with corpses. Mostly indigent paupers who couldn't afford a real grave. Four million…they must be bloody deep caves."

They were. They found the main entrance unguarded but locked. After a quick opening spell, the two slipped down into the dark—there were no light switches and Jack was forced to use a touch more of his power as he blew on a handful of dust filling the immense caverns with glowing particles of light. There were many caverns carved into the hill and a tremendous number of bones, all of which were stacked in rows, set out as if on display.

And what a sickening display. Skulls were stacked in great piles; sometimes shaped in pyramids and others in towers that went to the ceiling of the caverns fifty feet over their heads. Sometimes they were just ill-shaped mounds. Frequently the stacks of skulls were set on a lattice of smaller bones. There seemed to be a great number of femurs and arm bones, but few ribs and fewer hand bones.

"Will this even work?" Cyn asked as she knelt down to inspect the closest pile. "I can't tell if there's a full skeleton in any of this."

"Let's hope so," Jack answered. "Do you have any idea which way north is?" She didn't and they had to go back outside and orient on the North Star to get their bearings. Once they did, Jack began the first spell with a slice of his wrist. The blood came out of him in the exact number of drops needed to form the twin spells—the glyphs were perfect, their edges exact.

"That was...that was way too easy," Jack said. "*She* wants me to do this. I can feel her eagerness."

"And look at the glyphs," Cyn said, pointing with one hand and clutching her shotgun to her chest with the other. "Are they pulsing or is that a trick of the light?" They both knelt down to look at the glyphs from the side and they did seem to move and swell slightly. "Maybe we shouldn't do this," she said.

Jack reached out and touched the nearest glyph; it was his blood and yet it felt foreign. Standing up, he went around the twin circles, silently mouthing the words he had written. "It's the usual spell, there's nothing different about the wording. It should work like it always does."

"But what if the Mother has set a trap in the..."

He stopped her with a raised hand. "Then we deal with it. If we want to save Romanus, then we do this here and now. Our only other choice is for you to do the spell."

"You know I can't do it," she said, stepping back. "You know that I won't."

"Then we do this and we fight the Mother. We've done it before."

Cyn reluctantly agreed and they moved to the furthest cavern in the eastern part of the underground complex and repeated the spell with a new cut. The blood ran even faster now. The same was true in the southern cavern and again in the west. Jack cut the back of his left hand and the blood shot out in a painless spray.

Without any effort, the four sets of spells were complete. Now, there was only the final spell, the one that Jack would draw on his own flesh. It would link all the previous spells and would allow him to control what came through the gate.

There was only one problem; the spell was necromancy. Out of nowhere it created an unholy demand within him. It was a lust for blood and souls that he hadn't felt in a year and a half and it suddenly made him dangerous. "You should go," he said in a strangled voice. "Get out of here before…" His hand was suddenly on the hilt of his Holy sword and it was half drawn before he could stop it.

Cyn's eyes went wide when she saw the blade. "What is it? Is She in you?"

He couldn't answer her. Cyn was too close to him and he was almost overcome with the need to kill. It was so fantastic that it began to control him. He couldn't stop his eyes from going to her throat where the blood pumped just beneath the surface. He needed that blood and he needed the soul, and he would tear open her flesh with his teeth if he had to.

She saw the evil look and saw his hand struggling with his sword. "You can have my soul," she told him. "If you need a soul to open the gate, then take mine." She dropped to her knees and lifted her chin so that her throat was wide open to him. He could kill her in a flash, but just like that, he suddenly didn't want to.

"I could never," he said, speaking partly to himself and partly to her. It was a lie and it wasn't—just then it was both, but with every passing second it became the truth once again. The ugly desire for her soul was only a fading echo within him. Necromancy could only use a stolen soul, not one gifted.

"That was smart," he said, hiding his shaking hands behind his back.

"Why do you sound so surprised?" she asked. She tried to give him her trademark smirk; however, it failed after a second. "Are you going to be able to complete the spell without killing anyone?"

Before answering, he closed his eyes and explored the remains of the spell that the Mother had tricked him into accepting. There was still plenty of power wrapped up in the remaining words. "Yes, but you should still go. She's dangerous and she'll be extra dangerous with you near. She'll pit us against each other."

Although she agreed, she hesitated. "Remember that you love me."

A minute before, he had been on the verge of killing her, and yet he said: "I could never forget it." They kissed lightly. He felt anxiety in her lips and the way her breath came in a little tickle as though she was afraid to spook him by breathing normally.

She hurried from the bone-filled cavern and he wasted no time. He yanked off his armored vest and then opened the shirt beneath. With a quick breath, he cut himself once again. The blood didn't fly; it welled in the crook of his arm, looking black. Jack painted with his right index finger, drawing the glyphs on his chest.

When he was done, he spoke the words that opened the gate and there came a great metallic ringing sound and the rock within the circles turned jet black, and deep in the darkness motes of light began to race upward as the souls of the damned saw the way out of their hell. But then there was a shriek, a horrible sound that had the hair on Jack's arm lift up.

The motes backed away from the gate, as did Jack. He snatched up his vest and was desperately trying to get it on when *She* suddenly came up out of the darkness. The Mother of Demons stood within the twin circles, staring at Jack. She was young and naked. She was beautiful in a way that defied logic. She was perfect, all thirty feet of her. She was huge; her head brushed the ceiling and her arm span ran the length of the cavern.

Her flesh was white and silver; she sparkled in the gloom. Her eyes were opals and her smile diamonds. Jack found himself staring, his mouth hanging open, drool beginning to collect at the corners.

Time lost all meaning and he would have happily wasted his life away and turned into an old man staring at her if she hadn't chosen that moment to enter him. Effortlessly and without leaving the circle, she crossed over into his mind. There was a stab of pain and then there came what could laughably be called a contest of wills.

Hers was steel, while his was butter in comparison. In three seconds, he was crushed, his mind open to hers, his soul right at the surface, so vulnerable. It seemed as if she could reach out and snatch it out of his body if she wished. Her body and face was that of an angel, but what lay in her mind was absolutely horrifying. Pure terror ran throughout his body. It sapped his strength to the point that he couldn't run away as much as he wanted to, and he desperately wanted to. His legs were jelly and his heart rattled in his chest so heavily that he was sure it would seize up altogether.

"I did not call you!" he screamed, his hysterical voice reverberating off the walls and echoing throughout the cavern.

The pitiful scream was all the defiance he could muster. In his ears it was pathetic and cowardly. The scream showed just how weak he really was before her; yet she could not stand even this toddler's tantrum. Jack felt the pain of knives lance into the softest part of his stomach and then twist and turn. He fell, clutching himself, feeling his guts spill out through his fingers, feeling his hot blood pour onto the roughhewn rock floor.

But then the Mother smiled at Jack and it was as if the previous moment of terror had never happened. He sat up, trembling, sweat running into his eyes. He looked down at his stomach—the skin was unblemished. For a few crazy seconds, he sobbed with relief and felt the urge to actually thank her for not having really gutted him.

The Mother spoke: "You have done wonderfully my dear, Jonathan. I am so proud of you."

He looked up, confused. "You are?"

"Of course. Look how strong you are. Look how brave. You have come such a long way since your father's tragic death. No mother could be more proud of her son."

Jack's head swam with pride and confusion. "Thanks…but you are not my mother. My mother died and she didn't go to hell."

"Are you sure? Have you seen her in heaven? I think not. All you have is your father's word and men are such liars."

"My father is not a liar. My father was a good man."

"Sometimes good men lie. Wouldn't he want to spare you the pain of knowing that your mother came here to be with me? He would. He loves you. And I love you. I love all my children and that is wonderful and good." Her voice was like velvet and he could feel the love come off of her; however there was an underlying note to the emotion that felt false. It was as if there was a "but" mixed in with the love.

"You love me, only…what?" he asked. "Is there a condition I must meet?"

Her smile dipped at the edge and the golden glow of Jack's lights dimmed. "Of course not. I love you with all of my heart, can't you see how wonderful that is? And yet it saddens me that you do not love me. I have given you so much. Feel the power in you. That came from me and that is wonderful and good. I helped you, though you did not know it. Now, you turn from me."

"I'm not," Jack said, quickly. "I would never turn from you." He meant it. At that moment, he might have killed for the Mother if she asked.

As if hearing his thoughts, she pressed against the invisible barrier created by the first of the circles. "Yes, you are a good son and as a good son you should do as your mother tells you. Won't you free me?"

There was something behind the request, and it took Jack a moment to realize what it was. "Am I going to have to kill someone?" He had killed before. To save others, he had sacrificed three men. And to save himself from the necromancer he had committed murder, pure and simple. Metzger's face floated into his mind.

"Yes, you have killed before," the Mother said. "You have done so for selfish reasons. Now, you can do so for a noble one. You will kill to free your mother, and that is wonderful and good."

He had a sudden vision of stabbing some vague person; there was a scream and some blood and then small hands scratched at his armor and a voice begged for him to stop. The vision gave him a momentary notion of sadness, but then a new vision came to eclipse the old one. The gate to the netherworld opened and this time there wasn't an ugly black, oily patch on the ground. The gate was lit with a thousand suns. And there wasn't the rude sound of a tinny bell, there were trumpets of gold blaring, proclaiming the good news. And then *She* came out. It wasn't the Mother of Demons, but some wonderful cross between his own mother and this beautiful being before him.

"Who do I have to kill?" he asked, eagerly, not knowing what he was saying.

Chapter 33
Naples, Italy
Jack Dreyden

The Mother beamed at Jack and he grinned like an imbecile in return. She purred: "I need you to help Cynthia Childs to enter the Duat. Wouldn't that be wonderful? It is the way. Love for love; life for life. Free her from the cares of this world and free me from then chains of mine."

"Cynthia? Do you mean Cyn?" A second before, the idea of murder hadn't seemed all that bad. It was just killing and as the Mother had pointed out, hadn't he killed before? But now there was an actual face to go along with the blood and the screams, and what was worse, it was a face he knew and loved.

"But you also love me," the Mother insisted in a purring voice that had Jack's head swimming. "That you love me is wonderful and good."

And it was wonderful and good, but also confusing and intoxicating in a bad way. He found himself nodding and he didn't know exactly what he was nodding about. It felt as though he was being drugged. His mind was in a stupor of forced emotions and fear, and yet he understood on some level that this was her will going against his once more.

"I don't think I can," he managed to spit out in a groggy voice.

The glowing particles of Jack's spell disappeared altogether as the Mother grew angry. "You can. You are a killer. You can kill Cyn for me or you can die right here, right now." Without warning, the knives were back, sliding under his skin, going for his joints and his eyes and his testicles. He screamed, a haunting sound that echoed throughout the entire warren of tunnels.

The pain was unbearable. He screamed, twisting in knots on the rock floor until the Mother finally relented.

332

When she did, he lay in a heap, crying, snot and tears mingling on his face. "Do not make me kill you, Jonathan. You are my child and I would not want to kill my own child."

"I'm not going to kill Cyn, so you do what you have to do." In response, she hurt him. The pain was beyond anything he had experienced so far and how long it lasted, he didn't know. When she released him, she spoke words that didn't register. All he could think of was to crawl away. He made it two and half feet before he was tortured a third time.

The bones in their stacks rattled with his screams and dust sifted down and yet when she released him, he growled: "Is that all you got?" He had mouthed the cliche in an attempt to bolster his own flagging strength and had expected only pain in response. What he received; however, was a pause from the Mother. "*Is* that all you got?" he asked again, this time looking for an honest answer and receiving one when the Mother smiled, nastily.

Surprisingly, it was all she had. She could hurt him and could probably kill him, but she couldn't force him to do as she wished. "You need me to kill Cyn, voluntarily, don't you? Okay, I get it now. The power of sacrificing love is greater than the power of stealing souls."

"Yes. It's a delicious power. Though now I see that I won't be getting it from you. That's too bad. I could have made you one of the great ones…but maybe I still can. Would you like a taste of power?"

Before he could say no, the Mother looked him straight in the eyes. The air crackled between them and when the power entered Jack, his back bowed and his arms flung out. It was almost too much. The power raced electric over his flesh and in a way burned him.

While he squirmed in a mixture of ecstasy and pain, she only grinned. "I could have made you my chief lieutenant on this world. I could have given you such power." She put images in Jack's mind. He could see himself casting true bolts of lightning from his hands and lifting cars without effort. He saw fire rain down on his enemies at a word and the last image was of him standing with his boot on Robert's neck.

"So much power," she said. "You would be second only to me, your power unstoppable. Would you like that? Would you like to rule this world?" This was a much more difficult test for Jack. The first had been easy to pass; he would never murder Cyn under any circumstances. And the second test was, in a way, even easier; he had faced so much pain in the last year and a half that the threat of more was nothing.

But power? That was something he craved, it was something he needed. He found himself saying: "Yes," his voice only a whisper.

"Then you know what to do," she said, and now her voice matched his in tone, quiet, secretive. In his mind, he saw himself slitting Cyn's throat.

"No."

"She will feel nothing. She will be asleep. It will be easy for both of you. Say the words: *Arth-mallie-tyth-on* and her eyes will close and she will sleep, and with one touch of your knife they will never open again. And she will be eternally young, and her cares will be gone forever."

"But…"

"And the world will be safe," the Mother added quickly. "You will cast Robert into the flames, personally. And then you will take command of this world. Think about it! You can have peace in your time. No more war, no more strife, no more hunger. Isn't that worth one life?"

It was worth it, if it would actually happen. Yet this was Eve, the first in sin, the first in lies, the first temptress. "I can't," Jack said and as soon as the words left his mouth, he sagged and he felt the sweat cool on the back of his neck. Somehow he knew he had passed his test. He had been tempted and now he felt as though there was nothing more she could do to him.

He stood straight, waiting on her. Wondering what she had planned next. Would she offer him riches? He could handle it if she did. He had been absolutely dirt poor for most of his life and he had been happy. Perhaps she would attempt to seduce him. That would end in failure as well; he had Cyn and didn't want any other woman.

The Mother appraised him, cooly, her opal eyes at squints. "Okay, you are a tough nut." Her voice was no longer dripping with magical charm. She spoke plainly as if they were equals, maybe even friends. "I like toughness in a man. Too bad Robert isn't like you. Your cousin is weak. We both know that he'll do what I demand of him and then he will rule instead of you. Will he be as generous a leader as you? I doubt it. Will the world thrive under his greatness or will he be petty and vindictive? Tell me Jack, will blood run in the streets? Will you wake up to screams every morning?"

"I don't know."

The tremendous figure of the Mother laughed at this and the ground shook and skulls cascaded down from their stacks in an avalanche of bleached bone. "Are you lying to yourself or to me? We both know Robert's style. He kills without batting an eye. I know you think Cyn is the most precious thing this world has to offer, but you know that she is dead no matter what. One way or another her soul will be in hell. Robert will kill both of you as soon as he takes over and what a waste this nobility of yours will have been. Her screams of torment will ring in your ears. Hers and millions more; all on your head. One way or another, either you or Robert will free me. Because I respect you, Jack I'm offering you the chance to do some good in the world. Take this chance."

A grunting laugh escaped Jack as he stared up at the beautiful creature. "If you respect me, why are you treating me like an idiot? Robert can't free you. My cousin doesn't love anyone but himself. Who could he sacrifice to open the gate for you? No one. Now, since you are out of anything left to tempt me with, I need to ask you to leave. I have work to do."

Jack expected her to flare into anger, but she only laughed heartily, causing his dancing motes to reignite so that the bare walls of the catacombs and the ugly bleached bones were visible again.

"I really do like you, Jack," she said, grinning. "You are courageous to the point of insanity. It's refreshing. I'm almost tempted to tell you what Robert is really after."

He had been about to offer a witty retort when he was brought up short. There was one word that stuck out. "Really? What he's really after? You know what he's... wait, of course you know." This was no fake out. His and Robert's mortal machinations were likely child's play to someone nearly as old as the earth.

And yet, her words suggested some sort of trickery on Robert's part. What did he know of Robert's plan? Next to nothing. Everyone figured that he was going after someone or something in Naples; likely something that had to do with the Lance of Longinus—what was so tricky about that? "Unless he isn't going after something in Naples," Jack said, thinking out loud.

"You are getting warmer" the Mother said.

Since everything that came out of her mouth was suspect, Jack did his best to ignore her as he tried to analyze the situation. Question: did Robert's actions suggest he was after something in Naples? Yes, he had raised a demon army, but what was it doing? "It's trying to kill the Pope and all of his clergy," he said, answering himself. "Robert knew the Pope would come if there was a threat close enough to his front door. Is this a trap?"

The Mother gave Jack an exaggerated shrug which had him growling: "You're no help. Wait...what's west of here? Robert fled west. Maybe there's something to the west that he is after."

"The Mediterranean is two miles west of here," she suggested. "And after that is Spain and the Atlantic."

At first he was going to snap at her for being particularly unhelpful, but then he saw that she was spelling it out for him. Robert had laid a trap for the Pope and his cardinals not just to kill them but also to draw as many of them away as he could. The Vatican was wide open, easy pickings and hadn't the Pope himself said that there were many interesting and powerful objects there? The Mother had also pointed out Robert's path; he had gone west, meaning that he was going to Rome by sea, perhaps the quickest route with a zombie apocalypse tying up all the roads in this part of Italy.

"That has to be it," Jack said, but then immediately second guessed himself. "What if there really is someone or something he's after right in the Pope's backyard and he hadn't expected so vigorous of a response?"

"Very unlikely," the Mother said.

He wanted to agree, but he was so suspicious of her that he began to second guess his second guessing. What he needed was time to figure this out without her right there leering over him. And what he needed more than that was his army of corpses.

"Okay, thanks for all your help," Jack said to the Mother, after which there followed an awkward silence.

"I take it you are dismissing me?" she asked.

He shrugged. "Yeah, if you don't mind. I don't mean to be rude, but I have an army of demons to fight, and then I have to get up to Rome. I mean, this was nice and all, but I have work to do. I'm sure you understand."

"I do, more than you realize. Good bye, Jack Dreyden. I fear you will be on your knees begging me when we next meet. Don't expect me to be so cordial."

"Huh? What do you mean?" She did not answer, she only slid silently down into the inky black depths of the gate. When she had disappeared and the motes of lights appeared once more in the darkness, Jack whispered: "Then there better not be a next time."

He stepped back as the motes grew both in numbers and size. They came racing up to smear themselves like a bubble of wax, swelling the gate to tremendous size. Jack barely saw this. He was suddenly anxious that he was being played by the Mother. "What did she mean by begging? And should I stay here in Naples? Maybe Robert isn't after something in the Vatican…and even if he is after the lance, it's a fake."

Next to him the gate grew and the floor of the cavern swelled and cracked with the number of souls trying to get out. He was still trying to figure out if he had been double crossed by the Mother or triple crossed or quadruple crossed when the gate opened with a cosmic sigh and the souls poured out in the hundreds of thousands.

"Find the nearest corpse and then attack Robert's army. Drag it back to hell. Do not dawdle and do not harm any humans. Now go!" He said this with half his mind still on the puzzle before him. Perhaps because of his inattention, a demon of middling power challenged him.

It was a crude skeleton, missing half its bones. "What do you want?" Jack demanded.

"I want to hear your screams once more. And taste your tears and…"

Jack didn't have time for this. "Get your ass out of here," he growled, whipping out his Holy sword. At the sight of it, the bone-demon turned on his heel and left without another word. The rest went clacking along with him; rank upon rank, their numbers beyond count. For a good thirty minutes, the bones assembled themselves and filed out.

Jack pushed through them, needing to find Cyn and tell her about his conversation with the Mother. He found her sitting on the side of the hill with her knees drawn up and her feet tucked up under her. She was watching the parade of dead and nibbling on a croissant that had seen better days. It was smushed nearly flat.

"I heard you screaming," she said.

This stopped him. "She tested me," he admitted, keeping his eyes down at the tops of his boots. "I think I passed, but who knows? The Mother is so conniving that I don't where I stand on anything." He explained the tests she had put him through and then told her about Robert. "I don't know which way to go."

"That's easy, we go to the Vatican," Cyn answered without hesitation. "Naples is huge. We could spend a day or two looking for whatever he might be digging up. If he's at the Vatican, we'll know in minutes. Hell, if we get lucky, we could beat him there and trap him ourselves."

It was exactly the unhesitating advice he needed. As she called Captain Vance, the only person in a hundred miles whose number she knew, Jack focused on his army. It was an immense force, ten times the size of Robert's, which made Jack wonder why he hadn't chosen it.

"Maybe an army that big would have discouraged the Pope. Or maybe he has a control issue." Jack rarely had to issue more than one set of commands. It made controlling his army much easier.

Cyn came up and offered him a flattened croissant. "Captain Vance is worried that everyone will be mad that you raised this army. I told him not to be such a git."

"I don't know what that is," Jack admitted. "Is he going to send a helicopter?" That was all that mattered to him just then, or so he thought.

"He said he would do what he could. So…so you're supposed to kill me? You were going to inherit the world if you killed me? Sounds like the Mother doesn't know squat about haggling. She should have started with the moon or maybe Greenland in exchange for my soul."

Jack laughed. "She wasn't that bad at haggling. I demanded that she throw in a set of steak knives, but she held firm."

"You think I'm worth steak knives?"

"I think you are worth more than this planet and everything on it." She grinned up at him; they were close, armored chest to armored chest. He had a thousand things on his mind—she had one. She pulled him down until their lips met and they kissed in a surreal moment, standing above marching regiments of undead soldiers.

They were still at it when a beam of light transfixed them twenty minutes later. Vance and a team of *Raiders* had arrived. "Where too?" he asked when the two of them had climbed aboard the crowded chopper. "They have motels around here if you think there's time for a quickie."

That earned him a punch from Cyn that had him rubbing his arm. "Takes us to the Vatican," Jack ordered. "Robert has about an hour head start, but if he is traveling by boat, we might be able to overtake him. If not, is there anyone left there?"

"A few people, I think," Vance said. "His Holiness went 'all in.' The last I saw, there were a few very, very old priests and some janitors. I'll give them a heads up that trouble might be heading their way."

As he tried both his cell phone and the radio, they blazed north, while below them the night was alive. The remainder of the Pope's out of positioned forces were trucking it south to Naples, while the civilians in that city were a fear driven mob that was spreading out in all directions. The two groups clashed on the Autustrada del Sole, the main highway linking Rome and Naples. The ensuing traffic jam was immense. Seen from the air, it was like two rivers of light colliding.

"I'm not getting any answer from the frequency we had been using at the Vatican," Vance told them, a few minutes later. "And the Pope is surrounded by two armies of undead. He won't get any radio signals until he's free of the black cloud."

"What about the soldiers down there?" Cyn asked. "Can we get any of them to turn around?"

Vance gave her a pained look. "Probably not. The Pope made it very clear that he was in charge. None of the priests will countermand his orders. Not even the American priests." He jerked his thumb at the full chopper. "These are all soldiers. None of the priests would think about coming."

"Then we make do," Jack said, raising his voice so everyone could hear. "We can expect Robert to have brought a few demons with him. Hit them hard and fast. Use the shotguns to slow them down and the swords to finish them off. I know they won't stay down, but it'll take them longer to reform."

The soldiers shared a look and a few crossed themselves. No one wanted to go into battle against demons without a priest on hand for exorcisms and healing.

"One more thing," Jack announced. "There may be civilians with Robert…they need to be shot on sight."

This caused a murmur to spread throughout the chopper. Cyn pulled her hand from Jack's, and Vance stared as if he couldn't believe what he was hearing. "Civilians?" the captain demanded. "You mean humans. You mean you want us to murder innocent people, don't you?"

Jack met the captain's steely gaze. "In case you forgot, Robert is a necromancer. He gets his power from stealing souls. If we have any chance at defeating him, we need to make sure he can't keep replenishing his power and that means…"

"Screw that!" Vance spat. "That is not a valid order and no one is going to follow it." The soldiers all nodded and cast dark looks Jack's way. Cyn didn't look up. She kept her eyes steadily at the vibrating deck of the helicopter.

"Keep an open mind," Jack said, quieter now. "This may be our best shot at getting Robert. Think about what happens if he gets away. Think about what will happen if he finds the real Lance of Longinus. So please, do what you have to do."

No one answered his plea except with barely audible curses. Jack didn't blame them. These were all proud men, fighting on the side of good. They were Holy warriors and he was asking them to commit murder.

Cyn checked her shotgun. Vance made a point to stare past Jack to look down at the glowing city of Rome as it came into view. "One minute!" he cried. The soldiers all said near silent prayers and kissed the crosses that hung from their necks.

St. Peter's Basilica was a beacon of light, and they buzzed right for it. They were still two hundred yards out when Jack saw the bodies. Eight people were sprawled on the steps; their blood running into the square. "Hot LZ!" Vance yelled. The second he did, the helicopter dropped fifty feet, sending Jack's stomach into his throat. They bucked left and right, dropping so fast that he feared that they were going to crash.

At the last moment, the pilot flared and set down softly. All eleven of them leapt out in seconds. The soldiers spread out in a small circle, their weapons trained outward.

"No," cried Cyn. "Inside! I can feel them inside."

There were demons all right. Ten of them, and one was horribly familiar. "Hor," Jack whispered. Hor had been the very first demon he had ever faced. Jack had been beaten and survived only by running for his life. The next time they had met, Jack had been beaten again. "Not this time," he said and ran up the stairs with the others struggling to catch up.

He charged into the basilica and saw the last moments of a sadly one-sided battle. Three old men were being attacked from all sides. They were being picked at, nipped and torn. They were being worn down and readied for Robert's "last rites." He would take their souls and grow stronger.

"Stop!" Jack demanded, his voice rolling like thunder through the cavernous basilica, stopping the fight. The demons—rotting corpses with leering eyes and bloody teeth—paused in confusion. They could feel Jack's power.

Behind the demons stood the bone-creature that was Hor. He was tall compared to the others and his flesh was ancient leather, and the deep sockets of his eyes were dark with evil power. He wasn't afraid of Jack in the least. Somehow he managed to form the bone of his jaw into a grin.

Ten feet behind him, holding a girl child by the hair stood Jack's cousin Robert, looking sickly thin.

"I felt you coming," Robert said. He too was smiling as he pulled the girl close to him in a hideous mock embrace. It was a one-handed embrace. In the other hand he held a tall pole of wood, the top of which was tipped with a shining iron spike.

"Is that…" Jack asked.

Robert lifted the pole and swept the iron spear in Jack's direction. It was simple, sharp and deadly. It was a spear a soldier would carry, except this one was special. A cold wind from the spear splashed over Jack and the others, chilling their ardor and stopping them in their tracks.

"Yes, this is the Lance of Longinus," Robert said, his smile manic as if his teeth were about to burst out of his head. "I hear you've been shopping around for replicas. Too bad you didn't get to St. Martin's tomb before I did. Do you like it?"

He pointed it at Jack and the cold wind sunk into his bones. "I'll like it better when I take it from you and stick it in your guts," Jack answered.

"Always the rowdy American," Robert replied with a sneer. "But you blew it, Jack. You should have accepted what the Mother offered, because now it's too late for you."

Chapter 34
Rome, Italy
Jack Dreyden

"You've talked to the Mother?" Jack asked. This unnerved him more than facing the demons or the spear or Robert himself. What plot had been hatched between them? What malign spell had been given? Was Robert set to inherit the power that Jack had turned down?

He never found out.

Just as Robert opened his mouth to answer, Captain Vance pulled a Beretta and squeezed off five shots. There was sixty yards between them, virtually point blank range for someone of Vance's abilities, and yet not a single bullet struck Robert.

The air flashed silver, inches in front of his chest, as some spell of Robert's stopped the bullets.

"That wasn't very sporting," Robert chided and then pulled the girl behind him, shielding her.

Sporting or not, it hadn't been a smart move. Vance should have gone for the girl. "If you want sporting, why don't you and I settle this one-on-one," Jack challenged.

Robert pretended to think this over for a few seconds and then replied: "How about instead I have Hor kill you and drag your soul down into the pit?" In answer, Jack charged, the sword, Almacia raised. Time slowed at his command and he moved in a blur, flashing past the cringing priests and the demons, heading straight for his cousin.

Jack could end the fight with one swing of his sword; however, Hor was suddenly in front of him, matching his time. The demon blew out a gout of ice and Jack only saved himself by diving to the side. He wasn't fast enough. The cold bit his right leg, numbing it, turning it wooden.

"You are not the master," Hor said, and then clapped his bone hands together and Jack's spell failed. Time snapped back into place and the air was suddenly filled with flying lead and the sound of shotguns going off.

The soldiers charged after Jack, looking to save the priests, but too late. One of the demon-possessed corpses leapt among the old men and raked them with its long claws, tearing open throats and bellies. The soldiers blasted it with their shotguns, sending it flying while the other demons retched up sheets of ice.

Jack barely had a second to watch. Hor was all over him, slashing with claws that crackled and glowed with magical energy. He had to dodge and parry, steel against ancient bone. Somehow the bone resisted the magical blade. It should not have been possible. Hor should have been nothing but a pile of bones.

On the reverse side of the coin, Hor's magic was countered either by Jack's quickness or by the magic sword which ate up electrical energy. They fought under the great dome, their battle a stalemate. When Hor drenched the room in his magical darkness, Jack countered with a million particles of glowing light. When Jack stabbed with his shining sword straight through Hor's eye socket, the demon built up a magical barrier around the blade so that it felt like he was wielding a useless weighted golf club.

Around them the fight between the demons and soldiers was a draw as well. The men worked in teams: a gun fighter matching up with a swordsman. This kept the demons on their heels. The beasts retaliated, alternating between blasting out sheets of ice and poison fog. Men went down screaming. Some were revived with a splash of Holy Water, while others died, their bodies contorted in their final agonies.

They fought among a growing litter of bone as the demons were being rendered into scraps by the valiant soldiers, and yet these scraps were slowly come back together. Jack saw that the "draw" would only be temporary if he didn't do something to alter the course of the battle. Only Hor would not let him. The creature kept up the pressure, knowing that once the soldiers were all dead, the demons would be able to overwhelm Jack by sheer numbers.

Thankfully a splash of gold in his periphery caught his attention. "Shishin Ighn-Rahe!" Jack hissed, sending electricity coursing up his blade. Hor appraised the spell with a gleam in his eye. The demon made to dispel the magic, clapping his hands together, but Jack slowed time and lunged in.

Hor countered, slowing time as well. They were moving in a blur, while everyone around them looked to be in slow motion. When Cyn brought her shotgun up, it moved at an achingly torpid pace—a snail's pace right up until Hor clapped his hands, ruining both of Jack's spells.

The lightning fizzled and time returned to its normal pace, just as Cyn pulled the trigger of her shotgun. There was a deafening roar and Hor's head was vaporized. Two more shots turned him into a twitching pile of bone. Immediately, she pulled out a vial of Holy Water and began splashing it about.

"Go!" she cried

Jack was already turning, sword in hand. There were seven humans still standing, though three of them were only barely on their feet. They had their hands full fighting the six demons that were still mostly intact, while all around them bones were skittering across the gleaming marble. In seconds, the other four creatures would be whole again.

It wasn't something that Jack could allow. He slowed time once more and flashed in, dodging the ice and the poison gas and the savage claws. His sword was an explosion of light as he hacked here and there, rendering three of the creatures into nothing but rags of flesh and kindling.

But then his strength failed him and time returned to normal. He had exhausted his supply of magical energy; it felt like only a soft wisp in his chest. Still, he had managed to give the men a fighting chance and they rushed at the last three demons with their swords drawn.

Instead of fighting, one of the demons raised a putrid grey foot and then slammed it down. The marble beneath its foot cracked and the room shook. Another of the demons smiled, its blank eye sockets alive with evil glee. It too, stomped its foot.

Now, cracks ran up the stone walls. The third demon laughed and let loose, stomping over and over. The ground shook and the walls began to crumble, sending blocks of stone falling from hundreds of feet in the air to land with the sound of thunder. The ceiling was coming apart.

"Everyone get out of here!" Captain Vance yelled. The soldiers broke for the door. Jack went in the opposite direction. Cyn was directly under the dome keeping Hor from coming back together by blasting any bone that had the audacity to try to connect with another.

"Run!" Jack screamed as the walls failed completely. She turned to run deeper into the basilica, but a bony hand reached out and caught her foot. It was Hor; even dismembered the demon could fight. Cyn fell, her shotgun flying out of her hands. She tried to scramble to her feet, but Jack saw that she was going to be too late. The entire ceiling was falling now. They had all of three and a half seconds to get clear.

Jack had nothing left in the tank, but that didn't stop him from trying. Gritting his teeth from the pain of tearing the final nub of his soul, he slowed time and raced forward with tons of stone seemingly directly hanging over his head. He grabbed Cyn, hauled her to her feet and made it exactly twenty steps before he couldn't hold back time any more.

There was an explosion of sound from behind as if a bomb had exploded; the floor heaved and rocks of every size flew all around them. At least one struck Jack in the back of the head and he fell into a black world where he felt nothing and saw nothing.

He thought he had died, but the next thing he knew he was being shaken into consciousness. "Jack? Wake up, Jack." A strange version of Cyn knelt above him. She was as grey as the dead. Even her golden locks were grey. Only her eyes were of another color. They were wonderfully blue, like neon stars.

"What happened?" He could remember fighting Hor and the demons and then nothing. He tried to sit up and winced at the pain in his head. There was a lump half the size of his fist on the back of his skull. All around him was more grey; dust billowing in clouds that obscured everything.

"We have to get to Robert," Cyn told him, trying to pull him up to his feet. "He's killed that little girl and opened the gate again."

The idea that Robert had raised the dead within the basilica boggled Jack's mind even more than it had been. "Why? When? Why?" The why seemed very significant.

"It happened just now and I don't know why. But maybe…" She stopped speaking as two noises came to them. The first was a tremendous crash that shook the floor. It sounded as if it had practically come from beneath them.

The second noise was a weak voice, begging: "Help me." Although the crash beneath them portended something awful, they couldn't ignore the plea. Together they pushed through the clouds of billowing dust until they found a huge mound of stone that rose to a new ceiling of jumbled rock that hadn't been there a minute before.

At the closest end, they found a soldier who was mostly buried under blocks the size of boulders. Only his head and part of his torso jutted from beneath the rubble. Jack tottered to him and tried to budge the stone but only the smallest of them would move.

"It's got me, Jack," the soldier whispered.

Jack dropped down and peered into the grey face. "Captain Vance! I'll get you out of there. Hold on." He tried again pushing and pulling on stone blocks with all of his strength. They were hundreds of pounds in weight and didn't budge.

Vance cried out again: "It's got me! Jack! My leg. My leg. It has me."

Cyn had been straining at the rocks in equal futility, but now she dropped down next to Vance's head and asked: "What has you?"

"One of *them*. It's chewing. Oh damn it!"

In desperation, Jack tore at the rock cursing at the top of his lungs. His nails split and bent back; his fingers bled but the rocks would not move. "Try a spell," Cyn suggested.

Jack shook his head. "I don't have one for something like this and besides, I'm completely drained."

"Save me," Vance said in a harsh whisper. His face was screwed up in pain and fear, and tears ran streaks down through the grey dust, showing Jack that there was real living flesh beneath. "Jack, s-save me. You know what's going to happen. It's chewing in-into my l-leg. It'll get an artery, J-Jack. And you know what it'll happen then."

He knew. Vance would have his blood and then his soul sucked out of him. He would become the demon's plaything. Perhaps he would turn Vance into the living dead. Perhaps he would send Vance down to the pits.

Jack also knew what Vance wanted from him. Vance wanted Jack to kill him.

It's always me, Jack thought to himself, tasting bile come up the back of his throat. He bent down and picked up the Holy sword he had tossed aside.

"Not the sword," Cyn said. She pointed at Vance. His shoulder holster was just visible. "The gun will be quicker."

"Yes," Vance begged. "The gun…but first promise me you'll tell my kids something for me." He took a breath to go on only his face screwed up in a spasm of pain and a scream echoed throughout the room. Jack felt impotent fury rock him as next to him, Cyn sobbed.

After a few agonizing seconds, Vance was able to go on, speaking quickly, perhaps knowing he didn't have a lot of time left. "Tell them I died a good death. Lie for me, Jack. Okay?" Jack didn't know what a good death was, but nodded anyway and then tugged out the Beretta. He thumbed off the safety and paused as Vance added: "And w-watch over them, please. Don't let any of these things get them. P-promise me!"

"I will do my best," Jack said. He didn't think he could say the words: *I promise*, since as far as he could tell he was not only powerless, he was also trapped in the basilica with Robert and who knew how many demons. He'd be lucky to be alive in five minutes. For some reason that didn't bother him. He was numb and tired and mentally exhausted.

But not spiritually. He was about to kill another friend and the pain of it hurt worse than any torture. With his hand shaking, he brought the gun up. Vance turned to look at the floor, only before Jack could pull the trigger, Cyn put out a hand to stop him. She held one of her silver vials. She tipped it, wetting her finger with Holy Oil and then drew a glistening cross on Vance's forehead, saying: "May the Lord bless and guard your soul. And may you find your way to heaven."

Vance nodded once, said: "Thanks." He kept his eyes focused on what had been part of a ceiling fresco drawn by Michelangelo. It was a cherub, with a chubby belly and a satisfied smile. "That was nice," he said. "Now look away, Cyn. Let Jack do what he has to."

Again the thought: *It's always me.* And to it Jack added: *Do I even have a choice anymore?*

It didn't feel like it. Jack felt as if he was an actor in a play. His words written for him, his actions dictated, his footsteps chosen by another. He held the gun, waiting on his cue and when Cyn looked up to where the ceiling had once been, he knew that was it. He pulled the trigger, blasting out brain and blood to add color to the grey world.

It was the wrong color. It didn't brighten things; it only caused pain.

Wordlessly, he handed the pistol to Cyn and then stuffed the heels of both hands into his eyes and pushed as hard as he could until he was sure that he was on the verge of shoving his eyeballs into his head. He might have growled or cursed or screamed, but he didn't cry. He was too angry to cry.

In a cold fury, he pulled his hands away and bent to pick up his sword. It was time for the final act. It was time for either him or Robert to die. There was no other way, because there was no way out. The ceiling had collapsed, trapping them, two scorpions in a bottle. He wanted to tell Cyn to hide only he knew that she wouldn't. She was too tough to run.

Through the gloom and the hanging dust, they saw an open stairwell that led down. He knew what was down there. He had seen the tombs. There were fifty popes interred beneath the basilica. Robert could have a company of undead soldiers to greet them, but that didn't bother Jack. After all, his steps had been chosen for him.

They went to the stairs and paused as they heard Robert screech: "You bitch!"

Jack grinned, a smile that was entirely filled with hate. "So he's having his issues with the Mother as well. That bodes well for us. Try the gun right off the bat. Don't give him a second to think. Just shoot." She was a fair shot, much better than Jack, who never trained with any weapon except the sword.

"And if he's still protected with that spell?" she asked.

Then we die—that was obvious. "Then we figure it out." It was a stupid answer and yet she gave him a nod as though he had just spouted Zen wisdom.

The stairs were dark, but from below there came an intermittent flashing that guided them. The walls were cracked and the integrity of the basilica compromised. Water flowed like a river down the stairs, so that when they reached the bottom, they were knee-deep, leading Jack to think: *What if I die by drowning?*

It was a funny thought, just not a realistic one. No, he'd be killed by a demon and his soul tortured for all eternity. Still, he smiled grimly as he slogged through the water, following the sound of voices. Jack was full of piss and vinegar and yet their destination unnerved him: St. Peter's tomb.

The hallway they found themselves in had a ceiling of gorgeous tile that hung in a low curve above their heads. With the water so high, it didn't leave much room for fighting and Jack knew it would cut into his speed advantage. He went on, regardless, pausing only when the body of the little girl they had seen earlier floated by; she had been split up the middle. Cyn cursed under her breath and the hand holding the pistol shook in anger.

"Save it for Robert," Jack whispered. Despite that he had kept his tone low, the word 'Robert' echoed across the tile.

Thirty feet away, standing in an alcove, Robert heard and stepped out into the hall. He was a shadowy figure full of malice and yet his voice was light and easy. "Wild Jack. Wow, you look like warmed over death. I should…"

Without warning, Cyn started firing the pistol, cutting him off. Her aim was fantastic. They could see where each bullet struck Robert's protective barrier. The first two would have been perfect head shots. The next two would have blasted out Robert's heart, if he had one. And the final shot, one that showed her anger and frustration, was aimed straight into his crotch.

He glanced down as the air shimmered an inch from his groin. A laugh, what he thought would be mocking escaped him; however, there wasn't much energy to it. In fact, Jack thought his cousin looked utterly slagged. Robert leaned on the Lance of Longinus as though it were an old man's walking stick.

"The Mother drained you, didn't she?" Jack asked. "You're as weak as I am."

"She likes to play her games," Robert admitted. "And we're her pawns...but not for long. Very soon, I will be her equal."

Cyn snarled: "You are already her equal as an evil little git."

"What is evil and good to a god?" Robert asked. "They make the rules, Cyn, they aren't bound by them. And yes, I will be a god. My power is already almost equal to one. Look at me." He raised his hands, lifting the lance so that it almost scraped the ceiling. "The greatest powers in the world are arrayed against me and yet I am still standing. I am still thriving and my strength is still growing."

Jack laughed, a merciless sound. The dead girl was so close he could touch her, and he did, letting his warm fingers caress her cold ones. "You have no power of your own. You have to steal souls just to light a candle. You are a weak, little creature and the Mother did me a great favor by draining you."

He started forward, uncaring that Robert's smile had grown wicked. "Let me show you how 'weak' I am. Come here, Peter."

There was movement from the alcove and a tall skeletal figure came to stand in the hall. It wore moldy robes of crimson embroidered with silver and across it's thin bone-chest hung a heavy crucifix of gold. Both Jack and Cyn, overcome by awe, took a step back. This was no middling demon that had been summoned from the void, this was Saint Peter, the first Bishop of Rome, the first Pope, the first disciple of Jesus Christ. His power radiated off of him as if there was an invisible bonfire burning in his chest.

"But...but he's good," Cyn said. "You c-can't make him hurt us."

Robert laughed and again it was little more than a chuckle. "He's my slave, cousin. I told you my power is greater than you know. I can make him do anything I want.

If I wanted him to skin a baby alive, he'd have to do it. Give them a taste, Pete."

The skeleton raised an arm that was clean of any tissue whatsoever and out of its hand a blast of light shot straight at Jack. He flung up his sword, catching the light on its shining blade and absorbing most of its energy. The piercing glare instantly blinded him and the shock wave that came with the blast knocked him into the water.

St. Peter kept the light burning and in seconds, the sword glowed orange and the heat generated by it blistered his hand. With a cry, Jack dropped the sword and threw himself to the side, where he floundered in the water, helpless to another attack.

"That's good, Pete," Robert said, tapping the creature's arm. "We have made our point, I believe."

"And what point is that?" Cyn demanded. In one hand, she had the useless gun pointed at Robert and with the other she tried to pull Jack to his feet.

Jack fought her for a moment, desperately searching in the water for the Holy sword. He came up sputtering, brandishing the blade which now felt as useless as the gun. They clutched each other and the only thing going through Jack's mind was the realization that he had made a huge mistake trying to take Robert on as weak as he was.

Robert grinned at the pathetic display. "The point is I can kill you anytime I want, and I will, mind you, just as soon as you call off your army. I want you to destroy it, Jack."

For a brief moment, Jack had a wild hope that they could get out of the fight alive. Robert's request suggested he feared the army, though Jack didn't know why. It was fifty miles away and he and Cyn would be long dead before any of the demons could get halfway back to the Vatican.

"I don't get it," he asked. "Why do you care about a bunch of ghouls and demons?"

"I don't care, except that when you die, they'll be free. They'll go on a rampage, killing everything that moves.

And as sad as that is, the real issue is that it'll disrupt the timing of my plans. It's as simple as that. Send them back to their graves, be a hero in your last moments by saving a million people, and as a reward I'll make your death easy."

Cyn shook her head, stepping in front of Jack. "Don't listen to him, Jack, he's a liar. He's afraid. I don't know what of, but he's afraid of something."

Robert only lifted an eyebrow and waited in a silence that was broken by an unlikely source. Behind St. Peter stood another bone-creature. This one was much smaller. It too was fleshless and the ancient black cassock it wore hung off its shoulders, so that it appeared almost like a floating skull.

"The cabal. He fears the cabal of demons," it said in a sighing voice.

"Do you mind shutting up," Robert barked.

Jack pointed at the small bone creature. "That's Saint Gregory. What does he know? What's going to happen?"

"Like I said, your army is going to get out of control and, according to Gregory, most of Italy will be destroyed."

"And this cabal he spoke of, what's that?" Cyn demanded.

Robert shrugged. "You have dealt with stray demons here and there, but you've never dealt with them when they're banded together. They are far more powerful and… and some are strong enough to open their own portal into hell. What do you think will happen then?"

"The Mother," Jack breathed. "They'll try to bring forth the Mother."

"Or one of the other Gods of the Undead," Robert said. "Either way, the end result is mass death, tears, blood, blah, blah, blah. Generally, everyone has a bad day. My only option is to raise an even larger army and think about what will happen if I should die? The earth will be overrun. It's in your best interest to keep that from happening."

Jack and Cyn shared a look, and only when she nodded with painful reluctance did Jack say: "Okay, I'll send them back, but it'll take a few minutes."

"Two minutes," Robert said. "I know what it takes, Jack so don't try to fool me."

"Sure, two minutes. I can do two minutes," Jack said, slowly, trying to draw out the seconds in order to figure a way out of his predicament.

No answer came to him. No answer could. Robert held the trump card with Saint Peter. He was too strong. Even if Jack was at full strength, he had no chance against the awesome power of Saint Peter. No one did, not even the current "fighting pope" Romanus. Robert would be unstoppable.

"I've lost," Jack whispered to Cyn. "You need to run away."

She shook her head. "I've fought with you, I've loved you, I'll die with you."

Jack nodded, knowing that there was almost no chance that she would make it out of there no matter what he did.

He was about to open his mouth to insist when St. Gregory spoke: "One of the heirs of Lord Blackburn will die tonight. And only one."

Robert spun, his face livid as he demanded: "Which one?"

Gregory lifted a bony hand and swept it across the low-ceilinged hallway. The bony finger pointed at each of the heirs. It was the hand of death. When it passed over Robert, he shuddered. When it passed over Cyn, she grit her teeth and stepped forward in hard anger. When that bony claw passed over Jack, he smiled. He knew who would die.

Robert was too strong. Cyn was too tough. And Jack was ready. He had seen enough misery and he had been the cause of too much misery.

"One," was all Gregory answered.

Chapter 35
Rome, Italy
Jack Dreyden

Robert's first move was to lift the Lance of Longinus and sidle to his left so that the magnificent figure of St. Peter shielded him. Jack chortled at this display of cowardice. He was all set to die, in fact, he was kind of looking forward to it now that he knew Cyn would live. His burden had been too great for too long and, sure he was going to hell—murderers didn't get to go to heaven—but at least he would go out in a blaze of glory.

"One out of three are pretty good odds, if you ask me," he said, wagging the Holy sword, Almacia back and forth.

Cyn, who wouldn't stop trying to get in his way, laughed: "That's better odds that we've ever faced." She had her pistol and the steel in her spine and nothing else to fight Robert, his spear and St. Peter with, and yet she wasn't the least bit afraid.

"Call off your army, Jack," Robert demanded, the spear thrust out.

Jack hesitated as the cold wind rushed over him once again. Next to him, Cyn brazenly spat into the water, glared and said: "Don't do it. If he's that nervous about it, he'll let us go."

For once, Robert seemed unsure of himself and he kept glancing at the skeletal figure of St. Gregory; however, the little being remained quiet and still. Finally, he said: "Okay. This isn't a problem. There are more cemeteries and more souls. I was trying to be nice. The millions of deaths that will happen tonight will be on your head, Jack."

"There will only be one death on my conscience tonight and because he's a murderer, I doubt that I will lose too much sleep."

"I don't know whose life that will be since I'm not sticking around. Greg, come with me. St. Pete, kill them both."

Robert plunged further down the hall as St. Peter turned with aching slowness toward Jack and Cyn. There was unmistakable sadness in the depths of his eye sockets. Cyn stepped forward and she was spitting mad. "Coward!" she screamed at their cousin. "You are a damned coward."

Just before he took a turn that would take him into the crumbled labyrinth of the Vatican Grotto where there was a possible way out if the ceiling held, Robert stopped and waved a hand. "Yes, but I will be a live coward," he said. He then disappeared around the corner.

Cyn looked as though she wanted to scream a few choice curse words, but just then St. Peter turned his head to the cracked ceiling and said in a low, ghostly tone: "Lord, please forgive me for what I must do."

"You don't have to do this," Cyn begged. "Let us go. You have to fight this."

"I am fighting, dear child," St. Peter said, raising his hand once more. "I am compelled by a force greater than my own and I will be able to hold back for a few more seconds. You may try to run away if you wish."

Jack knew that a few seconds wouldn't even get them back to the stairwell. He grabbed Cyn and thrust her behind him. "Run! Don't look back. Only one of us has to die tonight."

Knowing that she would try to argue and knowing that they didn't have time, Jack forged ahead, hoping that Peter would hold off a little longer, allowing Jack a chance to get close enough to get in a few swings with his sword. A few swings were all he would have time for before he died.

There would be no beating the saint. His aura was as bright as the sun. St. Peter had the power of ten sorcerers, and just then, Jack had the power of none. Still, he had his sword. He made it all of ten feet and then Peter moaned as if in pain and suddenly a fury of white light shot forth from his hand.

Jack threw up his sword, catching the light. He was driven back, his feet sliding on the slick tile below the water. As before, the heat built up on the pommel of the sword, searing his hands, only now, he took the pain. It was agony. The white fire raced up the blade, up his arms and then went deep inside of his soul where it attacked his sins, torching them and in the process, torching him as well.

St. Peter's power was in the destruction of evil and there was just too much evil in Jack.

A scream tore out of his throat that reverberated along the tile and up the stairs and could be heard in the square above. The scream went on and on until a shadow moved in his periphery and suddenly Cyn stood before him taking the fire into herself.

Jack fell into the water, barely conscious, barely able to think. "No," he whispered. This was a wasted death. Cyn would die and then Jack would be fried where he knelt. He didn't have the strength to run. It was a struggle even to stand and when he got to his feet he stared in amazement.

Cyn was not being burned. She wasn't being driven back. She strode forward while all around her the water steamed and hissed. But she was untouched.

Hollow laughter filled the air. It was St. Peter. He shot light from his hand and laughed with joy. "You are without sin," he intoned. "You have repented and your soul is clean and untouchable. Narrow is the path you have chosen, Cynthia. The Lord loves you." In spite of his words, he tried all the harder to burn her down to nothing and yet the heat passed right through her and into the water. Steam filled the air and Jack had to back up to keep from being scalded.

The intensity of the light reached solar levels and then, slowly, became dimmer and dimmer until it was only a glow, and then the skeleton dropped his hand, letting loose with a long sigh.

"I must try to kill you with my hands and I am strong still," St. Peter said and then lurched forward, his bone feet uncertain on the slippery tile. Cyn made no move to protect herself. Her eyes were large and unblinking. She was too dazed to move. Jack splashed forward and caught St. Peter with his gleaming sword just as he swung a bony claw.

The saint was no warrior and in six seconds, Jack dismembered the skeleton, leaving only its head sitting on its shoulders. Using the tip of the sword, Jack parted the crimson robes. He had expected to have to search for the soul of the saint; however, Peter's soul was a white light filling his chest.

Jack raised his sword to pierce it, but Cyn stopped him. "What will happen to you?" she asked Peter. "Your soul, I mean."

"I do not know," he answered. "But do not concern yourself with that. Strike before I regain my strength."

"What about Robert?" Jack asked. "Why did he bring you back?"

Peter's bones started to slide back toward him. He was reforming faster than any demon Jack had ever come up against and the power of his soul was blooming once again, glaring in its purity to such an extent that Jack found himself squinting.

"He thought I knew secrets," Peter said. "He is searching for Eden. The original garden that the Lord laid out for his child. Robert searches for this land for the secrets it holds."

"The Tree of Knowledge," Cyn said in a whisper.

The skeleton nodded. "I do not know where the land was hidden, and this has infuriated, Robert. He will keep searching but he can not be allowed to find it. He would be unstoppable if he were to find it."

"It's guarded, isn't it?" Jack asked.

"By cherubs," Peter said. "Many of them, but Robert has the Lance. Its power is great, though he does not know yet how to wield it. Defeat him before he does. Now you must strike me down, Jack Dreyden. I have regained my strength, and my will to fight the command within me grows less with every second."

Despite the saint's warning, Jack paused. Here he was being asked to kill yet another innocent person…and this was no ordinary person. He was the first disciple. His feet had been washed by none other than Jesus Christ, and now Jack had to kill him just to save his own pathetic life. In misery, he raised the sword.

Cyn turned away and did not watch as Jack stabbed the beautiful soul. He felt a sting in his palm and then a glorious wind blasted up out of the skeleton, as the bones fell in on themselves. Cyn crossed herself and started mumbling a prayer, but Jack feeling empty, save for his self-hatred stopped her. "We don't have time. We have to find Robert. Remember what Gregory said: only one of us will die and I'm going to make sure that it's him." He pulled her along; she felt feather light, in spite of that she tripped over every shard of stone in their way. "Are you okay?" he asked.

"I didn't die," she answered. "I should have, but I didn't. I thought I was giving my life for yours, but I didn't die."

"Yeah, well, it was stupid," Jack growled, "and next time you won't be so lucky, so make sure there isn't a next time. I'm not going to have you die for my sorry ass. You're the one without sin. You're the one who is worthy of this life." She opened her mouth to reply, but he stopped her with a kiss. It had to be a short one. They were running out of time.

Despite his urgency, he felt her love in the softness of her lips. It made him falter and the quick kiss turned into a long one. But then a sound of rock falling came from ahead of them and the moment passed. "Come on," he said and then started running. As he ran down the hall and into the dim and frightening grotto where the ceiling was coming apart by the second, he spoke over his shoulder: "You go after Gregory. If he's like St. Peter, he won't be able to hurt you. I'll take on Robert. He's out of power and only has the spear as a weapon. We can do this, Cyn. This can be the end!"

"I think it will be," she said, but without his enthusiasm.

He stopped and looked into her china-blue eyes. "What is it?" Her answer surprised him.

"I'm afraid for you. Your soul is so dark. I saw it, Jack. When St. Peter had you transfixed by his light. I saw your soul and it was a sad and pitiful, shriveled-up thing. I can't have that be me."

"What are you saying?"

She gave a little shrug and kept her eyes averted. "You're going to want to join souls. You're going to want use some of my strength but I-I can't do that."

"Just one more time, Cyn," he insisted. He could feel his cousin not far ahead of them. The going was slow in this part of the sub-basement. The water poured away down deep cracks and what looked like endless crevices. Each had crumbling edges and had to be leapt over. Then they came to a maze of tombs and crisscrossing halls that were made all the more confusing by the darkness and the fact that in many places the ceiling had caved in.

When she didn't say anything, Jack whispered: "If he's figured out how to use that spear even a little, then we're going to need all the magic we can get on our side. This will be the last time, I swear."

"It'll never be one more time with you, Jack. Maybe one day you'll face the fact that you're a junky. You're hooked on power."

He stepped back, nudging against a dusty tomb and gave her a hard look, feeling the quick burn of resentment in his wasted chest. He wanted to tell her off for being so presumptuous. After all it had been Cyn who had brought up the entire concept of him taking her power; he hadn't said a word.

But it was in the back of your head, Jack, a voice within him spoke. *The idea has been lurking there all along. It's why you keep her near. It's not because of her fighting skills. It's because you can always take what you need when you need it.*

The word "take" had an ugly sound to it. It was too much like "steal" which was what necromancers did. The word cooled his anger.

"And you're okay with one of us dying?" he asked. "I doubt Gregory was wrong."

"No, I'm not afraid. There are no demons here," she answered. "If one of us dies, it'll be a natural death. Our souls will be safe. But let's make it Robert who has to worry about his soul. What do you think?" Somehow, in spite of the miserable predicament they were in, she was able to smirk at him just as she had the first moment she had met him, grubby and nervous in the Waldorf Hotel, a lifetime before.

Jack grabbed her in an embrace, squeezing her hard into his chest. He didn't want her to see the sudden fear that swept him. Her soul would be fine. She had been given a clean bill of health by no less than St. Peter, while Jack had a shriveled-up little thing for a soul.

"We'll make it Robert," he said and then forced a smile on his face before giving her another quick kiss.

Covered by a sudden weight of depression, he couldn't think of anything inspiring to say and so, with his Holy sword held out in front of him, he plunged deeper into the Vatican Grotto, following the pair of tracks that meandered through the new layer of dust and the mounds of debris. He followed after, feeling once again as though his steps had been chosen for him. This time it was almost literal; he was placing his feet in the prints left by his cousin.

Just as he knew they would, they caught up to Robert and Gregory who were trying to pull huge blocks of rock away from a stairwell exit and neither suspected that their enemies were near.

It would be their only opportunity and Jack tried his best to get close before he was noticed, but after three overly-pronounced and "sneaky" steps, his foot struck a piece of tile which went skittering away. Robert spun to face them; however, before he was halfway turned, Cyn fired her pistol only to be disappointed once more as the bullet struck the magical barrier around him.

Despite being protected, Robert jumped in surprise. The look of shock stayed on his face for only a few seconds before it was replaced by one of rage. "St. Peter!" he screamed. "Where are you? You will listen to me! Get over here right this sec…"

"Save your breath, Robert," Jack said, easing closer. "I killed him. Don't look so surprised. Haven't I defeated everything you've sent my way? The sorcerer, the necromancer, even the Mother. I have grown stronger and all you've done is kill innocent beings. Why don't you give up and make it easy on yourself? We can get you a solitary jail cell far from any cemeteries or corpses. You'll be safe and we'll be safe. Don't you see that this has gone too far? Weren't you the one who said that this whole thing was a mistake that got out of hand?"

"That was then, Jack. Now, there are too many evil things out there gunning for me. I can't just retire. And besides, I'm not exactly afraid of you. You have nothing in the tank and Cyn is, well she's a born-again necromancer and there's nothing more sad than that. So, I don't think I'll be accepting your offer of a jail cell, thank you. Gregory, clear that door while I take care of these two."

Without warning, he turned the spear's point toward Jack. From its tip a blast of what looked like concentrated air shot out. It was strange to see the air wobble as the force raced at Jack. He tried to dive to the side, but was caught in the left leg and spun like a frisbee.

He landed on the top of a crypt twenty feet away, shaken but not exactly hurt. With a grunt, he leapt down just as Robert pointed the spear in Cyn's direction. She tried to duck away, but was too slow and was caught full on and sent flying. When she landed in a heap, there was an ugly sound of bone striking rock and she remained motionless.

Seeing her lying there caused Jack to hesitate but only for a second, and then with a curse on his lips, he charged. As expected Robert pivoted and pointed his spear. Without hesitation, Jack dove to the side, rolling across the tile floor in a neat ball. Something passed near him and there was a crash behind him, and then there came the sound of rock falling.

Part of the ceiling had come crashing down, filling the darkened grotto with clouds of dust, making it that much harder to see. Jack could only pinpoint Robert by the gleam from the silver tip of his spear, which tracked Jack mercilessly as he dodged here and there, leaping away time and again as Robert sent blasts his way with excellent aim.

It was only after he had been struck a third partial blow, which left him clutching his side, that Jack realized that he would never be able to get close to his cousin as long as held a sword that glowed like a torch. He sheathed it and the gloom of the grotto became almost full on dark.

"What are you doing, Jack?" Robert asked. Where a second before, he had been grinning and confident as he fired his blasts, now he spun right and left in jerky moves. "Stop playing, Jack. Let's finish this."

Jack kept silent and still, hiding in the dark, hoping that his cousin would come closer so that he could spring out and strike him down. Robert refused to be drawn away; he kept to the middle of the hall between the low alcoves.

"Let me tell you how this is going to end," Robert said, his voice echoing in the dark. "Gregory is going to clear that door in a few minutes and then on my way out I'm going to use this spear to drop the roof on you and Cyn. Or we can fulfill Greg's prophecy. You come out of hiding and I'll kill just you. I'll leave Cyn out of this. I promise."

With great difficulty, Jack bit back another snarling curse. Robert had him over a barrel. Jack was stuck. He couldn't get close to his cousin to kill him and waiting only played into Robert's hands. It seemed he had only two choices: a desperate and useless charge across thirty feet of open space, or he could pray that Robert would actually keep his promise and not hurt Cyn anymore that she had been.

It wasn't much of a choice. Robert could not be trusted. "Please, God," Jack whispered and then jumped up from behind the tomb of some long dead pope and raced at his cousin. He should have been killed right then. Robert should have heard the sound of his boots kicking stone and tile. Robert should have triggered his spear; however, at that exact moment Cyn moaned and stirred.

"Jack?" she asked, her voice sounding ghostly in the dark as if she was only a spirit.

Robert spun to point the Lance at her, and that little move allowed Jack just enough time to get in close. He swept the Holy sword from its golden sheath and its light bathed the room in a fantastic blue-white glow and showed Jack that he had a perfect shot at ending the fight once and for all. Robert had jerked in surprise at the sudden light and seemed frozen in place by the fierce onslaught.

With a cry, Jack drove the sword down in a killing stroke, knowing that there was no way his cousin would be able to get the Lance around in time to block it.

And yet, astonishingly, he did.

Metal clanged on metal and sparks flew. Jack blinked in surprise. Robert had moved faster than his eye could follow. It had been magical, but the magic hadn't come from Robert. Feeling dread crawl into his gut that he was once again in way over his head, Jack attacked again, driving his sword under the spear.

Robert had the Lance held in an uncertain grip as if he was just as perplexed as Jack, and the sword thrust should have pierced Robert's heart—but again his cousin managed to twist the spear sending the sword point off to the side.

"Huh," Robert grunted, marveling at the spear. Jack used his distraction to attack again and again in a swirl of flashing metal. Never in his life had his strokes been so exact, his lunges so perfect. The Holy sword threw sparks and clanged metal on metal and the blade never got within an inch of Robert's skin.

After half a minute, he broke off and the two stood panting with only two feet separating them. "It's the spear," Robert said. He grinned like a child right into Jack's face as if Jack should be just as excited. "When the Romans went to break Christ's legs, they saw that he was already dead. Not believing it, one centurion, pierced Jesus' side with this spear and what came out?"

"Blood and water," Jack answered. "But it wasn't, really."

Robert's grin grew so that the wicked thing went from ear to ear. "No it wasn't. It was a part of him, perhaps a part of his immortality. Nothing could have harmed the Son of God, unless he allowed it. And he gave it up so he could give up his life. And who knew that anyone would stab his lifeless body? And who knew what would happen to the spear? Who knew that it would make whoever possesses it invincible?"

If Jack had known, he would never have come to Rome, but now he was there and only two feet from his death and yet something Robert had said triggered a thought.

"Possesses?" That suggested that its owner was fluid in nature. Immediately, Jack dropped his sword and latched onto the lance with both hands. He was so quick that he almost yanked it away from Robert in the first second. Grimly, he held on and the two, very much equal in size, tussled in the dark until Jack started to get the upper hand.

In desperation, Robert started triggering the power of the spear, sending out blasts at random. The ceiling rained rock and marble, walls crumbled and two support columns collapsed from direct hits. Above them the weight of the basilica pressing down, caused the ceiling to let out a loud groan. It was the only indication that all hell was about to break loose.

Jack let go of the spear and threw himself to the side, just as the ceiling came down. He rolled and rolled until he rammed up against a tomb and then he crawled up into its protective alcove until the ground stopped shaking. He found himself in near total darkness; the only light came straining through a wall of rock. It was meager and yet it drew him. He wobbled across an uneven ground until he could peer through a narrow opening the size of his fist.

"Cyn?" he whispered into the opening, his heart caught up in his throat, afraid that she was the death in Gregory's prediction.

"Jack?" she answered, matching his whisper. He almost collapsed in relief. He clutched the wall to hold himself up as she asked: "Where are you?"

He didn't know the answer to that. He felt as though he was in an alternant universe peering through a portal into the world…as if he was in hell looking through the gate. "Am I dead?" he whispered, touching himself, wondering what it felt like to be dead.

Cyn was bathed in a pale blue light—*the moon*, Jack thought. The ceiling on the other side of the wall of stone was completely gone and the moon shone down bright enough to cast shadows and one fell across her as she was trying to climb the pile of rocks toward him. It was Robert. His spear glinted as he used it as a club and knocked her legs out from beneath her. With a cry, she fell, rolling to the base of the mound.

"Leave her alone!" Jack thundered. "She can't hurt you, so just leave her out of this."

"She may not be able to hurt me, but she can help me," Robert answered. "I am drained and she is brimming with energy. I love it." He waved a hand just inches over her as she tried to sit up.

"Maybe you can love this," she replied. She had Vance's Beretta in her hand and without hesitation, shoved it up into his crotch and pulled the trigger. The blast echoed as did Robert's laughter.

"I'm invincible, Cyn darling. And pretty soon, I'll be all-powerful and you will help me with that, by giving me that precious soul of yours."

"Stop!" Jack screamed. "Take mine instead."

This had Robert crying with laughter. "Your soul? You don't have a soul. Instead of a soul, you have some sort of jigsaw puzzle. Pieces of this and that, of people you probably don't even know. There's so much ugliness inside of you that even I don't want any part of. But that doesn't mean I won't kill you. Give me a moment and after I take care of Cyn, I'll show you what true power looks like."

There was a sound of velcro tearing and then Cyn said: "You'll do no such thing." She had the Beretta in hand and had finally found a use for it—her armored vest was open and she had the gun pointed directly into her heart.

Jack went cold. "Cyn," he whispered. "Don't, please."

"What choice do I have?" she asked, through sudden tears. "My soul is doomed. If he kills me, my soul will go the Mother as payment for the spells he wields. That's how it works, right?"

Robert held up his hands, one empty, the other holding the spear. "Yes, but if you kill yourself, you'll be going to hell anyway. You see? At least this way someone gains from this unfortunate turn of events."

"Unfortunate?" she asked in harsh whisper. "That's what you call killing thousands of innocent people? Unfortunate?"

He sneered down a her. "It is what it is. Now go ahead and pull the trigger if you have the guts to damn yourself for all eternity. Which I doubt you will." He lifted the butt of the spear, looking to ram down ion her head.

"If it means stopping you, I will." Her face was rigid, held in determined, angry lines. Only a single tear belied her anguish. She turned away from Robert and looked toward the wall of rock, her eyes searching for Jack, hidden away in his little portal.

"Stop him, Jack, but don't lose yourself in the process."

Jack was in a perfect state of shock. He was beyond emotion. He was broken. He should have been crying and begging for her not to pull the trigger, only he knew that wouldn't save her. She was lost and now he was as well. Cyn was his anchor and now that she was on the verge of death, he felt disconnected from his body as if he was already a wandering spirit. It took all of his concentration just to form the words: "I will."

"I love you," she said and she too seemed to be losing her emotions. The words were hollow and hung, lifeless in the air. They were just words. She was almost gone.

He wanted to answer her. He desperately wanted to express the fullness of his love, but that would take hours and would never be contained in the mere words: *I love you*. He wanted to say something, anything but all that came out was her name.

"Cyn," he said in a whisper. As the word left his mouth, Robert desperately tried to bash her head with the blunt part of the spear in order to keep her from killing herself so that he could kill her his way. So that he could gain and grow.

He was too slow. She pulled the trigger, bucked from the violence and the shock as the bullet tore out her heart, and then she fell back, her eyes blank, her soul doomed.

Chapter 36
Rome, Italy
Jack Dreyden

The echoes seemed to go on and on, rattling the walls of the grotto and shaking Jack to the core of his being. "Robert," Jack said, when the ruinous sound had died away. "I think you had better run far away. I think you better run and you had better keep on running."

"She brought it on herself," Robert answered. "Just like you brought this on yourself." He pointed his spear at the wall and there were crashes and explosions and all light disappeared, and the air was filled with choking dust.

Jack could hear mumbled curses—they competed with the sound of a drum banging in his head. The drum wouldn't stop. It was a rhythm of hate. After a minute, the cursing faded and there were no more crashes. He could feel the soul of St. Gregory retreating.

Immediately, Jack went to work on the wall, not feeling the pain in his fingers as the rocks bit into his flesh. He felt nothing but the rage.

It took two hours to dig a hole through the wall. On a certain level, Jack knew he was exhausted beyond anything he had ever experienced, and he had experienced his fair share of exhaustion. But this was different. He was so dead inside that when he finally saw Cyn's lifeless body, he didn't breakdown crying as he had expected.

He'd been sure that when he found her, he'd be so overcome that he wouldn't be able to carry on. Instead, he knelt over her, studying every soft curve of her beautiful face until the sound of birds twittering sounded. The moon sat banked well over in the sky and on the opposite side of the world, the night was no longer the deep velvet it had been.

Dawn was coming; a new awakening.

His power had been coming back to him little by little and when the first light of the new day crept over the horizon, Jack cut himself. Drops of perfectly red blood fell in a pattern as he walked around Cyn's body and as they fell they formed intricate shapes. Not a drop went wasted.

He spoke each word of the spell clearly, precisely, deliberately. Jack wasn't about to let Cyn languish in hell, even if it drained him to death. And it was close. He reeled back in exhaustion as the broken and dirty floor beneath her body turned the deepest black and within that black was a single mote that grew until it took up the entire circle, and then the glow faded and Cyn began blinking her blue eyes.

"What happened?" she asked. Her voice came up out of her throat in a breathy rush. She stood quickly and looked down at herself. "Am I dead?"

"Just a little," Jack answered, laughing at the same time that tears ran through the grime on his face. "But we'll figure some way to fix that. I don't know if a priest can heal a dead body, but we'll find a way even if we have to use a voodoo priest. And then all we have to do is fuse your soul back in you and you'll be good to go."

He expected her to raise an eyebrow at that and when she didn't, he figured that she was having a little trouble controlling her body. Jack was so tired that it was a struggle to get to his feet and when he did he found that his body was shaking all over; it happened sometimes and he thought nothing of it; however, Cyn saw.

"You're cold? I'm cold too. Hold me, Jack. Hold me so I can feel something again."

"Sure," he said, tripping on the loose stones under feet. "I honestly thought that you would have more of a problem with this. I thought you'd fret over my soul and read me the riot act."

"Hell changes a girl," she answered and then held out her arms.

Jack stopped a foot away, worried for her. "How long were you there? I mean, is time different in hell? Is five hours equal to five centuries?"

"It was long enough for me to miss your touch." Her arms had not dropped, they stood straight out in front of her. The embrace would be awkward and stiff and very cold. He hesitated, fearing that his reaction wouldn't be what either of them were looking for.

"What are you waiting for? You did this to me. The least you could do is comfort me." The arms were still out.

Jack took a step back, suddenly wary. Hell certainly could change a person, but Cyn wasn't acting like the others that had been brought back. His father had still been his father and acted like it, and Dr Loret had been just as prissy as when he had been alive.

"If you want a hug, come to me." Jack stuck out his own arms in an ugly imitation of Cyn. She didn't budge. She remained in the circle and now she sneered. "Who are you, really?" Jack asked. "Are you the Mother?"

Cyn's demeanor changed in an instant. The faux anger was replaced by something which resembled her old impish smirk. "I almost suckered you in. I nearly got the ol' two for one deal."

"Where is Cyn?" Jack demanded. "I called her not you."

"Oh, she is down here somewhere, probably having a gay old time being raped or flayed or forced to eat her own intestines in an endless loop. I can find her for you, of course, except you've been so mean to me. Yelling at me and saying lies about me, and then there's the fact that you've said *no* to me time and again."

"I'm sorry about that," he answered, trying his best to remain calm. Losing his temper meant that he could lose Cyn for good. "All of that was a mistake and I'm sorry. So please let me have Cyn or…or just step aside and I'll call her. You won't have to do anything."

The Mother forced another sneer onto Cyn's beautiful lips. "Is that the best you have? Remember what I said the last time you were so rude to me? I said you would beg on your knees."

Jack didn't hesitate. He dropped down, clasped his hands together and debased himself in front of the Mother. He begged for Cyn's soul, shamelessly.

She let him go on for five minutes and then said: "No."

"I'll give you my soul for hers."

The sneer turned to a look of disgust. "Are you kidding me? Her soul is wonderful while yours is a joke. It's in pieces. It's nothing but rags. It would probably fall apart down here and leave me with a whole lot of nothing."

"Then what can I do? What can I give you for her soul?"

"You know what I want. Let me out of here! Find someone willing to sacrifice their true love. Only then will I let you use my gate to call Cyn. And you had better hurry. Cyn is everyone's favorite down here. Her screams are simply delicious. And it won't be long until she *changes*, if you know what I mean."

He didn't know and was about to ask when she waved Cyn's hand and left the body and the world.

Just like that, the endless black of the gate disappeared with a snapping sound, becoming only dirt and rock once again. Cyn's dead body fell as if all the bones in her body had become rubber and when she struck the ground her head knocked so hard against a rock that there was a grisly sound like a hammer striking bone.

"Oh Lord," Jack cried and rushed to her side. She was horribly cold and stiff…dead. "No, not yet!" For a minute, he inexplicably rubbed her limbs and blew on her hands as he cried over her.

Then as the stiffness refused to pass and her skin stayed cold, his anger returned. He slid his hands beneath her body, picking her up. She lolled in his arms, a loose bag of bones. It was horrible. He cried and raged as he stumbled up out of the ruins of the basilica.

The sun stood on point over the city and he let it beat into his face before he looked around him. The destruction seemed total; a few walls stood, none connected to another. The rest of the basilica consisted of jagged mounds of rock and glass. Jack mounted one a hundred feet in height and the sight below him took his breath away. The Vatican and the city around it swarmed with undead. Bone-creatures and skeletons and partial corpses in rags were everywhere, down every block and street—millions of them crushed together.

It was a moment before he realized that these were his soldiers. This was the army he had raised. In silence, they waited on his command.

Smack dab in the middle of the horde of dead were three helicopters sitting silent and still. In a ring around the machines were priests and Swiss guards, staring fearfully at the undead, gripping their guns and crosses with sweaty hands. The Pope was there. Jack could feel him, the light of his soul, the antithesis of his own.

He carried Cyn to the helicopters and for some reason, seeing the priests rekindled Jack's fury, but he stuffed it away. He had debased himself before the Mother of Demons and he would do the same for the Pope if it would help.

The undead parted allowing him to pass through. Strangely, even the priests and the soldiers stepped aside as well as if they had been expecting him. A battle weary cardinal greeted him, speaking in Italian, concern in his tired eyes for the girl in Jack's arms. He led Jack to Pope Romanus, who drew the sign of the cross over her.

"I need your help," Jack said, keeping his eyes down. "I need God's intervention."

The Pope sighed, tired and worn. "You come to the Lord as your second choice? And then you come with an impossible demand?"

The rage had Jack shaking, but he bit back the words of acid and said: "Nothing is impossible with God. That's what I've always been taught."

Romanus nodded. "Nothing is. But the Lord does not interfere with choice. Cynthia chose to commit suicide… and as a devout catholic, she knew the consequences."

Jack was suddenly in such a fury that he was afraid that he would dump Cyn on the ground in order to strangle the Pope. Gently, he lowered her and then knelt, spreading his fingers on the smooth pavement of the square and bowing his head. Through gritted teeth, he said: "That's where you're wrong, she had no choice."

"There is always a choice. A thousand choices led her here today. Just like a thousand led you to bring her here with you. Now, we are all out of choices."

It was a fight to keep his hand off the hilt of the Holy sword that Romanus had given him, but it was a much more difficult fight to keep the fire of anger out of his voice. "Pray. Please," Jack begged. "If God won't listen, pray to Gabriel or Michael. Pray to the heavenly host. There is a child in hell who is blameless and altogether good. She doesn't belong there."

Romanus shook his head. He had sad, weary eyes and his hands were maroon with the dried blood of priests and soldiers who had died in his arms. He spoke in full honesty and complete compassion when he said: "I'm sorry, there's nothing I can do."

Now the rage had Jack in a death grip. His splayed hands scritched across the pavement, his nails bending back and peeling away as his hands balled into fists. The pain was almost welcome and the truth was that he wished with all his heart that he could feel more pain. He wished that he could take away Cyn's pain and take it all on himself. But he couldn't.

"If you won't help, there are those who will," he said, picking Cyn up once more.

"Do not go down that path, my son," Romanus pleaded. "It is a false path. It is a road built of lies and it will only lead to more misery, for everyone."

Jack chomped down on the inside of his cheeks, tasting blood and enjoying it. He was drained of power, but that blood was a reminder of where he could get all the power he would ever need. Silently, he commanded a demon who stood nearby to take Cyn from his arms. "Do not let even a single hair on her head be harmed," he ordered and then turned his back on the Pope.

He strode through the crowd of skeletons, ignoring the stink and the static of their unnatural evil that hung around them in a cloud. Jack parted them and went through to the gate of the Vatican and then led his army into Rome. It was early morning and yet the city was in the throes of panic. The coming of his army, peaceful as it had been, had sent the city into a frenzy. They had abandoned everything and had fled empty-handed.

And that was good; there were *things* left behind that Jack needed. He stopped the demon holding Cyn's cold body and searched her pockets. The first thing he found was a red ponytail holder. He stuck it on his wrist, snuffled back snot and tears and went searching again. He found two candy bars, chapstick, five shotgun shells, lipstick and a whetstone, and then he found what he was looking for: her phone.

A five second Google search showed where he needed to go and a twenty-two minute walk got him to the closest *Case Di Reclusione Maschilirison*—a prison for male convicts.

The city had been abandoned; however the guards had not fled, though they seemed to be regretting it. They were hiding in their guard towers at the approach of millions of walking dead. Jack strode right up to the gate and yelled to a guard: "Open the gate or I'll tear it down."

In seconds the gate was open. First one guard, then a dozen of them ran. Only three held their ground beside the iron doors, thought they all looked on the verge of wetting themselves as Jack's army flooded the inner courtyard of the prison and flowed around the walls.

Although Jack admired their courage, he knew he would destroy the first man who wasted his time by making a gallant stand on principle. With the insolence of a Roman emperor, he ordered. "Fetch me the worst, most evil man you have. Bring him to me or I will break down these doors and get him myself."

Two of the guards looked to a third, whose fanciful uniform suggested that he possessed some sort of superior rank. He wasn't superior to Jack's power and after a quarter second he said: "Si…si," and fled inside.

The other two followed after, leaving Jack alone for five minutes. He knelt on the brick courtyard, his knees crying out in pain that went ignored as he looked up at the sky and, in all honestly, pleaded: "Please, Lord, help me. Help me to get her out of there. I'll take any sign whatsoever."

He waited and waited for an answer, but the only one he received was when the doors opened and a man in chains was thrust out. He was tall and thickly muscled, swarthy, scarred and tattooed. Under different circumstances, he might have been a bad man, a hard man.

Now he cringed and cried and begged.

"Seize him," Jack ordered. Fifty skeletons charged and with hateful glee, they grabbed the man and pinned him down. He shrieked like a frightened child as Jack stood above him. A part of Jack saw a fellow human, a man who had made terrible mistakes but who had also loved and laughed and cared.

"If you won't save Cyn," Jack cried, looking up at the heavens, "then save this man." When the skies failed to part, he shrugged and said to the man: "It seems God is forcing us to play our parts and yours is as sacrifice and mine…mine just might be as destroyer of worlds."

How the knife came to be in his hand, he did not know, but its blade glittered and its edge was wickedly sharp. It parted flesh with sensual, gentle ease. If God wouldn't right this injustice then Jack would have to do it and his way wasn't going to be easy. In fact, his way was going to be a bloody nightmare and it would start with sacrifices to beings as black as night, beings that were desperate to rival the Mother of Demons and the Father of all.

He called upon the Gods of the Undead.

The End

****

Author's note:

As always, I hope you've enjoyed the book and as always I humbly beg for an Amazon review and a quick mention on Facebook so that I can continue to write what I think are pretty good stories(Most people agree, except for those whose chests seize up over the occasional errant comma.)

I am frequently in need of names for my characters and if you would like your name to appear in one of my books, please contact me at petermeredith07@gmail.com. I try to use as many fan names as possible, but if your name is Willy Willoughby, maybe just write to say hello.

The third book in *The Gods of the Undead* series is being written right this moment(Yes, even if you are reading this note and two in the morning, chances are that I am up and writing!) As you desperately wait on book 3, how about you take a look at some of my other works. I would suggest my seven book series: The Undead World.

A Perfect America
The Sacrificial Daughter
The Apocalypse Crusade War of the Undead: Day One
The Apocalypse Crusade War of the Undead: Day Two
The Horror of the Shade: Trilogy of the Void 1
An Illusion of Hell: Trilogy of the Void 2
Hell Blade: Trilogy of the Void 3
The Punished
Sprite
The Blood Lure: The Hidden Land Book 1
The King's Trap: The Hidden Land Novel 2
To Ensnare A Queen: The Hidden Land Novel 3
The Apocalypse: The Undead World Novel 1
The Apocalypse Survivors: The Undead World Novel 2
The Apocalypse Outcasts: The Undead World Novel 3
The Apocalypse Fugitives: The Undead World Novel 4
The Apocalypse Renegades: The Undead World Novel 5
The Apocalypse Exile: The Undead World Novel 6
The Apocalypse War: The Undead World Novel 7
The Edge of Hell: Gods of the Undead 1
The Edge of Temptation: Gods of the Undead 2
Pen(Novella)
A Sliver of Perfection (Novella)
The Haunting At Red Feathers(Short Story)
The Haunting On Colonel's Row(Short Story)
The Drawer(Short Story)
The Eyes in the Storm(Short Story)
The Witch: Jillybean in the Undead World

www.ingramcontent.com/pod-product-compliance
Lightning Source LLC
Chambersburg PA
CBHW071203250626
47159CB00001B/180